Robert Silverberg was born in New York in 1935. He sold his first novel while still a student at Columbia University, and has been a full-time writer since graduation. He has published more than fifty novels, as well as serious works of history and archaeology, and has been nominated for more awards for his fiction than any other science-fiction writer. He and his wife live in the San Francisco area.

G000162427

The Bookshop Coleraine
21 Society Street
0777 6075176

The Collected Stories of Robert Silverberg

Volume Two: The Secret Sharer

Grafton

An Imprint of HarperCollins*Publishers*

Grafton
An Imprint of HarperCollins *Publishers*
77–85 Fulham Palace Road
Hammersmith, London W6 8JB

First published by Grafton 1993
9 8 7 6 5 4 3 2 1

A catalogue record for this book is
available from the British Library

ISBN 0 586 21370 8

Set in Times

Printed in Great Britain by
The Guernsey Press Co. Ltd, Guernsey, Channel Islands

For *Ellen Datlow*
Gardner Dozois
Martin H. Greenberg
Beth Meacham
Byron Preiss
Alice K. Turner
Chuck Miller and *Tim Underwood*

Acknowledgments

'The Pardoner's Tale', 'The Dead Man's Eyes', and 'A Sleep and a Forgetting' first appeared in *Playboy*.
'To the Promised Land' first appeared in *Omni*.
'The Asenion Solution' first appeared in *Foundation's Friends*.
'The Secret Sharer' first appeared as a limited-edition volume published by Underwood-Miller.
'The Iron Star' first appeared in *The Universe*.
'Chip Runner' first appeared in *The Microverse*.
'Enter a Soldier. Later: Enter Another' and 'We Are For the Dark' first appeared in *Isaac Asimov's Science Fiction Magazine*.
'House of Bones' first appeared in *Terry's Universe*.

Contents

Introduction

A couple of working definitions:

1) A short story is a piece of prose fiction in which just one significant thing happens.

2) A science-fiction short story is a piece of prose fiction in which just one extraordinary thing happens.

These are not definitions of my devising, nor are they especially recent. The first one was formulated by Edgar Allan Poe a century and a half ago, and the second by H. G. Wells about fifty years after that. Neither one is an absolute commandment: it's quite possible to violate one or both of these definitions and still produce a story that will fascinate its readers. But they're good basic working rules, and I've tried to keep them in mind throughout my writing career.

What Poe spoke of, actually, was the 'single effect' that every story should work towards. Every word in the story, he said, should work towards that effect. That might be interpreted as much as a stylistic rule as a structural one: the 'effect' could be construed as eldritch horror, farce, philosophical contemplation, whatever. But in fact Poe, both in theory and in practice, understood virtually in the hour of the birth of the short story that it must be constructed round one central point and only one. Like a painting, it must be capable of being taken in at a single glance, although close inspection or repeated viewings would reveal complexities and subtleties not immediately perceptible.

Thus Poe, in 'The Fall of the House of Usher', say, builds his story around the strange bond linking Roderick Usher and his sister, Lady Madeline. The baroque details of the story, rich and vivid, serve entirely to tell us that *the Ushers are very odd people and something extremely peculiar has been going on in their house*, and ultimately the truth is revealed. There are no sub-plots; but if there had been (Roderick Usher's dispute with the local vicar, or Lady Madeline's affair with her head gardener, or the narrator's anxiety over a stock-market manoeuvre) they would have had to be integrated with the main theme or the story's power would have been dissipated.

Similarly, in Guy de Maupassant's classic 'The Piece of String', one significant thing happens: Maître Hauchecome sees a piece of string on the ground, picks it up, and puts it in his pocket. As a result he is suspected of having found and kept a lost wallet full of cash, and he is driven to madness and an early death by the scorn of his fellow villagers. A simple enough situation, with no side-paths: but Maupassant manages, within a few thousand words which concentrate entirely on M. Hauchecome's unfortunate entanglement, to tell us a great many things about French village life, peasant thrift, the ferocity of bourgeois morality, and the ironies of life in general. A long disquisition about M. Hauchecome's unhappy early marriage or the unexpected death of his neighbour's grandchild would probably have added nothing and subtracted much from the impact of the story.

H. G. Wells, who towards the end of the nineteenth century employed the technique of the short story to deal with the thematic matter of what we now call science fiction – and did it so well that his stories still can hold their own with the best s-f of later generations – refined Poe's 'single-effect' concept with special application to the fantastic:

The thing that makes such imaginations [i.e., s-f themes] interesting is their translation into commonplace terms and a rigid exclusion of other marvels from the story. Then it becomes human. 'How would you feel and what might not happen to you?' is the typical question, if for instance pigs could fly and one came rocketing over a hedge at you. How would you feel and what might not happen to you if suddenly you were changed into an ass and couldn't tell anyone about it? Or if you suddenly became invisible? But no one would think twice about the answer if hedges and houses also began to fly, or if people changed into lions, tigers, cats, and dogs left and right, or if anyone could vanish anyhow. Nothing remains interesting where anything may happen.

Right on the mark: *Nothing remains interesting where anything may happen.* The science-fiction story is at its best when it deals with the consequences, however ramifying and multifarious, of a single fantastic assumption. What will happen the first time our spaceships meet those of another intelligent species? Suppose there were so many suns in the sky that the stars were visible only one night every two thousand years: what would that night be like? What if a twentieth-century doctor suddenly found himself in possession of a medical kit of the far future? What about *toys* from the far future falling into the hands of a couple of contemporary kids? One single wild assumption; one significant thing has happened. And from each hypothesis has come great science fiction: each of these four is a one-sentence summary of a story included in the definitive 1970 anthology, *The Science Fiction Hall of Fame*.

I think it's an effective way to construct a story, though not necessarily the only effective way, and in general I've kept the one-thing-happens precept in mind through close to forty years of writing them. The stories collected here, written between June of 1986 and September of 1988, demonstrate that I still believe in the classical unities. Of course, what seems to us a unity now might not have appeared that way when H. G. Wells was writing his wonderful stories late in the nineteenth century. Wells might have argued that my 'House of Bones', for example, is built around *two* speculative fantastic assumptions, one that it is possible to travel backwards in time, and the other that our 'primitive' prehistoric ancestors were actually far more complex and sophisticated human beings than we usually think them to be. But in fact the assumption that time-travel is possible, while still very much speculative and fantastic, no longer *seems* that way to those of us who read and write science fiction a century after Wells, because he and his successors have done so much to familiarize us with the time-travel concept that it no longer strikes us as a very daring speculation. It's part of the background, now. 'Oh, yes,' the reader says. 'A time-travel story. All right, what's new about it?' Simply to have my stranded time-traveller encounter men in shaggy loincloths who chase him around waving clubs would no longer be acceptable: it's necessary for me to come up with some unusual hypothesis about the world in which he finds himself. Technically speaking, the time-travel element of a science-fiction story has become part of the given; it's the next step in the assumption that forms the central matter of the plot.

Two of the stories in this book, 'The Secret Sharer' and 'We Are for the Dark', are actually not short stories at all, but novellas – a considerably different form, running three to five times as long as the traditional short story. The novella form is one of which I'm particularly fond, and one which I think lends itself particularly well to science-fiction use. But it too is bound by the single-effect single-assumption Poe/Wells prescriptions. A novel may sprawl; it may jump freely from character to character, from sub-plot to sub-plot, even from theme to countertheme. A short story, as we've already seen, is best held under rigid technical discipline. But the novella is an intermediate form, partaking of some of the discursiveness of the novel yet benefiting from the discipline of the short story. A single startling assumption; the rigorous exploration of that assumption's consequences; a resolution, eventually, of the problems that those consequences have engendered: the schema works as well for a novella as it does for a short story. The difference lies in texture, in detail, in breadth. In a novella the writer is free to construct a richly imagined background and to develop extensive insight into character as it manifests itself within a complex plot. In a short story those things, however virtuous, may blur and even ruin the effect the story strives to attain.

One story in this collection is neither fish nor fowl, and I point that out for whatever light it may cast on these problems of definition. 'Enter a Soldier. Later: Enter Another' may be considered either a very short novella or a very long short story, but in my mind it verges on being a novella without quite attaining a novella's full complexity, while at the same time being too intricate to be considered a short story. Its primary structure is that of a short story: one speculation is put forth ('What if computers were capable of creating artificial-intelligence replications of famous figures of history'?) and everything else stems from it. But because Pizarro and Socrates are such powerful characters, they launch into an extensive dialogue that carries the story far beyond the conventional limits of short fiction – without, however, leading the story into the complexities of plot that a novella might develop.

And yet I think the story, whatever it may be, is a success, an opinion backed by many readers. The credit, I think, should go to Socrates and Pizarro, who carry it all along. As a rule, I think it's ordinarily better to stick to the rules as I understand them. But, as we see, there are occasions when they can safely be abandoned.

Writing novels is an exhausting proposition: months and months of living with the same group of characters, the same background situation, the same narrative voice, trying to keep everything consistent day after day until the distant finish line is reached. When writing a novel, I yearn for the brevity and simplicity of short-story writing. But then comes the time of the year when the novel is over and short stories must be written, and I feel myself in the iron clamp of the disciplines which govern that remorseless form, and long for the range and expansiveness of novel-writing. So be it. I have spent decades now moving from one extreme of feeling to the other, and the only conclusion I can draw from it is that writing is tough work.

So is reading, sometimes. But we go on doing it. Herewith eleven stories that illustrate some of my notions of what science fiction ought to be attempting in the late twentieth century. Whether they'll last as long as those of Poe and Wells is a question I'd just as soon not spend much time contemplating;

13

but I can say quite certainly that they would not have been written as they were but for the work of those two early masters. Even in a field as supposedly revolutionary as science fiction, the hand of tradition still governs what we do.

Robert Silverberg
Oakland California
August 1990

The Pardoner's Tale

I wrote this story in June of 1986 for *Playboy*, the slick male-oriented magazine which is, I think, the highest paying market for fiction in the United States. Since about 1980 I've had at least one story published every year there, but rarely without a struggle, for *Playboy*'s fiction editor, Alice K. Turner, is formidably adroit in matters of narrative technique and she usually extends me to the limits of my abilities before she's satisfied with the manuscript at hand. Now and then she'll buy a story of mine without raising a single objection, but more often we find ourselves embroiled in elaborate debates over theme, viewpoint, length of expository matter, and such. Sometimes she wins, sometimes I do, sometimes we strike a truce. It's been splendid fun battling it out with her over the years and I wouldn't let a summer go by without it. (My favourite Alice Turner story concerns the time when I turned in a first-person story and she showed me a way of rewriting it *so that a different character was the first-person narrator* with just a few quick strokes necessary to effect the change. I still think I had picked the right narrator the first time, but the technical sleight-of-hand involved in her suggestion took my breath away.)

My 1985 story for her, 'Blindsight', had been one of the easy ones – we had some minor quibbles over futuristic terminology but none over the plot. And now it was time to tackle a project for Alice again. During the intervening eleven months I had been busy indeed. In the fall of 1985 had come the novella 'Gilgamesh in the Outback', which would win a Hugo for me at the 1987 World Science Fiction Convention. That was the first of the Afterworld stories that I eventually collected in the novel *To the Land of the Living*. Then some domestic rearrangements were required, for I had lured a young writer named Karen Haber out of her Texas domicile to live with me in far-off exotic California; and hardly had she unpacked her suitcase but I was embarked on the immense picaresque novel *Star of Gypsies*, which occupied me all during the winter and spring of 1986 and required any number of drafts before I was satisfied. And then, without pausing for breath, I did a second Afterworld novella about Gilgamesh, 'The Fascination of the Abomination'.

Some time off seemed in order, but in the spring of the year my thoughts invariably turn to writing something for *Playboy* and my 1986 project was 'The Pardoner's Tale', title courtesy of Chaucer, who'd probably be puzzled by the story appended to it. At that time the term 'cyberpunk' was being bandied about *ad nauseam* in the science-fiction world, and I suppose you could call this a cyberpunk story – Alice did, in her acceptance letter of 1 July, and I didn't quarrel with the description, although it wasn't exactly what I had thought I was writing.

She wanted about two pages of cuts – a line here, two lines there – in keeping with a dictum she had heard that quintessential cyberpunk featured 'the hottest of all the technological futures, fast action, tight construction, and a disdain for all that is slow and boring'. As usual, when Alice Turner thinks a line or two ought to be cut, I give heed to what she says. I did the cutting with scarcely a demur and the final version, sleek and taut, owes no little of its success to her nifty work with the scalpel. Gardner Dozois picked it for his 1988 year's-best anthology, my fifth appearance in a row in that collection, and Don Wollheim chose it also for his book, giving me one more sweep of the anthologies – although, since Terry Carr's anthology no longer appeared, it was only a double sweep this time. (I pay attention to such things, even if you don't. But they're my stories.)

'Key Sixteen, Housing Omicron Kappa, aleph sub-one,' I said to the software on duty at the Alhambra gate of the Los Angeles Wall.

Software isn't generally suspicious. This wasn't even very smart software. It was working off some great biochips – I could feel them jigging and pulsing as the electron stream flowed through them – but the software itself was just a kludge. Typical gatekeeper stuff.

I stood waiting as the picoseconds went ticking away by the millions.

'Name, please,' the gatekeeper said finally.

'John Doe. Beta Pi Upsilon 104324x.'

The gate opened. I walked into Los Angeles.

As easy as Beta Pi.

The wall that encircles LA is a hundred, a hundred fifty feet thick. Its gates are more like tunnels. When you consider that the wall runs completely around the LA basin from the San Gabriel Valley to the San Fernando Valley and then over the mountains and down the coast and back the far side past Long Beach, and that it's at least sixty feet high and all that distance deep, you can begin to appreciate the mass of it. Think of the phenomenal expenditure of human energy that went into building it – muscle and sweat, sweat and muscle. I think about that a lot.

I suppose the walls around our cities were put there mostly as symbols. They highlight the distinction between city and countryside, between citizen and uncitizen, between control and chaos, just as city walls did five thousand years ago. But mainly they serve to remind us that we are all slaves nowadays. You can't ignore the walls. You can't pretend they aren't there. *We made you build them*, is what they say, *and don't you ever forget that*. All the same, Chicago doesn't have a wall sixty feet high and a hundred fifty feet deep. Houston doesn't. Phoenix doesn't. They make do with less. But LA is the main city. I suppose the Los Angeles wall is a statement: *I am the Big Cheese. I am the Ham What Am*.

The walls aren't there because the Entities are afraid of attack. They know how invulnerable they are. We know it too. They just wanted to decorate their capital with something a little special. What the hell, it isn't *their* sweat that goes into

17

building the walls. It's ours. Not mine personally, of course. But ours.

I saw a few Entities walking around just inside the wall, preoccupied as usual with God knows what and paying no attention to the humans in the vicinity. These were low-caste ones, the kind with the luminous orange spots along their sides. I gave them plenty of room. They have a way sometimes of picking a human up with those long elastic tongues, like a frog snapping up a fly, and letting him dangle in mid-air while they study him with those saucer-sized yellow eyes. I don't care for that. You don't get hurt, but it isn't agreeable to be dangled in mid-air by something that looks like a fifteen-foot-high purple squid standing on the tips of its tentacles. Happened to me once in St Louis, long ago, and I'm in no hurry to have it happen again.

The first thing I did when I was inside LA was find me a car. On Valley Boulevard about two blocks in from the wall I saw a '31 Toshiba El Dorado that looked good to me, and I matched frequencies with its lock and slipped inside and took about ninety seconds to reprogram its drive control to my personal metabolic cues. The previous owner must have been fat as a hippo and probably diabetic: her glycogen index was absurd and her phosphines were wild.

Not a bad car, a little slow in the shift but what can you expect, considering the last time any cars were manufactured on this planet was the year 2034.

'Pershing Square,' I told it.

It had nice capacity, maybe sixty megabytes. It turned south right away and found the old freeway and drove off towards downtown. I figured I'd set up shop in the middle of things, work two or three pardons to keep my edge sharp, get myself a hotel room, a meal, maybe hire some companionship. And then think about the next move. It was winter, a nice time to be in LA. That golden sun, those warm breezes coming down the canyons.

I hadn't been out on the Coast in years. Working Florida mainly, Texas, sometimes Arizona. I hate the cold. I hadn't been in LA since '36. A long time to stay away, but maybe I'd been staying away deliberately. I wasn't sure. That last LA trip had left bad-tasting memories. There had been a woman who wanted a pardon and I sold her a stiff. You have to stiff the customers now and then or else you start looking too good, which can be dangerous; but she was young and pretty and full of hope and I could have stiffed the next one instead of her, only I didn't. Sometimes I've felt bad, thinking back over that. Maybe that's what had kept me away from LA all this time.

A couple of miles east of the big downtown interchange traffic began backing up. Maybe an accident ahead, maybe a roadblock. I told the Toshiba to get off the freeway.

Slipping through roadblocks is scary and calls for a lot of hard work. I knew that I probably could fool any kind of software at a roadblock and certainly any human cop, but why bother if you don't have to?

I asked the car where I was.

The screen lit up. Alameda near Banning, it said. A long walk to Pershing Square, looked like. I had the car drop me at Spring Street and went the rest of the way on foot. 'Pick me up at 1830 hours,' I told it. 'Corner of – umm – Sixth and Hill.' It went away to park itself and I headed for the Square to peddle some pardons.

It isn't hard for a good pardoner to find buyers. You can see it in their eyes: the tightly controlled anger, the smouldering resentment. And something else, sometimes intangible, a certain sense of having a shred or two of inner integrity left, that tells you right away, Here's somebody willing to risk a lot to regain some measure of freedom. I was in business within fifteen minutes.

The first one was an ageing surfer sort, barrel chest and that sun-bleached look. The Entities haven't allowed surfing for ten, fifteen years – they've got their plankton seines just off shore from Santa Barbara to San Diego, gulping in the marine nutrients they have to have, and any beach boy who tried to take a whack at the waves out there could be chewed right up. But this guy must have been one hell of a performer in his day. The way he moved through the park, making little balancing moves as if he needed to compensate for the irregularities of the Earth's rotation, you could see how he would have been in the water. Sat down next to me, began working on his lunch. Thick forearms, gnarled hands. A wall-labourer. Muscles knotting in his cheeks: the anger, forever simmering just below boil.

I got him talking, after a while. A surfer, yes. Lost in the far-away and gone. He began sighing to me about legendary beaches where the waves were tubes and they came pumping end to end. 'Trestle Beach,' he murmured. 'That's north of San Onofre. You had to sneak through Camp Pendleton. Sometimes the Marines would open fire, just warning shots. Or Hollister Ranch, up by Santa Barbara.' His blue eyes got misty. 'Huntington Beach. Oxnard. I got everywhere, man.' He flexed his huge fingers. 'Now these fucking Entity hodads own the shore. Can you believe it? They *own* it. And I'm pulling wall, my second time around, seven days a week next ten years.'

'Ten?' I said. 'That's a shitty deal.'

'You know anyone who doesn't have a shitty deal?'

'Some,' I said. 'They buy out.'

'Yeah.'

'It can be done.'

A careful look. You never know who might be a borgmann. Those stinking collaborators are everywhere.

'Can it?'

'All it takes is money,' I said.

'And a pardoner.'

'That's right.'

'One you can trust.'

I shrugged. 'You've got to go on faith, man.'

'Yeah,' he said. Then, after a while: 'I heard of a guy, he bought a three-year pardon and wall passage thrown in. Went up north, caught a krill trawler, wound up in Australia, on the Reef. Nobody's ever going to find him there. He's out of the system. Right out of the fucking system. What do you think that cost?'

'About twenty grand,' I said.

'Hey, that's a sharp guess!'

'No guess.'

'Oh?' Another careful look. 'You don't sound local.'

'I'm not. Just visiting.'

'That's still the price? Twenty grand?'

'I can't do anything about supplying krill trawlers. You'd be on your own once you were outside the wall.'

'Twenty grand just to get through the wall?'

'And a seven-year labour exemption.'

'I pulled ten,' he said.

'I can't get you ten. It's not in the configuration, you follow? But seven would work. You could get so far, in seven, that they'd lose you. You could goddamned *swim* to Australia. Come in low, below Sydney, no seines there.'

'You know a hell of a lot.'

'My business to know,' I said. 'You want me to run an asset check on you?'

'I'm worth seventeen five. Fifteen hundred real, the rest collat. What can I get for seventeen five?'

'Just what I said. Through the wall, and seven years' exemption.'

'A bargain rate, hey?'

'I take what I can get,' I said. 'Give me your wrist. And don't worry. This part is read-only.'

I keyed his data implant and patched mine in. He had fifteen hundred in the bank and a collateral rating of sixteen thou, exactly as he claimed. We eyed each other very carefully now. As I said, you never know who the borgmanns are.

'You can do it right here in the park?' he asked.

'You bet. Lean back, close your eyes, make like you're snoozing in the sun. The deal is that I take a thousand of the cash now and you transfer five thou of the collateral bucks to me, straight labour-debenture deal. When you get through the wall I get the other five hundred cash and five thou more on sweat security. The rest you pay off at three thou a year plus interest, wherever you are, quarterly key-ins. I'll program the whole thing, including beep reminders on payment dates. It's up to you to make your travel arrangements, remember. I can do pardons and wall transits but I'm not a goddamned travel agent. Are we on?'

He put his head back and closed his eyes.

'Go ahead,' he said.

It was fingertip stuff, straight circuit emulation, my standard hack. I picked up all his identification codes, carried them into central, found his records. He seemed real, nothing more or less than he had claimed. Sure enough, he had drawn a lulu of a labour tax, ten years on the wall. I wrote him a pardon good for the first seven of that. Had to leave the final three on the books, purely technical reasons, but the computers weren't going to be able to find him by then. I gave him a wall-transit pass, too, which meant writing in a new skills class for him, programmer third grade. He didn't think like a programmer and he didn't look like a programmer but the wall software wasn't going to figure that out. Now I had made him a member of the human élite, the relative handful of us who are free to go in and out of the walled cities as we wish. In return for these little favours I signed over his entire life savings to various accounts of mine, payable as arranged, part now, part later. He wasn't worth a nickel any more, but he was a free man. That's not such a terrible trade-off.

Oh, and the pardon was a valid one. I had decided not to write any stiffs while I was in Los Angeles. A kind of sentimental atonement, you might say, for the job I had done on that woman all those years back.

You absolutely have to write stiffs once in a while, you understand. So that you don't look too good, so that you don't give the Entities reason to hunt you down. Just as you have to ration the number of pardons you do. I didn't have to be writing pardons at all, of course. I could have just authorized the system to pay me so much a year, fifty thou, a hundred, and taken it easy forever. But where's the challenge in that?

So I write pardons, but no more than I need to cover my expenses, and I deliberately fudge some of them up, making myself look as incompetent as the rest so the Entities don't have a reason to begin trying to track the identifying marks of my work. My conscience hasn't been too sore about that. It's a matter of survival, after all. And most other pardoners are out-and-out frauds, you know. At least with me you stand a better than even chance of getting what you're paying for.

The next one was a tiny Japanese woman, the classic style, sleek, fragile, doll-like. Crying in big wild gulps that I thought might break her in half, while a grey-haired older man in a shabby business suit – her grandfather, you'd guess – was trying to comfort her. Public crying is a good indicator of Entity trouble. 'Maybe I can help,' I said, and they were both so distraught that they didn't even bother to be suspicious.

He was her father-in-law, not her grandfather. The husband was dead, killed by burglars the year before. There were two small kids. Now she had received her new labour-tax ticket. She had been afraid they were going to send her out to work on the wall, which of course wasn't likely to happen: the assignments are pretty random, but they usually aren't crazy, and what use would a ninety-pound girl be in hauling stone blocks around? The father-in-law had some friends who were in the know, and they managed to bring up the hidden encoding on her ticket. The computers hadn't sent her to the wall, no. They had sent her to Area Five. And they had given her a TTD classification.

'The wall would have been better,' the old man said. 'They'd see, right away, she wasn't strong enough for heavy work, and they'd find something else, something she could do. But Area Five? Who ever comes back from that?'

'You know what Area Five is?' I said.

'The medical experiment place. And this mark here, TTD. I know what that stands for too.'

She began to moan again. I couldn't blame her. TTD means Test To Destruction. The Entities want to find out how much work we can really do, and they feel that the only reliable way to discover that is to put us through tests that show where the physical limits are.

'I will die,' she wailed. 'My babies! My babies!'

'Do you know what a pardoner is?' I asked the father-in-law.

A quick excited response: sharp intake of breath, eyes going bright, head nodding vehemently. Just as quickly the excitement faded, giving way to bleakness, helplessness, despair.

'They all cheat you,' he said.

'Not all.'

'Who can say? They take your money, they give you nothing.'

'You know that isn't true. Everybody can tell you stories of pardons that came through.'

'Maybe. Maybe,' the old man said. The woman sobbed quietly. 'You know of such a person?'

'For three thousand dollars,' I said, 'I can take the TTD off her ticket. For five I can write an exemption from service good until her children are in high school.'

Sentimental me. A fifty per cent discount, and I hadn't even run an asset check. For all I knew the father-in-law was a millionaire. But no, he'd have been off cutting a pardon for her, then, and not sitting around like this in Pershing Square.

He gave me a long, deep, appraising look. Peasant shrewdness coming to the surface.

'How can we be sure of that?' he asked.

I might have told him that I was the king of my profession, the best of all pardoners, a genius hacker with the truly magic touch, who could slip into any computer ever designed and make it dance to my tune. Which would have been nothing more than the truth. But all I said was that he'd have to make up his own mind, that I couldn't offer any affidavits or guarantees, that I was available if he wanted me and otherwise it was all the same to me if she preferred to stick with her TTD ticket. They went off and conferred for a couple of minutes.

When they came back, he silently rolled up his sleeve and presented his implant to me. I keyed his credit balance: thirty thou or so, not bad. I transferred eight of it to my accounts, half to Seattle, the rest to Los Angeles. Then I took her wrist, which was about two of my fingers thick, and got into her implant and wrote her the pardon that would save her life. Just to be certain, I ran a double validation check on it. It's always possible to stiff a customer unintentionally, though I've never done it. But I didn't want this particular one to be my first.

'Go on,' I said. 'Home. Your kids are waiting for their lunch.'

Her eyes glowed. 'If I could only thank you somehow – '

'I've already banked my fee. Go. If you ever see me again, don't say hello.'

'This will work?' the old man asked.

'You say you have friends who know things. Wait seven days, then tell the data bank that she's lost her ticket. When you get the new one, ask your pals to decode it for you. You'll see. It'll be all right.'

I don't think he believed me. I think he was more than half sure I had swindled him out of one fourth of his life's savings, and I could see the hatred in his eyes. But that was his problem. In a week he'd find out that I really had saved his daughter-in-law's life, and then he'd rush down to the Square to tell me how sorry he was that he had had such terrible feelings towards me. Only by then I'd be somewhere else, far away.

They shuffled out the east side of the park, pausing a couple of times to peer over their shoulders at me as if they thought I was going to transform them into pillars of salt the moment their backs were turned. Then they were gone.

I'd earned enough now to get me through the week I planned to spend in LA. But I stuck around anyway, hoping for a little more. My mistake.

This one was Mr Invisible, the sort of man you'd never notice in a crowd, grey on grey, thinning hair, mild bland apologetic smile. But his eyes had a shine. I forget whether he started talking first to me, or me to him, but pretty soon we were jockeying around trying to find out things about each other. He told me he was from Silver Lake. I gave him a blank look. How in hell am I supposed to know all the zillion LA neighbourhoods? Said that he had come down here to see someone at the big government HQ on Figueroa Street. All right: probably an appeals case. I sensed a customer.

Then he wanted to know where I was from. Santa Monica? West LA? Something in my accent, I guess. 'I'm a travelling man,' I said. 'Hate to stay in one place.' True enough. I need to hack or I go crazy; if I did all my hacking in just one city I'd be virtually begging them to slap a trace on me sooner or later and that would be the end. I didn't tell him any of that. 'Came in from Utah last night. Wyoming before that.' Not true, either one. 'Maybe on to New York, next.' He looked at me as if I'd said I was planning a voyage to the moon. People out here, they don't go east a lot. These days most people don't go anywhere.

Now he knew that I had wall-transit clearance, or else that I had some way of getting it when I wanted it. That was what he was looking to find out. In no time at all we were down to basics.

He said he had drawn a new ticket, six years at the salt-field reclamation site out back of Mono Lake. People die like mayflies out there. What he wanted was a transfer to something softer, like Operations & Maintenance, and it had to be within the walls, preferably in one of the districts out by the ocean where the air is cool and clear. I quoted him a price and he accepted without a quiver.

'Let's have your wrist,' I said.

He held out his right hand, palm upwards. His implant access was a pale yellow plaque, mounted in the usual place but rounder than the standard kind and of a slightly smoother texture. I didn't see any great significance in that. As I had done maybe a thousand times before, I put my own arm over his, wrist to wrist, access to access. Our biocomputers made contact and instantly I knew that I was in trouble.

Human beings have been carrying biochip-based computers in their bodies for the last forty or fifty years or so – long before the Entity invasion, anyway – but for most people it's just something they take for granted, like the vaccination mark on their thighs. They use them for the things they're meant to be used for, and don't give them a thought beyond that. The biocomputer's just a commonplace tool for them, like a fork, like a shovel. You have to have the hacker sort of mentality to be willing to turn your biocomputer into something more. That's why, when the Entities came and took us over and made us build walls around our cities, most people reacted just like sheep, letting themselves be herded inside and politely staying there. The only ones who can move around freely now – because we know how to manipulate the mainframes through which the Entities rule us – are the hackers. And there aren't many of us. I could tell right away that I had hooked myself on to one now.

The moment we were in contact, he came at me like a storm.

The strength of his signal let me know I was up against something special, and that I'd been hustled. He hadn't been trying to buy a pardon at all. What he was looking for was a duel. Mr Macho behind the bland smile, out to show the new boy in town a few of his tricks.

No hacker had ever mastered me in a one-on-one anywhere. Not ever. I felt sorry for him, but not much.

He shot me a bunch of stuff, cryptic but easy, just by way of finding out my parameters. I caught it and stored it and laid an interrupt on him and took over the dialogue. My turn to test him. I wanted him to begin to see who he was fooling around with. But just as I began to execute he put an interrupt on *me*. That was a new experience. I stared at him with some respect.

Usually any hacker anywhere will recognize my signal in the first thirty seconds, and that'll be enough to finish the interchange. He'll know that there's no point in continuing. But this guy either wasn't able to identify me or just didn't care, and he came right back with his interrupt. Amazing. So was the stuff he began laying on me next.

27

He went right to work, really trying to scramble my architecture. Reams of stuff came flying at me up in the heavy megabyte zone.

– *jspike. dbltag. nslice. dzcnt.*

I gave it right back to him, twice as hard.

– *maxrrq. minpau. spktot. jspike.*

He didn't mind at all.

– *maxdz. spktim. falter. nslice.*

– *frqsum. eburst.*

– *iburst.*

– *prebst.*

– *nobrst.*

Mexican standoff. He was still smiling. Not even a trace of sweat on his forehead. Something eerie about him, something new and strange. This is some kind of borgmann hacker, I realized suddenly. He must be working for the Entities, roving the city, looking to make trouble for freelancers like me. Good as he was, and he was plenty good, I despised him. A hacker who had become a borgmann – now, that was truly disgusting. I wanted to short him. I wanted to burn him out, now. I had never hated anyone so much in my life.

I couldn't do a thing with him.

I was baffled. I was the Data King, I was the Megabyte Monster. All my life I had floated back and forth across a world in chains, picking every lock I came across. And now this nobody was tying me in knots. Whatever I gave him, he parried; and what came back from him was getting increasingly bizarre. He was working with an algorithm I had never seen before and was having serious trouble solving. After a little while I couldn't even figure out what he was doing to me, let alone what I was going to do to cancel it. It was getting so I could barely execute. He was forcing me inexorably towards a wetware crash.

'Who are you?' I yelled.

He laughed in my face.

And kept pouring it on. He was threatening the integrity of my implant, going at me down on the microcosmic level, attacking the molecules themselves. Fiddling around with electron shells, reversing charges and mucking up valences, clogging my gates, turning my circuits to soup. The computer that is implanted in my brain is nothing but a lot of organic chemistry, after all. So is my brain. If he kept this up the computer would go and the brain would follow, and I'd spend the rest of my life in the bibble-bibble academy.

This wasn't a sporting contest. This was murder.

I reached for the reserves, throwing up all the defensive blockages I could invent. Things I had never had to use in my life, but they were there when I needed them, and they did slow him down. For a moment I was able to halt his ballbreaking onslaught and even push him back. And give myself the breathing space to set up a few offensive combinations of my own. But before I could get them running, he shut me down once more and started to drive me towards crashville all over again. He was unbelievable.

I blocked him. He came back again. I hit him hard and he threw the punch into some other neural channel altogether and it went fizzling away.

I hit him again. Again he blocked it.

Then he hit me and I went reeling and staggering, and managed to get myself together when I was about three nanoseconds from the edge of the abyss.

I began to set up a new combination. But even as I did it, I was reading the tone of his data, and what I was getting was absolute cool confidence. He was waiting for me. He was ready for anything I could throw. He was in that realm beyond mere self-confidence into utter certainty.

What it was coming down to was this. I was able to keep him from ruining me, but only just barely, and I wasn't able to lay a glove on him at all. And he seemed to have infinite resources behind him. I didn't worry him. He was tireless. He didn't appear to degrade at all. He just took all I could give and kept throwing new stuff at me, coming at me from six sides at once.

Now I understood for the first time what it must have felt

like for all the hackers I had beaten. Some of them must have felt pretty cocky, I suppose, until they ran into me. It costs more to lose when you think you're good. When you *know* you're good. People like that, when they lose, they have to reprogram their whole sense of their relation to the universe.

I had two choices. I could go on fighting until he wore me down and crashed me. Or I could give up right now. In the end everything comes down to yes or no, on or off, one or zero, doesn't it?

I took a deep breath. I was staring straight into chaos.

'All right,' I said. 'I'm beaten. I quit.'

I wrenched my wrist free of his, trembled, swayed, went toppling down on the ground.

A minute later five cops jumped me and trussed me up like a turkey and hauled me away, with my implant arm sticking out of the package and a security lock wrapped around my wrist, as if they were afraid I was going to start pulling data right out of the air.

Where they took me was Figueroa Street, the big black marble ninety-storey job that is the home of the puppet city government. I didn't give a damn. I was numb. They could have put me in the sewer and I wouldn't have cared. I wasn't damaged – the automatic circuit check was still running and it came up green – but the humiliation was so intense that I felt crashed. I felt destroyed. The only thing I wanted to know was the name of the hacker who had done it to me.

The Figueroa Street building has ceilings about twenty feet high everywhere, so that there'll be room for Entities to move around. Voices reverberate in those vast open spaces like echoes in a cavern. The cops sat me down in a hallway, still all wrapped up, and kept me there for a long time. Blurred sounds went lalloping up and down the passage. I wanted to hide from them. My brain felt raw. I had taken one hell of a pounding.

Now and then a couple of towering Entities would come rumbling through the hall, tiptoeing on their tentacles in that weirdly dainty way of theirs. With them came a little entourage of humans whom they ignored entirely, as they always do. They know that we're intelligent but they just don't care to talk to us. They let their computers do that, via the Borgmann interface, and may his signal degrade forever for having sold us out. Not that they wouldn't have conquered us anyway, but Borgmann made it ever so much easier for them to push us around by showing them how to connect our little biocomputers to their huge mainframes. I bet he was very proud of himself, too: just wanted to see if his gadget would work, and to hell with the fact that he was selling us into eternal bondage.

Nobody has ever figured out why the Entities are here or what they want from us. They simply came, that's all. Saw. Conquered. Rearranged us. Put us to work doing godawful unfathomable tasks, like a bad dream.

And there wasn't any way we could defend ourselves against them. Didn't seem that way to us at first – we were cocky, we were going to wage guerrilla war and wipe them out – but we learned fast how wrong we were, and we are theirs for keeps. There's nobody left with anything close to freedom except the handful of hackers like me; and, as I've explained, we're not dopey enough to try any serious sort of counterattack. It's a big enough triumph for us just to be able to dodge around from one city to another without having to get authorization.

Looked like all that was finished for me, now. Right then I didn't give a damn. I was still trying to integrate the notion that I had been beaten; I didn't have capacity left over to work on a program for the new life I would be leading now.

'Is this the pardoner, over here?' someone said.

'That one, yeah.'

'She wants to see him now.'

'You think we should fix him up a little first?'

'She said now.'

A hand at my shoulder, rocking me gently. 'Up, fellow. It's interview time. Don't make a mess or you'll get hurt.'

I let them shuffle me down the hall and through a gigantic doorway and into an immense office with a ceiling high enough to give an Entity all the room it would want. I didn't say a word. There weren't any Entities in the office, just a woman in a black robe, sitting behind a wide desk at the far end. It looked like a toy desk in that colossal room. She looked like a toy woman. The cops left me alone with her. Trussed up like that, I wasn't any risk.

'Are you John Doe?' she asked.

I was halfway across the room, studying my shoes. 'What do you think?' I said.

'That's the name you gave upon entry to the city.'

'I give lots of names. John Smith, Richard Roe, Joe Blow. It doesn't matter much to the gate software what name I give.'

'Because you've gimmicked the gate?' She paused. 'I should tell you, this is a court of inquiry.'

'You already know everything I could tell you. Your borgmann hacker's been swimming around in my brain.'

'Please,' she said. 'This'll be easier if you cooperate. The accusation is illegal entry, illegal seizure of a vehicle, and illegal interfacing activity, specifically, selling pardons. Do you have a statement?'

'No.'

'You deny that you're a pardoner?'

'I don't deny, I don't affirm. What's the goddamned use.'

'Look up at me,' she said.

'That's a lot of effort.'

'Look up,' she said. There was an odd edge on her voice. 'Whether you're a pardoner or not isn't the issue. We know you're a pardoner. *I* know you're a pardoner.' And she called me by a name I hadn't used in a very long time. Not since '36, as a matter of fact.

I looked at her. Stared. Had trouble believing I was seeing what I saw. Felt a rush of memories come flooding up. Did some mental editing work on her face, taking out some lines here, subtracting a little flesh in a few places, adding some in others. Stripping away the years.

'Yes,' she said. 'I'm who you think I am.'

I gaped. This was worse than what the hacker had done to me. But there was no way to run from it.

'You work for them?' I asked.

'The pardon you sold me wasn't any good. You knew that, didn't you? I had someone waiting for me in San Diego, but when I tried to get through the wall they stopped me just like that, and dragged me away screaming. I could have killed you. I would have gone to San Diego and then we would have tried to make it to Hawaii in his boat.'

'I didn't know about the guy in San Diego,' I said.

'Why should you? It wasn't your business. You took my money, you were supposed to get me my pardon. That was the deal.'

Her eyes were grey with golden sparkles in them. I had trouble looking into them.

'You still want to kill me?' I asked. 'Are you planning to kill me now?'

'No and no.' She used my old name again. 'I can't tell you how astounded I was, when they brought you in here. A pardoner, they said. John Doe. Pardoners, that's my department. They bring all of them to me. I used to wonder years ago if they'd ever bring *you* in, but after a while I figured, no, not a chance, he's probably a million miles away, he'll never come back this way again. And then they brought in this John Doe, and I saw your face.'

'Do you think you could manage to believe,' I said, 'that I've felt guilty for what I did to you ever since? You don't have to believe it. But it's the truth.'

'I'm sure it's been unending agony for you.'

'I mean it. Please. I've stiffed a lot of people, yes, and sometimes I've regretted it and sometimes I haven't, but you were one that I regretted. You're the one I've regretted most. This is the absolute truth.'

She considered that. I couldn't tell whether she believed it even for a fraction of a second, but I could see that she was considering it.

'Why did you do it?' she asked after a bit.

'I stiff people because I don't want to seem too perfect,' I told her. 'You deliver a pardon every single time, word gets around, people start talking, you start to become legendary. And then you're known everywhere and sooner or later the Entities get hold of you, and that's that. So I always make sure to write a lot of stiffs. I tell people I'll do my best, but there aren't any guarantees, and sometimes it doesn't work.'

'You deliberately cheated me.'

'Yes.'

'I thought you did. You seemed so cool, so professional. So perfect. I was sure the pardon would be valid. I couldn't see how it would miss. And then I got to the wall and they grabbed me. So I thought, that bastard sold me out. He was too good just to have flubbed it up.' Her tone was calm but the anger was still in her eyes. 'Couldn't you have stiffed the next one? Why did it have to be me?'

I looked at her for a long time.

'Because I loved you,' I said.

'Shit,' she said. 'You didn't even know me. I was just some stranger who had hired you.'

'That's just it. There I was full of all kinds of crazy instant lunatic fantasies about you, all of a sudden ready to turn my nice orderly life upside down for you, and all you could see was somebody you had hired to do a job. I didn't know about the guy from San Diego. All I knew was I saw you and I wanted you. You don't think that's love? Well, call it something else, then, whatever you want. I never let myself feel it before. It isn't smart, I thought, it ties you down, the risks are too big. And then I saw you and I talked to you a little and I thought something could be happening between us and things started to change inside me, and I thought, Yeah, yeah, go with it this time, let it happen, this may make everything different. And you stood there not seeing it, not even beginning to notice, just jabbering on and on about how important the pardon was for you. So I stiffed you. And afterwards I thought, Jesus, I ruined that girl's life and it was just because I got myself into a snit, and that was a fucking petty thing to have done. So I've been sorry ever since. You don't have to believe that. I didn't know about San Diego. That makes it even worse for me.' She didn't say anything all this time, and the silence felt enormous. So after a moment I said, 'Tell me one thing, at least. That guy who wrecked me in Pershing Square: who is he?'

'He wasn't anybody,' she said.

'What does that mean?'

'He isn't a who. He's a *what*. It's an android, a mobile anti-pardoner unit, plugged right into the big Entity mainframe in Culver City. Something new that we have going around town.'

'Oh,' I said. 'Oh.'

'The report is that you gave it one hell of a workout.'

'It gave me one too. Turned my brain half to mush.'

'You were trying to drink the sea through a straw. For a while it looked like you were really going to do it, too. You're one goddamned hacker, you know that?'

'Why did you go to work for them?' I said.

She shrugged. 'Everybody works for them. Except people like you. You took everything I had and didn't give me my pardon. So what was I supposed to do?'

'I see.'

'It's not such a bad job. At least I'm not out there on the wall. Or being sent off for TTD.'

'No,' I said. 'It's probably not so bad. If you don't mind working in a room with such a high ceiling. Is that what's going to happen to me? Sent off for TTD?'

'Don't be stupid. You're too valuable.'

'To whom?'

'The system always needs upgrading. You know it better than anyone alive. You'll work for us.'

'You think I'm going to turn borgmann?' I said, amazed.

'It beats TTD,' she said.

I fell silent again. I was thinking that she couldn't possibly be serious, that they'd be fools to trust me in any kind of responsible position. And even bigger fools to let me near their computer.

'All right,' I said. 'I'll do it. On one condition.'

'You really have balls, don't you?'

'Let me have a rematch with that android of yours. I need to check something out. And afterwards we can discuss what kind of work I'd be best suited for here. Okay?'

'You know you aren't in any position to lay down conditions.'

'Sure I am. What I do with computers is a unique art. You can't make me do it against my will. You can't make me do anything against my will.'

She thought about that. 'What good is a rematch?'

'Nobody ever beat me before. I want a second try.'

'You know it'll be worse for you than before.'

'Let me find that out.'

'But what's the point?'

'Get me your android and I'll show you the point,' I said.

She went along with it. Maybe it was curiosity, maybe it was something else, but she patched herself into the computer net and pretty soon they brought in the android I had encountered in the park, or maybe another one with the same face. It looked me over pleasantly, without the slightest sign of interest.

Someone came in and took the security lock off my wrist and left again. She gave the android its instructions and it held out its wrist to me and we made contact. And I jumped right in.

I was raw and wobbly and pretty damned battered, still, but I knew what I needed to do and I knew I had to do it fast. The thing was to ignore the android completely – it was just a terminal, it was just a unit – and go for what lay behind it. So I bypassed the android's own identity program, which was clever but shallow. I went right around it while the android was still setting up its combinations, dived underneath, got myself instantly from the unit level to the mainframe level and gave the master Culver City computer a hearty handshake.

Jesus, that felt good!

All that power, all those millions of megabytes squatting there, and I was plugged right into it. Of course I felt like a mouse hitchhiking on the back of an elephant. That was all right. I might be a mouse but that mouse was getting a tremendous ride. I hung on tight and went soaring along on the hurricane winds of that colossal machine.

And as I soared, I ripped out chunks of it by the double handful and tossed them to the breeze.

It didn't even notice for a good tenth of a second. That's how big it was. There I was, tearing great blocks of data out of its gut, joyously ripping and rending. And it didn't even know it, because even the most magnificent computer ever assembled is still stuck with operating at the speed of light, and when the best you can do is 186,000 miles a second it can take quite a while for the alarm to travel the full distance down all your neural channels. That thing was *huge*. Mouse riding on elephant, did I say? Amoeba piggybacking on brontosaurus, was more like it.

God knows how much damage I was able to do. But of course the alarm circuitry did cut in eventually. Internal gates came clanging down and all sensitive areas were sealed away and I was shrugged off with the greatest of ease. There was no sense staying around waiting to get trapped, so I pulled myself free.

I had found out what I needed to know. Where the defences were, how they worked. This time the computer had kicked me out, but it wouldn't be able to, the next. Whenever I wanted, I could go in there and smash whatever I felt like.

The android crumpled to the carpet. It was nothing but an empty husk now.

Lights were flashing on the office wall.

She looked at me appalled. 'What did you *do*?'

'I beat your android,' I said. 'It wasn't all that hard, once I knew the scoop.'

'You damaged the main computer.'

'Not really. Not much. I just gave it a little tickle. It was surprised, seeing me get access in there, that's all.'

'I think you really damaged it.'

'Why would I want to do that?'

'The question ought to be why you haven't done it already.

Why you haven't gone in there and crashed the hell out of their programs.'

'You think I could do something like that?'

She studied me. 'I think maybe you could, yes.'

'Well, maybe so. Or maybe not. But I'm not a crusader, you know. I like my life the way it is. I move around, I do as I please. It's a quiet life. I don't start revolutions. When I need to gimmick things, I gimmick them just enough, and no more. And the Entities don't even know I exist. If I stick my finger in their eye, they'll cut my finger off. So I haven't done it.'

'But now you might,' she said.

I began to get uncomfortable. 'I don't follow you,' I said, although I was beginning to think that I did.

'You don't like risk. You don't like being conspicuous. But if we take your freedom away, if we tie you down in LA and put you to work, what the hell would you have to lose? You'd go right in there. You'd gimmick things but good.' She was silent for a time. 'Yes,' she said. 'You really would. I see it now, that you have the capability and that you could be put in a position where you'd be willing to use it. And then you'd screw everything up for all of us, wouldn't you?'

'What?'

'You'd fix the Entities, sure. You'd do such a job on their computer that they'd have to scrap it and start all over again. Isn't that so?'

She was on to me, all right.

'But I'm not going to give you the chance. I'm not crazy. There isn't going to be any revolution and I'm not going to be its heroine and you aren't the type to be a hero. I understand you now. It isn't safe to fool around with you. Because if anybody did, you'd take your little revenge, and you wouldn't care what you brought down on everybody else's head. You could ruin their computer but then they'd come down on us and they'd make things twice as hard for us as they already are, and you wouldn't care. We'd all suffer, but you wouldn't care. No. My life isn't so terrible that I need you to turn it upside down for me. You've already done it to me once. I don't need it again.'

She looked at me steadily and all the anger seemed to be gone from her and there was only contempt left.

After a little she said, 'Can you go in there again and gimmick things so that there's no record of your arrest today?'

'Yeah. Yeah, I could do that.'

'Do it, then. And then get going. Get the hell out of here, fast.'

'Are you serious?'

'You think I'm not?'

I shook my head. I understood. And I knew that I had won and I had lost, both at the same time.

She made an impatient gesture, a shoo-fly gesture.

I nodded. I felt very, very small.

'I just want to say – all that stuff about how much I regretted the thing I did to you back then – it was true. Every word of it.'

'It probably was,' she said. 'Look, do your gimmicking and edit yourself out and then I want you to start moving. Out of the building. Out of the city. Okay? Do it real fast.'

I hunted around for something else to say and couldn't find it. Quit while you're ahead, I thought. She gave me her wrist and I did the interface with her. As my implant access touched hers she shuddered a little. It wasn't much of a shudder but I noticed it. I felt it, all right. I think I'm going to feel it every time I stiff anyone, ever again. Any time I even think of stiffing anyone.

I went in and around the John Doe arrest entry and got rid of it, and then I searched out her civil service file and promoted her up two grades and doubled her pay. Not much of an atonement. But what the hell, there wasn't much I could do. Then I cleaned up my traces behind me and exited the program.

'All right,' I said. 'It's done.'

'Fine,' she said, and rang for her cops.

They apologized for the case of mistaken identity and let me out of the building and turned me loose on Figueroa Street. It was late afternoon and the street was getting dark and the air was cool. Even in Los Angeles winter is winter, of a sort. I went to a street access and summoned the Toshiba from wherever it had parked itself and it came driving up, five or ten minutes later, and I told it to take me north. The going was slow, rush-hour stuff, but that was okay. We came to the wall at the Sylmar gate, fifty miles or so out of town. The gate asked me my name. 'Richard Roe,' I said. 'Beta Pi Upsilon 104324x. Destination San Francisco.'

It rains a lot in San Francisco in the winter. Still, it's a pretty town. I would have preferred Los Angeles that time of year, but what the hell. Nobody gets all his first choices all the time. The gate opened and the Toshiba went through. Easy as Beta Pi.

The Iron Star

This was written for a project initiated by Byron Preiss, the New York book packager, with whom I've worked closely on all sorts of things over the years. His handsome glossy-paper book *The Planets*, in which I had had one piece of fiction and one scientific article, had sold very nicely, and now he was casting his net a little wider: a book called *The Universe*. As before, professional astronomers were doing most of the scientific essays and s-f writers were providing stories to match. Byron showed me the list of themes — stars, quasars, black holes, galaxies and clusters, and so forth — and I chose to write about supernova and pulsars.

One incidental bit of pleasure came from this for me. In Byron's book, my story was illustrated with a full-colour plate by Bob Eggleton. I sold magazine rights to the story to *Amazing Stories*, oldest of science-fiction magazines, and it drew a cover painting by Terry Lee. By coincidence both Lee and Eggleton chose to illustrate the same scene, the one in which the narrator first gets a look at the Nine Sparg captain on his television screen. The two paintings are quite different in mood and technique, yet each depicts my alien critter in a distinctive and powerful way, while remaining faithful to my prose description. It's one of science-fiction writing's special treats to see your verbal inventions brought to visual life this way.

The alien ship came drifting up from behind the far side of the neutron star just as I was going on watch. It looked a little like a miniature neutron star itself: a perfect sphere, metallic, dark. But neutron stars don't have six perky little out-thrust legs and the alien craft did.

While I paused in front of the screen the alien floated diagonally upward, cutting a swathe of darkness across the brilliantly starry sky like a fast-moving black hole. It even occulted the real black hole that lay thirty light-minutes away.

I stared at the strange vessel, fascinated and annoyed, wishing I had never seen it, wishing it would softly and suddenly vanish away. This mission was sufficiently complicated already. We hadn't needed an alien ship to appear on the scene. For five days now we had circled the neutron star in seesaw orbit with the aliens, a hundred eighty degrees apart. They hadn't said anything to us and we didn't know how to say anything to them. I didn't feel good about that. I like things direct, succinct, known.

Lina Sorabji, busy enhancing sonar transparencies over at our improvised archaeology station, looked up from her work and caught me scowling. Lina is a slender, dark woman from Madras whose ancestors were priests and scholars when mine were hunting bison on the Great Plains. She said, 'You shouldn't let it get to you like that, Tom.'

'You know what it feels like, every time I see it cross the screen? It's like having a little speck wandering around on the visual field of your eye. Irritating, frustrating, maddening – and absolutely impossible to get rid of.'

'You want to get rid of it?'

I shrugged. 'Isn't this job tough enough? Attempting to scoop a sample from the core of a neutron star? Do we really have to have an alien spaceship looking over our shoulders while we work?'

'Maybe it's not a spaceship at all,' Lina said cheerily. 'Maybe it's just some kind of giant spacebug.'

I suppose she was trying to amuse me. I wasn't amused. This was going to win me a place in the history of space exploration, sure: Chief Executive Officer of the first expedition from Earth ever to encounter intelligent extraterrestrial life. Terrific. But that wasn't what IBM/Toshiba had hired me to do. And I'm more interested in completing assignments than in making history. You don't get paid for making history.

Basically the aliens were a distraction from our real work, just as last month's discovery of a dead civilization on a nearby solar system had been, the one whose photographs Lina Sorabji now was studying. This was supposed to be a business venture involving the experimental use of new technology, not an archaeological mission or an exercise in interspecies diplomacy. And I knew that there was a ship from the Exxon/Hyundai combine loose somewhere in hyperspace right now working on the same task we'd been sent out to handle. If they brought it off first, IBM/Toshiba would suffer a very severe loss of face, which is considered very bad on the corporate level. What's bad for IBM/Toshiba would be exceedingly bad for me. For all of us.

I glowered at the screen. Then the orbit of the *Ben-wah Maru* carried us down and away and the alien disappeared from my line of sight. But not for long, I knew.

As I keyed up the log reports from my sleep period I said to Lina, 'You have anything new today?' She had spent the past three weeks analysing the dead-world data. You never know what the parent companies will see as potentially profitable.

'I'm down to hundred-metre penetration now. There's a system of broad tunnels wormholing the entire planet. Some kind of pneumatic transportation network, is my guess. Here, have a look.'

A holoprint sprang into vivid life in the air between us. It was a sonar scan that we had taken from ten thousand kilometres out, reaching a short distance below the surface of the dead world. I saw odd-angled tunnels lined with gleaming luminescent tiles that still pulsed with dazzling colours, centuries after the cataclysm that had destroyed all life there. Amazing decorative patterns of bright lines were plainly visible along the tunnel walls, lines that swirled and overlapped and entwined and beckoned my eye into some adjoining dimension.

Trains of sleek snub-nosed vehicles were scattered like caterpillars everywhere in the tunnels. In them and around them lay skeletons, thousands of them, millions, a whole continent full of commuters slaughtered as they waited at the station for the morning express. Lina touched the fine scan and gave me a close look: biped creatures, broad skulls tapering sharply at the sides, long apelike arms, seven-fingered hands with what seemed like an opposable thumb at each end, pelvises enlarged into peculiar bony crests jutting far out from their hips. It wasn't the first time a hyperspace exploring vessel had come across relics of extinct extraterrestrial races, even a fossil or two. But these weren't fossils. These beings had died only a few hundred years ago. And they had all died at the same time.

I shook my head sombrely. 'Those are some tunnels. They might have been able to convert them into pretty fair radiation shelters, is my guess. If only they'd had a little warning of what was coming.'

'They never knew what hit them.'

'No,' I said. 'They never knew a thing. A supernova brewing right next door and they must not have been able to tell what was getting ready to happen.'

Lina called up another print, and another, then another. During our brief fly-by last month our sensors had captured an amazing panoramic view of this magnificent lost civilization: wide streets, spacious parks, splendid public buildings, imposing private houses, the works. Bizarre architecture, all unlikely angles and jutting crests like its creators, but unquestionably grand, noble, impressive. There had been keen intelligence at work here, and high artistry. Everything was intact and in a remarkable state of preservation, if you make allowances for the natural inroads that time and weather and I suppose the occasional earthquake will bring over three or four hundred years. Obviously this had been a wealthy, powerful society, stable and confident.

And between one instant and the next it had all been stopped dead in its tracks, wiped out, extinguished, annihilated. Perhaps they had had a fraction of a second to realize that the end of the world had come, but no more than that. I saw what surely were family groups huddling together, skeletons clumped in threes or fours or fives. I saw what I took to be couples with their seven-fingered hands still clasped in a final exchange of love. I saw some kneeling in a weird elbows-down position that might have been one of – who can say? Prayer? Despair? Acceptance?

A sun had exploded and this great world had died. I shuddered, not for the first time, thinking of it.

It hadn't even been their own sun. What had blown up was this one, forty light-years away from them, the one that was now the neutron star about which we orbited and which once had been a main-sequence sun maybe three or four times as big as Earth's. Or else it had been the other one in this binary system, thirty light-minutes from the first, the blazing young giant companion star of which nothing remained except the black hole nearby. At the moment we had no way of knowing which of these two stars had gone supernova first. Whichever one it was, though, had sent a furious burst of radiation heading outward, a lethal flux of cosmic rays capable of destroying most or perhaps all life-forms within a sphere a hundred light-years in diameter.

The planet of the underground tunnels and the noble temples had simply been in the way. One of these two suns had come to the moment when all the fuel in its core had been consumed: hydrogen had been fused into helium, helium into carbon, carbon into neon, oxygen, sulphur, silicon, until at last a core of pure iron lay at its heart. There is no atomic nucleus more strongly bound than iron. The star had reached the point where its release of energy through fusion had to cease; and with the end of energy production the star no longer could withstand the gravitational pressure of its own vast mass. In a moment, in the twinkling of an eye, the core underwent a catastrophic collapse. Its matter was compressed – beyond the point of equilibrium. And rebounded. And sent forth an intense shock wave that went rushing through the star's outer layers at a speed of 15,000 kilometres a second.

Which ripped the fabric of the star apart, generating an explosion releasing more energy than a billion suns.

The shock wave would have continued outward and outward

across space, carrying debris from the exploded star with it, and interstellar gas that the debris had swept up. A fierce sleet of radiation would have been riding on that wave, too: cosmic rays, X-rays, radio waves, gamma rays, everything, all up and down the spectrum. If the sun that had gone supernova had had planets close by, they would have been vaporized immediately. Outlying worlds of that system might merely have been fried.

The people of the world of the tunnels, forty light-years distant, must have known nothing of the great explosion for a full generation after it had happened. But, all that while, the light of that shattered star was travelling towards them at a speed of 300,000 kilometres per second, and one night its frightful baleful unexpected glare must have burst suddenly into their sky in the most terrifying way. And almost in that same moment – for the deadly cosmic rays thrown off by the explosion move nearly at the speed of light – the killing blast of hard radiation would have arrived. And so these people and all else that lived on their world perished in terror and light.

All this took place a thousand light-years from Earth: that surging burst of radiation will need another six centuries to complete its journey towards our home world. At that distance, the cosmic rays will do us little or no harm. But for a time that long-dead star will shine in our skies so brilliantly that it will be visible by day, and by night it will cast deep shadows, longer than those of the Moon.

That's still in Earth's future. Here the fatal supernova, and the second one that must have happened not long afterwards, were some four hundred years in the past. What we had here now was a neutron star left over from one cataclysm and a black hole left over from the other. Plus the pathetic remains of a great civilization on a scorched planet orbiting a neighbouring star. And now a ship from some alien culture. A busy corner of the galaxy, this one. A busy time for the crew of the IBM/Toshiba hyperspace ship *Ben-wah Maru*.

I was still going over the reports that had piled up at my station during my sleep period – mass-and-output readings on the neutron star, progress bulletins on the setup procedures for the neutronium scoop, and other routine stuff of that nature – when the communicator cone in front of me started to glow. I flipped it on. Cal Bjornsen, our communications guru, was calling from Brain Central downstairs.

Bjornsen is mostly black African with some Viking genes salted in. The whole left side of his face is cyborg, the result of some extreme bit of teenage carelessness. The story is that he was gravity-vaulting and lost polarity at sixty metres. The mix of ebony skin, blue eyes, blond hair, and sculpted titanium is an odd one, but I've seen a lot of faces less friendly than Cal's. He's a good man with anything electronic.

He said, 'I think they're finally trying to send us messages, Tom.'

I sat up fast. 'What's that?'

'We've been pulling in signals of some sort for the past ninety minutes that didn't look random, but we weren't sure about it. A dozen or so different frequencies all up and down the line, mostly in the radio band, but we're also getting what seem to be infra-red pulses, and something flashing in the ultraviolet range. A kind of scattershot noise effect, only it isn't noise.'

'Are you sure of that?'

'The computer's still chewing on it,' Bjornsen said. The fingers of his right hand glided nervously up and down his smooth metal cheek. 'But we can see already that there are clumps of repetitive patterns.'

'Coming from them? How do you know?'

'We didn't, at first. But the transmissions conked out when we lost line-of-sight with them, and started up again when they came back into view.'

'I'll be right down,' I said.

Bjornsen is normally a calm man, but he was running in frantic circles when I reached Brain Central three or four minutes later. There was stuff dancing on all the walls: sine waves, mainly, but plenty of other patterns jumping around on the monitors. He had already pulled in specialists from practically every department – the whole astronomy staff, two of the math guys, a couple from the external maintenance team, and somebody from engines. I felt preempted. Who was CEO on this ship, anyway? They were all babbling at once. 'Fourier series,' someone said, and someone yelled back, 'Dirichlet factor,' and someone else said, 'Gibbs phenomenon!' I heard Angie Seraphin insisting vehemently, ' – continuous except possibly for a finite number of finite discontinuities in the interval -pi to pi – '

'Hold it,' I said. 'What's going on?'

More babble, more gibberish. I got them quiet again and repeated my question, aiming it this time at Bjornsen.

'We have the analysis now,' he said.

'So?'

'You understand that it's only guesswork, but Brain Central gives good guess. The way it looks, they seem to want us to broadcast a carrier wave they can tune in on, and just talk to them while they lock in with some sort of word-to-word translating device of theirs.'

'That's what Brain Central thinks they're saying?'

'It's the most plausible semantic content of the patterns they're transmitting,' Bjornsen answered.

I felt a chill. The aliens had word-to-word translating devices? That was a lot more than we could claim. Brain Central is one very smart computer, and if it thought that it had correctly deciphered the message coming in, then in all likelihood it had. An astonishing accomplishment, taking a bunch of ones and zeros put together by an alien mind and culling some sense out of them.

But even Brain Central wasn't capable of word-to-word translation out of some unknown language. Nothing in our technology is. The alien message had been *designed* to be easy: put together, most likely, in a careful high-redundancy manner, the computer equivalent of picture-writing. Any race able to undertake interstellar travel ought to have a computer powerful enough to sweat the essential meaning out of a message like that, and we did. We couldn't go farther than that, though. Let the entropy of that message – that is, the unexpectedness of it, the unpredictability of its semantic content – rise just a little beyond the picture-writing level, and Brain Central would be lost. A computer that knows French should be able to puzzle out Spanish, and maybe even Greek. But Chinese? A tough proposition. And an *alien* language? Languages may start out logical, but they don't stay that way. And when its underlying grammatical assumptions were put together in the first place by beings with nervous systems that were wired up in ways entirely different from our own, well, the notion of instantaneous decoding becomes hopeless.

Yet our computer said that their computer could do word-to-word. That was scary.

On the other hand, if we couldn't talk to them, we wouldn't begin to find out what they were doing here and what threat, if any, they might pose to us. By revealing our language to them we might be handing them some sort of advantage, but I couldn't be sure of that, and it seemed to me we had to take the risk.

It struck me as a good idea to get some backing for that decision, though. After a dozen years as CEO aboard various corporate ships I knew the protocols. You did what you thought was right, but you didn't go all the way out on the limb by yourself if you could help it.

'Request a call for a meeting of the corporate staff,' I told Bjornsen.

It wasn't so much a scientific matter now as a political one. The scientists would probably be gung-ho to go blasting straight ahead with making contact. But I wanted to hear what the Toshiba people would say, and the IBM people, and the military people. So we got everyone together and I laid the situation out and asked for a Consensus Process. And let them go at it, hammer and tongs.

Instant polarization. The Toshiba people were scared silly of the aliens. We must be cautious, Nakamura said. Caution, yes, said her cohort Nagy-Szabo. There may be danger to Earth. We have no knowledge of the aims and motivations of these beings. Avoid all contact with them, Nagy-Szabo said.

Nakamura went even further. We should withdraw from the area immediately, she said, and return to Earth for additional instructions. That drew hot opposition from Jorgensen and Kalliotis, the IBM people. We had work to do here, they said. We should do it. They grudgingly conceded the need to be wary, but strongly urged continuation of the mission and advocated a circumspect opening of contact with the other ship. I think they were already starting to think about alien marketing demographics. Maybe I do them an injustice. Maybe.

The military people were about evenly divided between the two factions. A couple of them, the hair-splitting career-minded ones, wanted to play it absolutely safe and clear out of here fast, and the others, the up-and-away hero types, spoke out in favour of forging ahead with contact and to hell with the risks.

I could see there wasn't going to be any consensus. It was going to come down to me to decide.

By nature I am cautious. I might have voted with Nakamura in favour of immediate withdrawal, however that would have made my ancient cold-eyed Sioux forebears howl. Yet in the end what swayed me was an argument that came from Bryce-Williamson, one of the fiercest of the military sorts. He said that we didn't dare turn tail and run for home without making contact, because the aliens would take that either as a hostile act or a stupid one, and either way they might just slap some kind of tracer on us that ultimately would enable them to discover the location of our home world. True caution, he said, required us to try to find out what these people were all about before we made any move to leave the scene. We couldn't just run and we couldn't simply ignore them.

I sat quietly for a long time, weighing everything.

'Well?' Bjornsen asked. 'What do you want to do, Tom?'

'Send them a broadcast,' I said. 'Give them greetings in the name of Earth and all its peoples. Extend to them the benevolent warm wishes of the board of directors of IBM/Toshiba. And then we'll wait and see.'

We waited. But for a long while we didn't see.

Two days, and then some. We went round and round the neutron star, and they went round and round the neutron star, and no further communication came from them. We beamed them all sorts of messages at all sorts of frequencies along the spectrum, both in the radio band and via infra-red and ultra-violet as well, so that they'd have plenty of material to work with. Perhaps their translator gadget wasn't all that good, I told myself hopefully. Perhaps it was stripping its gears trying to fathom the pleasant little packets of semantic data that we had sent them.

On the third day of silence I began feeling restless. There was no way we could begin the work we had been sent here to do, not with aliens watching. The Toshiba people – the Ultra Cautious faction – got more and more nervous. Even the IBM representatives began to act a little twitchy. I started to question the wisdom of having overruled the advocates of a no-contact policy. Although the parent companies hadn't seriously expected us to run into aliens, they had covered their eventuality in our instructions, and we were under orders to do minimum tipping of our hands if we found ourselves observed by strangers. But it was too late to call back our messages and I was still eager to find out what would happen next. So we watched and waited, and then we waited and watched. Round and round the neutron star.

We had been parked in orbit for ten days now around the neutron star, an orbit calculated to bring us no closer to its surface than 9000 kilometres at the closest skim. That was close enough for us to carry out our work, but not so close that we would be subjected to troublesome and dangerous tidal effects.

The neutron star had been formed in the supernova explosion that had destroyed the smaller of the two suns in what had once been a binary star system here. At the moment of the cataclysmic collapse of the stellar sphere, all its matter had come rushing inward with such force that electrons and protons were driven into each other to become a soup of pure neutrons. Which then were squeezed so tightly that they were forced virtually into contact with one another, creating a smooth globe of the strange stuff that we call neutronium, a billion billion times denser than steel and a hundred billion billion times more incompressible.

That tiny ball of neutronium glowing dimly in our screens was the neutron star. It was just eighteen kilometres in diameter but its mass was greater than that of Earth's sun. That gave it a gravitational field a quarter of a billion billion times as strong as that of the surface of Earth. If we could somehow set foot on it, we wouldn't just be squashed flat, we'd be instantly reduced to fine powder by the colossal tidal effects – the difference in gravitational pull between the soles of our feet and the tops of our heads, stretching us towards and away from the neutron star's centre with a kick of eighteen billion kilograms.

A ghostly halo of electromagnetic energy surrounded the neutron star: X-rays, radio waves, gammas, and an oily, crackling flicker of violet light. The neutron star was rotating on its axis some 550 times a second, and powerful jets of electrons were spouting from its magnetic poles at each sweep, sending forth a beacon-like pulsar broadcast of the familiar type that we have been able to detect since the middle of the twentieth century.

Behind that zone of fiercely outflung radiation lay the neutron star's atmosphere: an envelope of gaseous iron a few centimetres thick. Below that, our scan had told us, was a two-kilometres-thick crust of normal matter, heavy elements only, ranging from molybdenum on up to transuranics with atomic numbers as high as 140. And within that was the neutronium zone, the stripped nuclei of iron packed unimaginably close together, an ocean of strangeness nine kilometres deep. What lay at the heart of *that*, we could only guess.

We had come here to plunge a probe into the neutronium zone and carry off a spoonful of star-stuff that weighed 100 billion tons per cubic centimetre.

No sort of conventional landing on the neutron star was possible or even conceivable. Not only was the gravitational pull beyond our comprehension – anything that was capable of withstanding the tidal effects would still have to cope with an escape velocity requirement of 200,000 kilometres per second when it tried to take off, two thirds the speed of light – but the neutron star's surface temperature was something like 3.5 million degrees. The surface temperature of our own sun is six *thousand* degrees and we don't try to make landings there. Even at this distance, our heat and radiation shields were straining to the limits to keep us from being cooked. We didn't intend to go any closer.

What IBM/Toshiba wanted us to do was to put a miniature hyperspace ship into orbit around the neutron star: an astonishing little vessel no bigger than your clenched fist, powered by a fantastically scaled-down version of the drive that had carried us through the space-time manifold across a span of a thousand light-years in a dozen weeks. The little ship was a slave-drone; we would operate it from the *Ben-wah Maru*. Or, rather, Brain Central would. In a manoeuvre that had taken fifty computer-years to program, we would send the miniature into hyperspace and bring it out again *right inside the neutron star*. And keep it there a billionth of a second, long enough for it to gulp the spoonful of neutronium we had been sent here to collect. Then we'd head for home, with the miniature ship following us along the same hyperpath.

We'd head for home, that is, unless the slave-drone's brief intrusion into the neutron star released disruptive forces that splattered us all over this end of the galaxy. IBM/Toshiba didn't really think that was going to happen. In theory a neutron star is one of the most stable things there is in the universe, and the math didn't indicate that taking a nip from its interior would cause real problems. This neighbourhood had already had its full quota of giant explosions, anyway.

Still, the possibility existed. Especially since there was a black hole just thirty light-minutes away, a souvenir of the second and much larger supernova bang that had happened here in the recent past. Having a black hole nearby is a little like playing with an extra wild card whose existence isn't made known to the players until some randomly chosen moment midway through the game. If we destabilized the neutron star in some way not anticipated by the scientists back on Earth, we might just find ourselves going for a visit to the event horizon instead of getting to go home. Or we might not. There was only one way of finding out.

I didn't know, by the way, what use the parent companies planned to make of the neutronium we had been hired to bring them. I hoped it was a good one.

But obviously we weren't going to tackle any of this while there was an alien ship in the vicinity. So all we could do was wait. And see. Right now we were doing a lot of waiting, and no seeing at all.

Two days later Cal Bjornsen said, 'We're getting a message back from them now. Audio only. In English.'

We had wanted that, we had even hoped for that. And yet it shook me to learn that it was happening.

'Let's hear it,' I said.

'The relay's coming over ship channel seven.'

I tuned in. What I heard was an obviously synthetic voice, no undertones or overtones, not much inflection. They were trying to mimic the speech rhythms of what we had sent them, and I suppose they were actually doing a fair job of it, but the result was still unmistakably mechanical-sounding. Of course there might be nothing on board that ship but a computer, I thought, or maybe robots. I wish now that they had been robots.

It had the absolute and utter familiarity of a recurring dream. In stiff, halting, but weirdly comprehensible English came the first greetings of an alien race to the people of the planet of Earth. 'This who speak be First of Nine Sparg,' the voice said. Nine Sparg, we soon realized from context, was the name of their planet. First might have been the speaker's name, or his – hers, its? – title; that was unclear, and stayed that way. In an awkward pidgin-English that we nevertheless had little trouble understanding, First expressed gratitude for our transmission and asked us to send more words. To send a dictionary, in fact:

now that they had the algorithm for our speech they needed more content to jam in behind it, so that we could go on to exchange more complex statements than Hello and How are you.

Bjornsen queried me on the override. 'We've got an English program that we could start feeding them,' he said. 'Thirty thousand words: that should give them plenty. You want me to put it on for them?'

'Not so fast,' I said. 'We need to edit it first.'

'For what?'

'Anything that might help them find the location of Earth. That's in our orders, under Eventuality of Contact with Extra-terrestrials. Remember, I have Nakamura and Nagy-Szabo breathing down my neck, telling me that there's a ship full of boogiemen out there and we mustn't have anything to do with them. I don't believe that myself. But right now we don't know how friendly these Spargs are and we aren't supposed to bring strangers home with us.'

'But how could a dictionary entry – '

'Suppose the sun – *our* sun – is defined as a yellow G2 type star,' I said. 'That gives them a pretty good beginning. Or something about the constellations as seen from Earth. I don't know, Cal. I just want to make sure we don't accidentally hand these beings a road-map to our home planet before we find out what sort of critters they are.'

Three of us spent half a day screening the dictionary, and we put Brain Central to work on it too. In the end we pulled seven words – you'd laugh if you knew which they were, but we wanted to be careful – and sent the rest across to the Spargs. They were silent for nine or ten hours. When they came back on the air their command of English was immensely more fluent. Frighteningly more fluent. Yesterday First had sounded like a tourist using a Fifty Handy Phrases program. A day later, First's command of English was as good as that of an intelligent Japanese who has been living in the United States for ten or fifteen years.

It was a tense, wary conversation. Or so it seemed to me,

the way it began to seem that First was male and that his way of speaking was brusque and bluntly probing. I may have been wrong on every count.

First wanted to know who we were and why we were here. Jumping right in, getting down to the heart of the matter. I felt a little like a butterfly collector who has wandered onto the grounds of a fusion plant and is being interrogated by a security guard. But I kept my tone and phrasing as neutral as I could, and told him that our planet was called Earth and that we had come on a mission of exploration and investigation.

So had they, he told me. Where is Earth?

Pretty straightforward of him, I thought. I answered that I lacked at this point a means of explaining galactic positions to him in terms that he would understand. I did volunteer the information that Earth was not anywhere close at hand.

He was willing to drop that line of inquiry for the time being. He shifted to the other obvious one:

What were we investigating?

Certain properties of collapsed stars, I said, after a bit of hesitation.

And which properties were those?

I told him that we didn't have enough vocabulary in common for me to try to explain that either.

The Nine Sparg captain seemed to accept that evasion too. And provided me with a pause that indicated that it was my turn. Fair enough.

When I asked him what *he* was doing here, he replied without any apparent trace of evasiveness that he had come on a mission of historical inquiry. I pressed for details. It has to do with the ancestry of our race, he said. We used to live in this part of the galaxy, before the great explosion. No hesitation at all about telling me that. It struck me that First was being less reticent about dealing with my queries than I was with his; but of course I had no way of judging whether I was hearing the truth from him.

'I'd like to know more,' I said, as much as a test as anything else. 'How long ago did your people flee this great explosion?

56

And how far from here is your present home world?'

A long silence: several minutes. I wondered uncomfortably if I had overplayed my hand. If they were as edgy about our finding their home world as I was about their finding ours, I had to be careful not to push them into an overreaction. They might just think that the safest thing to do would be to blow us out of the sky as soon as they had learned all they could from us.

But when First spoke again it was only to say, 'Are you willing to establish contact in the visual band?'

'Is such a thing possible?'

'We think so,' he said.

I thought about it. Would letting them see what we looked like give them any sort of clue to the location of Earth? Perhaps, but it seemed far-fetched. Maybe they'd be able to guess that we were carbon-based oxygen-breathers, but the risk of allowing them to know that seemed relatively small. And in any case we'd find out what *they* looked like. An even trade, right?

I had my doubts that their video transmission system could be made compatible with our receiving equipment. But I gave First the go-ahead and turned the microphone over to the communications staff. Who struggled with the problem for a day and a half. Sending the signal back and forth was no big deal, but breaking it down into information that would paint a picture on a cathode-ray tube was a different matter. The communications people at both ends talked and talked and talked, while I fretted about how much technical information about us we were revealing to the Spargs. The tinkering went on and on and nothing appeared on screen except occasional strings of horizontal lines. We sent them more data about how our television system worked. They made further adjustments in their transmission devices. This time we got spots instead of lines. We sent even more data. Were they leading us on? And were we telling them too much? I came finally to the position that trying to make the video link work had been a bad idea, and started to tell Communications that. But then the haze of drifting spots on my screen abruptly cleared and I found myself looking into the face of an alien being.

An alien face, yes. Extremely alien. Suddenly this whole interchange was kicked up to a new level of reality.

A hairless wedge-shaped head, flat and broad on top, tapering to a sharp point below. Corrugated skin that looked as thick as heavy rubber. Two chilly eyes in the centre of that wide forehead and two more at its extreme edges. Three mouths, vertical slits, side by side: one for speaking and the other two, maybe for separate intake of fluids and solids. The whole business supported by three long columnar necks as thick as a man's wrist, separated by open spaces two or three centimetres wide. What was below the neck we never got to see. But the head alone was plenty.

They probably thought we were just as strange.

With video established, First and I picked up our conversation right where we had broken it off the day before. Once more he was not in the least shy about telling me things.

He had been able to calculate in our units of time the date of the great explosion that had driven his people far from home world: it had taken place 387 years ago. He didn't use the word 'supernova', because it hadn't been included in the 30,000-word vocabulary we had sent them, but that was obviously what he meant by 'the great explosion'. The 387-year figure squared pretty well with our own calculations, which were based on an analysis of the surface temperature and rate of rotation of the neutron star.

The Nine Sparg people had had plenty of warning that their sun was behaving oddly – the first signs of instability had become apparent more than a century before the blow-up – and they had devoted all their energy for several generations to the job of packing up and clearing out. It had taken many years, it seemed, for them to accomplish their migration to the distant new world they had chosen for their new home. Did that mean, I asked myself, that their method of interstellar travel was much slower than ours, and that they had needed decades or even a century to cover fifty or a hundred light-years? Earth had less to worry about, then. Even if they wanted to make trouble for us, they wouldn't be able easily to reach us, a thousand light-years from here. Or was First saying that their new world was *really* distant – all the way across the galaxy, perhaps, seventy or eighty thousand light-years away, or even in some other galaxy altogether? If that was the case, we were up against truly superior beings. But there was no easy way for me to question him about such things without telling him things about our own hyperdrive and our distance from this system that I didn't care to have him know.

After a long and evidently difficult period of settling in on the new world, First went on, the Nine Sparg folk finally were well enough established to launch an inquiry into the condition of their former home planet. Thus his mission to the supernova site.

'But we are in great mystery,' First admitted, and it seemed to me that a note of sadness and bewilderment had crept into his mechanical-sounding voice. 'We have come to what certainly is the right location. Yet nothing seems to be correct here. We find only this little iron star. And of our former planet there is no trace.'

I stared at that peculiar and unfathomable four-eyed face, that three-columned neck, those tight vertical mouths, and to my surprise something close to compassion awoke in me. I had been dealing with this creature as though he were a potential enemy capable of leading armadas of war to my world and conquering it. But in fact he might be merely a scholarly explorer who was making a nostalgic pilgrimage, and running into problems with it. I decided to relax my guard just a little.

'Have you considered,' I said, 'that you might not be in the right location after all?'

'What do you mean?'

'As we were completing our journey towards what you call the iron star,' I said, 'we discovered a planet forty light-years from here that beyond much doubt had had a great civilization, and which evidently was close enough to the exploding star system here to have been devastated by it. We have pictures of it that we could show you. Perhaps *that* was your home world.'

Even as I was saying it the idea started to seem foolish to me. The skeletons we had photographed on the dead world had had broad tapering heads that might perhaps have been similar to those of First, but they hadn't shown any evidence of this unique triple-neck arrangement. Besides, First had said that his people had had several generations to prepare for evacuation. Would they have left so many millions of their people behind to die? It looked obvious from the way those skeletons were scattered around that the inhabitants of that planet hadn't had the slightest clue that doom was due to overtake them that day. And finally, I realized that First had plainly said that it was his own world's sun that had exploded, not some neighbouring star. The supernova had happened here. The dead world's sun was still intact.

'Can you show me your pictures?' he said.

It seemed pointless. But I felt odd about retracting my offer. And in the new rapport that had sprung up between us I could see no harm in it.

I told Lina Sorabji to feed her sonar transparencies into the relay pickup. It was easy enough for Cal Bjornsen to shunt them into our video transmission to the alien ship.

The Nine Sparg captain withheld his comment until we had shown him the batch.

Then he said, 'Oh, that was not our world. That was the world of the Garvalekkinon people.'

'The Garvalekkinon?'

'We knew them. A neighbouring race, not related to us. Sometimes, on rare occasions, we traded with them. Yes, they must all have died when the star exploded. It is too bad.'

'They look as though they had no warning,' I said. 'Look: can you see them there, waiting in the train stations?'

The triple mouths fluttered in what might have been the Nine Sparg equivalent of a nod.

'I suppose they did not know the explosion was coming.'

'You suppose? You mean you didn't tell them?'

All four eyes blinked at once. Expression of puzzlement.

'Tell them? Why should we have told them? We were busy with our preparations. We had no time for them. Of course the radiation would have been harmful to them, but why was that our concern? They were not related to us. They were nothing to us.'

I had trouble believing I had heard him correctly. A neighbouring people. Occasional trading partners. Your sun is about to blow up, and it's reasonable to assume that nearby solar systems will be affected. You have fifty or a hundred years of advance notice yourselves, and you can't even take the trouble to let these other people know what's going to happen?

I said, 'You felt no need at all to warn them? That isn't easy for me to understand.'

Again the four-eyed shrug.

'I have explained it to you already,' said First. 'They were not of our kind. They were nothing to us.'

I excused myself on some flimsy excuse and broke contact. And sat and thought a long long while. Listening to the words of the Nine Sparg captain echoing in my mind. And thinking of the millions of skeletons scattered like straws in the tunnels of that dead world that the supernova had baked. A whole people left to die because it was inconvenient to take five minutes to send them a message. Or perhaps because it simply never had occurred to anybody to bother.

The families, huddling together. The children reaching out. The husbands and wives with hands interlocked.

A world of busy, happy, intelligent, people. Boulevards and temples. Parks and gardens. Paintings, sculpture, poetry, music. History, philosophy, science. And a sudden star in the sky, and everything gone in a moment.

Why should we have told them? They were nothing to us.

I knew something of the history of my own people. We had experienced casual extermination too. But at least when the white settlers had done it to us it was because they had wanted our land.

For the first time I understood the meaning of alien.

I turned on the external screen and stared out at the unfamiliar sky of this place. The neutron star was barely visible, a dull red dot, far down in the lower left quadrant; and the black hole was high.

Once they had both been stars. What havoc must have attended their destruction! It must have been the Sparg sun that blew first, the one that had become the neutron star. And then, fifty or a hundred years later, perhaps, the other, larger star had gone the same route. Another titanic supernova, a great flare of killing light. But of course everything for hundreds of light-years around hàd perished already in the first blast.

The second sun had been too big to leave a neutron star behind. So great was its mass that the process of collapse had continued on beyond the neutron-star stage, matter crushing in upon itself until it broke through the normal barriers of space and took on a bizarre and almost unthinkable form, creating an object of infinitely small volume that was nevertheless of infinite density: a black hole, a pocket of incomprehensibility where once a star had been.

I stared now at the black hole before me.

I couldn't see it, of course. So powerful was the surface gravity of that grotesque thing that nothing could escape from it, not even electromagnetic radiation, not the merest particle of light. The ultimate in invisibility cloaked that infinitely deep hole in space.

But though the black hole itself was invisible, the effects that its presence caused were not. That terrible gravitational pull would rip apart and swallow any solid object that came too close; and so the hole was surrounded by a bright ring of dust and gas several hundred kilometres across. These shimmering particles constantly tumbled towards that insatiable mouth, colliding as they spiralled in, releasing flaring fountains of radiation, red-shifted into the visual spectrum by the enormous gravity: the bright green of helium, the majestic purple of hydrogen, the crimson of oxygen. That outpouring of energy was the death-cry of doomed matter. That rainbow whirlpool of blazing light was the beacon marking the maw of the black hole.

I found it oddly comforting to stare at that thing. To contemplate that zone of eternal quietude from which there was no escape. Pondering so inexorable and unanswerable an infinity was more soothing than thinking of a world of busy people destroyed by the indifference of their neighbours. Black holes offer no choices, no complexities, no shades of disagreement. They are absolute.

Why should we have told them? They were nothing to us.

After a time I restored contact with the Nine Sparg ship. First came to the screen at once, ready to continue our conversation.

'There is no question that our world once was located here,' he said at once. 'We have checked and rechecked the coordinates. But the changes have been extraordinary.'

'Have they?'

'Once there were two stars here, our own and the brilliant blue one that was nearby. Our history is very specific on that point: a brilliant blue star that lit the entire sky. Now we have only the iron star. Apparently it has taken the place of our sun. But where has the blue one gone? Could the explosion have destroyed it too?'

I frowned. Did they really not know? Could a race be capable of attaining an interstellar spacedrive and an interspecies translating device, and nevertheless not have arrived at any understanding of the neutron star/black hole cosmogony?

Why not? They were aliens. They had come by all their understanding of the universe via a route different from ours. They might well have overlooked this feature or that of the universe about them.

'The blue star – ' I began.

But First spoke right over me, saying, 'It is a mystery that we must devote all our energies to solving, or our mission will be fruitless. But let us talk of other things. You have said little

63

of your own mission. And of your home world. I am filled with great curiosity, Captain, about those subjects.'

I'm sure you are, I thought.

'We have only begun our return to space travel,' said First. 'Thus far we have encountered no other intelligent races. And so we regard this meeting as fortunate. It is our wish to initiate contact with you. Quite likely some aspects of your technology would be valuable to us. And there will be much that you wish to purchase from us. Therefore we would be glad to establish trade relations with you.'

As you did with the Garvalekkinon people, I said to myself.

I said, 'We can speak of that tomorrow, Captain. I grow tired now. But before we break contact for the day, allow me to offer you the beginning of a solution to the mystery of the disappearance of the blue sun.'

The four eyes widened. The slitted mouths parted in what seemed surely to be excitement.

'Can you do that?'

I took a deep breath.

'We have some preliminary knowledge. Do you see the place opposite the iron star, where energies boil and circle in the sky? As we entered this system, we found certain evidence there that may explain the fate of your former blue sun. You would do well to centre your investigations on that spot.'

'We are most grateful,' said First.

'And now, Captain, I must bid you good night. Until tomorrow, Captain.'

'Until tomorrow,' said the alien.

I was awakened in the middle of my sleep period by Lina Sorabji and Bryce-Williamson, both of them looking flushed and sweaty. I sat up, blinking and shaking my head.

'It's the alien ship,' Bryce-Williamson blurted. 'It's approaching the black hole.'

'Is it, now?'

'Dangerously close,' said Lina. 'What do they think they're doing? Don't they know?'

'I don't think so,' I said. 'I suggested that they go exploring there. Evidently they don't regard it as a bad idea.'

'You sent them there?' she said incredulously.

With a shrug I said, 'I told them that if they went over there they might find the answer to the question of where one of their missing suns went. I guess they've decided to see if I was right.'

'We have to warn them,' said Bryce-Williamson. 'Before it's too late. Especially if we're responsible for sending them there. They'll be furious with us once they realize that we failed to warn them of the danger.'

'By the time they realize it,' I replied calmly, 'it *will* be too late. And then their fury won't matter, will it? They won't be able to tell us how annoyed they are with us. Or to report to their home world, for that matter, that they had an encounter with intelligent aliens who might be worth exploiting.'

He gave me an odd look. The truth was starting to sink in.

I turned on the external screens and punched up a close look at the black hole region. Yes, there was the alien ship, the little metallic sphere, the six odd outthrust legs. It was in the zone of criticality now. It seemed hardly to be moving at all. And it was growing dimmer and dimmer as it slowed. The gravitational field had it, and it was being drawn in. Blacking out, becoming motionless. Soon it would have gone beyond the point where outside observers could perceive it. Already it was beyond the point of turning back.

I heard Lina sobbing behind me. Bryce-Williamson was muttering to himself: praying, perhaps.

I said, 'Who can say what they would have done to us – in their casual, indifferent way – once they came to Earth? We know now that Spargs worry only about Spargs. Anybody else is just so much furniture.' I shook my head. 'To hell with them. They're gone, and in a universe this big we'll probably never come across any of them again, or they us. Which is just fine. We'll be a lot better off having nothing at all to do with them.'

'But to die that way – ' Lina murmured. 'To sail blindly into a black hole – '

'It is a great tragedy,' said Bryce-Williamson.

'A tragedy for them,' I said. 'For us, a reprieve, I think. And tomorrow we can get moving on the neutronium-scoop project.' I tuned up the screen to the next level. The boiling cloud of matter around the mouth of the black hole blazed fiercely. But of the alien ship there was nothing to be seen.

Yes, a great tragedy, I thought. The valiant exploratory mission that had sought the remains of the Nine Sparg home world has been lost with all hands. No hope of rescue. A pity that they hadn't known how unpleasant black holes can be.

But why should we have told them? They were nothing to us.

The Secret Sharer

I make no secret of my admiration for the work of Joseph Conrad. (Or for Conrad himself, the tough, stubborn little man who, although English was only his third language, after Polish and French, not only was able to pass the difficult oral qualifying exam to become a captain in the British merchant marine, but then, a decade or so later, transformed himself into one of the greatest figures in twentieth-century English literature.) Most of what I owe to Conrad as a writer is buried deep in the substructure of my stories – a way of looking at narrative, a way of understanding character. But occasionally I've made the homage more visible. My novel *Downward to the Earth* of 1969 is a kind of free transposition of his novella 'Heart of Darkness' to science fiction, a borrowing which I signalled overtly by labelling my most tormented character with the name of Kurtz. 'Heart of Darkness', when I first encountered it as a reader forty years ago, had been packaged as half of a two-novella paperback collection, the other story being 'The Secret Sharer'. And some time late in 1986, I know not why – a love of symmetry? A compulsion towards completion? – I felt the urge to finish what I had begun in *Downward to the Earth* by writing a story adapted from the other great novella of that paperback of long ago.

This time I was less subtle than before, announcing my intentions not by using one of Conrad's character names but by appropriating his story's actual title. (This produced a pleasantly absurd result when my story was published in *Isaac Asimov's Science Fiction Magazine* and a reader wrote to the editor, somewhat indignantly, to ask whether I knew that the title had already been used by Joseph Conrad!) I swiped not only the title but Conrad's basic story

67

situation, that of the ship captain who finds a stowaway on board and eventually is drawn into a strange alliance with him. (Her, in my story.) But otherwise I translated the Conrad into purely science-fictional terms and produced something that I think represents completely original work, however much it may owe to the structure of a classic earlier story.

'Translate' is perhaps not the appropriate term for what I did. A 'translation', in the uncompromising critical vocabulary set forth by Damon Knight and James Blish in the 1950s upon which I based much of my own fiction-writing aesthetic, is an adaptation of a stock format of mundane fiction into s-f by a simple one-for-one substitution of science-fictiony noises for the artefacts of the mundane field. That is, change 'Colt .44' to 'laser pistol' and 'horse' to 'greeznak' and 'Comanche' to 'Sloogl' and you can easily generate s-f out of a standard western story, complete with cattle-rustlers, scalpings, and cavalry rescues. But you don't get science fiction; you don't get anything *new*, just a western story with greeznaks and Sloogls. Change 'Los Angeles Police Department' to 'Drylands Patrol' and 'crack dealer' to 'canal-dust dealer' and you've got a crime story set on Mars, but so what? Change 'the canals of Venice' to 'the marshy streets of Venusburg' and the sinister agents of SMERSH to the sinister agents of AAAARGH and you've got a James Bond story set on the second planet, but it's still a James Bond story.

I don't think that's what I've done here. The particular way in which Vox stows away aboard the *Sword of Orion* is nothing that Joseph Conrad could have understood, and arises, I think, purely out of the science-fictional inventions at the heart of the story. The way she leaves the ship is very different from anything depicted in Conrad's maritime fiction. The starwalk scene provides visionary possibilities quite unlike those afforded by a long stare into the vastness of the trackless Pacific. And so on: 'The Secret Sharer' by Robert Silverberg is, or so I believe, a new and unique *science-fiction* story set, for reasons of the author's private amusement, within the framework of a well-known century-old masterpiece of the sea by Joseph Conrad that happens to have the same title.

'The Secret Sharer' – mine, not Conrad's – was a Nebula and

Hugo nominee in 1988 as best novella of the year, but didn't get the trophies. It did win the third of the major s-f honours, the *Locus* award. Usually most of the *Locus* winners go on to get Hugos as well, but that year it didn't happen. I regretted that. But Joseph Conrad's original version of the story didn't win a Hugo or a Nebula either. You take your lumps in this business and you go bravely onward: it's the only way.

1.

It was my first time to heaven and I was no one at all, no one at all, and this was the voyage that was supposed to make me someone.

But though I was no one at all I dared to look upon the million worlds and I felt a great sorrow for them. There were all about me, humming along on their courses through the night, each of them believing it was actually going somewhere. And each one wrong, of course, for worlds go nowhere, except around and around and around, pathetic monkeys on a string, forever tethered in place. They seem to move, yes. But really they stand still. And I – I who stared at the worlds of heaven and was swept with compassion for them – I knew that though I seemed to be standing still, I was in fact moving. For I was aboard a ship of heaven, a ship of the Service, that was spanning the light-years at a speed so incomprehensibly great that it might as well have been no speed at all.

I was very young. My ship, then as now, was the *Sword of Orion*, on a journey out of Kansas Four bound for Cul-de-Sac and Strappado and Mangan's Bitch and several other worlds, via the usual spinarounds. It was my first voyage and I was in command. I thought for a long time that I would lose my soul on that voyage; but now I know that what was happening aboard that ship was not the losing of a soul but the gaining of one. And perhaps of more than one.

2.

Roacher thought I was sweet. I could have killed him for that; but of course he was dead already.

You have to give up your life when you go to heaven. What you get in return is for me to know and you, if you care, to find out; but the inescapable thing is that you leave behind anything that ever linked you to life on shore, and you become something else. We say that you give up the body and you get your soul. Certainly you can keep your body too, if you want it. Most do. But it isn't any good to you any more, not in the ways that you think a body is good to you. I mean to tell you how it was for me on my first voyage aboard the *Sword of Orion*, so many years ago.

I was the youngest officer on board, so naturally I was captain.

They put you in command right at the start, before you're anyone. That's the only test that means a damn: they throw you in the sea and if you can swim you don't drown, and if you can't you do. The drowned ones go back in the tank and they serve their own useful purposes, as push-cells or downloaders or mind-wipers or Johnny-scrub-and-scour or whatever. The ones that don't drown go on to other commands. No one is wasted. The Age of Waste has been over a long time.

On the third virtual day out from Kansas Four, Roacher told me that I was the sweetest captain he had ever served under. And he had served under plenty of them, for Roacher had gone up to heaven at least two hundred years before, maybe more.

'I can see it in your eyes, the sweetness. I can see it in the angle you hold your head.'

He didn't mean it as a compliment.

'We can put you off ship at Ultima Thule,' Roacher said. 'Nobody will hold it against you. We'll put you in a bottle and send you down, and the Thuleys will catch you and decant you and you'll be able to find your way back to Kansas Four in

70

twenty or fifty years. It might be the best thing.'

Roacher is small and parched, with brown skin and eyes that shine with the purple luminescence of space. Some of the worlds he has seen were forgotten a thousand years ago.

'Go bottle yourself, Roacher,' I told him.

'Ah, Captain, Captain! Don't take it the wrong way. Here, Captain, give us a touch of the sweetness.' He reached out a claw, trying to stroke me along the side of my face. 'Give us a touch, Captain, give us just a little touch!'

'I'll fry your soul and have it for breakfast, Roacher. There's sweetness for you. Go scuttle off, will you? Go jack yourself to the mast and drink hydrogen, Roacher. Go. Go.'

'So sweet,' he said. But he went. I had the power to hurt him. He knew I could do it, because I was captain. He also knew I wouldn't; but there was always the possibility he was wrong. The captain exists in that margin between certainty and possibility. A crewman tests the width of that margin at his own risk. Roacher knew that. He had been a captain once himself, after all.

There were seventeen of us to heaven that voyage, staffing a ten-kilo Megaspore-class ship with full annexes and extensions and all virtualities. We carried a bulging cargo of the things regarded in those days as vital in the distant colonies: pre-read vapour chips, artificial intelligences, climate nodes, matrix jacks, mediq machines, bone banks, soil converters, transit spheres, communication bubbles, skin-and-organ synthesizers, wildlife domestication plaques, gene replacement kits, a sealed consignment of obliteration sand and other proscribed weapons, and so on. We also had fifty billion dollars in the form of liquid currency pods, central-bank-to-central-bank transmission. In addition there was a passenger load of seven thousand colonists. Eight hundred of these were on the hoof and the others were stored in matrix form for body transplant on the worlds of destination. A standard load, in other words. The crew worked on commission, also as per standard, one per cent of bill-of-lading value divided in customary lays. Mine was the fiftieth lay – that is, two per cent of the net profits of the voyage – and that included a bonus for serving as captain; otherwise I would have had the hundredth lay or something even longer. Roacher had the tenth lay and his jackmate Bulgar the fourteenth, although they weren't even officers. Which demonstrates the value of seniority in the Service. But seniority is the same thing as survival, after all, and why should survival not be rewarded? On my most recent voyage I drew the nineteenth lay. I will have better than that on my next.

3.

You have never seen a starship. We keep only to heaven; when we are to worldward, shoreships come out to us for the downloading. The closest we ever go to planetskin is a million shiplengths. Any closer and we'd be shaken apart by that terrible strength which emanates from worlds.

We don't miss landcrawling, though. It's a plague to us. If I had to step to shore now, after having spent most of my lifetime in heaven, I would die of the drop-death within an hour. That is a monstrous way to die; but why would I ever go ashore? The likelihood of that still existed for me at the time I first sailed the *Sword of Orion,* you understand, but I have long since given it up. That is what I mean when I say that you give up your life when you go to heaven. But of course what also goes from you is any feeling that to be ashore has anything to do with being alive. If you could ride a starship, or even see one as we see them, you would understand. I don't blame you for being what you are.

Let me show you the *Sword of Orion.* Though you will never see it as we see it.

What would you see, if you left the ship as we sometimes do to do the starwalk in the Great Open?

The first thing you would see is the light of the ship. A starship gives off a tremendous insistent glow of light that splits heaven like the blast of a trumpet. That great light both precedes and follows. Ahead of the ship rides a luminescent cone of brightness bellowing in the void. In its wake the ship leaves a photonic track so intense that it could be gathered up and weighed. It is the stardrive that issues this light: a ship eats space, and light is its offthrow.

Within the light you would see a needle ten kilometres long. That is the ship. One end tapers to a sharp point and the other has the Eye, and it is several days' journey by foot from end to end through all the compartments that lie between. It is a world self-contained. The needle is a flattened one. You could walk about easily on the outer surface of the ship, the skin of the top deck, what we call Skin Deck. Or just as easily on Belly Deck, the one on the bottom side. We call one the top deck and the other the bottom, but when you are outside the ship these distinctions have no meaning. Between Skin and Belly lie Crew Deck, Passenger Deck, Cargo Deck, Drive Deck. Ordinarily no one goes from one deck to another. We stay where we belong. The engines are in the Eye. So are the captain's quarters.

That needle is the ship, but it is not the whole ship. What you will not be able to see are the annexes and extensions and virtualities. These accompany the ship, enfolding it in a webwork of intricate outstructures. But they are of a subordinate level of reality and therefore they defy vision. A ship tunnels into the void, spreading far and wide to find room for all that it must carry. In these outlying zones are kept our supplies and provisions, our stores of fuel, and all cargo travelling at second-class rates. If the ship transports prisoners, they will ride in an annexe. If the ship expects to encounter severe probability turbulence during the course of the voyage, it will arm itself with stabilizers, and those will be carried in the virtualities, ready to be brought into being if needed. These are the mysteries of our profession. Take them on faith, or ignore them, as you will: they are not meant for you to know.

A ship takes forty years to build. There are two hundred seventy-one of them in service now. New ones are constantly under construction. They are the only link binding the Mother Worlds and the eight hundred ninety-eight Colonies and the colonies of the Colonies. Four ships have been lost since the beginning of the Service. No one knows why. The loss of a starship is the worst disaster I can imagine. The last such event occurred sixty virtual years ago.

A starship never returns to the world from which it was launched. The galaxy is too large for that. It makes its voyage and it continues onward through heaven in an endless open circuit. That is the service of the Service. There would be no point in returning, since thousands of worldward years sweep by behind us as we make our voyages. We live outside of time. We must, for there is no other way. That is our burden and our privilege. That is the service of the Service.

4.

On the fifth virtual day of the voyage I suddenly felt a tic, a nibble, a subtle indication that something had gone wrong. It was a very trifling thing, barely perceptible, like the scatter of eroded pebbles that tells you that the palaces and towers of a great ruined city lie buried beneath the mound on which you climb. Unless you are looking for such signals you will not see them. But I was primed for discovery that day. I was eager for it. A strange kind of joy came over me when I picked up that fleeting signal of wrongness.

I keyed the intelligence on duty and said, 'What was that tremor on Passenger Deck?'

The intelligence arrived instantly in my mind, a sharp grey-green presence with a halo of tingling music.

'I am aware of no tremor, sir.'

'There was a distinct tremor. There was a data-spurt just now.'

'Indeed, sir? A data-spurt, sir?' The intelligence sounded aghast, but in a condescending way. It was humouring me. 'What action shall I take, sir?'

I was being invited to retreat.

The intelligence on duty was a 49 Henry Henry. The Henry

74

series affects a sort of slippery innocence that I find disingenuous. Still, they are very capable intelligences. I wondered if I had misread the signal. Perhaps I was too eager for an event, any event, that would confirm my relationship with the ship.

There is never a sense of motion or activity aboard a starship: we float in silence on a tide of darkness, cloaked in our own dazzling light. Nothing moves, nothing seems to live in all the universe. Since we had left Kansas Four I had felt that great silence judging me. Was I really captain of this vessel? Good: then let me feel the weight of duty upon my shoulders.

We were past Ultima Thule by this time, and there could be no turning back. Borne on our cloak of light, we would roar through heaven for week after virtual week until we came to worldward at the first of our destinations, which was Cul-de-Sac in the Vainglory Archipelago, out by the Spook Clusters. Here in free space I must begin to master the ship, or it would master me.

'Sir?' the intelligence said.

'Run a data uptake,' I ordered. 'All Passenger Deck input for the past half-hour. There was movement. There was a spurt.'

I knew I might be wrong. Still, to err on the side of caution may be naïve, but it isn't a sin. And I knew that at this stage in the voyage nothing I could say or do would make me seem other than naïve to the crew of the *Sword of Orion*. What did I have to lose by ordering a recheck, then? I was hungry for surprises. Any irregularity that 49 Henry Henry turned up would be to my advantage; the absence of one would make nothing worse for me.

'Begging your pardon, sir,' 49 Henry Henry reported after a moment, 'but there was no tremor, sir.'

'Maybe I overstated it, then. Calling it a tremor. Maybe it was just an anomaly. What do you say, 49 Henry Henry?' I wondered if I was humiliating myself, negotiating like this with an intelligence. 'There was something. I'm sure of that. An unmistakable irregular burst in the data-flow. An anomaly, yes. What do you say, 49 Henry Henry?'

'Yes, sir.'

'Yes what?'

'The record does show an irregularity, sir. Your observation was quite acute, sir.'

'Go on.'

'No cause for alarm, sir. A minor metabolic movement, nothing more. Like turning over in your sleep.' You bastard, what do you know about sleep? 'Extremely unusual, sir, that you should be able to observe anything so small. I commend you, sir. The passengers are all well, sir.'

'Very good,' I said. 'Enter this exchange in the log, 49 Henry Henry.'

'Already entered, sir,' the intelligence said. 'Permission to decouple, sir?'

'Yes, you can decouple,' I told it.

The shimmer of music that signalled its presence grew tinny and was gone. I could imagine it smirking as it went about its ghostly flitting rounds deep in the neural conduits of the ship. Scornful software, glowing with contempt for its putative master. The poor captain, it was thinking. The poor hopeless silly boy of a captain. A passenger sneezes and he's ready to seal all bulkheads.

Well, let it smirk, I thought. I have acted appropriately and the record will show it.

I knew that all this was part of my testing.

You may think that to be captain of such a ship as the *Sword of Orion* in your first voyage to heaven is an awesome responsibility and an inconceivable burden. So it is, but not for the reason you think.

In truth the captain's duties are the least significant of anyone's aboard the ship. The others have well-defined tasks that are essential to the smooth running of the voyage, although the ship could, if the need arose, generate virtual replacements for any and every crew member and function adequately on its own. The captain's task, though, is fundamentally abstract.

His role is to witness the voyage, to embody it in his own consciousness, to give it coherence, continuity, by reducing it to a pattern of decisions and responses. In that sense the captain is simply so much software: he is the coding through which the voyage is expressed as a series of linear functions. If he fails to perform that duty adequately, others will quietly see to it that the voyage proceeds as it should. What is destroyed, in the course of a voyage that is inadequately captained, is the captain himself, not the voyage. My pre-flight training made that absolutely clear. The voyage can survive the most feeble of captains. As I have said, four starships have been lost since the Service began, and no one knows why. But there is no reason to think that any of those catastrophes were caused by failings of the captain. How could they have been? The captain is only the vehicle through which others act. It is not the captain who makes the voyage, but the voyage which makes the captain.

5.

Restless, troubled, I wandered the eye of the ship. Despite Henry Henry's suave mockery I was still convinced there was trouble on board, or about to be.

Just as I reached Outerscreen Level I felt something strange touch me a second time. It was different this time, and deeply disturbing.

The Eye, as it makes the complete descent from Skin Deck to Belly Deck, is lined with screens that provide displays, actual or virtual, of all aspects of the ship both internal and external. I came up to the great black bevel-edged screen that provided our simulated view of the external realspace environment and was staring at the dwindling wheel of the Ultima Thule relay point when the new anomaly occurred. The other had been the merest of subliminal signals, a nip, a tickle. This was more like an attempted intrusion. Invisible fingers seemed to brush lightly over my brain, probing, seeking entrance. The fingers withdrew; a moment later there was a sudden stabbing pain in my left temple.

I stiffened. 'Who's there?'

'Help me,' a silent voice said.

I had heard wild tales of passenger matrixes breaking free of their storage circuits and drifting through the ship like ghosts, looking for an unguarded body that they might infiltrate. The sources were unreliable, old scoundrels like Roacher or Bulgar. I dismissed such stories as fables, the way I dismissed what I had heard of the vast tentacular krakens that were said to swim the seas of space, or the beckoning mermaids with shining breasts who danced along the force-lines at spinaround points. But I had felt this. The probing fingers, the sudden sharp pain. And the sense of someone frightened, frightened but strong, stronger than I, hovering close at hand.

'Where are you?'

There was no reply. Whatever it was, if it had been anything at all, had slipped back into hiding after that one furtive thrust.

But was it really gone?

'You're still here somewhere,' I said. 'I know that you are.'

Silence. Stillness.

'You asked for help. Why did you disappear so fast?'

No response. I felt anger rising.

'Whoever you are. Whatever. Speak up.'

Nothing. Silence. Had I imagined it? The probing, the voiceless voice?

No. No. I was certain that there was something invisible and unreal hovering about me. And I found it infuriating, not to be able to regain contact with it. To be toyed with this way, to be mocked like this.

This is my ship, I thought. I want no ghosts aboard my ship.

'You can be detected,' I said. 'You can be contained. You can be eradicated.'

As I stood there blustering in my frustration, it seemed to me that I felt that touch against my mind again, a lighter one this time, wistful, regretful. Perhaps I invented it. Perhaps I have supplied it retroactively.

But it lasted only a part of an instant, if it happened at all, and then I was unquestionably alone again. The solitude was real and total and unmistakable. I stood gripping the rail of the screen, leaning forward into the brilliant blackness and swaying dizzily as if I were being pulled forward through the wall of the ship into space.

'Captain?'

The voice of 49 Henry Henry, tumbling out of the air behind me.

'Did you feel something that time?' I asked.

The intelligence ignored my question. 'Captain, there's trouble on Passenger Deck. Hands-on alarm: will you come?'

'Set up a transit track for me,' I said. 'I'm on my way.'

Lights began to glow in mid-air, yellow, blue, green. The interior of the ship is a vast opaque maze and moving about within it is difficult without an intelligence to guide you. 49 Henry Henry constructed an efficient route for me down the curve of the Eye and into the main body of the ship, and thence around the rim of the leeward wall to the elevator down to Passenger Deck. I rode an air-cushion tracker keyed to the lights. The journey took no more than fifteen minutes. Unaided I might have needed a week.

Passenger Deck is an echoing nest of coffins, hundreds of them, sometimes even thousands, arranged in rows three abreast. Here our live cargo sleeps until we arrive and decant the stored sleepers into wakefulness. Machinery sighs and murmurs all around them, coddling them in their suspension. Beyond, far off in the dim distance, is the place for passengers of a different sort – a spiderwebbing of sensory cables that holds our thousands of disembodied matrixes. Those are the colonists who have left their bodies behind when going into space. It is a dark and forbidding place, dimly lit by swirling velvet comets that circle overhead emitting sparks of red and green.

The trouble was in the suspension area. Five crewmen were there already, the oldest hands on board: Katkat, Dismas, Rio de Rio, Gavotte, Roacher. Seeing them all together, I knew this must be some major event. We move on distant orbits within the immensity of the ship: to see as many as three members of the crew in the same virtual month is extraordinary. Now here were five. I felt an oppressive sense of community among them. Each of these five had sailed the seas of heaven more years than I had been alive. For at least a dozen voyages now they had been together as a team. I was the stranger in their midst, unknown, untried, lightly regarded, insignificant. Already Roacher had indicted me for my sweetness, by which he meant, I knew, a basic incapacity to act decisively. I thought he was wrong. But perhaps he knew me better than I knew myself.

They stepped back, opening a path between them. Gavotte, a great hulking thick-shouldered man with a surprisingly delicate and precise way of conducting himself, gestured with open hands: Here, Captain, see? See?

What I saw were coils of greenish smoke coming up from a passenger housing, and the glass door of the housing half open, cracked from top to bottom, frosted by temperature differentials. I could hear a sullen dripping sound. Blue fluid fell in thick steady gouts from a shattered support line. Within the housing itself was the pale naked figure of a man, eyes wide open, mouth agape as if in a silent scream. His left arm was raised, his fist was clenched. He looked like an anguished statue.

They had body-salvage equipment standing by. The hapless passenger would be disassembled and all usable parts stored as soon as I gave the word.

'Is he irretrievable?' I asked.

'Take a look,' Katkat said, pointing to the housing readout. All the curves pointed down. 'We have nineteen per cent degradation already, and rising. Do we disassemble?'

'Go ahead,' I said. 'Approved.'

The lasers glinted and flailed. Body parts came into view, shining, moist. The coiling metallic arms of the body-salvage equipment rose and fell, lifting organs that were not yet beyond repair and putting them into storage. As the machine laboured the men worked around it, shutting down the broken housing, tying off the disrupted feeders and refrigerator cables.

I asked Dismas what had happened. He was the mind-wiper for this sector, responsible for maintenance on the suspended passengers. His face was open and easy, but the deceptive cheeriness about his mouth and cheeks was mysteriously negated by his bleak, shadowy eyes. He told me that he had been working much farther down the deck, performing routine service on the Strappado-bound people, when he felt a sudden small disturbance, a quick tickle of wrongness.

'So did I,' I said. 'How long ago was that?'

'Half an hour, maybe. I didn't make a special note of it. I thought it was something in my gut, Captain. You felt it too, you say?'

I nodded. 'Just a tickle. It's in the record.' I heard the distant music of 49 Henry Henry. Perhaps the intelligence was trying to apologize for doubting me. 'What happened next?' I asked.

'Went back to work. Five, ten minutes, maybe. Felt another jolt, a stronger one.' He touched his forehead, right at the temple, showing me where. 'Detectors went off, broken glass. Came running, found this Cul-de-Sac passenger here undergoing convulsions. Rising from his bindings, thrashing around. Pulled himself loose from everything, went smack against the housing window. Broke it. It's a very fast death.'

'Matrix intrusion,' Roacher said.

The skin of my scalp tightened. I turned to him.

'Tell me about that.'

He shrugged. 'Once in a long while someone in the storage circuits gets to feeling footloose, and finds a way out and goes roaming the ship. Looking for a body to jack into, that's what they're doing. Jack into me, jack into Katkat, even jack into you, Captain. Anybody handy, just so they can feel flesh around them again. Jacked into this one here and something went wrong.'

The probing fingers, yes. The silent voice. *Help me.*

'I never heard of anyone jacking into a passenger in suspension,' Dismas said.

81

'No reason why not,' said Roacher.

'What's the good? Still stuck in a housing, you are. Frozen down, that's no better than staying matrix.'

'Five to two it was matrix intrusion,' Roacher said, glaring.

'Done,' Dismas said. Gavotte laughed and came in on the bet. So too did sinuous little Katkat, taking the other side. Rio de Rio, who had not spoken a word to anyone in his last six voyages, snorted and gestured obscenely at both factions.

I felt like an idle spectator. To regain some illusion of command I said, 'If there's a matrix loose, it'll show up on ship inventory. Dismas, check with the intelligence on duty and report to me. Katkat, Gavotte, finish cleaning up this mess and seal everything off. Then I want your reports in the log and a copy to me. I'll be in my quarters. There'll be further instructions later. The missing matrix, if that's what we have on our hands, will be identified, located, and recaptured.'

Roacher grinned at me. I thought he was going to lead a round of cheers.

I turned and mounted my tracker, and rode it following the lights, yellow, blue, green, back up through the maze of decks and out to the Eye.

As I entered my cabin something touched my mind and a silent voice said, 'Please help me.'

6.

Carefully I shut the door behind me, locked it, loaded the privacy screens. The captain's cabin aboard a Megaspore starship of the Service is a world in itself, serene, private, immense. In mine, spiral galaxies whirled and sparkled on the walls. I had a stream, a lake, a silver waterfall beyond it. The air was soft and glistening. At a touch of my hand I could have light, music, scent, colour, from any one of a thousand hidden orifices. Or I could turn the walls translucent and let the luminous splendour of starspace come flooding through.

Only when I was fully settled in, protected and insulated and comfortable, did I say, 'All right. What are you?'

'You promise you won't report me to the captain?'

'I don't promise anything.'

'You will help me, though?' The voice seemed at once frightened and insistent, urgent and vulnerable.

'How can I say? You give me nothing to work with.'

'I'll tell you everything. But first you have to promise not to call the captain.'

I debated with myself for a moment and opted for directness.

'I am the captain,' I said.

'No!'

'Can you see this room? What do you think it is? Crew quarters? The scullery?'

I felt turbulent waves of fear coming from my invisible companion. And then nothing. Was it gone? Then I had made a mistake in being so forthright. This phantom had to be confined, sealed away, perhaps destroyed, before it could do more damage. I should have been more devious. And also I knew that I would regret it in another way if it had slipped away: I was taking a certain pleasure in being able to speak to someone – something – that was neither a member of my crew nor an omnipotent, contemptuous artificial intelligence.

'Are you still there?' I asked after a while.

Silence.

Gone, I thought. Sweeping through the *Sword of Orion* like a gale of wind. Probably down at the far end of the ship by this time.

Then, as if there had been no break in the conversation: 'I just can't believe it. Of all the places I could have gone, I had to walk right into the captain's cabin.'

'So it seems.'

'And you're actually the captain?'

'Yes. Actually.'

Another pause.

'You seem so young,' it said. 'For a captain.'

'Be careful,' I told it.

'I didn't mean anything by that, Captain.' With a touch of bravado, even defiance, mingling with uncertainty and anxiety. 'Captain *sir*.'

Looking towards the ceiling, where shining resonator nodes shimmered all up and down the spectrum as slave-light leaped from junction to junction along the illuminator strands, I searched for a glimpse of it, some minute electromagnetic clue. But there was nothing.

I imagined a web of impalpable force, a dancing will-o'-the-wisp, flitting erratically about the room, now perching on my shoulder, now clinging to some fixture, now extending itself to fill every open space: an airy thing, a sprite, playful and capricious. Curiously, not only was I unafraid but I found myself strongly drawn to it. There was something strangely appealing about this quick vibrating spirit, so bright with contradictions. And yet it had caused the death of one of my passengers.

'Well?' I said. 'You're safe here. But when are you going to tell me what you are?'

'Isn't that obvious? I'm a matrix.'

'Go on.'

'A free matrix, a matrix on the loose. A matrix who's in big trouble. I think I've hurt someone. Maybe killed him.'

'One of the passengers?' I said.

'So you know?'

'There was a dead passenger, yes. We're not sure what happened.'

'It wasn't my fault. It was an accident.'

'That may be,' I said. 'Tell me about it. Tell me everything.'

'Can I trust you?'

'More than anyone else on this ship.'

'But you're the captain.'

'That's why,' I said.

7.

Her name was Leeleaine, but she wanted me to call her Vox. That means 'voice', she said, in one of the ancient languages of Earth. She was seventeen years old, from Jaana Head, which is an island off the coast of West Palabar on Kansas Four. Her father was a glass-farmer, her mother operated a gravity hole, and she had five brothers and three sisters, all of them much older than she was.

'Do you know what that's like, Captain? Being the youngest of nine? And both your parents working all the time, and your cross-parents just as busy? Can you imagine? And growing up on Kansas Four, where it's a thousand kilometres between cities, and you aren't even in a city, you're on an *island*?'

'I know something of what that's like,' I said.

'Are you from Kansas Four too?'

'No,' I said. 'Not from Kansas Four. But a place much like it, I think.'

She spoke of a troubled, unruly childhood, full of loneliness and anger. Kansas Four, I have heard, is a beautiful world, if you are inclined to find beauty in worlds: a wild and splendid place, where the sky is scarlet and the bare basalt mountains rise in the east like a magnificent black wall. But to hear Vox speak of it, it was squalid, grim, bleak. For her it was a loveless place where she led a loveless life. And yet she told me of pale violet seas aglow with brilliant yellow fish, and trees that erupted with a shower of dazzling crimson fronds when they were in bloom, and warm rains that sang in the air like harps. I was not then so long in heaven that I had forgotten the beauty of seas or trees or rains, which by now are nothing but hollow words to me. Yet Vox had found her life on Kansas Four so hateful that she had been willing to abandon not only her native world but her body itself. That was a point of kinship between us: I too had given up my world and my former life, if not my actual flesh. But I had chosen heaven, and the Service. Vox had volunteered to exchange one landcrawling servitude for another.

85

'The day came,' she said, 'when I knew I couldn't stand it any more. I was so miserable, so empty: I thought about having to live this way for another two hundred years or even more, and I wanted to pick up the hills and throw them at each other. Or get into my mother's plummeter and take it straight to the bottom of the sea. I made a list of ways I could kill myself. But I knew I couldn't do it, not this way or that way or any way. I wanted to live. But I didn't want to live like *that*.'

On that same day, she said, the soul-call from Cul-de-Sac reached Kansas Four. A thousand vacant bodies were available there and they wanted soul-matrixes to fill them. Without a moment's hesitation Vox put her name on the list.

There is a constant migration of souls between the worlds. On each of my voyages I have carried thousands of them, setting forth hopefully towards new bodies on strange planets.

Every world has a stock of bodies awaiting replacement souls. Most were the victims of sudden violence. Life is risky on shore, and death lurks everywhere. Salvaging and repairing a body is no troublesome matter, but once a soul has fled it can never be recovered. So the empty bodies of those who drown and those who are stung by lethal insects and those who are thrown from vehicles and those who are struck by falling branches as they work are collected and examined. If they are beyond repair they are disassembled and their usable parts set aside to be installed in others. But if their bodies can be made whole again, they are, and they are placed in holding chambers until new souls become available for them.

And then there are those who vacate their bodies voluntarily, perhaps because they are weary of them, or weary of their worlds, and wish to move along. They are the ones who sign up to fill the waiting bodies on far worlds, while others come behind them to fill the bodies they have abandoned. The least costly way to travel between the worlds is to surrender your body and go in matrix form, thus exchanging a discouraging life for an unfamiliar one. That was what Vox had done. In pain and despair she had agreed to allow the essence of herself, everything she had ever seen or felt or thought or dreamed, to

86

be converted into a lattice of electrical impulses that the *Sword of Orion* would carry on its voyage from Kansas Four to Cul-de-Sac. A new body lay reserved for her there. Her own discarded body would remain in suspension on Kansas Four. Some day it might become the home of some wandering soul from another world; or, if there were no bids for it, it might eventually be disassembled by the body-salvagers, and its parts put to some worthy use. Vox would never know; Vox would never care.

'I can understand trading an unhappy life for a chance at a happy one,' I said. 'But why break loose on ship? What purpose could that serve? Why not wait until you got to Cul-de-Sac?'

'Because it was torture,' she said.

'Torture? What was?'

'Living as a matrix.' She laughed bitterly. 'Living? It's worse than death could ever be!'

'Tell me.'

'You've never done matrix, have you?'

'No,' I said. 'I chose another way to escape.'

'Then you don't know. You can't know. You've got a ship full of matrixes in storage circuits but you don't understand a thing about them. Imagine that the back of your neck itches, Captain. But you have no arms to scratch with. Your thigh starts to itch. Your chest. You lie there itching everywhere. And you can't scratch. Do you understand me?'

'How can a matrix feel an itch? A matrix is simply a pattern of electrical – '

'Oh, you're impossible! You're *stupid*! I'm not talking about actual literal itching. I'm giving you a suppose, a for-instance. Because you'd never be able to understand the real situation. Look: you're in the storage circuit. All you are is electricity. That's all a mind really is, anyway: electricity. But you used to have a body. The body had sensation. The body had feelings. You remember them. You're a prisoner. A prisoner remembers all sorts of things that used to be taken for granted. You'd give anything to feel the wind in your hair again, or the taste of cool milk, or the scent of flowers. Or even the pain of a cut finger. The saltiness of your blood when you lick the cut. Anything. I hated my body, don't you see? I couldn't wait to be rid of it. But once it was gone I missed the feelings it had. I missed the sense of flesh pulling at me, holding me to the ground, flesh full of nerves, flesh that could feel pleasure. Or pain.'

'I understand,' I said, and I think that I truly did. 'But the voyage to Cul-de-Sac is short. A few virtual weeks and you'd be there, and out of storage and into your new body, and – '

'Weeks? Think of that itch on the back of your neck, Captain. The itch that you can't scratch. How long do you think you could stand it, lying there feeling that itch? Five minutes? An hour? *Weeks*?'

It seemed to me that an itch left unscratched would die of its own, perhaps in minutes. But that was only how it seemed to me. I was not Vox; I had not been a matrix in a storage circuit.

I said, 'So you let yourself out? How?'

'It wasn't that hard to figure. I had nothing else to do but think about it. You align yourself with the polarity of the circuit. That's a matrix too, an electrical pattern holding you in crosswise bands. You change the alignment. It's like being tied up, and slipping the ropes around until you can slide free. And then you can go anywhere you like. You key into any bioprocessor aboard the ship and you draw your energy from that instead of from the storage circuit, and it sustains you. I can move anywhere around this ship at the speed of light. Anywhere. In just the time you blinked your eye, I've been everywhere. I've been to the far tip and out on the mast, and I've been down through the lower decks, and I've been in the crew quarters and the cargo places and I've even been a little way off into something that's right outside the ship but isn't quite real, if you know what I mean. Something that just seems to be a cradle of probability waves surrounding us. It's like being a ghost. But it doesn't solve anything. Do you see? The torture still goes on. You want to feel, but you can't. You want to be connected again, your senses, your inputs. That's why I tried to get into the passenger, do you see? But he wouldn't let me.'

I began to understand at last.

Not everyone who goes to the worlds of heaven as a colonist travels in matrix form. Ordinarily anyone who can afford to take his body with him will do so; but relatively few can afford it. Those who do travel in suspension, the deepest of sleeps. We carry no waking passengers in the Service, not at any price. They would be trouble for us, poking here, poking there, asking questions, demanding to be served and pampered. They would shatter the peace of the voyage. And so they go down into their coffins, their housings, and there they sleep the voyage away, all life-processes halted, a death-in-life that will not be reversed until we bring them to their destinations.

And poor Vox, freed of her prisoning circuit and hungry for sensory data, had tried to slip herself into a passenger's body.

I listened, appalled and sombre, as she told of her terrible odyssey through the ship. Breaking free of the circuit: that had been the first strangeness I felt, that tic, that nibble at the threshold of my consciousness.

Her first wild moment of freedom had been exhilarating and joyous. But then had come the realization that nothing really had changed. She was at large, but still she was incorporeal, caught in that monstrous frustration of bodilessness, yearning for a touch. Perhaps such torment was common among matrixes; perhaps that was why, now and then, they broke free as Vox had done, to roam ships like sad troubled spirits. So Roacher had said. *Once in a long while someone in the storage circuits gets to feeling footloose, and finds a way out and goes roaming the ship. Looking for a body to jack into, that's what they're doing. Jack into me, jack into Katkat, even jack into you, Captain. Anybody handy, just so they can feel flesh around them again.* Yes.

That was the second jolt, the stronger one, that Dismas and I had felt, when Vox, selecting a passenger at random, suddenly, impulsively, had slipped herself inside his brain. She had realized her mistake at once. The passenger, lost in whatever dreams may come to the suspended, reacted to her intrusion with wild terror. Convulsions swept him; he rose, clawing at the equipment that sustained his life, trying desperately to evict the succubus that had penetrated him. In this frantic struggle he smashed the case of his housing and died. Vox, fleeing, frightened, careened about the ship in search of refuge, encountered me standing by the screen in the Eye, and made an abortive attempt to enter my mind. But just then the death of the passenger registered on 49 Henry Henry's sensors and when the intelligence made contact with me to tell me of the emergency Vox fled again, and hovered dolefully until I returned to my cabin. She had not meant to kill the passenger, she said. She was sorry that he had died. She felt some embarrassment, now, and fear. But no guilt. She rejected guilt for it almost defiantly. He had died? Well, so he had died. That was too bad. But how could she have known any such thing was going to happen? She was only looking for a body to take refuge in. Hearing that from her, I had a sense of her as someone utterly unlike me, someone volatile, unstable, perhaps violent. And yet I felt a strange kinship with her, even an identity. As though we were two parts of the same spirit; as though she and I were one and the same. I barely understood why.

'And what now?' I asked. 'You say you want help. How?'

'Take me in.'

'What?'

'Hide me. In you. If they find me, they'll eradicate me. You said so yourself, that it could be done, that I could be detected, contained, eradicated. But it won't happen if you protect me.'

'I'm the *captain*,' I said, astounded.

'Yes.'

'How can I – '

'They'll all be looking for me. The intelligences, the crewmen. It scares them, knowing there's a matrix loose. They'll want to destroy me. But if they can't find me, they'll start to forget about me after a while. They'll think I've escaped into space, or something. And if I'm jacked into you, nobody's going to be able to find me.'

'I have a responsibility to – '

'Please,' she said. 'I could go to one of the others, maybe. But I feel closest to you. Please. Please.'

'Closest to me?'

'You aren't happy. You don't belong. Not here, not anywhere. You don't fit in, any more than I did on Kansas Four. I could feel it the moment I first touched your mind. You're a new captain, right? And the others on board are making it hard for you. Why should you care about *them*? Save me. We have more in common than you do with them. Please? You can't just let them eradicate me. I'm young. I didn't mean to hurt anyone. All I want is to get to Cul-de-Sac and be put in the body that's waiting for me there. A new start, my first start, really. Will you?'

'Why do you bother asking permission? You can simply enter me through my jack whenever you want, can't you?'

'The last one died,' she said.

'He was in suspension. You didn't kill him by entering him. It was the surprise, the fright. He killed himself by thrashing around and wrecking his housing.'

'Even so,' said Vox. 'I wouldn't try that again, an unwilling host. You have to say you'll let me, or I won't come in.'

I was silent.

'Help me?' she said.

'Come,' I told her.

8.

It was just like any other jacking: an electrochemical mind-to-mind bond, a linkage by way of the implant socket at the base of my spine. The sort of thing that any two people who wanted to make communion might do. There was just one difference, which was that we didn't use a jack. We skipped the whole intricate business of checking bandwidths and voltages and selecting the right transformer-adapter. She could do it all, simply by matching evoked potentials. I felt a momentary sharp sensation and then she was with me.

'Breathe,' she said. 'Breathe real deep. Fill your lungs. Rub your hands together. Touch your cheeks. Scratch behind your left ear. Please. Please. It's been so long for me since I've *felt* anything.'

Her voice sounded the same as before, both real and unreal. There was no substance to it, no density of timbre, no sense that it was produced by the vibrations of vocal cords atop a column of air. Yet it was clear, firm, substantial in some essential way, a true voice in all respects except that there was no speaker to utter it. I suppose that while she was outside me she had needed to extend some strand of herself into my neural system in order to generate it. Now that was unnecessary. But I still perceived the voice as originating outside me, even though she had taken up residence within.

She overflowed with needs.

'Take a drink of water,' she urged. 'Eat something. Can you make your knuckles crack? Do it, oh, do it! Put your hand between your legs and squeeze. There's so much I want to feel. Do you have music here? Give me some music, will you? Something loud, something really hard.'

I did the things she wanted. Gradually she grew more calm.

I was strangely calm myself. I had no special awareness then of her presence within me, no unfamiliar pressure in my skull, no slitherings along my spine. There was no mingling of her thoughtstream and mine. She seemed not to have any way of controlling the movements or responses of my body. In these respects our contact was less intimate than any ordinary human jacking communion would have been. But that, I would soon discover, was by her choice. We would not remain so carefully compartmentalized for long.

'Is it better for you now?' I asked.

'I thought I was going to go crazy. If I didn't start feeling something again soon.'

'You can feel things now?'

'Through you, yes. Whatever you touch, I touch.'

'You know I can't hide you for long. They'll take my command away if I'm caught harbouring a fugitive. Or worse.'

'You don't have to speak out loud to me any more,' she said.

'I don't understand.'

'Just *send* it. We have the same nervous system now.'

'You can read my thoughts?' I said, still aloud.

'Not really. I'm not hooked into the higher cerebral centres. But I pick up motor, sensory stuff. And I get subvocalizations. You know what those are? I can hear your thoughts if you want me to. It's like being in communion. You've been in communion, haven't you?'

'Once in a while.'

'Then you know. Just open the channel to me. You can't go around the ship talking out loud to somebody invisible, you know. *Send* me something. It isn't hard.'

'Like this?' I said, visualizing a packet of verbal information sliding through the channels of my mind.

'You see? You can do it!'

'Even so,' I told her. 'You still can't stay like this with me for long. You have to realize that.'

She laughed. It was unmistakable, a silent but definite laugh. 'You sound so serious. I bet you're still surprised you took me in in the first place.'

'I certainly am. Did you think I would?'

'Sure I did. From the first moment. You're basically a very kind person.'

'Am I, Vox?'

'Of course. You just have to let yourself do it.' Again the silent laughter. 'I don't even know your name. Here I am right inside your head and I don't know your name.'

'Adam.'

'That's a nice name. Is that an Earth name?'

'An old Earth name, yes. Very old.'

'And are you from Earth?' she asked.

'No. Except in the sense that we're all from Earth.'

'Where, then?'

'I'd just as soon not talk about it,' I said.

She thought about that. 'You hated the place where you grew up that much?'

'Please, Vox – '

'Of course you hated it. Just like I hated Kansas Four. We're two of a kind, you and me. We're one and the same. You got all the caution and I got all the impulsiveness. But otherwise we're the same person. That's why we share so well. I'm glad I'm sharing with you, Adam. You won't make me leave, will you? We belong with each other. You'll let me stay until we reach Cul-de-Sac. I know you will.'

'Maybe. Maybe not.' I wasn't at all sure, either way.

'Oh, you will. You will, Adam. I know you better than you know yourself.'

9.

So it began. I was in some new realm outside my established sense of myself, so far beyond my notions of appropriate behaviour that I could not even feel astonishment at what I had done. I had taken her in, that was all. A stranger in my skull. She had turned to me in appeal and I had taken her in. It was as if her recklessness was contagious. And though I didn't mean to shelter her any longer than was absolutely necessary, I could already see that I wasn't going to make any move to eject her until her safety was assured.

But how was I going to hide her?

Invisible she might be, but not undetectable. And everyone on the ship would be searching for her.

There were sixteen crewmen on board who dreaded a loose matrix as they would a vampire. They would seek her as long as she remained at large. And not only the crew. The intelligences would be monitoring for her too, not out of any kind of fear but simply out of efficiency: they had nothing to fear from Vox but they would want the cargo manifests to come out in balance when we reached our destination.

The crew didn't trust me in the first place. I was too young, too new, too green, too *sweet*. I was just the sort who might be guilty of giving shelter to a secret fugitive. And it was altogether likely that her presence within me would be obvious to others in some way not apparent to me. As for the intelligence, they had access to all sorts of data as part of their routine maintenance operations. Perhaps they could measure tiny physiological changes, differences in my reaction times or circulatory efficiency or whatever, that would be a tipoff to the truth. How would I know? I would have to be on constant guard against discovery of the secret sharer of my consciousness.

The first test came less than an hour after Vox had entered me. The communicator light went on and I heard the far-off music of the intelligence on duty.

This one was 612 Jason, working the late shift. Its aura was golden, its music deep and throbbing. Jasons tend to be more brusque and less condescending than the Henry series, and in general I prefer them. But it was terrifying now to see that light, to hear that music, to know that the ship's intelligence wanted to speak with me. I shrank back at a tense awkward angle, the way one does when trying to avoid a face-to-face confrontation with someone.

But of course the intelligence had no face to confront. The intelligence was only a voice speaking to me out of a speaker grid, and a stew of magnetic impulses somewhere on the control levels of the ship. All the same, I perceived 612 Jason now as a great glowing eye, staring through me to the hidden Vox.

'What is it?' I asked.

'Report summary, Captain. The dead passenger and the missing matrix.'

Deep within me I felt a quick plunging sensation, and then the skin of my arms and shoulders began to glow as the chemicals of fear went coursing through my veins in a fierce tide. It was Vox, I knew, reacting in sudden alarm, opening the petcocks of my hormonal system. It was the thing I had dreaded.

How could 612 Jason fail to notice that flood of endocrine response?

'Go on,' I said, as coolly as I could.

But noticing was one thing, interpreting the data something else. Fluctuations in a human being's endocrine output might have any number of causes. To my troubled conscience everything was a glaring signal of my guilt. 612 Jason gave no indication that it suspected a thing.

The intelligence said, 'The dead passenger was Hans Eger Olafssen, fifty-four years of age, a native of – '

'Never mind his details. You can let me have a printout on that part.'

'The missing matrix,' 612 Jason went on imperturbably. 'Leeleaine Eliani, seventeen years of age, a native of Kansas Four, bound for Cul-de-Sac, Vainglory Archipelago, under Transmission Contract No. D-14871532, dated the twenty-seventh day of the third month of – '

'Printout on that too,' I cut in. 'What I want to know is where she is now.'

'That information is not available.'

'That isn't a responsive answer, 612 Jason.'

'No better answer can be provided at this time, Captain. Tracer circuits have been activated and remain in constant search mode.'

'And?'

'We have no data on the present location of the missing matrix.'

Within me Vox reacted instantly to the intelligence's calm flat statement. The hormonal response changed from one of fear to one of relief. My blazing skin began at once to cool. Would 612 Jason notice that too, and from that small clue be able to assemble the subtext of my body's responses into a sequence that exposed my criminal violation of regulations?

'Don't relax too soon,' I told her silently. 'This may be some sort of trap.'

To 612 Jason I said, 'What data *do* you have, then?'

'Two things are known: the time at which the Eliani matrix

achieved negation of its storage circuitry and the time of its presumed attempt at making neural entry into the suspended passenger Olafssen. Beyond that no data has been recovered.'

'It's *presumed* attempt?' I said.

'There is no proof, Captain.'

'Olafssen's convulsions? The smashing of the storage housing?'

'We know that Olafssen responded to an electrical stimulus, Captain. The source of the stimulus is impossible to trace, although the presumption is that it came from the missing matrix Eliani. These are matters for the subsequent inquiry. It is not within my responsibilities to assign definite causal relationships.'

Spoken like a true Jason-series intelligence, I thought.

I said, 'You don't have any effective way of tracing the movements of the Eliani matrix, is that what you're telling me?'

'We're dealing with extremely minute impedances, sir. In the ordinary functioning of the ship it is very difficult to distinguish a matrix manifestation from normal surges and pulses in the general electrical system.'

'You mean, it might take something as big as the matrix trying to climb back into its own storage circuit to register on the monitoring system?'

'Very possibly, sir.'

'Is there any reason to think the Eliani matrix is still on the ship at all?'

'There is no reason to think that it is not, Captain.'

'In other words, you don't know anything about anything concerning the Eliani matrix.'

'I have provided you with all known data at this point. Trace efforts are continuing, sir.'

'You still think this is a trap?' Vox asked me.

'It's sounding better and better by the minute. But shut up and don't distract me, will you?'

To the intelligence I said, 'All right, keep me posted on the situation. I'm preparing for sleep, 612 Jason. I want the end-of-day status report, and then I want you to clear off and leave me alone.'

'Very good, sir. Fifth virtual day of voyage. Position of ship sixteen units beyond last port of call, Kansas Four. Scheduled rendezvous with relay forces at Ultima Thule spinaround point was successfully achieved at the hour of – '

The intelligence droned on and on: the usual report of the routine events of the day, broken only by the novelty of an entry for the loss of a passenger and one for the escape of a matrix, then returning to the standard data, fuel levels and velocity soundings and all the rest. On the first four nights of the voyage I had solemnly tried to absorb all this torrent of ritualized downloading of the log as though my captaincy depended on committing it all to memory, but this night I barely listened, and nearly missed my cue when it was time to give it my approval before clocking out for the night. Vox had to prod me and let me know that the intelligence was waiting for something. I gave 612 Jason the confirm-and-clock-out and heard the welcome sound of its diminishing music as it decoupled the contact.

'What do you think?' Vox asked. 'It doesn't know, does it?'

'Not yet,' I said.

'You really are a pessimist, aren't you?'

'I think we may be able to bring this off,' I told her. 'But the moment we become overconfident, it'll be the end. Everyone on this ship wants to know where you are. The slightest slip and we're both gone.'

'Okay. Don't lecture me.'

'I'll try not to. Let's get some sleep now.'

'I don't need to sleep.'

'Well, I do.'

'Can we talk for a while first?'

'Tomorrow,' I said.

But of course sleep was impossible. I was all too aware of the stranger within me, perhaps prowling the most hidden places of my psyche at this moment. Or waiting to invade my dreams once I drifted off. For the first time I thought I could feel her presence even when she was silent: a hot node of identity pressing against the wall of my brain. Perhaps I imagined it. I lay stiff and tense, as wide awake as I have ever been in my life. After a time I had to call 612 Jason and ask it to put me under the wire; and even then my sleep was uneasy when it came.

10.

Until that point in the voyage I had taken nearly all of my meals in my quarters. It seemed a way of exerting my authority, such as it was, aboard ship. By my absence from the dining hall I created a presence, that of the austere and aloof captain; and I avoided the embarrassment of having to sit in the seat of command over men who were much my senior in all things. It was no great sacrifice to me. My quarters were more than comfortable, the food was the same as that which was available in the dining hall, the servo-steward that brought it was silent and efficient. The question of isolation did not arise. There has always been something solitary about me, as there is about most who are of the Service.

But when I awoke the next morning after what had seemed like an endless night, I went down to the dining hall for breakfast.

It was nothing like a deliberate change of policy, a decision that had been rigorously arrived at through careful reasoning. It wasn't a decision at all. Nor did Vox suggest it, though I'm sure she inspired it. It was purely automatic. I arose, showered, and dressed. I confess that I had forgotten all about the events of the night before. Vox was quiet within me. Not until I was under the shower, feeling the warm comforting ultrasonic vibration, did I remember her: there came a disturbing sensation of being in two places at once, and, immediately afterwards, an astonishingly odd feeling of shame at my own nakedness. Both those feelings passed quickly. But they did indeed bring to mind that extraordinary thing which I had managed to suppress for some minutes, that I was no longer alone in my body.

She said nothing. Neither did I. After last night's astounding alliance I seemed to want to pull back into wordlessness, unthinkingness, a kind of automaton consciousness. The need for breakfast occurred to me and I called up a tracker to take me down to the dining hall. When I stepped outside the room I was surprised to encounter my servo-steward, already on its way up with my tray. Perhaps it was just as surprised to see me going out, though of course its blank metal face betrayed no feelings.

'I'll be having breakfast in the dining hall today,' I told it.

'Very good, sir.'

My tracker arrived. I climbed into its seat and it set out at once on its cushion of air towards the dining hall.

The dining hall of the *Sword of Orion* is a magnificent room at the Eye end of Crew Deck, with one glass wall providing a view of all the lights of heaven. By some whim of the designers we sit with that wall below us, so that the stars and their tethered worlds drift beneath our feet. The other walls are of some silvery metal chased with thin swirls of gold, everything shining by the reflected light of the passing star-clusters. At the centre is a table of black stone, with places allotted for each of the seventeen members of the crew. It is a splendid if somewhat ridiculous place, a resonant reminder of the wealth and power of the Service.

Three of my shipmates were at their places when I entered. Pedregal was there, the supercargo, a compact, sullen man whose broad dome of a head seemed to rise directly from his shoulders. And there was Fresco, too, slender and elusive, the navigator, a lithe dark-skinned person of ambiguous sex who alternated from voyage to voyage, so I had been told, converting from male to female and back again according to some private rhythm. The third person was Raebuck, whose sphere of responsibility was communications, an older man whose flat, chilly gaze conveyed either boredom or menace, I could never be sure which.

'Why, it's the captain,' said Pedregal calmly. 'Favouring us with one of his rare visits.'

All three stared at me with that curious testing intensity which I was coming to see was an inescapable part of my life aboard ship: a constant hazing meted out to any newcomer to the Service, an interminable probing for the place that was most vulnerable. Mine was a parsec wide and I was certain they would discover it at once. But I was determined to match them stare for stare, ploy for ploy, test for test.

'Good morning, gentlemen,' I said. Then, giving Fresco a level glance, I added, 'Good morning, Fresco.'

I took my seat at the table's head and rang for service.

I was beginning to realize why I had come out of my cabin that morning. In part it was a reflection of Vox's presence within me, an expression of that new component of rashness and impulsiveness that had entered me with her. But mainly it was, I saw now, some stratagem of my own, hatched on some inaccessible subterranean level of my double mind. In order to conceal Vox most effectively, I would have to take the offensive: rather than skulking in my quarters and perhaps awakening perilous suspicions in the minds of my shipmates, I must come forth, defiantly, challengingly, almost flaunting the thing that I had done, and go among them, pretending that nothing unusual was afoot and forcing them to believe it. Such aggressiveness was not natural to my temperament. But perhaps I could draw on some reserves provided by Vox. If not, we both were lost.

Raebuck said, to no one in particular, 'I suppose yesterday's disturbing events must inspire a need for companionship in the captain.'

I faced him squarely. 'I have all the companionship I require, Raebuck. But I agree that what happened yesterday was disturbing.'

'A nasty business,' Pedregal said, ponderously shaking his neckless head. 'And a strange one, a matrix trying to get into a passenger. That's new to me, a thing like that. And to lose the passenger besides – that's bad. That's very bad.'

'It does happen, losing a passenger,' said Raebuck.

'A long time since it happened on a ship of mine,' Pedregal rejoined.

'We lost a whole batch of them on the *Emperor of Callisto*,' Fresco said. 'You know the story? It was thirty years ago. We were making the run from Van Buren to the San Pedro Cluster. We picked up a supernova pulse and the intelligence on duty went into flicker. Somehow dumped a load of aluminium salts in the feed-lines and killed off fifteen, sixteen passengers. I saw the bodies before they went into the converter. Beyond salvage, they were.'

'Yes,' said Raebuck. 'I heard of that one. And then there was the *Queen Astarte*, a couple of years after that. Tchelitchev was her captain, little green-eyed Russian woman from one of the Troika worlds. They were taking a routine inventory and two digits got transposed, and a faulty delivery signal slipped through. I think it was six dead, premature decanting, killed by air poisoning. Tchelitchev took it very badly. *Very* badly. Somehow the captain always does.'

'And then that time on the *Hecuba*,' said Pedregal. 'No ship of mine, thank God. That was the captain who ran amok, thought the ship was too quiet, wanted to see some passengers moving around and started awakening them – '

Raebuck showed a quiver of surprise. 'You know about that? I thought that was supposed to be hushed up.'

'Things get around,' Pedregal said, with something like a smirk. 'The captain's name was Catania-Szu, I believe, a man from Mediterraneo, very high-strung, the way all of them are there. I was working the *Valparaiso* then, out of Mendax Nine bound for Scylla and Charybdis and neighbouring points, and when we stopped to download some cargo in the Seneca system I got the whole story from a ship's clerk named – '

'You were on the *Valparaiso*?' Fresco asked. 'Wasn't that the ship that had a free matrix, too, ten or eleven years back? A real soul-eater, so the report went – '

'After my time,' said Pedregal, blandly waving his hand. 'But I did hear of it. You get to hear about everything, when you're downloading cargo. Soul-eater, you say, reminds me of the time – '

And he launched into some tale of horror at a spinaround station in a far quadrant of the galaxy. But he was no more than halfway through it when Raebuck cut in with a gorier reminiscence of his own, and then Fresco, seething with impatience, broke in on him to tell of a ship infested by three free matrixes at once. I had no doubt that all this was being staged for my enlightenment, by way of showing me how seriously such events were taken in the Service, and how the captains under whom they occurred went down in the folklore of the starships with ineradicable black marks. But their attempts to unsettle me, if that is what they were, left me undismayed. Vox, silent within me, infused me with a strange confidence that allowed me to ignore the darker implications of these anecdotes.

I simply listened, playing my role: the neophyte fascinated by the accumulated depth of spacegoing experience that their stories implied.

Then I said, finally, 'When matrixes get loose, how long do they generally manage to stay at large?'

'An hour or two, generally,' said Raebuck. 'As they drift around the ship, of course, they leave an electrical trail. We track it and close off access routes behind them and eventually we pin them down in close quarters. Then it's not hard to put them back in their bottles.'

'And if they've jacked into some member of the crew?'

'That makes it even easier to find them.'

Boldly I said, 'Was there ever a case where a free matrix jacked into a member of the crew and managed to keep itself hidden?'

'Never,' said a new voice. It belonged to Roacher, who had just entered the dining hall. He stood at the far end of the long table, staring at me. His strange luminescent eyes, harsh and probing, came to rest on mine. 'No matter how clever the matrix may be, sooner or later the host will find some way to call for help.'

'And if the host doesn't choose to call for help?' I asked.

Roacher studied me with great care.

Had I been too bold? Had I given away too much?

'But that would be a violation of regulations!' he said, in a tone of mock astonishment. 'That would be a criminal act!'

11.

She asked me to take her starwalking, to show her the full view of the Great Open.

It was the third day of her concealment within me. Life aboard the *Sword of Orion* had returned to routine, or, to be more accurate, it had settled into a new routine in which the presence on board of an undetected and apparently undetectable free matrix was a constant element.

As Vox had suggested, there were some who quickly came to believe that the missing matrix must have slipped off into space, since the watchful ship-intelligences could find no trace of it. But there were others who kept looking over their shoulders, figuratively or literally, as if expecting the fugitive to attempt to thrust herself without warning into the spinal jacks that gave access to their nervous systems. They behaved exactly as if the ship were haunted. To placate those uneasy ones, I ordered round-the-clock circuit sweeps that would report every vagrant pulse and random surge. Each such anomalous electrical event was duly investigated, and, of course, none of these investigations led to anything significant. Now that Vox resided in my brain instead of the ship's wiring, she was beyond any such mode of discovery.

Whether anyone suspected the truth was something I had no way of knowing. Perhaps Roacher did; but he made no move to denounce me, nor did he so much as raise the issue of the missing matrix with me at all after that time in the dining hall. He might know nothing whatever; he might know everything, and not care; he might simply be keeping his own counsel for the moment. I had no way of telling.

I was growing accustomed to my double life, and to my daily duplicity. Vox had quickly come to seem as much a part of me as my arm, or my leg. When she was silent – and often I heard nothing from her for hours at a time – I was no more aware of her than I would be, in any special way, of my arm or my leg; but nevertheless I knew somehow that she was there. The boundaries between her mind and mine were eroding steadily. She was learning how to infiltrate me. At times it seemed to me that what we were were joint tenants of the same dwelling, rather than I the permanent occupant and she a guest. I came to perceive my own mind as something not notably different from hers, a mere web of electrical force which for the moment was housed in the soft moist globe that was the brain of the captain of the *Sword of Orion*. Either of us, so it seemed, might come and go within that soft moist globe as we pleased, flitting casually in or out after the wraithlike fashion of matrixes.

At other times it was not at all like that: I gave no thought to her presence and went about my tasks as if nothing had changed for me. Then it would come as a surprise when Vox announced herself to me with some sudden comment, some quick question. I had to learn to guard myself against letting my reaction show, if it happened when I was with other members of the crew. Though no one around us could hear anything when she spoke to me, or I to her, I knew it would be the end for our masquerade if anyone caught me in some unguarded moment of conversation with an unseen companion.

How far she had penetrated my mind began to become apparent to me when she asked to go on a starwalk.

'You know about that?' I said, startled, for starwalking is the private pleasure of the spacegoing and I had not known of it myself before I was taken into the Service.

Vox seemed amazed by my amazement. She indicated casually that the details of starwalking were common knowledge everywhere. But something rang false in her tone. Were the landcrawling folk really so familiar with our special pastime? Or had she picked what she knew of it out of the hitherto private reaches of my consciousness?

I chose not to ask. But I was uneasy about taking her with me into the Great Open, much as I was beginning to yearn for it myself. She was not one of us. She was planetary; she had not passed through the training of the Service.

I told her that.

'Take me anyway,' she said. 'It's the only chance I'll ever have.'

'But the training – '

'I don't need it. Not if you've had it.'

'What if that's not enough?'

'It will be,' she said. 'I know it will, Adam. There's nothing to be afraid of. You've had the training, haven't you? And I am you.'

12.

Together we rode the transit track out of the Eye and down to Drive Deck, where the soul of the ship lies lost in throbbing dreams of the far galaxies as it pulls us ever onward across the unending night.

We passed through zones of utter darkness and zones of cascading light, through places where wheeling helixes of silvery radiance burst like auroras from the air, through passages so crazed in their geometry that they reawakened the terrors of the womb in anyone who traversed them. A starship is the mother of mysteries. Vox crouched, frozen with awe, within that portion of our brain that was hers. I felt the surges of her awe, one after another, as we went downward.

'Are you really sure you want to do this?' I asked.

'Yes!' she cried fiercely. 'Keep going!'

'There's the possibility that you'll be detected,' I told her.

'There's the possibility that I won't be,' she said.

We continued to descend. Now we were in the realm of the three cyborg push-cells, Gabriel, Banquo, and Fleece. Those were three members of the crew whom we would never see at the table in the dining hall, for they dwelled here in the walls of Drive Deck, permanently jacked in, perpetually pumping their energies into the ship's great maw. I have already told you of our saying in the Service, that when you enter you give up the body and you get your soul. For most of us that is only a figure of speech: what we give up, when we say farewell forever to planetskin and take up our new lives in starships, is not the body itself but the body's trivial needs, the sweaty things so dear to shore people. But some of us are more literal in their renunciations. The flesh is a meaningless hindrance to them; they shed it entirely, knowing that they can experience starship life just as fully without it. They allow themselves to be transformed into extensions of the stardrive. From them comes the raw energy out of which is made the power that carries us hurtling through heaven. Their work is unending; their reward is a sort of immortality. It is not a choice I could make, nor, I think, you: but for them it is bliss. There can be no doubt about that.

'Another starwalk so soon, Captain?' Banquo asked. For I had been here on the second day of the voyage, losing no time in availing myself of the great privilege of the Service.

'Is there any harm in it?'

'No, no harm,' said Banquo. 'Just isn't usual, is all.'

'That's all right,' I said. 'That's not important to me.'

Banquo is a gleaming metallic ovoid, twice the size of a human head, jacked into a slot in the wall. Within the ovoid is the matrix of what had once been Banquo, long ago on a world called Sunrise where night is unknown. Sunrise's golden dawns and shining days had not been good enough for Banquo, apparently. What Banquo had wanted was to be a gleaming metallic ovoid, hanging on the wall of Drive Deck aboard the *Sword of Orion*.

Any of the three cyborgs could set up a starwalk. But Banquo was the one who had done it for me that other time and it seemed best to return to him. He was the most congenial of the three. He struck me as amiable and easy. Gabriel, on my first visit, had seemed austere, remote, incomprehensible. He is an early model who had lived the equivalent of three human lifetimes as a cyborg aboard starships and there was not much about him that was human any more. Fleece, much younger, quick-minded and quirky, I mistrusted: in her weird edgy way she might just somehow be able to detect the hidden other who would be going along with me for the ride.

You must realize that when we starwalk we do not literally leave the ship, though that is how it seems to us. If we left the ship even for a moment we would be swept away and lost forever in the abyss of heaven. Going outside a starship of heaven is not like stepping outside an ordinary planet-launched shoreship that moves through normal space. But even if it were possible, there would be no point in leaving the ship. There is nothing to see out there. A starship moves through utter empty darkness.

But though there may be nothing to see, that does not mean that there is nothing out there. The entire universe is out there. If we could see it while we are travelling across the special space that is heaven we would find it flattened and curved, so that we had the illusion of viewing everything at once, all the far-flung galaxies back to the beginning of time. This is the Great Open, the totality of the continuum. Our external screens show it to us in simulated form, because we need occasional assurance that it is there.

A starship rides along the mighty lines of force which cross that immense void like the lines of the compass rose on an ancient mariner's map. When we starwalk, we ride those same lines, and we are held by them, sealed fast to the ship that is carrying us onward through heaven. We seem to step forth into space; we seem to look down on the ship, on the stars, on all the worlds of heaven. For the moment we become little starships flying along beside the great one that is our mother. It is magic; it is illusion; but it is magic that so closely approaches what we perceive as reality that there is no way to measure the difference, which means that in effect there is no difference.

'Ready?' I asked Vox.

'Absolutely.'

Still I hesitated.

'Are you *sure*?'

'Go on,' she said impatiently. 'Do it!'

I put the jack to my spine myself. Banquo did the matching of impedances. If he were going to discover the passenger I carried, this would be the moment. But he showed no sign that anything was amiss. He queried me; I gave him the signal to proceed; there was a moment of sharp warmth at the back of my neck as my neural matrix, and Vox's travelling with it, rushed out through Banquo and hurtled downward towards its merger with the soul of the ship.

We were seized and drawn in and engulfed by the vast force that is the ship. As the coils of the engine caught us we were spun around and around, hurled from vector to vector, mercilessly stretched, distended by an unimaginable flux. And then there was a brightness all about us, a brightness that cried out in heaven with a mighty clamour. We were outside the ship. We were starwalking.

'Oh,' she said. A little soft cry, a muted gasp of wonder.

The blazing mantle of the ship lay upon the darkness of heaven like a white shadow. That great cone of cold fiery light reached far out in front of us, arching awesomely towards heaven's vault, and behind us it extended beyond the limits of our sight. The slender tapering outline of the ship was clearly visible within it, the needle and its Eye, all ten kilometres of it easily apparent to us in a single glance.

And there were the stars. And there were the worlds of heaven.

The effect of the stardrive is to collapse the dimensions, each one in upon the other. Thus inordinate spaces are diminished and the galaxy may be spanned by human voyagers. There is no logic, no linearity of sequence, to heaven as it appears to our eyes. Wherever we look we see the universe bent back upon itself, revealing its entirety in an infinite series of infinite segments of itself. Any sector of stars contains all stars. Any demarcation of time encompasses all of time past and time to come. What we behold is altogether beyond our understanding, which is exactly as it should be; for what we are given, when we look through the Eye of the ship at the naked heavens, is a god's-eye view of the universe. And we are not gods.

'What are we seeing?' Vox murmured within me.

I tried to tell her. I showed her how to define her relative position so there would be an up and a down for her, a backward, a forward, a flow of time and event from beginning to end. I pointed out the arbitrary coordinate axes by which we locate ourselves in this fundamentally incomprehensible arena. I found known stars for her, and known worlds, and showed them to her.

She understood nothing. She was entirely lost.

I told her that there was no shame in that.

I told her that I had been just as bewildered, when I was undergoing my training in the simulator. That everyone was; and that no one, not even if he spent a thousand years aboard the starships that plied the routes of heaven, could ever come to anything more than a set of crude equivalents and approximations of understanding what starwalking shows us. Attaining actual understanding itself is beyond the best of us.

I could feel her struggling to encompass the impact of all that rose and wheeled and soared before us. Her mind was agile, though still only half formed, and I sensed her working out her own system of explanations and assumptions, her analogies, her equivalencies. I gave her no more help. It was best for her to do these things by herself; and in any case I had no more help to give.

I had my own astonishment and bewilderment to deal with, on this my second starwalk in heaven.

Once more I looked down upon the myriad worlds turning in their orbits. I could see them easily, the little bright globes rotating in the huge night of the Great Open: red worlds, blue worlds, green ones, some turning their full faces to me, some showing mere slivers of a crescent. How they cleaved to their appointed tracks! How they clung to their parent stars!

I remembered that other time, only a few virtual days before, when I had felt such compassion for them, such sorrow. Knowing that they were condemned forever to follow the same path

110

about the same star, a hopeless bondage, a meaningless retracing of a perpetual route. In their own eyes they might be footloose wanderers, but to me they had seemed the most pitiful of slaves. And so I had grieved for the worlds of heaven; but now, to my surprise, I felt no pity, only a kind of love. There was no reason to be sad for them. They were what they were, and there was a supreme rightness in those fixed orbits and their obedient movements along them. They were content with being what they were. If they were loosed even a moment from that bondage, such chaos would arise in the universe as could never be contained. Those circling worlds are the foundations upon which all else is built; they know that and they take pride in it; they are loyal to their tasks and we must honour them for their devotion to their duty. And with honour comes love.

This must be Vox speaking within me, I told myself.

I had never thought such thoughts. Love the planets in their orbits? What kind of notion was that? Perhaps no stranger than my earlier notion of pitying them because they weren't starships; but that thought had arisen from the spontaneous depths of my own spirit and it had seemed to make a kind of sense to me. Now it had given way to a wholly other view.

I loved the worlds that moved before me and yet did not move, in the great night of heaven.

I loved the strange fugitive girl within me who beheld those worlds and loved them for their immobility.

I felt her seize me now, taking me impatiently onwards, outwards, into the depths of heaven. She understood now; she knew how it was done. And she was far more daring than ever I would have allowed me to be. Together we walked the stars. Not only walked but plunged and swooped and soared, travelling among them like gods. Their hot breath singed us. Their throbbing brightness thundered at us. Their serene movements boomed a mighty music at us. On and on we went, hand in hand, Vox leading, I letting her draw me, deeper and deeper into the shining abyss that was the universe. Until at last we halted, floating in mid-cosmos, the ship nowhere to be seen, only the two of us surrounded by a shield of suns.

In that moment a sweeping ecstasy filled my soul. I felt all eternity within my grasp. No, that puts it the wrong way around and makes it seem that I was seized by delusions of imperial grandeur, which was not at all the case. What I felt was myself within the grasp of all eternity, enfolded in the loving embrace of a complete and perfect cosmos in which nothing was out of place, or ever could be.

It is this that we go starwalking to attain. This sense of belonging, this sense of being contained in the divine perfection of the universe.

When it comes, there is no telling what effect it will have; but inner change is what it usually brings. I had come away from my first starwalk unaware of any transformation; but within three days I had impulsively opened myself to a wandering phantom, violating not only regulations but the nature of my own character as I understood it. I have always, as I think I have said, been an intensely private man. Even though I had given Vox refuge, I had been relieved and grateful that her mind and mine had remained separate entities within our shared brain.

Now I did what I could to break down whatever boundary remained between us.

I hadn't let her know anything, so far, of my life before going to heaven. I had met her occasional questions with coy evasions, with half-truths, with blunt refusals. It was the way I had always been with everyone, a habit of secrecy, an unwillingness to reveal myself. I had been even more secretive, perhaps, with Vox than with all the others, because of the very closeness of her mind to mine. As though I feared that by giving her any interior knowledge of me I was opening the way for her to take me over entirely, to absorb me into her own vigorous, undisciplined soul.

But now I offered my past to her in a joyous rush. We began to make our way slowly backwards from that apocalyptic place at the centre of everything; and as we hovered on the breast of the Great Open, drifting between the darkness and the brilliance of the light that the ship created, I told her everything about myself that I had been holding back.

I suppose they were mere trivial things, though to me they were all so highly charged with meaning. I told her the name of my home planet. I let her see it, the sea the colour of lead, the sky the colour of smoke. I showed her the sparse and scrubby grey headlands behind our house, where I would go running for hours by myself, a tall slender boy pounding tirelessly across the crackling sands as though demons were pursuing him.

I showed her everything: the sombre child, the troubled youth, the wary, overcautious young man. The playmates who remained forever strangers, the friends whose voices were drowned in hollow babbling echoes, the lovers whose love seemed without substance or meaning. I told her of my feeling that I was the only one alive in the world, that everyone about me was some sort of artificial being full of gears and wires. Or that the world was only a flat colourless dream in which I somehow had become trapped, but from which I would eventually awaken into the true world of light and colour and richness of texture. Or that I might not be human at all, but had been abandoned in the human galaxy by creatures of another form entirely, who would return for me some day far in the future.

I was lighthearted as I told her these things, and she received them lightly. She knew them for what they were – not symptoms of madness, but only the bleak fantasies of a lonely child, seeking to make sense out of an incomprehensible universe in which he felt himself to be a stranger and afraid.

'But you escaped,' she said. 'You found a place where you belonged!'

'Yes,' I said. 'I escaped.'

And I told her of the day when I had seen a sudden light in the sky. My first thought then had been that my true parents had come back for me; my second, that it was some comet passing by. That light was a starship of heaven that had come to worldward in our system. And as I looked upward through the darkness on that day long ago, straining to catch a glimpse of the shoreships that were going up to it bearing cargo and passengers to be taken from our world to some unknowable place at the other end of the galaxy, I realized that that starship was my true home. I realized that the Service was my destiny.

And so it came to pass, I said, that I left my world behind, and my name, and my life, such as it had been, to enter the company of those who sail between the stars. I let her know that this was my first voyage, explaining that it is the peculiar custom of the Service to test all new officers by placing them in command at once. She asked me if I had found happiness here; and I said, quickly, Yes, I had, and then I said a moment later, Not yet, not yet, but I see at least the possibility of it.

She was quiet for a time. We watched the worlds turning and the stars like blazing spikes of colour racing towards their far-off destinations, and the fiery white light of the ship itself streaming in the firmament as if it were the blood of some alien god. The thought came to me of all that I was risking by hiding her like this within me. I brushed it aside. This was neither the place nor the moment for doubt or fear or misgiving.

Then she said, 'I'm glad you told me all that, Adam.'

'Yes. I am too.'

'I could feel it from the start, what sort of person you were. But I needed to hear it in your own words, your own thoughts. It's just like I've been saying. You and I, we're two of a kind. Square pegs in a world of round holes. You ran away to the Service and I ran away to a new life in somebody else's body.'

I realized that Vox wasn't speaking of my body, but of the new one that waited for her on Cul-de-Sac.

And I realized too that there was one thing about herself that she had never shared with me, which was the nature of the flaw in her old body that had caused her to discard it. If I knew her more fully, I thought, I could love her more deeply: imperfections and all, which is the way of love. But she had shied away from telling me that, and I had never pressed her on it. Now, out here under the cool gleam of heaven, surely

114

we had moved into a place of total trust, of complete union of soul.

I said, 'Let me see you, Vox.'

'See me? How could you – '

'Give me an image of yourself. You're too abstract for me this way. *Vox*. A voice. Only a voice. You talk to me, you live within me, and I still don't have the slightest idea what you look like.'

'That's how I want it to be.'

'Won't you show me how you look?'

'I won't look like anything. I'm a matrix. I'm nothing but electricity.'

'I understand that. I mean how you looked *before*. Your old self, the one you left behind on Kansas Four.'

She made no reply.

I thought she was hesitating, deciding; but some time went by, and still I heard nothing from her. What came from her was silence, only silence, a silence that had crashed down between us like a steel curtain.

'Vox?'

Nothing.

Where was she hiding? What had I done?

'What's the matter? Is it the thing I asked you?'

No answer.

'It's all right, Vox. Forget about it. It isn't important at all. You don't have to show me anything you don't want to show me.'

Nothing. Silence.

'Vox? Vox?'

The worlds and stars wheeled in chaos before me. The light of the ship roared up and down the spectrum from end to end. In growing panic I sought for her and found no trace of her presence within me. Nothing. Nothing.

'Are you all right?' came another voice. Banquo, from inside the ship. 'I'm getting some pretty wild signals. You'd better come in. You've been out there long enough as it is.'

Vox was gone. I had crossed some uncrossable boundary and I had frightened her away.

Numbly I gave Banquo the signal, and he brought me back inside.

13.

Alone, I made my way upwards level by level through the darkness and mystery of the ship, towards the Eye. The crash of silence went on and on, like the falling of some colossal wave on an endless shore. I missed Vox terribly. I had never known such complete solitude as I felt now. I had not realized how accustomed I had become to her being there, nor what impact her leaving would have on me. In just those few days of giving her sanctuary, it had somehow come to seem to me that to house two souls within one brain was the normal condition of mankind, and that to be alone in one's skull as I was now was a shameful thing.

As I neared the place where Crew Deck narrows into the curve of the Eye a slender figure stepped without warning from the shadows.

'Captain.'

My mind was full of the loss of Vox and he caught me unaware. I jumped back, badly startled.

'For the love of God, man!'

'It's just me. Bulgar. Don't be so scared, Captain. It's only Bulgar.'

'Let me be,' I said, and brusquely beckoned him away.

'No. Wait, Captain. Please, wait.'

He clutched at my arm, holding me as I tried to go. I halted and turned towards him, trembling with anger and surprise.

Bulgar, Roacher's jackmate, was a gentle, soft-voiced little man, wide-mouthed, olive-skinned, with huge sad eyes. He and Roacher had sailed the skies of heaven together since before I was born. They complemented each other. Where Roacher was small and hard, like fruit that has been left to dry in the sun

116

for a hundred years, his jackmate Bulgar was small and tender, with a plump, succulent look about him. Together they seemed complete, an unassailable whole: I could readily imagine them lying together in their bunk, each jacked to the other, one person in two bodies, linked more intimately even than Vox and I had been.

With an effort I recovered my poise. Tightly I said, 'What is it, Bulgar?'

'Can we talk a minute, Captain?'

'We are talking. What do you want with me?'

'That loose matrix, sir.'

My reaction must have been stronger than he was expecting. His eyes went wide and he took a step or two back from me.

Moistening his lips, he said, 'We were wondering, Captain – wondering how the search is going – whether you had any idea where the matrix might be – '

I said stiffly, 'Who's *we*, Bulgar?'

'The men. Roacher. Me. Some of the others. Mainly Roacher, sir.'

'Ah. So Roacher wants to know where the matrix is.'

The little man moved closer. I saw him staring deep into me as though searching for Vox behind the mask of my carefully expressionless face. Did he know? Did they all? I wanted to cry out, *She's not there any more, she's gone, she left me, she ran off into space*. But apparently what was troubling Roacher and his shipmates was something other than the possibility that Vox had taken refuge with me.

Bulgar's tone was soft, insinuating, concerned. 'Roacher's very worried, Captain. He's been on ships with loose matrixes before. He knows how much trouble they can be. He's really worried, Captain. I have to tell you that. I've never seen him so worried.'

'What does he think the matrix will do to him?'

'He's afraid of being taken over,' Bulgar said.

'Taken over?'

'The matrix coming into his head through his jack. Mixing itself up with his brain. It's been known to happen, Captain.'

117

'And why should it happen to Roacher, out of all the men on this ship? Why not you? Why not Pedregal? Or Rio de Rio? Or one of the passengers again?' I took a deep breath. 'Why not me, for that matter?'

'He just wants to know, sir, what's the situation with the matrix now. Whether you've discovered anything about where it is. Whether you've been able to trap it.'

There was something strange in Bulgar's eyes. I began to think I was being tested again. This assertion of Roacher's alleged terror of being infiltrated and possessed by the wandering matrix might simply be a roundabout way of finding out whether that had already happened to me.

'Tell him it's gone,' I said.

'Gone, sir?'

'Gone. Vanished. It isn't anywhere on the ship any more. Tell him that, Bulgar. He can forget about her slithering down his precious jackhole.'

'*Her*?'

'Female matrix, yes. But that doesn't matter now. She's gone. You can tell him that. Escaped. Flew off into heaven. The emergency's over.' I glowered at him. I yearned to be rid of him, to go off by myself to nurse my new grief. 'Shouldn't you be getting back to your post, Bulgar?'

Did he believe me? Or did he think that I had slapped together some transparent lie to cover my complicity in the continued absence of the matrix? I had no way of knowing. Bulgar gave me a little obsequious bow and started to back away.

'Sir,' he said. 'Thank you, sir. I'll tell him, sir.'

He retreated into the shadows. I continued uplevel.

I passed Katkat on my way, and, a little while afterwards, Raebuck. They looked at me without speaking. There was something reproachful but almost loving about Katkat's expression, but Raebuck's icy, baleful stare brought me close to flinching. In their different ways they were saying, *Guilty, guilty, guilty*. But of what?

Before, I had imagined that everyone whom I encountered

aboard ship was able to tell at a single glance that I was harbouring the fugitive, and was simply waiting for me to reveal
myself with some foolish slip. Now everything was reversed.
They looked at me and I told myself that they were thinking,
*He's all alone by himself in there, he doesn't have anyone else
at all*, and I shrank away, shamed by my solitude. I knew that
this was the edge of madness. I was overwrought, overtired;
perhaps it had been a mistake to go starwalking a second time
so soon after my first. I needed to rest. I needed to hide.

I began to wish that there was someone aboard the *Sword
of Orion* with whom I could discuss these things. But who,
though? Roacher? 612 Jason? I was altogether isolated here.
The only one I could speak to on this ship was Vox. And she
was gone.

In the safety of my cabin I jacked myself into the mediq rack
and gave myself a ten-minute purge. That helped. The phantom
fears and intricate uncertainties that had taken possession of
me began to ebb.

I keyed up the log and ran through the list of my captainly
duties, such as they were, for the rest of the day. We were
approaching a spinaround point, one of those nodes of force
positioned equidistantly across heaven which a starship in transit must seize and use in order to propel itself onward through
the next sector of the universe. Spinaround acquisition is performed automatically but at least in theory the responsibility
for carrying it out successfully falls to the captain: I would give
the commands, I would oversee the process from initiation
through completion.

But there was still time for that.

I accessed 49 Henry Henry, who was the intelligence on
duty, and asked for an update on the matrix situation.

'No change, sir,' the intelligence reported at once.

'What does that mean?'

'Trace efforts continue as requested, sir. But we have not
detected the location of the missing matrix.'

'No clues? Not even a hint?'

'No data at all, sir. There's essentially no way to isolate

the minute electromagnetic pulse of a free matrix from the background noise of the ship's entire electrical system.'

I believed it. 612 Jason had told me that in nearly the same words.

I said, 'I have reason to think that the matrix is no longer on the ship, 49 Henry Henry.'

'Do you, sir?' said 49 Henry Henry in its usual aloof, half-mocking way.

'I do, yes. After a careful study of the situation, it's my opinion that the matrix exited the ship earlier this day and will not be heard from again.'

'Shall I record that as an official position, sir?'

'Record it,' I said.

'Done, sir.'

'And therefore, 49 Henry Henry, you can cancel search mode immediately and close the file. We'll enter a debit for one matrix and the Service bookkeepers can work it out later.'

'Very good, sir.'

'Decouple,' I ordered the intelligence.

49 Henry Henry went away. I sat quietly amid the splendours of my cabin, thinking back over my starwalk and reliving that sense of harmony, of love, of oneness with the worlds of heaven, that had come over me while Vox and I drifted on the bosom of the Great Open. And feeling once again the keen slicing sense of loss that I had felt since Vox's departure from me. In a little while I would have to rise and go to the command centre and put myself through the motions of overseeing spin-around acquisition; but for the moment I remained where I was, motionless, silent, peering deep into the heart of my solitude.

'I'm not gone,' said an unexpected quiet voice.

It came like a punch beneath the heart. It was a moment before I could speak.

'Vox?' I said at last. 'Where are you, Vox?'

'Right here.'

'Where?' I asked.

'Inside. I never went away.'

'You never – '

'You upset me. I just had to hide for a while.'

'You knew I was trying to find you?'

'Yes.'

Colour came to my cheeks. Anger roared like a stream in spate through my veins. I felt myself blazing.

'You knew how I felt, when you – when it seemed that you weren't there any more.'

'Yes,' she said, even more quietly, after a time.

I forced myself to grow calm. I told myself that she owed me nothing, except perhaps gratitude for sheltering her, and that whatever pain she had caused me by going silent was none of her affair. I reminded myself also that she was a child, unruly and turbulent and undisciplined.

After a bit I said, 'I missed you. I missed you more than I want to say.'

'I'm sorry,' she said, sounding repentant, but not very. 'I had to go away for a time. You upset me, Adam.'

'By asking you to show me how you used to look?'

'Yes.'

'I don't understand why that upset you so much.'

'You don't have to,' Vox said. 'I don't mind now. You can see me, if you like. Do you still want to? Here. This is me. This is what I used to be. If it disgusts you don't blame me. Okay? Okay, Adam? Here. Have a look. Here I am.'

14.

There was a wrenching within me, a twisting, a painful yanking sensation, as of some heavy barrier forcibly being pulled aside. And then the glorious radiant scarlet sky of Kansas Four blossomed on the screen of my mind.

She didn't simply show it to me. She took me there. I felt the soft moist wind on my face, I breathed the sweet, faintly pungent air, I heard the sly rustling of glossy leathery fronds that dangled from bright yellow trees. Beneath my bare feet the black soil was warm and spongy.

I was Leeleaine, who liked to call herself Vox. I was seventeen years old and swept by forces and compulsions as powerful as hurricanes.

I was her from within and also I saw her from outside.

My hair was long and thick and dark, tumbling down past my shoulders in an avalanche of untended curls and loops and snags. My hips were broad, my breasts were full and heavy: I could feel the pull of them, the pain of them. It was almost as if they were stiff with milk, though they were not. My face was tense, alert, sullen, aglow with angry intelligence. It was not an unappealing face. Vox was not an unappealing girl.

From her earlier reluctance to show herself to me I had expected her to be ugly, or perhaps deformed in some way, dragging herself about in a coarse, heavy, burdensome husk of flesh that was a constant reproach to her. She had spoken of her life on Kansas Four as being so dreary, so sad, so miserable, that she saw no hope in staying there. And had given up her body to be turned into mere electricity, on the promise that she could have a new body – any body – when she reached Cul-de-Sac. *I hated my body*, she had told me. *I couldn't wait to be rid of it.* She had refused even to give me a glimpse of it, retreating instead for hours into a desperate silence so total that I thought she had fled.

All that was a mystery to me now. The Leeleaine that I saw, that I was, was a fine sturdy-looking girl. Not beautiful, no, too strong and strapping for that, I suppose, but far from ugly: her eyes were warm and intelligent, her lips full, her nose finely modelled. And it was a healthy body, too, robust, vital. Of course she had no deformities; and why had I thought she had, when it would have been a simple matter of retrogenetic surgery to amend any bothersome defect? No, there was nothing wrong with the body that Vox had abandoned and for which she professed such loathing, for which she felt such shame.

Then I realized that I was seeing her from outside. I was seeing her as if by relay, filtering and interpreting the information she was offering me by passing it through the mind of an objective observer: myself. Who understood nothing, really, of what it was like to be anyone but himself.

Somehow – it was one of those automatic, unconscious adjustments – I altered the focus of my perceptions. All old frames of reference fell away and I let myself lose any sense of the separateness of our identities.

I was her. Fully, unconditionally, inextricably.

And I understood.

Figures flitted about her, shadowy, baffling, maddening. Brothers, sisters, parents, friends: they were all strangers to her. Everyone on Kansas Four was a stranger to her. And always would be.

She hated her body not because it was weak or unsightly but because it was her prison. She was enclosed within it as though within narrow stone walls. It hung about her, a cage of flesh, holding her down, pinning her to this lovely world called Kansas Four where she knew only pain and isolation and estrangement. Her body – her perfectly acceptable, healthy body – had become hateful to her because it was the emblem and symbol of her soul's imprisonment. Wild and incurably restless by temperament, she had failed to find a way to live within the smothering predictability of Kansas Four, a planet where she would never be anything but an internal outlaw. The only way she could leave Kansas Four was to surrender the body that tied her to it; and so she had turned against it with fury and loathing, rejecting it, abandoning it, despising it, detesting it. No one could ever understand that who beheld her from the outside.

But I understood.

I understood much more than that, in that one flashing moment of communion that she and I had. I came to see what she meant when she said that I was her twin, her double, her other self. Of course we were wholly different, I the sober, staid, plodding, diligent man, and she the reckless, volatile, impulsive, tempestuous girl. But beneath all that we were the same: misfits, outsiders, troubled wanderers through worlds we

123

had never made. We had found vastly differing ways to cope with our pain. Yet we were one and the same, two halves of a single entity.

We will remain together always now, I told myself.

And in that moment our communion broke. She broke it – it must have been she, fearful of letting this new intimacy grow too deep – and I found myself apart from her once again, still playing host to her in my brain but separated from her by the boundaries of my own individuality, my own selfhood. I felt her nearby, within me, a warm but discrete presence. Still within me, yes. But separate again.

15.

There was shipwork to do. For days, now, Vox's invasion of me had been a startling distraction. But I dared not let myself forget that we were in the midst of a traversal of heaven. The lives of us all, and of our passengers, depended on the proper execution of our duties: even mine. And worlds awaited the bounty that we bore. My task of the moment was to oversee spinaround acquisition.

I told Vox to leave me temporarily while I went through the routines of acquisition. I would be jacked to other crewmen for a time; they might very well be able to detect her within me; there was no telling what might happen. But she refused. 'No,' she said. 'I won't leave you. I don't want to go out there. But I'll hide, deep down, the way I did when I was upset with you.'

'Vox – ' I began.

'No. Please. I don't want to talk about it.'

There was no time to argue the point. I could feel the depth and intensity of her stubborn determination.

'Hide, then,' I said. 'If that's what you want to do.'

I made my way down out of the Eye to Engine Deck.

The rest of the acquisition team was already assembled in the Great Navigation Hall: Fresco, Raebuck, Roacher.

Raebuck's role was to see to it that communications channels were kept open, Fresco's to set up the navigation coordinates, and Roacher, as power engineer, would monitor fluctuations in drain and input-output cycling. My function was to give the cues at each stage of acquisition. In truth I was pretty much redundant, since Raebuck and Fresco and Roacher had been doing this sort of thing a dozen times a voyage for scores of voyages and they had little need of my guidance. The deeper truth was that they were redundant too, for 49 Henry Henry would oversee us all, and the intelligence was quite capable of setting up the entire process without any human help. Nevertheless there were formalities to observe, and not inane ones.

Intelligences are far superior to humans in mental capacity, interfacing capability, and reaction time, but even so they are nothing but servants, and artificial servants at that, lacking in any real awareness of human fragility or human ethical complexity. They must only be used as tools, not decision-makers. A society which delegates responsibilities of life and death to its servants will eventually find the servants' hands at its throat. As for me, novice that I was, my role was valid as well: the focal point of the enterprise, the prime initiator, the conductor and observer of the process. Perhaps anyone could perform those functions, but the fact remained that *someone* had to, and by tradition that someone was the captain. Call it a ritual, call it a highly stylized dance, if you will. But there is no getting away from the human need for ritual and stylization. Such aspects of a process may not seem essential, but they are valuable and significant, and ultimately they can be seen to be essential as well.

'Shall we begin?' Fresco asked.

We jacked up, Roacher directly into the ship, Raebuck into Roacher, Fresco to me, me into the ship.

'Simulation,' I said.

Raebuck keyed in the first code and the vast echoing space that was the Great Navigation Hall came alive with pulsing light: a representation of heaven all about us, the lines of force, the spinaround nodes, the stars, the planets. We moved unhinderedly in free fall, drifting as casually as angels. We could easily have believed we were starwalking.

The simulacrum of the ship was a bright arrow of fierce light just below us and to the left. Ahead, throbbing like a nest of twining angry serpents, was the globe that represented the Lasciate Ogni Speranza spinaround point, tightly-wound dull grey cables shot through with strands of fierce scarlet.

'Enter approach mode,' I said. 'Activate receptors. Begin threshold equalization. Begin momentum comparison. Prepare for acceleration uptick. Check angular velocity. Begin spin consolidation. Enter displacement select. Extend mast. Prepare for acquisition receptivity.'

At each command the proper man touched a control key or pressed a directive panel or simply sent an impulse shooting through the jack hookup by which he was connected, directly or indirectly, to the mind of the ship. Out of courtesy to me, they waited until the commands were given, but the speed with which they obeyed told me that their minds were already in motion even as I spoke.

'It's really exciting, isn't it?' Vox said suddenly.

'For God's sake, Vox! What are you trying to do?'

For all I knew, the others had heard her outburst as clearly as though it had come across a loudspeaker.

'I mean,' she went on, 'I never imagined it was anything like this. I can feel the whole – '

I shot her a sharp, anguished order to keep quiet. Her surfacing like this, after my warning to her, was a lunatic act. In the silence that followed I felt a kind of inner reverberation, a sulky twanging of displeasure coming from her. But I had no time to worry about Vox's moods now.

Arcing patterns of displacement power went ricocheting through the Great Navigation Hall as our mast came forth – not the underpinning for a set of sails, as it would be on a vessel that plied planetary seas, but rather a giant antenna to link us to the spinaround point ahead – and the ship and the spinaround point reached towards one another like grappling many-armed wrestlers. Hot streaks of crimson and emerald and

126

gold and amethyst speared the air, vaulting and rebounding. The spinaround point, activated now and trembling between energy states, was enfolding us in its million tentacles, capturing us, making ready to whirl on its axis and hurl us swiftly onward towards the next way-station in our journey across heaven.

'Acquisition,' Raebuck announced.

'Proceed to capture acceptance,' I said.

'Acceptance,' said Raebuck.

'Directional mode,' I said. 'Dimensional grid eleven.'

'Dimensional grid eleven,' Fresco repeated.

The whole hall seemed on fire now.

'Wonderful,' Vox murmured. 'So beautiful – '

'*Vox!*'

'Request spin authorization,' said Fresco.

'Spin authorization granted,' I said. 'Grid eleven.'

'Grid eleven,' Fresco said again. 'Spin achieved.'

A tremor went rippling through me – and through Fresco, through Raebuck, through Roacher. It was the ship, in the persona of 49 Henry Henry, completing the acquisition process. We had been captured by Lasciate Ogni Speranza, we had undergone velocity absorption and redirection, we had had new spin imparted to us, and we had been sent soaring off through heaven towards our upcoming port of call. I heard Vox sobbing within me, not a sob of despair but one of ecstasy, of fulfilment.

We all unjacked. Raebuck, that dour man, managed a little smile as he turned to me.

'Nicely done, Captain,' he said.

'Yes,' said Fresco. 'Very nice. You're a quick learner.'

I saw Roacher studying me with those little shining eyes of his. Go on, you bastard, I thought. You give me a compliment too now, if you know how.

But all he did was stare. I shrugged and turned away. What Roacher thought or said made little difference to me, I told myself.

As we left the Great Navigation Hall in our separate directions Fresco fell in alongside me. Without a word we trudged together towards the transit trackers that were waiting for us.

127

Just as I was about to board mine he – or was it she? – said softly, 'Captain?'

'What is it, Fresco?'

Fresco leaned close. Soft sly eyes, tricksy little smile; and yet I felt some warmth coming from the navigator.

'It's a very dangerous game, Captain.'

'I don't know what you mean.'

'Yes, you do,' Fresco said. 'No use pretending. We were jacked together in there. I felt things. I know.'

There was nothing I could say, so I said nothing.

After a moment Fresco said, 'I like you. I won't harm you. But Roacher knows too. I don't know if he knew before, but he certainly knows now. If I were you, I'd find that very troublesome, Captain. Just a word to the wise. All right?'

16.

Only a fool would have remained on such a course as I had been following. Vox saw the risks as well as I. There was no hiding anything from anyone any longer; if Roacher knew, then Bulgar knew, and soon it would be all over the ship. No question, either, but that 49 Henry Henry knew. In the intimacies of our navigation-hall contact, Vox must have been as apparent to them as a red scarf around my forehead.

There was no point in taking her to task for revealing her presence within me like that during acquisition. What was done was done. At first it had seemed impossible to understand why she had done such a thing; but then it became all too easy to comprehend. It was the same sort of unpredictable, unexamined, impulsive behaviour that had led her to go barging into a suspended passenger's mind and cause his death. She was simply not one who paused to think before acting. That kind of behaviour has always been bewildering to me. She was my opposite as well as my double. And yet had I not done a Vox-like thing myself, taking her into me, when she appealed to me for sanctuary, without stopping at all to consider the consequences?

'Where can I go?' she asked, desperate. 'If I move around the ship freely again they'll track me and close me off. And then they'll eradicate me. They'll – '

'Easy,' I said. 'Don't panic. I'll hide you where they won't find you.'

'Inside some passenger?'

'We can't try that again. There's no way to prepare the passenger for what's happening to him, and he'll panic. No. I'll put you in one of the annexes. Or maybe one of the virtualities.'

'The what?'

'The additional cargo area. The subspace extensions that surround the ship.'

She gasped. 'Those aren't even real! I was in them, when I was travelling around the ship. Those are just clusters of probability waves!'

'You'll be safe there,' I said.

'I'm afraid. It's bad enough that *I'm* not real any more. But to be stored in a place that isn't real either – '

'You're as real as I am. And the outstructures are just as real as the rest of the ship. It's a different quality of reality, that's all. Nothing bad will happen to you out there. You've told me yourself that you've already been in them, right? And got out again without any problems. They won't be able to detect you there, Vox. But I tell you this, that if you stay in me, or anywhere else in the main part of the ship, they'll track you down and find you and eradicate you. And probably eradicate me right along with you.'

'Do you mean that?' she said, sounding chastened.

'Come on. There isn't much time.'

On the pretext of a routine inventory check – well within my table of responsibilities – I obtained access to one of the virtualities. It was the storehouse where the probability stabilizers were kept. No one was likely to search for her there. The chances of our encountering a zone of probability turbulence between here and Cul-de-Sac were minimal; and in the ordinary course of a voyage nobody cared to enter any of the virtualities.

I had lied to Vox, or at least committed a half-truth, by leading her to believe that all our outstructures are of an equal level of reality. Certainly the annexes are tangible, solid; they differ from the ship proper only in the spin of their dimensional polarity. They are invisible except when activated, and they involve us in no additional expenditure of fuel, but there is no uncertainty about their existence, which is why we entrust valuable cargo to them, and on some occasions even passengers.

The extensions are a level further removed from basic reality. They are skewed not only in dimensional polarity but in temporal contiguity: that is, we carry them with us under time displacement, generally ten to twenty virtual years in the past or future. The risks of this are extremely minor and the payoff in reduction of generating cost is great. Still, we are measurably more cautious about what sort of cargo we keep in them.

As for the virtualities –

Their name itself implies their uncertainty. They are purely probabilistic entities, existing most of the time in the stochastic void that surrounds the ship. In simpler words, whether they are actually there or not at any given time is a matter worth wagering on. We know how to access them at the time of greatest probability, and our techniques are quite reliable, which is why we can use them for overflow ladings when our cargo uptake is unusually heavy. But in general we prefer not to entrust anything very important to them, since a virtuality's range of access times can fluctuate in an extreme way, from a matter of microseconds to a matter of megayears, and that can make quick recall a chancy affair.

Knowing all this, I put Vox in a virtuality anyway.

I had to hide her. And I had to hide her in a place where no one would look. The risk that I'd be unable to call her up again because of virtuality fluctuation was a small one. The risk was much greater that she would be detected, and she and I both punished, if I let her remain in any area of the ship that had a higher order of probability.

'I want you to stay here until the coast is clear,' I told her sternly. 'No impulsive journeys around the ship, no excursions into adjoining outstructures, no little trips of any kind, regardless of how restless you get. Is that clear? I'll call you up from here as soon as I think it's safe.'

'I'll miss you, Adam.'

'The same here. But this is how it has to be.'

'I know.'

'If you're discovered, I'll deny I know anything about you. I mean that, Vox.'

'I understand.'

'You won't be stuck in here long. I promise you that.'

'Will you visit me?'

'That wouldn't be wise,' I said.

'But maybe you will anyway.'

'Maybe. I don't know.' I opened the access channel. The virtuality gaped before us. 'Go on,' I said. 'In with you. In. Now. Go, Vox. Go.'

I could feel her leaving me. It was almost like an amputation. The silence, the emptiness, that descended on me suddenly was ten times as deep as what I had felt when she had merely been hiding within me. She was gone, now. For the first time in days, I was truly alone.

I closed off the virtuality.

When I returned to the Eye, Roacher was waiting for me near the command bridge.

'You have a moment, Captain?'

'What is it, Roacher?'

'The missing matrix. We have proof it's still on board ship.'

'Proof?'

'You know what I mean. You felt it just like I did while we were doing acquisition. It said something. It spoke. It was right in there in the navigation hall with us, Captain.'

I met his luminescent gaze levelly and said in an even voice, 'I was giving my complete attention to what we were doing, Roacher. Spinaround acquisition isn't second nature to me the way it is to you. I had no time to notice any matrixes floating around in there.'

'You didn't?'

'No. Does that disappoint you?'

'That might mean that you're the one carrying the matrix,' he said.

'How so?'

'If it's in you, down on a subneural level, you might not even be aware of it. But we would be. Raebuck, Fresco, me. We all detected something, Captain. If it wasn't in us it would have to be in you. We can't have a matrix riding around inside our captain, you know. No telling how that could distort his judgement. What dangers that might lead us into.'

'I'm not carrying any matrixes, Roacher.'

'Can we be sure of that?'

'Would you like to have a look?'

'A jackup, you mean? You and me?'

The notion disgusted me. But I had to make the offer.

'A – jackup, yes,' I said. 'Communion. You and me, Roacher. Right now. Come on, we'll measure the bandwidths and do the matching. Let's get this over with.'

He contemplated me a long while, as if calculating the likelihood that I was bluffing. In the end he must have decided that I was too naïve to be able to play the game out to so hazardous a turn. He knew that I wouldn't bluff, that I was confident he would find me untenanted or I never would have made the offer.

'No,' he said finally. 'We don't need to bother with that.'

'Are you sure?'

'If you say you're clean – '

'But I might be carrying her and not even know it,' I said. 'You told me that yourself.'

'Forget it. You'd know, if you had her in you.'

'You'll never be certain of that unless you look. Let's jack up, Roacher.'

He scowled. 'Forget it,' he said again, and turned away. 'You must be clean, if you're this eager for jacking. But I'll tell you this, Captain. We're going to find her, wherever she's hiding. And when we do – '

He left the threat unfinished. I stood staring at his retreating form until he was lost to view.

17.

For a few days everything seemed back to normal. We sped onward towards Cul-de-Sac. I went through the round of my regular tasks, however meaningless they seemed to me. Most of them did. I had not yet achieved any sense that the *Sword of Orion* was under my command in anything but the most hypothetical way. Still, I did what I had to do.

No one spoke of the missing matrix within my hearing. On those rare occasions when I encountered some other member of the crew while I moved about the ship, I could tell by the hooded look of his eyes that I was still under suspicion. But they had no proof. The matrix was no longer in any way evident on board. The ship's intelligences were unable to find the slightest trace of its presence.

I was alone, and oh! it was a painful business for me.

I suppose that once you have tasted that kind of round-the-clock communion, that sort of perpetual jacking, you are never the same again. I don't know: there is no real information available on cases of possession by free matrix, only shipboard folklore, scarcely to be taken seriously. All I can judge by is my own misery now that Vox was actually gone. She was only a half-grown girl, a wild coltish thing, unstable, unformed; and yet, and yet, she had lived within me and we had come towards one another to construct the deepest sort of sharing, what was almost a kind of marriage. You could call it that.

After five or six days I knew I had to see her again. Whatever the risks.

I accessed the virtuality and sent a signal into it that I was coming in. There was no reply; and for one terrible moment I feared the worst, that in the mysterious workings of the virtuality she had somehow been engulfed and destroyed. But that was not the case. I stepped through the glowing pink-edged field of light that was the gateway to the virtuality, and instantly I felt her near me, clinging tight, trembling with joy.

She held back, though, from entering me. She wanted me to tell her it was safe. I beckoned her in; and then came that sharp warm sensation I remembered so well, as she slipped down into my neural network and we became one.

'I can only stay a little while,' I said. 'It's still very chancy for me to be with you.'

'Oh, Adam, Adam, it's been so awful for me in here – '

'I know. I can imagine.'

'Are they still looking for me?'

'I think they're starting to put you out of their minds,' I said. And we both laughed at the play on words that that phrase implied.

I didn't dare remain more than a few minutes. I had only wanted to touch souls with her briefly, to reassure myself that she was all right and to ease the pain of separation. But it was irregular for a captain to enter a virtuality at all. To stay in one for any length of time exposed me to real risk of detection.

But my next visit was longer, and the one after that longer still. We were like furtive lovers meeting in a dark forest for hasty delicious trysts. Hidden there in that not-quite-real out-structure of the ship we would join our two selves and whisper together with urgent intensity until I felt it was time for me to leave. She would always try to keep me longer; but her resistance to my departure was never great, nor did she ever suggest accompanying me back into the stable sector of the ship. She had come to understand that the only place we could meet was in the virtuality.

We were nearing the vicinity of Cul-de-Sac now. Soon we would go to worldward and the shoreships would travel out to meet us, so that we could download the cargo that was meant for them. It was time to begin considering the problem of what would happen to Vox when we reached our destination.

That was something I was unwilling to face. However I tried,

I could not force myself to confront the difficulties that I knew lay just ahead.

But she could.

'We must be getting close to Cul-de-Sac now,' she said.

'We'll be there soon, yes.'

'I've been thinking about that. How I'm going to deal with that.'

'What do you mean?'

'I'm a lost soul,' she said. 'Literally. There's no way I can come to life again.'

'I don't under – '

'Adam, don't you see?' she cried fiercely. 'I can't just float down to Cul-de-Sac and grab myself a body and put myself on the roster of colonists. And you can't possibly smuggle me down there while nobody's looking. The first time anyone ran an inventory check, or did passport control, I'd be dead. No, the only way I can get there is to be neatly packed up again in my original storage circuit. And even if I could figure out how to get back into that, I'd be simply handing myself over for punishment or even eradication. I'm listed as missing on the manifest, right? And I'm wanted for causing the death of that passenger. Now I turn up again, in my storage circuit. You think they'll just download me nicely to Cul-de-Sac and give me the body that's waiting for me there? Not very likely. Not likely that I'll ever get out of that circuit alive, is it, once I go back in? Assuming I *could* go back in in the first place. I don't know how a storage circuit is operated, do you? And there's nobody you can ask.'

'What are you trying to say, Vox?'

'I'm not trying to say anything. I'm saying it. I have to leave the ship on my own and disappear.'

'No. You can't do that!'

'Sure I can. It'll be just like starwalking. I can go anywhere I please. Right through the skin of the ship, out into heaven. And keep on going.'

'To Cul-de-Sac?'

'You're being stupid,' she said. 'Not to Cul-de-Sac, no. Not to anywhere. That's all over for me, the idea of getting a new body. I have no legal existence any more. I've messed myself up. All right: I admit it. I'll take what's coming to me. It won't be so bad, Adam. I'll go starwalking. Outward and outward and outward, forever and ever.'

'You mustn't,' I said. 'Stay here with me.'

'Where? In this empty storage unit out here?'

'No,' I told her. 'Within me. The way we are right now. The way we were before.'

'How long do you think we could carry that off?' she asked. I didn't answer.

'Every time you have to jack into the machinery I'll have to hide myself down deep,' she said. 'And I can't guarantee that I'll go deep enough, or that I'll stay down there long enough. Sooner or later they'll notice me. They'll find me. They'll eradicate me and they'll throw you out of the Service, or maybe they'll eradicate you too. No, Adam. It couldn't possibly work. And I'm not going to destroy you with me. I've done enough harm to you already.'

'Vox – '

'No. This is how it has to be.'

18.

And this is how it was. We were deep in the Spook Cluster now, and the Vainglory Archipelago burned bright on my realspace screen. Somewhere down there was the planet called Cul-de-Sac. Before we came to worldward of it, Vox would have to slip away into the great night of heaven.

Making a worldward approach is perhaps the most difficult manoeuvre a starship must achieve; and the captain must go to the edge of his abilities along with everyone else. Novice at my trade though I was, I would be called on to perform complex and challenging processes. If I failed at them, other crewmen might cut in and intervene, or, if necessary, the ship's intelligences might override; but if that came to pass my career would be destroyed, and there was the small but finite possibility, I suppose, that the ship itself could be gravely damaged or even lost.

I was determined, all the same, to give Vox the best send-off I could.

On the morning of our approach I stood for a time on Outerscreen Level, staring down at the world that called itself Cul-de-Sac. It glowed like a red eye in the night. I knew that it was the world Vox had chosen for herself, but all the same it seemed repellent to me, almost evil. I felt that way about all the worlds of the shore people now. The Service had changed me; and I knew that the change was irreversible. Never again would I go down to one of those worlds. The starship was my world now.

I went to the virtuality where Vox was waiting.

'Come,' I said, and she entered me.

Together we crossed the ship to the Great Navigation Hall.

The approach team had already gathered: Raebuck, Fresco, Roacher, again, along with Pedregal, who would supervise the downloading of cargo. The intelligence on duty was 612 Jason. I greeted them with quick nods and we jacked ourselves together in approach series.

Almost at once I felt Roacher probing within me, searching for the fugitive intelligence that he still thought I might be harbouring. Vox shrank back, deep out of sight. I didn't care. Let him probe, I thought. This will all be over soon.

'Request approach instructions,' Fresco said.

'Simulation,' I ordered.

The fiery red eye of Cul-de-Sac sprang into vivid representation before us in the hall. On the other side of us was the simulacrum of the ship, surrounded by sheets of white flame that rippled like the blaze of the aurora.

I gave the command and we entered approach mode.

We could not, of course, come closer to planetskin than a million shiplengths, or Cul-de-Sac's inexorable forces would rip us apart. But we had to line the ship up with its extended mast aimed at the planet's equator, and hold ourselves firm in that position while the shoreships of Cul-de-Sac came swarming up from their red world to receive their cargo from us.

612 Jason fed me the coordinates and I gave them to Fresco, while Raebuck kept the channels clear and Roacher saw to it that we had enough power for what we had to do. But as I passed the data along to Fresco, it was with every sign reversed. My purpose was to aim the mast not downward to Cul-de-Sac but outward towards the stars of heaven.

At first none of them noticed. Everything seemed to be going serenely. Because my reversals were exact, only the closest examination of the ship's position would indicate our 180-degree displacement.

Floating in the free fall of the Great Navigation Hall, I felt almost as though I could detect the movements of the ship. An illusion, I knew. But a powerful one. The vast ten-kilometre-long needle that was the *Sword of Orion* seemed to hang suspended, motionless, and then to begin slowly, slowly to turn, tipping itself on its axis, reaching for the stars with its mighty mast. Easily, easily, slowly, silently –

What joy that was, feeling the ship in my hand!

The ship was mine. I had mastered it.

'Captain,' Fresco said softly.

'Easy on, Fresco. Keep feeding power.'

'Captain, the signs don't look right – '

'Easy on. Easy.'

'Give me a coordinates check, Captain.'

'Another minute,' I told him.

'But – '

'Easy on, Fresco.'

Now I felt restlessness too from Pedregal, and a slow chilly stirring of interrogation from Raebuck; and then Roacher probed me again, perhaps seeking Vox, perhaps simply trying to discover what was going on. They knew something was wrong, but they weren't sure what it was.

We were nearly at full extension, now. Within me there was an electrical trembling: Vox rising through the levels of my mind, nearing the surface, preparing for departure.

'Captain, we're turned the wrong way!' Fresco cried.

'I know,' I said. 'Easy on. We'll swing around in a moment.'

'He's gone crazy!' Pedregal blurted.

I felt Vox slipping free of my mind. But somehow I found myself still aware of her movements, I suppose because I was jacked into 612 Jason and 612 Jason was monitoring everything. Easily, serenely, Vox melted into the skin of the ship.

'*Captain!*' Fresco yelled, and began to struggle with me for control.

I held the navigator at arm's length and watched in a strange and wonderful calmness as Vox passed through the ship's circuitry all in an instant and emerged at the tip of the mast, facing the stars. And cast herself adrift.

Because I had turned the ship around, she could not be captured and acquired by Cul-de-Sac's powerful navigational grid, but would be free to move outward into heaven. For her it would be a kind of floating out to sea, now. After a time she would be so far out that she could no longer key into the shipboard bioprocessors that sustained the patterns of her consciousness, and, though the web of electrical impulses that was the Vox matrix would travel outward and onward forever, the set of identity responses that was Vox herself would lose focus soon, would begin to waver and blur. In a little while, or perhaps not so little, but inevitably, her sense of herself as an independent entity would be lost. Which is to say, she would die.

I followed her as long as I could. I saw a spark travelling across the great night. And then nothing.

'All right,' I said to Fresco. 'Now let's turn the ship the right way around and give them their cargo.'

19.

That was many years ago. Perhaps no one else remembers those events, which seem so dreamlike now even to me. The *Sword of Orion* has carried me nearly everywhere in the galaxy since then. On some voyages I have been captain; on others, a downloader, a supercargo, a mind-wiper, even sometimes a push-cell. It makes no difference how we serve, in the Service.

I often think of her. There was a time when thinking of her meant coming to terms with feelings of grief and pain and irrecoverable loss, but no longer, not for many years. She must be long dead now, however durable and resilient the spark of her might have been. And yet she still lives. Of that much I am certain. There is a place within me where I can reach her warmth, her strength, her quirky vitality, her impulsive suddenness. I can feel those aspects of her, those gifts of her brief time of sanctuary within me, as a living presence still, and I think I always will, as I make my way from world to tethered world, as I journey onward everlastingly spanning the dark light-years in this great ship of heaven.

House of Bones

Terry Carr was a first-rate editor, who was responsible for the publication of such masterpieces of science fiction as *The Left Hand of Darkness*, *And Chaos Died*, and *Neuromancer*. He was a much underrated writer, who published one classic story ('The Dance of the Changer and the Three') and a number of fine ones that received less attention than they deserved. He was also a warm-hearted, funny, decent human being who was one of my closest friends for almost thirty years.

The one thing he wasn't was physically durable. Though he was tall and athletic-looking, his body began to give out by the time he was about forty-five, and in the spring of 1987 he died, two months after his fiftieth birthday, after a melancholy period of accelerating decline that for the most part had remained unknown beyond his immediate circle.

Beth Meacham, the editor-in-chief of Tor Books, was one of many in the science-fiction field who had learned her craft by working with Terry and by emulating his precepts. In the weeks after his death she sought to find some way of showing her gratitude; and quickly she hit upon the idea of assembling an anthology of original stories by writers who had had some professional association with Terry and who felt that his impact on their careers had been substantial. I was one of those invited to contribute, along with Fritz Leiber, Kate Wilhelm, Ursula K. Le Guin, Gene Wolfe, Roger Zelazny, and a dozen or so others.

I had just finished writing 'House of Bones'. Terry was keenly interested in prehistory, and had a fundamental belief that human beings were basically good, however unlikely that might seem judging by surface appearance alone. 'House of Bones' seemed to me to

141

be the perfect story for the memorial anthology, and I sent it to Beth. *Terry's Universe* was published in May of 1988, thirteen months after his death. 'House of Bones' was the first story in the book.

After the evening meal Paul starts tapping on his drum and chanting quietly to himself, and Marty picks up the rhythm, chanting too. And then the two of them launch into that night's instalment of the tribal epic, which is what happens, sooner or later, every evening.

It all sounds very intense but I don't have a clue to the meaning. They sing the epic in the religious language, which I've never been allowed to learn. It has the same relation to the everyday language, I guess, as Latin does to French or Spanish. But it's private, sacred, for insiders only. Not for the likes of me.

'Tell it, man!' BJ yells. 'Let it roll!' Danny shouts.

Paul and Marty are really getting into it. Then a gust of fierce stinging cold whistles through the house as the reindeer-hide flap over the doorway is lifted, and Zeus comes stomping in.

Zeus is the chieftain. Big burly man, starting to run to fat a little. Mean-looking, just as you'd expect. Heavy black beard streaked with grey and hard, glittering eyes that glow like rubies in a face wrinkled and carved by windburn and time. Despite the Palaeolithic cold, all he's wearing is a cloak of black fur, loosely draped. The thick hair on his heavy chest is turning grey too. Festoons of jewellery announce his power and status: necklaces of seashells, bone beads, and amber, a pendant of yellow wolf teeth, an ivory headband, bracelets carved from bone, five or six rings.

Sudden silence. Ordinarily when Zeus drops in at BJ's house it's for a little roistering and tale-telling and butt-pinching, but tonight he has come without either of his wives, and he looks troubled, grim. Jabs a finger towards Jeanne.

'You saw the stranger today? What's he like?'

There's been a stranger lurking near the village all week,

leaving traces everywhere – footprints in the permafrost, hastily covered-over campsites, broken flints, scraps of charred meat. The whole tribe's keyed. Strangers aren't common. I was the last one, a year and a half ago. God only knows why they took me in: because I seemed so pitiful to them, maybe. But the way they've been talking, they'll kill this one on sight if they can. Paul and Marty composed a Song of the Stranger last week and Marty sang it by the campfire two different nights. It was in the religious language so I couldn't understand a word of it. But it sounded terrifying.

Jeanne is Marty's wife. She got a good look at the stranger this afternoon, down by the river while netting fish for dinner. 'He's short,' she tells Zeus. 'Shorter than any of you, but with big muscles, like Gebravar.' Gebravar is Jeanne's name for me. The people of the tribe are strong, but they didn't pump iron when they were kids. My muscles fascinate them. 'His hair is yellow and his eyes are grey. And he's ugly. Nasty. Big head, big flat nose. Walks with his shoulders hunched and his head down.' Jeanne shudders. 'He's like a pig. A real beast. A goblin. Trying to steal fish from the net, he was. But he ran away when he saw me.'

Zeus listens, glowering, asking a question now and then – did he say anything, how was he dressed, was his skin painted in any way? Then he turns to Paul.

'What do you think he is?'

'A ghost,' Paul says. These people see ghosts everywhere. And Paul, who is the bard of the tribe, thinks about them all the time. His poems are full of ghosts. He feels the world of ghosts pressing in, pressing in. 'Ghosts have grey eyes,' he says. 'This man has grey eyes.'

'A ghost, maybe, yes. But what kind of ghost?'

'What *kind*?'

Zeus glares. 'You should listen to your own poems,' he snaps. 'Can't you see it? This is a Scavenger Folk man prowling around. Or the ghost of one.'

General uproar and hubbub at that.

I turn to Sally. Sally's my woman. I still have trouble saying

143

that she's my wife, but that's what she really is. I call her Sally because there once was a girl back home who I thought I might marry, and that was her name, far from here in another geological epoch.

I ask Sally who the Scavenger Folk are.

'From the old times,' she says. 'Lived here when we first came. But they're all dead now. They – '

That's all she gets a chance to tell me. Zeus is suddenly looming over me. He's always regarded me with a mixture of amusement and tolerant contempt, but now there's something new in his eye. 'Here is something you will do for us,' he says to me. 'It takes a stranger to find a stranger. This will be your task. Whether he is a ghost or a man, we must know the truth. So you, tomorrow: you will go out and you will find him and you will take him. Do you understand? At first light you will go to search for him, and you will not come back until you have him.'

I try to say something, but my lips don't want to move. My silence seems good enough for Zeus, though. He smiles and nods fiercely and swings around, and goes stalking off into the night.

They all gather around me, excited in that kind of animated edgy way that comes over you when someone you know is picked for some big distinction. I can't tell whether they envy me or feel sorry for me. BJ hugs me, Danny punches me in the arm, Paul runs up a jubilant-sounding number on his drum. Marty pulls a wickedly sharp stone blade about nine inches long out of his kit-bag and presses it into my hand.

'Here. You take this. You may need it.'

I stare at it as if he had handed me a live grenade.

'Look,' I say. 'I don't know anything about stalking and capturing people.'

'Come *on*,' BJ says. 'What's the problem?'

BJ is an architect. Paul's a poet. Marty sings, better than Pavarotti. Danny paints and sculpts. I think of them as my special buddies. They're all what you could loosely call Cro-

Magnon men. I'm not. They treat me just like one of the gang, though. We five, we're some bunch. Without them I'd have gone crazy here. Lost as I am, cut off as I am from everything I used to be and know.

'You're strong and quick,' Marty says. 'You can do it.'

'And you're pretty smart, in your crazy way,' says Paul. 'Smarter than *he* is. We aren't worried at all.'

If they're a little condescending sometimes, I suppose I deserve it. They're highly skilled individuals, after all, proud of the things they can do. To them I'm a kind of retard. That's a novelty for me. I used to be considered highly skilled too, back where I came from.

'You go with me,' I say to Marty. 'You and Paul both. I'll do whatever has to be done but I want you to back me up.'

'No,' Marty says. 'You do this alone.'

'BJ? Danny?'

'No,' they say. And their smiles harden, their eyes grow chilly. Suddenly it doesn't look so chummy around here. We may be buddies but I have to go out there by myself. Or I may have misread the whole situation and we aren't such big buddies at all. Either way this is some kind of test, some rite of passage maybe, an initiation. I don't know. Just when I think these people are exactly like us except for a few piddling differences of customs and languages, I realize how alien they really are. Not savages, far from it. But they aren't even remotely like modern people. They're something entirely else. Their bodies and their minds are pure *Homo sapiens* but their souls are different from ours by 20,000 years.

To Sally I say, 'Tell me more about the Scavenger Folk.'

'Like animals, they were,' she says. 'They could speak but only in grunts and belches. They were bad hunters and they ate dead things that they found on the ground, or stole the kills of others.'

'They smelled like garbage,' says Danny. 'Like an old dump where everything was rotten. And they didn't know how to paint or sculpt.'

'This was how they screwed,' says Marty, grabbing the

nearest woman, pushing her down, pretending to hump her from behind. Everyone laughs, cheers, stamps his feet.

'And they walked like this,' says BJ, doing an ape-shuffle, banging his chest with his fists.

There's a lot more, a lot of locker-room stuff about the ugly shaggy stupid smelly disgusting Scavenger Folk. How dirty they were, how barbaric. How the pregnant women kept the babies in their bellies twelve or thirteen months and they came out already hairy, with a full mouth of teeth. All ancient history, handed down through the generations by bards like Paul in the epics. None of them has ever actually seen a Scavenger. But they sure seem to detest them.

'They're all dead,' Paul says. 'They were killed in the migration wars long ago. That has to be a ghost out there.'

Of course I've guessed what's up. I'm no archaeologist at all – West Point, fourth generation. My skills are in electronics, computers, time-shift physics. There was such horrible political infighting among the archaeology boys about who was going to get to go to the past that in the end none of them went and the gig wound up going to the military. Still, they sent me here with enough crash-course archaeology to be able to see that the Scavengers must have been what we call the Neanderthals, that shambling race of also-rans that got left behind in the evolutionary sweepstakes.

So there really had been a war of extermination between the slow-witted Scavengers and clever *Homo sapiens* here in Ice Age Europe. But there must have been a few survivors left on the losing side, and one of them, God knows why, is wandering around near this village.

Now I'm supposed to find the ugly stranger and capture him. Or kill him, I guess. Is that what Zeus wants from me? To take the stranger's blood on my head? A very civilized tribe, they are, even if they do hunt huge woolly elephants and build houses out of their whitened bones. Too civilized to do their own murdering, and they figure they can send me out to do it for them.

'I don't think he's a Scavenger,' Danny says. 'I think he's

146

from Naz Glesim. The Naz Glesim people have grey eyes. Besides, what would a ghost want with fish?'

Naz Glesim is a land far to the north-east, perhaps near what will some day be Moscow. Even here in the Palaeolithic the world is divided into a thousand little nations. Danny once went on a great solo journey through all the neighbouring lands: he's a kind of tribal Marco Polo.

'You better not let the chief hear that,' BJ tells him. 'He'll break your balls. Anyway, the Naz Glesim people aren't ugly. They look just like us except for their eyes.'

'Well, there's that,' Danny concedes. 'But I still think – '

Paul shakes his head. That gesture goes way back, too. 'A Scavenger ghost,' he insists.

BJ looks at me. 'What do you think, Pumangiup?' That's his name for me.

'Me?' I say. 'What do I know about these things?'

'You come from far away. You ever see a man like that?'

'I've seen plenty of ugly men, yes.' The people of the tribe are tall and lean, brown hair and dark shining eyes, wide faces, bold cheekbones. If they had better teeth they'd be gorgeous. 'But I don't know about this one. I'd have to see him.'

Sally brings a new platter of grilled fish over. I run my hand fondly over her bare haunch. Inside this house made of mammoth bones nobody wears very much clothing, because the structure is well insulated and the heat builds up even in the dead of winter. To me Sally is far and away the best-looking woman in the tribe, high firm breasts, long supple legs, alert, inquisitive face. She was the mate of a man who had to be killed last summer because he became infested with ghosts. Danny and BJ and a couple of the others bashed his head in, by way of a mercy killing, and then there was a wild six-day wake, dancing and wailing around the clock. Because she needed a change of luck they gave Sally to me, or me to her, figuring a holy fool like me must carry the charm of the gods. We have a fine time, Sally and I. We were two lost souls when we came together, and together we've kept each other from tumbling even deeper into the darkness.

'You'll be all right,' BJ says. 'You can handle it. The gods love you.'

'I hope that's true,' I tell him.

Much later in the night Sally and I hold each other as though we both know that this could be our last time. She's all over me, hot, eager. There's no privacy in the bone-house and the others can hear us, four couples and I don't know how many kids, but that doesn't matter. It's dark. Our little bed of fox-pelts is our own little world.

There's nothing esoteric, by the way, about these people's style of love-making. There are only so many ways that a male human body and a female human body can be joined together, and all of them, it seems had already been invented by the time the glaciers came.

At dawn, by first light, I am on my way, alone, to hunt the Scavenger man. I rub the rough strange wall of the house of bones for luck, and off I go.

The village stretches for a couple of hundred yards along the bank of a cold, swiftly-flowing river. The three round bone-houses where most of us live are arranged in a row, and the fourth one, the long house that is the residence of Zeus and his family and also serves as the temple and house of parliament, is just beyond them. On the far side of it is the new fifth house that we've been building this past week. Further down, there's a workshop where tools are made and hides are scraped, and then a butchering area, and just past that there's an immense garbage dump and a towering heap of mammoth bones for future construction projects.

A sparse pine forest lies east of the village, and beyond it are the rolling hills and open plains where the mammoths and rhinos graze. No one ever goes into the river, because it's too cold and the current is too strong, and so it hems us in like a wall on our western border. I want to teach the tribesfolk how to build kayaks one of these days. I should also try to teach them how to swim, I guess. And maybe a few years farther along I'd like to see if we can chop down some trees and build

a bridge. Will it shock the pants off them when I come out
with all this useful stuff? They think I'm an idiot, because I
don't know about the different grades of mud and frozen
ground, the colours of charcoal, the uses and qualities of antler,
bone, fat, hide, and stone. They feel sorry for me because I'm
so limited. But they like me all the same. And the gods *love*
me. At least BJ thinks so.

I start my search down by the riverfront, since that's where
Jeanne saw the Scavenger yesterday. The sun, at dawn on this
Ice Age autumn morning, is small and pale, a sad little lemon
far away. But the wind is quiet now. The ground is still soft
from the summer thaw, and I look for tracks. There's permafrost five feet down, but the topsoil, at least, turns spongy in
May and gets downright muddy by July. Then it hardens again
and by October it's like steel, but by October we live mostly
indoors.

There are footprints all over the place. We wear leather
sandals, but a lot of us go barefoot much of the time, even
now, in forty-degree weather. The people of the tribe have
long, narrow feet with high arches. But down by the water near
the fish nets I pick up a different spoor, the mark of a short,
thick, low-arched foot with curled-under toes. It must be my
Neanderthal. I smile. I feel like Sherlock Holmes. 'Hey, look,
Marty,' I say to the sleeping village. 'I've got the ugly bugger's
track. BJ? Paul? Danny? You just watch me. I'm going to find
him faster than you could believe.'

Those aren't their actual names. I just call them that, Marty,
Paul, BJ, Danny. Around here everyone gives everyone else
his own private set of names. Marty's name for BJ is Ungklava.
He calls Danny Tisbalalak and Paul is Shibgamon. Paul calls
Marty Dolibog. His name for BJ is Kalamok. And so on all
around the tribe, a ton of names, hundreds and hundreds of
names for just forty or fifty people. It's a confusing system.
They have reasons for it that satisfy them. You learn to live
with it.

A man never reveals his true name, the one his mother

149

whispered when he was born. Not even his father knows that, or his wife. You could put hot stones between his legs and he still wouldn't tell you that true name of his, because that'd bring every ghost from Cornwall to Vladivostok down on his ass to haunt him. The world is full of angry ghosts, resentful of the living, ready to jump on anyone who'll give them an opening and plague him like leeches, like bedbugs, like every malign and perverse bloodsucking pest rolled into one.

We are somewhere in western Russia, or maybe Poland. The landscape suggests that: flat, bleak, a cold grassy steppe with a few oaks and birches and pines here and there. Of course a lot of Europe must look like that in this glacial epoch. But the clincher is the fact that these people build mammoth-bone houses. The only place that was ever done was Eastern Europe, so far as anybody down the line knows. Possibly they're the oldest true houses in the world.

What gets me is the immensity of this prehistoric age, the spans of time. It goes back and back and back and all of it is alive for these people. We think it's a big deal to go to England and see a cathedral a thousand years old. They've been hunting on this steppe thirty times as long. Can you visualize 30,000 years? To you, George Washington lived an incredibly long time ago. George is going to have his 300th birthday very soon. Make a stack of books a foot high and tell yourself that that stands for all the time that has gone by since George was born in 1732. Now go on stacking up the books. When you've got a pile as high as a ten-storey building, that's 30,000 years.

A stack of years almost as high as that separates me from you, right this minute. In my bad moments, when the loneliness and the fear and the pain and the remembrance of all that I have lost start to operate on me, I feel that stack of years pressing on me with the weight of a mountain. I try not to let it get me down. But that's a hell of a weight to carry. Now and then it grinds me right into the frozen ground.

The flatfooted track leads me up to the north, around the garbage dump, and towards the forest. Then I lose it. The prints go round and round, double back to the garbage dump, then to the butchering area, then towards the forest again, then all the way over to the river. I can't make sense of the pattern. The poor dumb bastard just seems to have been milling around, foraging in the garbage for anything edible, then taking off again but not going far, checking back to see if anything's been caught in the fish net, and so on. Where's he sleeping? Out in the open, I guess. Well, if what I heard last night is true, he's as hairy as a gorilla; maybe the cold doesn't bother him much.

Now that I've lost the trail, I have some time to think about the nature of the mission, and I start getting uncomfortable.

I'm carrying a long stone knife. I'm out here to kill. I picked the military for my profession a long time ago, but it wasn't with the idea of killing anyone, and certainly not in hand-to-hand combat. I guess I see myself as a representative of civilization, somebody trying to hold back the night, not as anyone who would go creeping around planning to stick a sharp flint blade into some miserable solitary tramp.

But I might well be the one that gets killed. He's wild, he's hungry, he's scared, he's primitive. He may not be very smart, but at least he's shrewd enough to have made it to adulthood, and he's out here earning his living by his wits and his strength. This is his world, not mine. He may be stalking me even while I'm stalking him, and when we catch up with each other he won't be fighting by any rules I ever learned. A good argument for turning back right now.

On the other hand if I come home in one piece with the Scavenger still at large, Zeus will hang my hide on the bone-house wall for disobeying him. We may all be great buddies here but when the chief gives the word, you hop to it or else. That's the way it's been since history began and I have no reason to think it's any different back here.

I simply have to kill the Scavenger. That's all there is to it.

I don't want to get killed by a wild man in this forest, and I don't want to be nailed up by a tribal court-martial either. I want to live to get back to my own time. I still hang on to the faint chance that the rainbow will come back for me and take

151

me down the line to tell my tale in what I have already started to think of as the future. I want to make my report.

The news I'd like to bring you people up there in the world of the future is that these Ice Age folk don't see themselves as primitive. They know, they absolutely *know*, that they're the crown of creation. They have a language – two of them, in fact – they have history, they have music, they have poetry, they have technology, they have art, they have architecture. They have religion. They have laws. They have a way of life that has worked for thousands of years, that will go on working for thousands more. You may think it's all grunts and war-clubs back here, but you're wrong. I can make this world real to you, if I could only get back there to you.

But even if I can't ever get back, there's a lot I want to do here. I want to learn that epic of theirs and write it down for you to read. I want to teach them about kayaks and bridges, and maybe more. I want to finish building the bone-house we started last week. I want to go on horsing around with my buddies BJ and Danny and Marty and Paul. I want Sally. Christ, I might even have kids by her, and inject my own futuristic genes into the Ice Age gene pool.

I don't want to die today trying to fulfil a dumb murderous mission in this cold bleak prehistoric forest.

The morning grows warmer, though not warm. I pick up the trail again, or think I do, and start off towards the east and north, into the forest. Behind me I hear the sounds of laughter and shouting and song as work gets going on the new house, but soon I'm out of earshot. Now I hold the knife in my hand, ready for anything. There are wolves in here, as well as a frightened half-man who may try to kill me before I can kill him.

I wonder how likely it is that I'll find him. I wonder how long I'm supposed to stay out here, too – a couple of hours, a day, a week? – and what I'm supposed to use for food, and how I keep my ass from freezing after dark, and what Zeus will say or do if I come back empty-handed.

I'm wandering around randomly now. I don't feel like Sherlock Holmes any longer.

Working on the bone-house, that's what I'd rather be doing now. Winter is coming on and the tribe has grown too big for the existing four houses. BJ directs the job and Marty and Paul sing and chant and play the drum and flute, and about seven of us do the heavy labour.

'Pile those jawbones chin down,' BJ will yell, as I try to slip one into the foundation the wrong way around. '*Chin down*, bozo! That's better.' Paul bangs out a terrific riff on the drum to applaud me for getting it right the second time. Marty starts making up a ballad about how dumb I am, and everyone laughs. But it's loving laughter. 'Now that backbone over there,' BJ yells to me. I pull a long string of mammoth vertebrae from the huge pile. The bones are white, old bones that have been lying around a long time. They're dense and heavy. 'Wedge it down in there good! Tighter! Tighter!' I huff and puff under the immense weight of the thing, and stagger a little, and somehow get it where it belongs, and jump out of the way just in time as Danny and two other men come tottering towards me carrying a gigantic skull.

The winter-houses are intricate and elaborate structures that require real ingenuity of design and construction. At this point in time BJ may well be the best architect the world has ever known. He carries around a piece of ivory on which he has carved a blueprint for the house, and makes sure everybody weaves the bones and skulls and tusks into the structure just the right way. There's no shortage of construction materials. After 30,000 years of hunting mammoths in this territory, these people have enough bones lying around to build a city the size of Los Angeles.

The houses are warm and snug. They're round and domed, like big igloos made out of bones. The foundation is a circle of mammoth skulls with maybe a hundred mammoth jawbones stacked up over them in fancy herringbone patterns to form the wall. The roof is made of hides stretched over enormous tusks mounted overhead as arches. The whole thing is supported by a wooden frame and smaller bones are chinked in to seal the openings in the walls, plus a plastering of red clay. There's an entranceway made up of gigantic thighbones set up on end. It may all sound bizarre but there's a weird kind of beauty to it and you have no idea, once you're inside, that the bitter winds of the Pleistocene are howling all around you.

The tribe is semi-nomadic and lives by hunting and gathering. In the summer, which is about two months long, they roam the steppe, killing mammoths and rhinos and musk oxen, and bagging up berries and nuts to get them through the winter. Towards what I would guess is August the weather turns cold and they start to head for their village of bone-houses, hunting reindeer along the way. By the time the really bad weather arrives – think Minnesota-and-a-half – they're settled in for the winter with six months' worth of meat stored in deep-freeze pits in the permafrost. It's an orderly, rhythmic life. There's a real community here. I'd be willing to call it a civilization. But – as I stalk my human prey out here in the cold – I remind myself that life here is harsh and strange. Alien. Maybe I'm doing all this buddy-buddy nickname stuff simply to save my own sanity, you think? I don't know.

If I get killed out here today the thing I'll regret most is never learning their secret religious language and not being able to understand the big historical epic that they sing every night. They just don't want to teach it to me. Evidently it's something outsiders aren't meant to understand.

The epic, Sally tells me, is an immense account of everything that's ever happened: the *Iliad* and the *Odyssey* and the *Encyclopaedia Britannica* all rolled into one, a vast tale of gods and kings and men and warfare and migrations and vanished empires and great calamities. The text is so big and Sally's recounting of it is so sketchy that I have only the foggiest idea of what it's about, but when I hear it I want desperately to understand it. It's the actual history of a forgotten world, the tribal annals of thirty millennia, told in a forgotten language, all of it as lost to us as last year's dreams.

If I could learn it and translate it I would set it all down in writing so that maybe it would be found by archaeologists thousands of years from now. I've been taking notes on these people already, an account of what they're like and how I happen to be living among them. I've made twenty tablets so far, using the same clay that the tribe uses to make its pots and sculptures, and firing it in the same beehive-shaped kiln. It's a godawful slow job writing on slabs of clay with my little bone knife. I bake my tablets and bury them in the cobblestone floor of the house. Somewhere in the twenty-first or twenty-second century a Russian archaeologist will dig them up and they'll give him one hell of a jolt. But of their history, their myths, their poetry, I don't have a thing, because of the language problem. Not a damned thing.

Noon has come and gone. I find some white berries on a glossy-leaved bush and, after only a moment's hesitation, gobble them down. There's a faint sweetness there. I'm still hungry even after I pick the bush clean.

If I were back in the village now, we'd have knocked off work at noon for a lunch of dried fruit and strips of preserved reindeer meat, washed down with mugs of mildly fermented fruit juice. The fermentation is accidental, I think, an artefact of their storage methods. But obviously there are yeasts here and I'd like to try to invent wine and beer. Maybe they'll make me a god for that. This year I invented writing, but I did it for my sake and not for theirs and they aren't much interested in it. I think they'll be more impressed with beer.

A hard, nasty wind has started up out of the east. It's September now and the long winter is clamping down. In half an hour the temperature has dropped fifteen degrees, and I'm freezing. I'm wearing a fur parka and trousers, but that thin icy wind cuts right through. And it scours up the fine dry loose topsoil and flings it in our faces. Some day that light yellow dust will lie thirty feet deep over this village, and over BJ and Marty and Danny and Paul, and probably over me as well.

Soon they'll be quitting for the day. The house will take eight or ten more days to finish, if early-season snowstorms don't interrupt. I can imagine Paul hitting the drum six good raps to wind things up and everybody making a run for indoors, whooping and hollering. These are high-spirited guys. They jump and shout and sing, punch each other playfully on the arms, brag about the goddesses they've screwed and the holy rhinos they've killed. Not that they're kids. My guess is that they're twenty-five, thirty years old, senior men of the tribe. The life expectancy here seems to be about forty-five. I'm thirty-four. I have a grandmother alive back in Illinois. Nobody here could possibly believe that. The one I call Zeus, the oldest and richest man in town, looks to be about fifty-three, probably is younger than that, and is generally regarded as favoured by the gods because he's lived so long. He's a wild old bastard, still full of bounce and vigour. He lets you know that he keeps those two wives of his busy all night long, even at his age. These are robust people. They lead a tough life, but they don't know that, and so their souls are buoyant. I definitely will try to turn them on to beer next summer, if I last that long and if I can figure out the technology. This could be one hell of a party town.

Sometimes I can't help feeling abandoned by my own time. I know it's irrational. It has to be just an accident that I'm marooned here. But there are times when I think the people up there in 2013 simply shrugged and forgot about me when things went wrong, and it pisses me off tremendously until I get it under control. I'm a professionally trained hard-ass. But I'm 20,000 years from home and there are times when it hurts more than I can stand.

Maybe beer isn't the answer. Maybe what I need is a still. Brew up some stronger stuff than beer, a little moonshine to get me through those very black moments when the anger and the really heavy resentment start breaking through.

In the beginning the tribe looked on me, I guess, as a moron.

156

Of course I was in shock. The time trip was a lot more traumatic than the experiments with rabbits and turtles had led us to think.

There I was, naked, dizzy, stunned, blinking and gaping, retching and puking. The air had a bitter acid smell to it – who expected that, that the air would smell different in the past? – and it was so cold it burned my nostrils. I knew at once that I hadn't landed in the pleasant France of the Cro-Magnons but in some harsher, bleaker land far to the east. I could still see the rainbow glow of the Zeller Ring, but it was vanishing fast, and then it was gone.

The tribe found me ten minutes later. That was an absolute fluke. I could have wandered for months, encountering nothing but reindeer and bison. I could have frozen; I could have starved. But no, the men I would come to call BJ and Danny and Marty and Paul were hunting near the place where I dropped out of the sky and they stumbled on me right away. Thank God they didn't see me arrive. They'd have decided that I was a supernatural being and would have expected miracles from me, and I can't do miracles. Instead they simply took me for some poor dope who had wandered so far from home that he didn't know where he was, which after all was essentially the truth.

I must have seemed like one sad case. I couldn't speak their language or any other language they knew. I carried no weapons. I didn't know how to make tools out of flints or sew a fur parka or set up a snare for a wolf or stampede a herd of mammoths into a trap. I didn't know anything, in fact, not a single useful thing. But instead of spearing me on the spot they took me to their village, fed me, clothed me, taught me their language. Threw their arms around me and told me what a great guy I was. They made me one of them. That was a year and a half ago. I'm a kind of holy fool for them, a sacred idiot.

I was supposed to be here just four days and then the Zeller Effect rainbow would come for me and carry me home. Of course within a few weeks I realized that something had gone wonky at the uptime end, that the experiment had malfunctioned and that I probably wasn't ever going to get home. There was that risk all along. Well, here I am, here I stay. First came stinging pain and anger and I suppose grief when the truth finally caught up with me. Now there's just a dull ache that won't go away.

In early afternoon I stumble across the Scavenger man. It's pure dumb luck. The trail has long since given out – the forest floor is covered with soft pine duff here, and I'm not enough of a hunter to distinguish one spoor from another in that – and I'm simply moving aimlessly when I see some broken branches, and then I get a whiff of burning wood, and I follow that scent twenty or thirty yards over a low rise and there he is, hunkered down by a hastily thrown-together little hearth roasting a couple of ptarmigans on a green spit. A Scavenger he may be, but he's a better man than I am when it comes to skulling ptarmigans.

He's really ugly. Jeanne wasn't exaggerating at all.

His head is huge and juts back a long way. His mouth is like a muzzle and his chin is hardly there at all and his forehead slopes down to huge brow-ridges like an ape's. His hair is like straw, and it's all over him, though he isn't really shaggy, no hairier than a lot of men I've known. His eyes are grey, yes, and small, deep-set. He's built low and thick, like an Olympic weightlifter. He's wearing a strip of fur around his middle and nothing else. He's an honest-to-God Neanderthal, straight out of the textbooks, and when I see him a chill runs down my spine as though up till this minute I had never really believed that I had travelled 20,000 years in time and now, holy shit, the whole concept has finally become real to me.

He sniffs and gets my wind, and his big brows knit and his whole body goes tense. He stares at me, checking me out, sizing me up. It's very quiet here and we are primordial enemies, face to face with no one else around. I've never felt anything like that before.

We are maybe twenty feet from each other. I can smell him and he can smell me, and it's the smell of fear on both sides.

I can't begin to anticipate his move. He rocks back and forth a little, as if getting ready to spring up and come charging, or maybe bolt off into the forest.

But he doesn't do that. The first moment of tension passes and he eases back. He doesn't try to attack, and he doesn't get up to run. He just sits there in a kind of patient, tired way, staring at me, waiting to see what I'm going to do. I wonder if I'm being suckered, set up for a sudden onslaught.

I'm so cold and hungry and tired that I wonder if I'll be able to kill him when he comes at me. For a moment I almost don't care.

Then I laugh at myself for expecting shrewdness and trickery from a Neanderthal man. Between one moment and the next all the menace goes out of him for me. He isn't pretty but he doesn't seem like a goblin, or a demon, just an ugly thick-bodied man sitting alone in a chilly forest.

And I know that sure as anything I'm not going to try to kill him, not because he's so terrifying but because he isn't.

'They sent me out here to kill you,' I say, showing him the flint knife.

He goes on staring. I might just as well be speaking English, or Sanskrit.

'I'm not going to do it,' I tell him. 'That's the first thing you ought to know. I've never killed anyone before and I'm not going to begin with a complete stranger. Okay? Is that understood?'

He says something now. His voice is soft and indistinct, but I can tell that he's speaking some entirely other language.

'I can't understand what you're telling me,' I say, 'and you don't understand me. So we're even.'

I take a couple of steps towards him. The blade is still in my hand. He doesn't move. I see now that he's got no weapons and even though he's powerfully built and could probably rip my arms off in two seconds, I'd be able to put the blade into him first. I point to the north, away from the village, and make a broad sweeping gesture. 'You'd be wise to head off that way,' I say, speaking very slowly and loudly, as if that would matter.

'Get yourself out of the neighbourhood. They'll kill you other-wise. You understand? *Capisce*? *Verstehen Sie*? Go. Scat. Scram. I won't kill you, but they will.'

I gesture some more, vociferously pantomiming his route to the north. He looks at me. He looks at the knife. His enormous cavernous nostrils widen and flicker. For a moment I think I've misread him in the most idiotically naïve way, that he's been simply biding his time getting ready to jump me as soon as I stop making speeches.

Then he pulls a chunk of meat from the bird he's been roasting, and offers it to me.

'I come here to kill you, and you give me lunch?'

He holds it out. A bribe? Begging for his life?

'I can't,' I say. 'I came here to kill you. Look, I'm just going to turn around and go back, all right? If anybody asks, I never saw you.' He waves the meat at me and I begin to salivate as though it's pheasant under glass. But no, no, I can't take his lunch. I point to him, and again to the north, and once more indicate that he ought not to let the sun set on him in this town. Then I turn and start to walk away, wondering if this is the moment when he'll leap up and spring on me from behind and choke the life out of me.

I take five steps, ten, and then I hear him moving behind me.

So this is it. We really are going to fight.

I turn, my knife at the ready. He looks down at it sadly. He's standing there with the piece of meat still in his hand, coming after me to give it to me anyway.

'Jesus,' I say. 'You're just lonely.'

He says something in that soft blurred language of his and holds out the meat. I take it and bolt it down fast, even though it's only half cooked – dumb Neanderthal! – and I almost gag. He smiles. I don't care what he looks like, if he smiles and shares his food then he's human by me. I smile too. Zeus is going to murder me. We sit down together and watch the other ptarmigan cook, and when it's ready we share it, neither of us saying a word. He has trouble getting a wing off, and I hand him my knife, which he uses in a clumsy way and hands back to me.

After lunch I get up and say, 'I'm going back now. I wish to hell you'd head off to the hills before they catch you.'

And I turn, and go.

And he follows me like a lost dog who has just adopted a new owner.

So I bring him back to the village with me. There's simply no way to get rid of him short of physically attacking him, and I'm not going to do that. As we emerge from the forest a sickening wave of fear sweeps over me. I think at first it's the roast ptarmigan trying to come back up, but no, it's downright terror, because the Scavenger is obviously planning to stick with me right to the end, and the end is not going to be good. I can see Zeus's blazing eyes, his furious scowl. The thwarted Ice Age chieftain in a storm of wrath. Since I didn't do the job, they will. They'll kill him and maybe they'll kill me too, since I've revealed myself to be a dangerous moron who will bring home the very enemy he was sent out to eliminate.

'This is dumb,' I tell the Neanderthal. 'You shouldn't be doing this.'

He smiles again. You don't understand shit, do you, fellow?

We are past the garbage dump now, past the butchering area. BJ and his crew are at work on the new house. BJ looks up when he sees me and his eyes are bright with surprise.

He nudges Marty and Marty nudges Paul, and Paul taps Danny on the shoulder. They point to me and to the Neanderthal. They look at each other. They open their mouths but they don't say anything. They whisper, they shake their heads. They back off a little, and circle around us, gaping, staring.

Christ. Here it comes.

I can imagine what they're thinking. They're thinking that I have really screwed up. That I've brought a ghost home for dinner. Or else an enemy that I was supposed to kill. They're thinking that I'm an absolute lunatic, that I'm an idiot, and now they've got to do the dirty work that I was too dumb to do. And I wonder if I'll try to defend the Neanderthal against them, and what it'll be like if I do. What am I going to do, take them all on at once? And go down swinging as my four sweet buddies close in on me and flatten me into the permafrost? I will. If they force me to it, by God I will. I'll go for their guts with Marty's long stone blade if they try anything on the Neanderthal, or on me.

I don't want to think about it. I don't want to think about any of this.

Then Marty points and claps his hands and jumps about three feet in the air.

'Hey!' he yells. 'Look at that! He brought the ghost back with him!'

And then they move in on me, just like that, the four of them, swarming all around me, pressing close, pummelling hard. There's no room to use the knife. They come on too fast. I do what I can with elbows, knees, even teeth. But they pound me from every side, open fists against my ribs, sides of hands crashing against the meat of my back. The breath goes from me and I come close to toppling as pain breaks out all over me at once. I need all of my strength, and then some, to keep from going down under their onslaught, and I think, this is a dumb way to die, beaten to death by a bunch of berserk cave men in 20,000 B.C.

But after the first few wild moments things become a bit quieter and I get myself together and manage to push them back from me a little way, and I land a good one that sends Paul reeling backwards with blood spouting from his lip, and I whirl towards BJ and start to take him out, figuring I'll deal with Marty on the rebound. And then I realize that they aren't really fighting with me any more, and in fact that they never were.

It dawns on me that they were smiling and laughing as they worked me over, that their eyes were full of laughter and love, that if they had truly wanted to work me over it would have taken the four of them about seven and a half seconds to do it.

They're just having fun. They're playing with me in a jolly roughhouse way.

They step back from me. We all stand there quietly for a moment, breathing hard, rubbing our cuts and bruises. The thought of throwing up crosses my mind and I push it away.

'You brought the ghost back,' Marty says again.

'Not a ghost,' I say. 'He's real.'

'Not a ghost?'

'Not a ghost, no. He's live. He followed me back here.'

'Can you believe it?' BJ cries. 'Live! Followed him back here! Just came marching right in here with him!' He turns to Paul. His eyes are gleaming and for a second I think they're going to jump me all over again. If they do I don't think I'm going to be able to deal with it. But he says simply, 'This has to be a song by tonight. This is something special.'

'I'm going to get the chief,' says Danny, and runs off.

'Look, I'm sorry,' I say. 'I know what the chief wanted. I just couldn't do it.'

'Do what?' BJ asks. 'What are you talking about?' says Paul.

'Kill him,' I say. 'He was just sitting there by his fire, roasting a couple of birds, and he offered me a chunk, and – '

'*Kill* him?' BJ says. 'You were going to kill him?'

'Wasn't that what I was supposed – '

He goggles at me and starts to answer, but just then Zeus comes running up, and pretty much everyone else in the tribe, the women and the kids too, and they sweep up around us like the tide. Cheering, yelling, dancing, pummelling me in that cheerful bone-smashing way of theirs, laughing, shouting. Forming a ring around the Scavenger man and throwing their hands in the air. It's a jubilee. Even Zeus is grinning. Marty begins to sing and Paul gets going on the drum. And Zeus comes over to me and embraces me like the big old bear that he is.

'I had it all wrong, didn't I?' I say later to BJ. 'You were all just testing me, sure. But not to see how good a hunter I am.'

He looks at me without any comprehension at all and doesn't answer. BJ, with that crafty architect's mind of his that takes in everything.

'You wanted to see if I was really human, right? If I had compassion, if I could treat a lost stranger the way I was treated myself.'

Blank stares. Deadpan faces.

'Marty? Paul?'

They shrug. Tap their foreheads: the timeless gesture, ages old.

Are they putting me on? I don't know. But I'm certain that I'm right. If I had killed the Neanderthal they almost certainly would have killed me. That must have been it. I need to believe that that was it. All the time that I was congratulating them for not being the savages I had expected them to be, they were wondering how much of a savage *I* was. They had tested the depth of my humanity; and I had passed. And they finally see that I'm civilized too.

At any rate the Scavenger man lives with us now. Not as a member of the tribe, of course, but as a sacred pet of some sort, a tame chimpanzee, perhaps. He may very well be the last of his kind, or close to it; and though the tribe looks upon him as something dopey and filthy and pathetic, they're not going to do him any harm. To them he's a pitiful bedraggled savage who'll bring good luck if he's treated well. He'll keep the ghosts away. Hell, maybe that's why they took me in, too.

As for me, I've given up what little hope I had of going home. The Zeller rainbow will never return for me, of that I'm altogether sure. But that's all right. I've been through some changes. I've come to terms with it.

We finished the new house yesterday and BJ let me put the last tusk in place, the one they call the ghost-bone, that keeps dark spirits outside. It's apparently a big honour to be the one who sets up the ghost-bone. Afterwards the four of them sang the Song of the House, which is sort of dedication. Like all their other songs, it's in the old language, the secret one, the sacred one. I couldn't sing it with them, not having the words, but I came in with oom-pahs on the choruses and that seemed to go down pretty well.

I told them that by the next time we need to build a house, I will have invented beer, so that we can all go out when it's finished and get drunk to celebrate properly.

Of course they didn't know what the hell I was talking about, but they looked pleased anyway.

And tomorrow, Paul says, he's going to begin teaching me the other language. The secret one. The one that only the members of the tribe may know.

The Dead Man's Eyes

A crime story, one of the few I've ever written. (Crime fiction, for some reason, has never interested me even as a reader, let alone as a writer. I've read the Sherlock Holmes stories with pleasure, yes, and some Simenons, and in 1985 I suddenly read seven or eight Elmore Leonard books in one unceasing burst. But such masters of the genre as P. D. James or John D. MacDonald inspire only yawns in me, which is not to say that they aren't masters, only that the thing they do so well is a thing that basically does not speak to any of my concerns. Doubtless a lot of mystery writers feel the same way about even the best science fiction.) 'The Dead Man's Eyes' isn't a detective story, but it *is* crime fiction, to the extent that it seems actually to have been in the running for the Edgar award given out by the Mystery Writers of America. It's also science fiction, though, built as it is around a concept of detection that exists today as the wildest scientific speculation.

I wrote it in a moment of agreeable ease and fluency in the summer of 1987, and Alice Turner of *Playboy* bought it in an equally uncomplicated way. I'm never enthusiastic about complications, but the summer is a time when I particularly like everything to go smoothly. This one did.

On a crisp afternoon of high winds late in the summer of 2017 Frazier murdered his wife's lover, a foolish deed that he immediately regretted. To murder anyone was stupid, when there were so many more effective alternatives available; but even so, if murder was what he had to do, why murder the *lover*? Two levels of guilt attached there: not only the taking

166

of a life, but the taking of an irrelevant life. If you had to kill someone, he told himself immediately afterwards, then you should have killed *her*. She was the one who had committed the crime against the marriage, after all. Poor Hurwitt had been only a means, a tool, virtually an innocent bystander. Yes, kill *her*, not him. Kill yourself, even. But Hurwitt was the one he had killed, a dumb thing to do and done in a dumb manner besides.

It had all happened very quickly, without premeditation. Frazier was attending a meeting of the museum trustees, to discuss expanding the Hall of Mammals. There was a recess; and because the day was so cool, the air so crystalline and bracing, he stepped out on the balcony that connected the old building with the Pilgersen Extension for a quick breather. Then the sleek bronze door of the Pilgersen opened far down the way and a dark-haired man in a grubby blue-grey lab coat appeared. Frazier saw at once, by the rigid set of his high shoulders and the way his long hair fluttered in the wind, that it was Hurwitt.

He wants to see me, Frazier thought. He knows I'm attending the meeting today and he's come out here to stage the confrontation at last, to tell me that he loves my famous and beautiful wife, to ask me bluntly to clear off and let him have her all to himself.

Frazier's pulse began to rise, his face grew hot. Even while he was thinking that it was oddly old-fashioned to talk of *letting* Hurwitt have Marianne, that in fact Hurwitt had probably already had Marianne in every conceivable way and vice versa but that if now he had some idea of setting up housekeeping with her – unbelievable, unthinkable! – this was hardly the appropriate place to discuss it with him, another and more primordial area of his brain was calling forth torrents of adrenaline and preparing him for mortal combat.

But no: Hurwitt didn't seem to have ventured onto the balcony for any man-to-man conference with his lover's husband. Evidently he was simply taking the short-cut from his lab in the Pilgersen to the fourth-floor cafeteria in the old building.

He walked with his head down, his brows knitted, as though pondering some abstruse detail of trilobite anatomy, and he took no notice of Frazier at all.

'Hurwitt?' Frazier said finally, when the other man was virtually abreast of him.

Caught by surprise, Hurwitt looked up, blinking. He appeared not to recognize Frazier for a moment. For that moment he was frozen in mid-blink, his unkempt hair a dark halo about him, his awkward rangy body off balance between strides, his peculiar glinting eyes flashing like yellow beacons. In fury Frazier imagined this man's bony nakedness, pale and gaunt, probably with sparse ropy strands of black hair sprouting on a white chest, imagined those long arms wrapped around Marianne, imagined those huge knobby fingers cupping her breasts, imagined that thin-lipped wide mouth covering hers. Imagined the grubby lab coat lying crumpled at the foot of the bed, and her silken orange wrap beside it. That was what sent Frazier over the brink, not the infidelities themselves, not the thought of the sweaty embraces – there was plenty of that in each of her films, and it had never meant a thing to him, for he knew it was only well-paid make-believe – and not the rawboned look of the man or his uncouth stride or even the manic glint of those strange off-colour eyes, those eerie topaz eyes, but the lab coat, stained and worn with a button missing and a pocket-flap dangling, lying beside Marianne's discarded silk. For her to take such a lover, a pathetic dreary poker of fossils, a hollow-chested laboratory drudge – no, no, no –

'Hello, Loren,' Hurwitt said. He smiled amiably, he offered his hand. His eyes, though, narrowed and seemed almost to glow. It must be those weird eyes, Frazier thought, that Marianne has fallen in love with. 'What a surprise, running into you out here.'

And stood there smiling, and stood there holding out his hand, and stood there with his frayed lab coat flapping in the breeze.

Suddenly Frazier was unable to bear the thought of sharing the world with this man an instant longer. He watched himself as though from a point just behind his own right ear as he went rushing forward, seized not Hurwitt's hand but his wrist, and pushed rather than pulled, guiding him swiftly backwards towards the parapet and tipping him up and over. It took perhaps a quarter of a second. Hurwitt, gaping, astonished, rose as though floating, hovered for an instant, began to descend. Frazier had one last look at Hurwitt's eyes, bright as glass, staring straight into his own, photographing his assailant's face; and then Hurwitt went plummeting downwards.

My God, Frazier thought, peering over the edge. Hurwitt lay face down in the courtyard five storeys below, arms and legs splayed, lab coat billowing about him.

He was at the airport an hour later, with a light suitcase that carried no more than a day's change of clothing and a few cosmetic items. He flew first to Dallas, endured a ninety-minute layover, went on to San Francisco, doubled back to Calgary as darkness descended, and caught a midnight special to Mexico City, where he checked into a hotel using the legal commercial alias that he employed when doing business in Macao, Singapore, and Hong Kong. Standing on the terrace of a tower thirty storeys above the Zona Rosa, he inhaled musky smog, listened to the squeals of traffic and the faint sounds of far-off drums, watched flares of green lightning in the choking sky above Popocatepetl, and wondered whether he should jump. Ultimately he decided against it. He wanted to share nothing whatever with Hurwitt, not even the manner of his death. And suicide would be an overreaction anyway. First he had to find out how much trouble he was really in.

The hotel had InfoLog. He dialled in and was told that queries were billed at five million pesos an hour, pro rated. Vaguely he wondered whether that was as expensive as it sounded. The peso was practically worthless, wasn't it? What could that be in dollars, a hundred bucks, five hundred, maybe? Nothing.

'I want Harvard Legal,' he told the screen. 'Criminology.

Forensics. Technical. Evidence technology.' Grimly he menued down and down until he was near what he wanted. 'Eyeflash,' he said. 'Theory, techniques. Methods of detail recovery. Acceptance as evidence. Reliability of record. Frequency of reversal on appeal. Supreme Court rulings, if any.'

Back to him, in surreal fragments which, at an extra charge of three million pesos per hour, pro rated, he had printed out for him, came blurts of information:

Perceptual pathways in outer brain layers . . . broad-scale optical architecture . . . images imprinted on striate cortex, or primary visual cortex . . . inferior temporal neurons . . . cf. McDermott and Brunetti, 2007, utilization of lateral geniculate body as storage for visual data . . . inferior temporal cortex . . . uptake of radioactive glucose . . . downloading . . . degrading of signal . . . degeneration period . . . Pilsudski signal-enhancement filter . . . Nevada vs Bensen, 2011 . . . hippocampus simulation . . . amygdala . . . acetylcholine . . . US Supreme Court, 23 March 2012 . . . cf Gross and Bernstein, 13 Aug 2003 . . . Mishkin . . . Appenzeller . . .

Enough. He shuffled the printouts in a kind of hard-edged stupor until dawn; and then, after a hazy calculation of time-zone differentials, he called his lawyer in New York. It took four bounces, but the telephone tracked him down in the commute, driving in from Connecticut.

Frazier keyed in the privacy filter. All the lawyer would know was that some client was calling; the screen image would be a blur, the voice would be rendered universal, generalized, unidentifiable. It was more for the lawyer's protection than Frazier's: there had been nasty twists in jurisprudence lately, and lawyers were less and less willing to run the risk of being named accomplices after the fact. Immediately came a query about the billing. Bill to my hotel room, Frazier replied, and the screen gave him a go-ahead.

'Let's say I'm responsible for causing a fatal injury and the victim had a good opportunity to see me as the act was occurring. What are the chances that they can recover eyeflash pictures?'

'Depends on how much damage was received in the process of the death. How did it happen?'

'Privileged communication?'

'Sorry. No.'

'Even under filter?'

'Even. If the mode of death was unique or even highly distinctive and unusual, how can I help but draw the right conclusion? And then I'll know more than I want to know.'

'It wasn't unique,' Frazier said. 'Or distinctive, or unusual. But I still won't go into details. I can tell you that the injury wasn't the sort that would cause specific brain trauma. I mean, nothing like a bullet between the eyes, or falling into a vat of acid, or – '

'All right. I follow. This take place in a major city?'

'Major, yes.'

'In Missouri, Alabama, or Kentucky?'

'None of those,' said Frazier. 'It took place in a state where eyeflash recovery is legal. No question of that.'

'And the body? How long after death do you estimate it would have been found?'

'Within minutes, I'd say.'

'And when was that?'

Frazier hesitated. 'Within the past twenty-four hours.'

'Then there's almost total likelihood that there's a readily recoverable photograph in your victim's brain of whatever he saw at the moment of death. Beyond much doubt it's already been recovered. Are you sure he was looking at you as he died?'

'Straight at me.'

'My guess is there's probably a warrant out for you already. If you want me to represent you, kill the privacy filter so I can confirm who you are, and we'll discuss our options.'

'Later,' Frazier said. 'I think I'd rather try to make a run for it.'

'But the chances of your getting away with – '

'This is something I need to do,' said Frazier. 'I'll talk to you some other time.'

* * *

171

He was almost certainly cooked. He knew that. He had wasted critical time running frantically back and forth across the continent yesterday, when he should have been transferring funds, setting up secure refuges, and such. The only question now was whether they were already looking for him, in which case there'd be blocks on his accounts everywhere, a passport screen at every airport, worldwide interdicts of all sorts. But if that was so they'd already have traced him to this hotel. Evidently they hadn't, which meant that they hadn't yet uncovered the Southeast Asian trading alias and put interdicts on that. Well, it was just a lousy manslaughter case, or maybe second-degree at worst: they had more serious things to worry about, he supposed.

Checking out of the hotel without bothering about breakfast, he headed for the airport and used his corporate credit card to buy himself a flight to Belize. There he bought a ticket to Surinam, and just before his plane was due to leave he tried his personal card in the cash disburser and was pleasantly surprised to find that it hadn't yet been yanked. He withdrew the maximum. Of course now there was evidence that Loren Frazier had been in Belize this day, but he wasn't travelling as Frazier, and he'd be in Surinam before long, and by the time they traced him there, assuming that they could, he'd be somewhere else, under some other name entirely. Maybe if he kept dodging for six or eight months he'd scramble his trail so thoroughly that they'd never be able to find him. Did they pursue you forever, he wondered? A time must come when they file and forget. Of course, he might not want to keep running forever, either. Already he missed Marianne. Despite what she had done.

He spent three days in Surinam at a little pastel-green Dutch hotel at the edge of Paramaribo, eating spicy noodle dishes and waiting to be arrested. Nobody bothered him. He used a cash machine again, keying up one of his corporate accounts and transferring a bundle of money into the account of Andreas Schmidt of Zurich, which was a name he had used seven years ago for some export-import manoeuvres involving Zimbabwe and somehow, he knew not why, had kept alive for eventualities unknown. This was an eventuality, now. When he checked the Schmidt account he found that there was money in it already, significant money, and that his Swiss passport had not yet expired. The Swiss chargé-d'affaires in Guyana was requested to prepare a duplicate for him. A quick boat trip up the Marowijne River took him to St Laurent on the French Guiana side of the river, where he was able to hire a driver to take him to Cayenne, and from there he flew to Georgetown in Guyana. A smiling proxy lawyer named Chatterji obligingly picked up his passport for him from the Swiss, and under the name of Schmidt he went on to Buenos Aires. There he destroyed all his Frazier documentation. He resisted the temptation to find out whether there was a Frazier interdict out yet. No sense handing them a trail extending down to Buenos Aires just to gratify his curiosity. If they weren't yet looking for him because he had murdered Hurwitt, they'd be looking for him on a simple missing-persons hook by this time. One way or another, it was best to forget about his previous identity and operate as Schmidt from here on.

This is almost fun, he thought.

But he missed his wife terribly.

While sitting in sidewalk cafés on the broad Avenida de 9 Julio, feasting on huge parrilladas sluiced down by carafe after carafe of red wine, he brooded obsessively on Marianne's affair. It made no sense. The world-famous actress and the awkward rawboned palaeontologist: why? How was it possible? She had been making a commercial at the museum – Frazier, in fact, had helped to set the business up in his capacity as member of the board of trustees – and Hurwitt, who was the head of the department of invertebrate palaeontology, or some such thing, had volunteered to serve as the technical consultant. Very kind of him, everyone said. Taking time away from his scientific work. He seemed so bland, so juiceless: who could suspect him of harbouring lust for the glamorous film personality? Nobody would have imagined it. But things must have started almost at once. Some chemistry between them, beyond all understanding. People began to notice, and then to give Frazier strange little knowing looks. Eventually even he caught on. A truly loving husband is generally just about the last one to know, because he will always put the best possible interpretation on the data. But after a time the accumulation of data becomes impossible to overlook or deny or reason away. There are always small changes when something like that has begun: they start to read books of a kind they've never read before, they talk of different things, they may even show some new moves in bed. Then comes the real carelessness, the seemingly unconscious slips that scream the actual nature of the situation. Frazier was forced finally to an acceptance of the truth. It tore at his heart. There was no room in their marriage for such stuff. Despite his money, despite his power, he had never gone in for the casual morality of the intercontinental set, and neither, so he thought, had Marianne. This was the second marriage for each: the one that was supposed to carry them happily on to the finish. And now look.

'Señor? Another carafe?'

'No,' he said. 'Yes. Yes.' He stared at his plate. It was full of sausages, sweetbreads, grilled steak. Where had all that come from? He was sure he had eaten everything. It must have grown back. Moodily he stabbed a plump blood sausage and ate without noticing. Took a drink. They mixed the wine with seltzer water here, half and half. Maybe it helped you put away those tons of meat more easily.

Afterwards, strolling along the narrow, glittering Calle Florida with the stylish evening promenade flowing past him on both sides, he caught sight of Marianne coming out of a jeweller's shop. She wore gaucho leathers, emerald earrings, skin-tight trousers of gold brocade. He grunted as though he had been struck and pressed his elbows against his sides as one might do if expecting a second blow. Then an elegant young Argentinian uncoiled himself from a kerbside table and trotted quickly towards her, and they laughed and embraced and ran off arm in arm, sweeping right past him without even a glance.

He remembered, now: women all over the world were wearing Marianne's face this season. This one, in fact, was too tall by half a head. But he would have to be prepared for such incidents wherever he went. Mariannes everywhere, bludgeoning him with their beauty and never even knowing what they had done. He found himself wishing that the one who had been sleeping with that museum man was just another Marianne clone, that the real one was at home alone now, waiting for him, wondering, wondering.

In Montreal six weeks later, using a privacy filter and one of his corporate cards, he risked putting through a call to his apartment and discovered that there was an interdict on his line. When he tried the office number an android mask appeared on the screen and he was blandly told that Mr Frazier was unavailable. The android didn't know when Mr Frazier would be available. Frazier asked for Markman, his executive assistant, and a moment later a bleak, harried, barely recognizable face looked out at him. Frazier explained that he was a representative of the Bucharest account, calling about a highly sensitive matter. 'Don't you know?' Markman said. 'Mr Frazier's disappeared. The police are looking for him.' Frazier asked why, and Markman's face dissolved in an agony of shame, bewilderment, protective zeal. 'There's a criminal charge against him,' Markman whispered, nearly in tears.

He called his lawyer next and said, 'I'm calling about the Frazier case. I don't want to kill the filter but I imagine you won't have much trouble figuring out who I am.'

'I imagine I won't. Just don't tell me where you are, okay?'

The situation was about as he expected. They had recovered the murder prints from the dead man's eyes: a nice shot, embedded deep in the cortical tissue, Frazier looming up against Hurwitt, nose to nose, a quick cut to the hand reaching for Hurwitt's arm, a wild free-form pan to the sky as Frazier lifted Hurwitt up and over the parapet. 'Pardon me for saying this, but you looked absolutely deranged,' the lawyer told him. 'The prints were on all the networks the next day. Your eyes

– it was really scary. I'm absolutely sure we could get impairment of faculties, maybe even crime of passion. Suspended sentence, but of course there'd be rehabilitation. I don't see any way around that, and it could last a year or two, and you might not be as effective in your profession afterwards, but considering the circumstances – '

'How's my wife?' Frazier said. 'Do you know anything about what she's been doing?'

'Well, of course I don't represent her, you realize. But she does get in the news. She's said to be travelling.'

'Where?'

'I couldn't say. Look, I can try to find out, if you'd like to call back this time tomorrow. Only I suggest that for your own good you call me at a different number, which is – '

'For my good or for yours?' Frazier said.

'I'm trying to help,' said the lawyer, sounding annoyed.

He took refresher courses in French, Italian, and German to give himself a little extra plausibility in the Andreas Schmidt identity, and cultivated a mild Teutonic accent. So long as he didn't run up against any real Swiss who wanted to gabble with him in Romansch or Schwyzerdeutsch he suspected he'd make out all right. He kept on moving, Strasbourg, Athens, Haifa, Tunis. Even though he knew that no further fund transfers were possible, there was enough money stashed under the Schmidt accounts to keep him going nicely for ten or fifteen years, and by then he hoped to have this thing figured out.

He saw Mariannes in Tel Aviv, in Heraklion on Crete, and in Sidi bou Said, just outside Tunis. They were all clones, of course. He recognized that after just a quick queasy instant. Still, seeing that delicate high-bridged nose once again, those splendid amethyst eyes, those tight auburn ringlets, it was all he could do to keep himself from going up to them and throwing his arms around them, and he had to force himself each time to turn away, biting down hard on his lip.

In London, outside the Connaught, he saw the real thing. The Connaught was where they had spent their wedding trip back in '07, and he winced at the sight of its familiar grand façade, and winced even more when Marianne came out, young and radiant, wearing a shimmering silver cloud. Dazzling light streamed from her. He had no doubt that this was no trendy clone but the true Marianne: she moved in that easy confident way, with that regal joy in her own beauty, that no cosmetic surgeon could ever impart even to the most intent imitator. The pavement itself seemed to do her homage. But then Frazier saw that the man on whose arm she walked was himself, young and radiant too, the Loren Frazier of that honeymoon journey of seven years back, his hair dark and thick, his love of life and success and his magnificent new wife cloaking him like an imperial mantle; and Frazier realized that he must merely be hallucinating, that the breakdown had moved on to a new and more serious stage. He stood gaping while Mr and Mrs Frazier swept through him like the phantoms they were and away in the direction of Grosvenor Square, and then he staggered and nearly fell. To the Connaught doorman he admitted that he was unwell, and because he was well dressed and spoke with the hint of an accent and was able to find a twenty-sovereign piece in the nick of time the doorman helped him into a cab and expressed his deepest concern. Back at his own hotel, ten minutes over on the other side of Mayfair, he had three quick gins in a row and sat shivering for an hour before the image faded from his mind.

'I advise you to give yourself up,' the lawyer said, when Frazier called him from Nairobi. 'Of course you can keep on running as long as you like. But you're wearing yourself out, and sooner or later someone will spot you, so why keep on delaying the inevitable?'

'Have you spoken to Marianne lately?'

'She wishes you'd come back. She wants to write to you, or call you, or even come and see you, wherever you are. But I've told her you refuse to provide me with any information about your location. Is that still your position?'

'I don't want to see her or hear from her.'

'She loves you.'

'I'm a homicidal maniac. I might do the same thing to her that I did to Hurwitt.'

'Surely you don't really believe – '

'No,' Frazier said. 'Not really.'

'Then let me give her an address for you, at least, and she can write to you.'

'It could be a trap, couldn't it?'

'Surely you can't possibly believe – '

'Who knows? Anything's possible.'

'A postal box in Caracas, say,' the lawyer suggested, 'and let's say that you're in Rio, for the sake of the discussion, and I arrange an intermediary to pick up the letter and forward it care of American Express in Lima, and then on some day of your own choosing, known to nobody else, you make a quick trip in and out of Peru and – '

'And they grab me the moment I collect the letter,' Frazier said. 'How stupid do you think I am? You could set up forty intermediaries and I'd still have to create a trail leading to myself if I want to get the letter. Besides, I'm not in South America any more. That was months ago.'

'It was only for the sake of the dis – ' the lawyer said, but Frazier was gone already.

He decided to change his face and settle down somewhere. The lawyer was right: all this compulsive travelling was wearing him down. But by staying in one place longer than a week or two he was multiplying the chance of being detected, so long as he went on looking like himself. He had always wanted a longer nose anyway, and not quite so obtrusive a chin, and thicker eyebrows. He fancied that he looked too Slavic, though he had no Eastern European ancestry at all. All one long rainy evening at the mellow old Addis Ababa Hilton he sketched a face for himself that he thought looked properly Swiss: rugged, passionate, with the right mix of French elegance, German stolidity, Italian passion. Then he went downstairs and showed the printout to the bartender, a supple little Portuguese.

'Where would you say this man comes from?' Frazier asked.

'Lisbon,' the bartender replied at once. 'That long jaw, those lips – unmistakably Lisbon, though perhaps his grandmother on his mother's side is of the Algarve. A man of considerable distinction, I would say. But I do not know him, Senhor Schmidt. He is no one I know. You would like your dry martini, as usual?'

'Make it a double,' Frazier said.

He had the work done in Vienna. Everyone agreed that the best people for that sort of surgery were in Geneva, but Switzerland was the one country in the world he dared not enter, so he used his Zurich banking connections to get him the name of the second-best people, who were said to be almost as good, remarkably good, he was told. That seemed high praise indeed, Frazier thought, considering it was a Swiss talking about Austrians. The head surgeon at the Vienna clinic, though, turned out to be Swiss himself, which provided Frazier with a moment of complete terror, pretending as he was to be a native of Zurich. But the surgeon had been at his trade long enough to know that a man who wants his perfectly good face transformed into something entirely different does not wish to talk about his personal affairs. He was a big, cheerful extrovert named Randegger, with a distinct limp. Skiing accident, the surgeon explained. Surely getting your leg fixed must be easier than getting your face changed, Frazier thought, but he decided that Randegger was simply waiting for the off season to undergo repair. 'This will be no problem at all,' Randegger told him, studying Frazier's printout. 'I have just a few small suggestions.' He went deftly to work with a light-pen, broadening the cheekbones, moving the ears downwards and forwards. Frazier shrugged. Whatever you want, Dr Randegger, he thought. Whatever you want. I'm putty in your hands.

It took six weeks from first cut to final healing. The results seemed fine to him – suave, convincing, an authoritative face – though at the beginning he was afraid it would all come apart if he smiled, and it was hard to get used to looking in a mirror and seeing someone else. He stayed at the clinic the whole six weeks. One of the nurses wore the Marianne face, but the body was all wrong, wide hips, startling steatopygous rump, short muscular legs. Near the end of his stay she lured him into bed. He was sure he'd be impotent with her, but he was wrong. There was only one really bad moment, when she reared above him and he couldn't see her body at all, only her beautiful, passionate, familiar face.

Even now, he couldn't stop running. Belgrade, Sydney, Rabat, Barcelona, Milan: they went by in a blur of identical airports, interchangeable hotels, baffling shifts of climate. Almost everywhere he went he saw Mariannes, and sometimes was puzzled that they never recognized him, until he remembered that he had altered his face: why should they know him now, even after the seven years of their marriage? As he travelled he began to see another ubiquitous face, dark and Latin and pixyish, and realized that Marianne's vogue must be beginning to wane. He hoped that some of the Mariannes would soon be converting themselves to this newer look. He had never really felt at ease with all these simulacra of his wife, whom he still loved beyond all measure.

That love, though, had become inextricably mixed with anger. He could not even now stop thinking about her incomprehensible, infuriating violation of the sanctity of their covenant. It had been the best of marriages, amiable, passionate, close, a true union on every level. He had never even thought of wanting another woman. She was everything he wanted; and he had every reason to think that his feelings were reciprocated. That was the worst of it, not the furtive little couplings she and Hurwitt must have enjoyed, but the deeper treason, the betrayal of their seeming harmony, her seemingly whimsical destruction of the hermetic seal that enclosed their perfect world.

He had overreacted, he knew. He wished he could call back the one absurd impulsive act that had thrust him from his smooth and agreeable existence into this frantic wearisome fugitive life. And he felt sorry for Hurwitt, who probably had been caught up in emotions beyond his depth, swept away by the astonishment of finding himself in Marianne's arms. How could he have stopped to worry, at such a time, about what he might be doing to someone else's marriage? How ridiculous it had been to kill him! And to stare right into Hurwitt's eyes, incontrovertibly incriminating himself, while he did! If he needed any proof of his temporary insanity, the utter foolishness of the murder would supply it.

But there was no calling any of it back. Hurwitt was dead; he had lived on the run for – what, two years, three? – and Marianne was altogether lost to him. So much destruction achieved in a single crazy moment. He wondered what he would do if he ever saw Marianne again. Nothing violent, no, certainly not. He had a sudden image of himself in tears, hugging her knees, begging her forgiveness. For what? For killing her lover? For bringing all sorts of nasty mess and the wrong kind of publicity into her life? For disrupting the easy rhythms of their happy marriage? No, he thought, astonished, aghast. What do I have to be forgiven for? From her, nothing. She's the one who should go down on her knees before me. I wasn't the one who was fooling around. And then he thought, No, no, we must forgive each other. And after that he thought, Best of all, I must take care never to have anything to do with her for the rest of my life. And that thought cut through him like a blade, like Dr Randegger's fiery scalpel.

Six months later he was walking through the cavernous, ornate lobby of the Hôtel de Paris in Monte Carlo when he saw a Marianne standing in front of a huge stack of suitcases against a marble pillar no more than twenty feet from him. He was inured to Mariannes by this time and at first the sight of her had no impact; but then he noticed the familiar monogram on the luggage, and recognized the intricate little bows of red plush cord with which the baggage tags were tied on, and he realized that this was the true Marianne at last. Nor was this any hallucination like the Connaught one. She was visibly older, with a vertical line in her left cheek that he had never seen before. Her hair was a darker shade and somehow more ordinary in its cut, and she was dressed simply, no radiance at all. Even so, people were staring at her and whispering. Frazier swayed, gripped a nearby pillar with his suddenly clammy hand, fought back the impulse to run. He took a deep breath and went towards her, walking slowly, impressively, his carefully cultivated distinguished-looking-Swiss-businessman walk.

'Marianne?' he said.

She turned her head slightly and stared at him without any show of recognition.

'I do look different, yes,' he said, smiling.

'I'm sorry, but I don't – '

A slender, agile-looking man five or six years younger than she, wearing sunglasses, appeared from somewhere as though conjured out of the floor. Smoothly he interpolated himself between Frazier and Marianne. A lover? A bodyguard? Simply part of her entourage? Pleasantly but forcefully he presented himself to Frazier as though saying, Let's not have any trouble now, shall we?

'Listen to my voice,' Frazier said. 'You haven't forgotten my voice. Only the face is different.'

Sunglasses came a little closer. Looked a little less pleasant. Marianne stared.

'You haven't forgotten, have you, Marianne?' Frazier said.

Sunglasses began to look definitely menacing.

'Wait a minute,' Marianne said, as he glided into a nose-to-nose with Frazier. 'Step back, Aurelio.' She peered through the shadows. 'Loren?' she said.

Frazier nodded. He went towards her. At a gesture from Marianne, Sunglasses faded away like a genie going back into the bottle. Frazier felt strangely calm now. He could see Marianne's upper lip trembling, her nostrils flickering a little. 'I thought I never wanted to see you again,' he said. 'But I was wrong about that. The moment I saw you and knew it was really you, I realized that I had never stopped thinking about

182

you, never stopped wanting you. Wanting to put it all back together.'

Her eyes widened. 'And you think you can?'

'Maybe.'

'What a damned fool you are,' she said, gently, almost lovingly, after a long moment.

'I know. I really messed myself up, doing what I did.'

'I don't mean that,' she said. 'You messed us both up with that. Not to mention him, the poor bastard. But that can't be undone, can it? If you only knew how often I prayed to have it not have happened.' She shook her head. 'It was nothing, what he and I were doing. Nothing. Just a silly fling, for Christ's sake. How could you possibly have cared so much?'

'What?'

'To *kill* a man, for something like that? To wreck three lives in half a second? For *that*?'

'What?' he said again. 'What are you telling me?'

Sunglasses suddenly was in the picture again. 'We're going to miss the car to the airport, Marianne.'

'Yes. Yes. All right, let's go.'

Frazier watched, numb, immobile. Sunglasses beckoned and a swarm of porters materialized to carry the luggage outside. As she reached the vast doorway Marianne turned abruptly and looked back, and in the dimness of the great lobby her eyes suddenly seemed to shift in colour, to take on the same strange topaz glint that he had imagined he had seen in Hurwitt's. Then she swung around and was gone.

An hour later he went down to the Consulate to turn himself in. They had a little trouble locating him in the list of wanted fugitives, but he told them to keep looking, going back a few years, and finally they came upon his entry. He was allowed half a day to clear up his business affairs, but he said he had none to clear up, so they set about the procedure of arranging his passage to the States, while he watched like a tourist who is trying to replace a lost passport.

Coming home was like returning to a foreign country that

he had visited a long time before. Everything was familiar, but in an unfamiliar way. There were endless hearings, conferences, psychological examinations. His lawyers were excessively polite, as if they feared that one wrong word would cause him to detonate, but behind their silkiness he saw the contempt that the orderly have for the self-destructive. Still, they did their job well. Eventually he drew a suspended sentence and two years of rehabilitation, after which, they told him, he'd need to move to some other city, find some appropriate line of work, and establish a stable new existence for himself. The rehabilitation people would help him. There would be a probation period of five years when he'd have to report for progress conferences every week.

At the very end one of the rehab officers came to him and told him that his lawyers had filed a petition asking the court to let him have his original face back. That startled him. For a moment Frazier felt like a fugitive again, wearily stumbling from airport to airport, from hotel to hotel.

'No,' he said. 'I don't think that's a good idea at all. The man who had that face, he's somebody else. I think I'm better off keeping this one. What do you say?'

'I think so too,' said the rehab man.

Chip Runner

Byron Preiss, having produced those two magnificent illustrated anthologies *The Planets* and *The Universe*, now turned his attention the other way, to the world of the infinitely small. *The Microverse* was his new project, and I, who had contributed material to both of the previous books, was invited to write something for this one too.

The scientific part of the story was easy enough to put together: required by the nature of the book to deal with the universe on the subatomic level, I rummaged around in *Scientific American* to see what the current state of thinking about electrons and protons and such might be. In the course of my rummaging I stumbled on some information about microchip technology, and that led me to the fictional component of the story. All about me in the San Francisco Bay Area are bright boys (and a few girls) with a deep, all-consuming, and spooky passion for computers. I happen to know something, also, about the prevalence of such eating disorders as bulimia and anorexia in Bay Area adolescents – disorders mainly involving girls, but not exclusively so. Everything fit together swiftly: an anorexic computer kid who has conceived the wild idea of entering the subatomic world by starving down to it. The rest was a matter of orchestrating theme and plot and character and style – of writing the story, that is. Byron had Ralph McQuarrie illustrate it with a fine, terrifying painting when he published it in *The Microverse*. Gardner Dozois bought the story also for *Isaac Asimov's Science Fiction Magazine*, and Don Wollheim selected it for his annual *World's Best SF* anthology.

He was fifteen, and looked about ninety, and a frail ninety at that. I knew his mother and his father, separately – they were Silicon Valley people, divorced, very important in their respective companies – and separately they had asked me to try to work with him. His skin was blue-grey and tight, drawn cruelly close over the jutting bones of his face. His eyes were grey too, and huge, and they lay deep within their sockets. His arms were like sticks. His thin lips were set in an angry grimace.

The chart before me on my desk told me that he was five feet eight inches tall and weighed seventy-one pounds. He was in his third year at one of the best private schools in the Palo Alto district. His IQ was 161. He crackled with intelligence and intensity. That was a novelty for me right at the outset. Most of my patients are depressed, withdrawn, uncertain of themselves, elusive, shy: virtual zombies. He wasn't anything like that. There would be other surprises ahead.

'So you're planning to go into the hardware end of the computer industry, your parents tell me,' I began. The usual let's-build-a-relationship procedure.

He blew it away instantly with a single sour glare. 'Is that your standard opening? "Tell me all about your favourite hobby, my boy"? If you don't mind I'd rather skip all the bullshit, Doctor, and then we can both get out of here faster. You're supposed to ask me about my eating habits.'

It amazed me to see him taking control of the session this way within the first thirty seconds. I marvelled at how different he was from most of the others, the poor sad wispy creatures who force me to fish for every word.

'Actually I do enjoy talking about the latest developments in the world of computers, too,' I said, still working hard at being genial.

'But my guess is you don't talk about them very often, or you wouldn't call it "the hardware end". Or "the computer industry". We don't use mundo phrases like those any more.' His high thin voice sizzled with barely suppressed rage. 'Come on, Doctor. Let's get right down to it. You think I'm anorexic, don't you?'

'Well – '

'I know about anorexia. It's a mental disease of girls, a vanity thing. They starve themselves because they want to look beautiful and they can't bring themselves to realize that they're not too fat. Vanity isn't the issue for me. And I'm not a girl, Doctor. Even you ought to be able to see that right away.'

'Timothy – '

'I want to let you know right out front that I don't have an eating disorder and I don't belong in a shrink's office. I know exactly what I'm doing all the time. The only reason I came today is to get my mother off my back, because she's taken it into her head that I'm trying to starve myself to death. She said I had to come here and see you. So I'm here. All right?'

'All right,' I said, and stood up. I am a tall man, deep-chested, very broad through the shoulders. I can loom when necessary. A flicker of fear crossed Timothy's face, which was the effect I wanted to produce. When it's appropriate for the therapist to assert authority, simpleminded methods are often the most effective. 'Let's talk about eating, Timothy. What did you have for lunch today?'

He shrugged. 'A piece of bread. Some lettuce.'

'That's all?'

'A glass of water.'

'And for breakfast?'

'I don't eat breakfast.'

'But you'll have a substantial dinner, won't you?'

'Maybe some fish. Maybe not. I think food is pretty gross.'

I nodded. 'Could you operate your computer with the power turned off, Timothy?'

'Isn't that a pretty condescending sort of question, Doctor?'

'I suppose it is. Okay, I'll be more direct. Do you think you can run your body without giving it any fuel?'

'My body runs just fine,' he said, with a defiant edge.

'Does it? What sports do you play?'

'Sports?' It might have been a Martian word.

'You know, the normal weight for someone of your age and height ought to be – '

187

'There's nothing normal about me, Doctor. Why should my weight be any more normal than the rest of me?'

'It was until last year, apparently. Then you stopped eating. Your family is worried about you, you know.'

'I'll be okay,' he said sullenly.

'You want to stay healthy, don't you?'

He stared at me for a long chilly moment. There was something close to hatred in his eyes, or so I imagined.

'What I want is to disappear,' he said.

That night I dreamed I was disappearing. I stood naked and alone on a slab of grey metal in the middle of a vast empty plain under a sinister coppery sky and I began steadily to shrink. There is often some carry-over from the office to a therapist's own unconscious life: we call it counter-transference. I grew smaller and smaller. Pores appeared on the surface of the metal slab and widened into jagged craters, and then into great crevices and gullies. A cloud of luminous dust shimmered about my head. Grains of sand, specks, mere motes, now took on the aspect of immense boulders. Down I drifted, gliding into the darkness of a fathomless chasm. Creatures I had not noticed before hovered about me, astonishing monsters, hairy, many-legged. They made menacing gestures, but I slipped away, downwards, downwards, and they were gone. The air was alive now with vibrating particles, inanimate, furious, that danced in frantic zigzag patterns, veering wildly past me, now and again crashing into me, knocking my breath from me, sending me ricocheting for what seemed like miles. I was floating, spinning, tumbling with no control. Pulsating waves of blinding light pounded me. I was falling into the infinitely small, and there was no halting my descent. I would shrink and shrink and shrink until I slipped through the realm of matter entirely and was lost. A mob of contemptuous glowing things – electrons and protons, maybe, but how could I tell? – crowded close around me, emitting fizzy sparks that seemed to me like jeers and laughter. They told me to keep moving along, to get myself out of their kingdom, or I would meet a terrible death.

'To see a world in a grain of sand,' Blake wrote. Yes. And Eliot wrote, 'I will show you fear in a handful of dust.'

I went on downwards, and downwards still. And then I awoke gasping, drenched in sweat, terrified, alone.

Normally the patient is uncommunicative. You interview parents, siblings, teachers, friends, anyone who might provide a clue or an opening wedge. Anorexia is a life-threatening matter. The patients – girls, almost always, or young women in their twenties – have lost all sense of normal body-image and feel none of the food-deprivation prompts that a normal body gives its owner. Food is the enemy. Food must be resisted. They eat only when forced to, and then as little as possible. They are unaware that they are frighteningly gaunt. Strip them and put them in front of a mirror and they will pinch their sagging empty skin to show you imaginary fatty bulges. Sometimes the process of self-skeletonization is impossible to halt, even by therapy. When it reaches a certain point the degree of organic damage becomes irreversible and the death-spiral begins.

'He was always tremendously bright,' Timothy's mother said. She was fifty, a striking woman, trim, elegant, almost radiant, vice president for finance at one of the biggest Valley companies. I knew her in that familiarly involuted California way: her present husband used to be married to my first wife. 'A genius, his teachers all said. But strange, you know? Moody. Dreamy. I used to think he was on drugs, though of course none of the kids do that any more.' Timothy was her only child by her first marriage. 'It scares me to death to watch him wasting away like that. When I see him I want to take him and shake him and force ice cream down his throat, pasta, milkshakes, anything. And then I want to hold him, and I want to cry.'

'You'd think he'd be starting to shave by now,' his father said. Technical man, working on nanoengineering projects at the Stanford AI lab. We often played racquetball together. 'I was. You too, probably. I got a look at him in the shower, three or four months ago. Hasn't even reached puberty yet.

Fifteen and not a hair on him. It's the starvation, isn't it? It's retarding his physical development, right?'

'I keep trying to get him to like eat something, anything,' his step-brother Mick said. 'He lives with us, you know, on the weekends, and most of the time he's downstairs playing with his computers, but sometimes I can get him to go out with us, and we buy like a chili dog for him, or, you know, a burrito, and he goes, Thank you, thank you, and pretends to eat it, but then he throws it away when he thinks we're not looking. He is *so* weird, you know? And scary. You look at him with those ribs and all and he's like something out of a horror movie.'

'What I want is to disappear,' Timothy said.

He came every Tuesday and Thursday for one-hour sessions. There was at the beginning an undertone of hostility and suspicion to everything he said. I asked him, in my layman way, a few things about the latest developments in computers, and he answered me in monosyllables at first, not at all bothering to hide his disdain for my ignorance and my innocence. But now and again some question of mine would catch his interest and he would forget to be irritated, and reply at length, going on and on into realms I could not even pretend to understand. Trying to find things of that sort to ask him seemed my best avenue of approach. But of course I knew I was unlikely to achieve anything of therapeutic value if we simply talked about computers for the whole hour.

He was very guarded, as was only to be expected, when I would bring the conversation around to the topic of eating. He made it clear that his eating habits were his own business and he would rather not discuss them with me, or anyone. Yet there was an aggressive glow on his face whenever we spoke of the way he ate that called Kafka's hunger artist to my mind: he seemed proud of his achievements in starvation, even eager to be admired for his skill at shunning food.

Too much directness in the early stages of therapy is generally counterproductive where anorexia is the problem. The patient *loves* her syndrome and resists any therapeutic approach that might deprive her of it. Timothy and I talked mainly of his studies, his classmates, his step-brothers. Progress was slow, circuitous, agonizing. What was most agonizing was my realization that I didn't have much time. According to the report from his school physician he was already running at dangerously low levels, bones weakening, muscles degenerating, electrolyte balance cockeyed, hormonal systems in disarray. The necessary treatment before long would be hospitalization, not psychotherapy, and it might almost be too late even for that.

He was aware that he was wasting away and in danger. He didn't seem to care.

I let him see that I wasn't going to force anything on him. So far as I was concerned, I told him, he was basically free to starve himself to death if that was what he was really after. But as a psychologist whose role it is to help people, I said, I had some scientific interest in finding out what made him tick – not particularly for his sake, but for the sake of other patients who might be more interested in being helped. He could relate to that. His facial expressions changed. He became less hostile. It was the fifth session now, and I sensed that his armour might be ready to crack. He was starting to think of me not as a member of the enemy but as a neutral observer, a dispassionate investigator. The next step was to make him see me as an ally. You and me, Timothy, standing together against *them*. I told him a few things about myself, my childhood, my troubled adolescence: little nuggets of confidence, offered by way of trade.

'When you disappear,' I said finally, 'where is it that you want to go?'

The moment was ripe and the breakthrough went beyond my highest expectations.

'You know what a microchip is?' he asked.

'Sure.'

'I go down into them.'

Not I *want* to go down into them. But I *do* go down into them.

'Tell me about that,' I said.

'The only way you can understand the nature of reality,' he said, 'is to take a close look at it. To really and truly take a look, you know? Here we have these fantastic chips, a whole processing unit smaller than your little toenail with fifty times the data-handling capacity of the old mainframes. What goes on inside them? I mean, what *really* goes on? I go into them and I look. It's like a trance, you know? You sharpen your concentration and you sharpen it and sharpen it and then you're moving downwards, inwards, deeper and deeper.' He laughed harshly. 'You think this is all mystical ka-ka, don't you? Half of you thinks I'm just a crazy kid mouthing off, and the other half thinks here's a kid who's smart as hell, feeding you a line of malarkey to keep you away from the real topic. Right, Doctor? Right?'

'I had a dream a couple of weeks ago abou shrinking down into the infinitely small,' I said. 'A nightmare, really. But a fascinating one. Fascinating and frightening both. I went all the way down to the molecular level, past grains of sand, past bacteria, down to electrons and protons, or what I suppose were electrons and protons.'

'What was the light like, where you were?'

'Blinding. It came in pulsing waves.'

'What colour?'

'Every colour all at once,' I said.

He stared at me. 'No shit!'

'Is that the way it looks for you?'

'Yes. No.' He shifted uneasily. 'How can I tell if you saw what I saw? But it's a stream of colours, yes. Pulsing. And – all the colours at once, yes, that's how you could describe it – '

'Tell me more.'

'More what?'

'When you go downwards – tell me what it's like, Timothy.'

He gave me his lofty look, his pedagogic look. 'You know how small a chip is? A MOSFET, say?'

'MOSFET?'

'Metal-oxide-silicon field-effect-transistor,' he said. 'The newest ones have a minimum feature size of about a micrometre. Ten to the minus sixth metres. That's a millionth of a metre, all right? Small. It isn't down there on the molecular level, no. You could fit 200 amoebas into a MOSFET channel one micrometre long. Okay? Okay? Or a whole army of viruses. But it's still plenty small. That's where I go. And run, down the corridors of the chips, with electrons whizzing by me all the time. Of course I can't see them. Even a lot smaller, you can't see electrons, you can only compute the probabilities of their paths. But you can feel them. *I* can feel them. And I run among them, everywhere, through the corridors, through the channels, past the gates, past the open spaces in the lattice. Getting to know the territory. Feeling at home in it.'

'What's an electron like, when you feel it?'

'You dreamed it, you said. You tell me.'

'Sparks,' I said. 'Something fizzy, going by in a blur.'

'You read about that somewhere, in one of your journals?'

'It's what I saw,' I said. 'What I felt, when I had that dream.'

'But that's it! That's it exactly!' He was perspiring. His face was flushed. His hands were trembling. His whole body was ablaze with a metabolic fervour I had not previously seen in him. He looked like a skeleton who had just trotted off a basketball court after a hard game. He leaned towards me and said, looking suddenly vulnerable in a way that he had never allowed himself to seem with me before, 'Are you sure it was only a dream? Or do you go there too?'

Kafka had the right idea. What the anorexic wants is to demonstrate a supreme ability. 'Look,' she says. 'I am a special person. I have an extraordinary gift. I am capable of exerting total control over my body. By refusing food I take command of my destiny. I display supreme force of will. Can you achieve that sort of discipline? Can you even begin to understand it? Of course you can't. But I can.' The issue isn't really one of worrying about being too fat. That's just a superficial problem. The real issue is one of exhibiting strength of purpose, of proving that you can accomplish something remarkable, of showing the world what a superior person you really are. So what we're dealing with isn't merely a perversely extreme form of dieting. The deeper issue is one of gaining control – over your body, over your life, even over the physical world itself.

He began to look healthier. There was some colour in his cheeks now, and he seemed more relaxed, less twitchy. I had the feeling that he was putting on a little weight, although the medical reports I was getting from his school physician didn't confirm that in any significant way – some weeks he'd be up a pound or two, some weeks down, and there was never any net gain. His mother reported that he went through periods when he appeared to be showing a little interest in food, but these were usually followed by periods of rigorous fasting or at best his typical sort of reluctant nibbling. There was nothing in any of this that I could find tremendously encouraging, but I had the definite feeling that I was starting to reach him, that I was beginning to win him back from the brink.

Timothy said, 'I have to be weightless in order to get there. I mean, literally weightless. Where I am now, it's only a beginning. I need to lose all the rest.'

'Only a beginning,' I said, appalled, and jotted a few quick notes.

'I've attained takeoff capability. But I can never get far enough. I run into a barrier on the way down, just as I'm entering the truly structural regions of the chip.'

'Yet you do get right into the interior of the chip.'

'Into it, yes. But I don't attain the real understanding that I'm after. Perhaps the problem's in the chip itself, not in me. Maybe if I tried a quantum-well chip instead of a MOSFET I'd get where I want to go, but they aren't ready yet, or if they are I don't have any way of getting my hands on one. I want to ride the probability waves, do you see? I want to be small enough to grab hold of an electron and stay with it as it zooms through the lattice.' His eyes were blazing. 'Try talking about this stuff with my brother. Or anyone. The ones who don't understand think I'm crazy. So do the ones who do.'

'You can talk here, Timothy.'

'The chip, the integrated circuit – what we're really talking about is transistors, microscopic ones, maybe a billion of them arranged side by side. Silicon or germanium, doped with impurities like boron, arsenic, sometimes other things. On one side are the N-type charge carriers, and the P-type ones are on the other, with an insulating layer between; and when the voltage comes through the gate, the electrons migrate to the P-type side, because it's positively charged, and the holes, the zones of positive charge, go to the N-type side. So your basic logic circuit – ' He paused. 'You following this?'

'More or less. Tell me about what you feel as you start to go downwards into a chip.'

It begins, he said, with a rush, an upward surge of almost ecstatic force: he is not descending but floating. The floor falls away beneath him as he dwindles. Then comes the intensifying of perception, dust-motes quivering and twinkling in what had a moment before seemed nothing but empty air, and the light taking on strange new refractions and shimmerings. The solid world begins to alter. Familiar shapes – the table, a chair, the computer before him – vanish as he comes closer to their essence. What he sees now is detailed structure, the intricacy of surfaces: no longer a forest, only trees. Everything is texture and there is no solidity. Wood and metal become strands and webs and mazes. Canyons yawn. Abysses open. He goes inwards, drifting, tossed like a feather on the molecular breeze.

It is no simple journey. The world grows grainy. He fights his way through a dust-storm of swirling granules of oxygen and nitrogen, an invisible blizzard battering him at every step. Ahead lies the chip he seeks, a magnificent thing, a gleaming radiant Valhalla. He begins to run towards it, heedless of obstacles. Giant rainbows sweep the sky: dizzying floods of pure colour, hammering down with a force capable of deflecting the wandering atoms. And then – then –

The chip stands before him like some temple of Zeus rising on the Athenian plain. Giant glowing columns – yawning gateways –

dark beckoning corridors – hidden sanctuaries, beyond access, beyond comprehension. It glimmers with light of many colours. A strange swelling music fills the air. He feels like an explorer taking the first stumbling steps into a lost world. And he is still shrinking. The intricacies of the chip swell, surging like metal fungi filling with water after a rain: they spring higher and higher, darkening the sky, concealing it entirely. Another level downwards and he is barely large enough to manage the passage across the threshold, but he does, and enters. Here he can move freely. He is in a strange canyon whose silvery walls, riven with vast fissures, rise farther than he can see. He runs. He runs. He has infinite energy; his legs move like springs. Behind him the gates open, close, open, close. Rivers of torrential current surge through, lifting him, carrying him along. He senses, does not see, the vibrating of the atoms of silicon or boron; he senses, does not see, the electrons and the not-electrons flooding past, streaming towards the sides, positive or negative, to which they are inexorably drawn.

But there is more. He runs on and on and on. There is infinitely more, a world within this world, a world that lies at his feet and mocks him with its inaccessibility. It swirls before him, a whirlpool, a maelstrom. He would throw himself into it if he could, but some invisible barrier keeps him from it. This is as far as he can go. This is as much as he can achieve. He yearns to reach out as an electron goes careering past, and pluck it from its path, and stare into its heart. He wants to step inside the atoms and breathe the mysterious air within their boundaries. He longs to look upon their hidden nuclei. He hungers for the sight of mesons, quarks, neutrinos. There is more, always more, an unending series of worlds within worlds, and he is huge, he is impossibly clumsy, he is a lurching reeling mountainous titan, incapable of penetrating beyond this point –

So far, and no farther –

No farther –

He looked up at me from the far side of the desk. Sweat was

streaming down his face and his light shirt was clinging to his skin. That sallow cadaverous look was gone from him entirely. He looked transfigured, aflame, throbbing with life: more alive than anyone I had ever seen, or so it seemed to me in that moment. There was a Faustian fire in his look, a world-swallowing urgency. Magellan must have looked that way sometimes, or Newton, or Galileo. And then in a moment more it was gone, and all I saw before me was a miserable scrawny boy, shrunken, feeble, pitifully frail.

I went to talk to a physicist I knew, a friend of Timothy's father who did advanced research at the university. I said nothing about Timothy to him.

'What's a quantum well?' I asked him.

He looked puzzled. 'Where'd you hear of those?'

'Someone I know. But I couldn't follow much of what he was saying.'

'Extremely small switching device,' he said. 'Experimental, maybe five, ten years away. Less if we're very lucky. The idea is that you use two different semiconductive materials in a single crystal lattice, a superlattice, something like a three-dimensional checkerboard. Electrons tunnelling between squares could be made to perform digital operations at tremendous speeds.'

'And how small would this thing be, compared with the sort of transistors they have on chips now?'

'It would be down in the nanometre range,' he told me. 'That's a billionth of a metre. Smaller than a virus. Getting right down there close to the theoretical limits for semiconductivity. Any smaller and you'll be measuring things in angstroms.'

'Angstroms?'

'One ten-billionth of a metre. We measure the diameter of atoms in angstrom units.'

'Ah,' I said. 'All right. Can I ask you something else?'

He looked amused, patient, tolerant.

'Does anyone know much about what an electron looks like?'

'*Looks* like?'

'Its physical appearance. I mean, has any sort of work been done on examining them, maybe even photographing them – '

'You know about the Uncertainty Principle?' he asked.

'Well – not much, really – '

'Electrons are very damned tiny. They've got a mass of – ah – about nine times ten to the minus twenty-eight grams. We need light in order to see, in any sense of the word. We see by receiving light radiated by an object, or by hitting it with light and getting a reflection. The smallest unit of light we can use, which is the photon, has such a long wavelength that it would completely hide an electron from view, so to speak. And we can't use radiation of shorter wavelength – gammas, let's say, or X-rays – for making our measurements, either, because the shorter the wavelength the greater the energy, and so a gamma ray would simply kick any electron we were going to inspect to hell and gone. So we can't "see" electrons. The very act of determining their position imparts new velocity to them, which alters their position. The best we can do by way of examining electrons is make an enlightened guess, a probabilistic determination, of where they are and how fast they're moving. In a very rough way that's what we mean by the Uncertainty Principle.'

'You mean, in order to look an electron in the eye, you'd virtually have to be the size of an electron yourself? Or even smaller?'

He gave me a strange look. 'I suppose that question makes sense,' he said. 'And I suppose I could answer yes to it. But what the hell are we talking about, now?'

I dreamed again that night: a feverish, disjointed dream of gigantic grotesque creatures shining with a fluorescent glow against a sky blacker than any night. They had claws, tentacles, eyes by the dozen. Their swollen asymmetrical bodies were bristling with thick red hairs. Some were clad in thick armour, others were equipped with ugly shining spikes that jutted in rows of ten or twenty from their quivering skins. They were pursuing me through the airless void. Wherever I ran there were more of them, crowding close. Behind them I saw the walls of the cosmos beginning to shiver and flow. The sky itself was dancing. Colour was breaking through the blackness: eddying bands of every hue at once, interwoven like great chains. I ran, and I ran, and I ran, but there were monsters on every side, and no escape.

Timothy missed an appointment. For some days now he had been growing more distant, often simply sitting silently, staring at me for the whole hour out of some hermetic sphere of unapproachability. That struck me as nothing more than predictable passive-aggressive resistance, but when he failed to show up at all I was startled: such blatant rebellion wasn't his expectable mode. Some new therapeutic strategies seemed in order: more direct intervention, with me playing the role of a gruff, loving older brother, or perhaps family therapy, or some meetings with his teachers and even classmates. Despite his recent aloofness I still felt I could get to him in time. But this business of skipping appointments was unacceptable. I phoned his mother the next day, only to learn that he was in the hospital; and after my last patient of the morning I drove across town to see him. The attending physician, a chunky-faced resident, turned frosty when I told him that I was Timothy's therapist, that I had been treating him for anorexia. I didn't need to be telepathic to know that he was thinking, *You didn't do much of a job on him, did you*? 'His parents are with him now,' he told me. 'Let me find out if they want you to go in. It looks pretty bad.'

Actually they were all there, parents, step-parents, the various children by the various second marriages. Timothy seemed to be no more than a waxen doll. They had brought him books, tapes, even a lap-top computer, but everything was pushed to the corners of the bed. The shrunken figure in the middle barely raised the level of the coverlet a few inches. They had him on an IV unit and a whole webwork of other lines and cables ran to him from the array of medical machines surrounding him. His eyes were open, but he seemed to be staring into some other world, perhaps that same world of rampaging bacteria and quivering molecules that had haunted my sleep a few nights before. He seemed perhaps to be smiling.

'He collapsed at school,' his mother whispered.

'In the computer lab, no less,' said his father, with a nervous ratcheting laugh. 'He was last conscious about two hours ago, but he wasn't talking coherently.'

'He wants to go inside his computer,' one of the little boys said. 'That's crazy, isn't it?' He might have been seven.

'Timothy's going to die, Timothy's going to die,' chanted somebody's daughter, about seven.

'Christopher! Bree! Shhh, both of you!' said about three of the various parents, all at once.

I said, 'Has he started to respond to the IV?'

'They don't think so. It's not at all good,' his mother said. 'He's right on the edge. He lost three pounds this week. We thought he was eating, but he must have been sliding the food into his pocket, or something like that.' She shook her head. 'You can't be a policeman.'

Her eyes were cold. So were her husband's, and even those of the step-parents. Telling me, *This is your fault, we counted on you to make him stop starving himself.* What could I say? You can only heal the ones you can reach. Timothy had been determined to keep himself beyond my grasp. Still, I felt the keenness of their reproachful anger, and it hurt.

'I've seen worse cases than this come back under medical treatment,' I told them. 'They'll build up his strength until he's capable of talking with me again. And then I'm certain I'll be able to lick this thing. I was just beginning to break through his defences when – when he – '

Sure. It costs no more to give them a little optimism. I gave them what I could: experience with other cases of severe food deprivation, positive results following a severe crisis of this nature, et cetera, et cetera, the man of science dipping into his reservoir of experience. They all began to brighten as I spoke. They even managed to convince themselves that a little colour was coming into Timothy's cheeks, that he was stirring, that he might soon be regaining consciousness as the machinery surrounding him pumped the nutrients into him that he had so conscientiously forbidden himself to have.

'Look,' this one said, or that one. 'Look how he's moving his hands! Look how he's breathing. It's better, isn't it!'

I actually began to believe it myself.

But then I heard his dry thin voice echoing in the caverns of my mind. *I can never get far enough. I have to be weightless in order to get there. Where I am now, it's only a beginning. I need to lose all the rest.*

I want to disappear.

That night, a third dream, vivid, precise, concrete. I was falling and running at the same time, my legs pistoning like those of a marathon runner in the twenty-sixth mile, while simultaneously I dropped in free fall through airless dark towards the silver-black surface of some distant world. And fell and fell and fell, in utter weightlessness, and hit the surface easily and kept on running, moving not forwards but downwards, the atoms of the ground parting for me as I ran. I became smaller as I descended, and smaller yet, and even smaller, until I was a mere phantom, a running ghost, the bodiless idea of myself. And still I went downwards towards the dazzling heart of things, shorn now of all impediments of the flesh.

I phoned the hospital the next morning. Timothy had died a little after dawn.

Did I fail with him? Well, then, I failed. But I think no one could possibly have succeeded. He went where he wanted to go; and so great was the force of his will that any attempts at impeding him must have seemed to him like the mere buzzing of insects, meaningless, insignificant.

So now his purpose is achieved. He has shed his useless husk. He has gone on, floating, running, descending: downwards, inwards, towards the core, where knowledge is absolute and uncertainty is unknown. He is running among the shining electrons, now. He is down there among the angstrom units at last.

To the Promised Land

As with many of my stories, this one was initiated by a request from outside. Gregory Benford and Martin H. Greenberg were editing an anthology of parallel-world stories called *What Might Have Been* and invited me to contribute. Each story was supposed to deal with the consequences of altering one major event of world history.

I worked backwards to generate my story idea, first imagining a variant world, then trying to explain what alteration of history had summoned it into being. It was autumn of 1987. I had been reading in the history of Imperial Rome – no particular reason, just recreational reading. But Rome was on my mind when the request for a story arrived. What if the Roman Empire hadn't fallen before the barbarians in the fifth century A.D., I asked myself, but somehow had survived and endured, on into our own era?

All right. A good starting point. But to what cause was I going to attribute the fall of Rome?

The rise of Christianity, I told myself. One could put forth all sorts of other reasons, such as the tendency to hire mercenary soldiers of barbarian ancestry for the army; but for the sake of the speculation I stuck with the idea that Christianity, spreading upwards until it reached the highest levels of the Empire, had so sapped the Imperial virtues of the Romans that they were easy prey to their enemies.

How, in my story, was I going to prevent Christianity from developing and taking over Rome, then?

Well, I could have Jesus die of measles at the age of five. But that was too obvious and too trivial. Besides, how would I ever communicate that to the reader without simply dragging it in by brute force? ('Meanwhile, in Nazareth, the carpenter Joseph and his wife Mary were mourning the death of their little boy Jesus . . .')

No. Even if Jesus had died in childhood, some other prophet might well have arisen in Palestine and filled His historical niche. I had to take the problem back a stage. If the monotheistic Jews had never reached that part of the Middle East in the first place, there'd have been no Jesus or Jesus-surrogate figure to give rise to the troublesome and ultimately destructive new religion. Well, then, should I suppose the Jews had gone somewhere else when they made their Exodus from Egypt? Have them build their Holy Land down in the Congo, say, safely beyond contact with Rome? Have them sail off to China? Settle in Australia? No, too far-fetched, all of them. The best idea was simply to leave them in Egypt, a backwater province of the Roman Empire. The Exodus must have miscarried, somehow. Pharaoh's soldiers had caught up with Moses and his people before they reached the Red Sea. So the Philistines had remained in possession of the land that would otherwise become the Kingdom of Israel, and the Jews would continue to be an unimportant sect, serving as scribes and such among the Egyptians.

There it was. No Exodus. Now come up to the other-world equivalent of our twentieth century. The scene is Egypt; the narrator is a Jewish historian; a new Moses has arisen, planning a very modern kind of Exodus. Everything was in place and I had my story.

Magazine publication rights went to Ellen Datlow for *Omni*. But, as I sometimes tend to do, I had got a little carried away doing the background details, and Ellen asked for four or five pages of cuts. I would sooner sell my cats into slavery than let anybody else cut my work without having the right to the result, but I'm perfectly willing to listen to an editor's suggestions. Ellen, during the course of a *very* long phone call, pointed out all sorts of places where the story would benefit from a little trimming. Here and there I stuck to my text, but mainly I found myself in agreement with her, and slashed away. I'm glad I did.

When the story appeared later in the Benford-Greenberg anthology, it was illustrated on the book's cover by a moody, brooding painting of the twentieth-century Memphis that I had created. The artist's vision was of something a little like the world of the film *Blade Runner*, plus sphinxes, Egyptian temples, and a giant pyramid-shaped hotel next to the downtown freeway. A man named Paul Swendsen painted it. I think it's a marvel.

They came for me at high noon, the hour of Apollo, when only a crazy man would want to go out into the desert. I was hard at work and in no mood to be kidnapped. But to get them to listen to reason was like trying to get the Nile to flow south. They weren't reasonable men. Their eyes had a wild metallic sheen and they held their jaws and mouths clamped in that special constipated way that fanatics like to affect. As they swaggered about in my little cluttered study, poking at the tottering stacks of books and pawing through the manuscript of my nearly finished history of the collapse of the Empire, they were like two immense irresistible forces, as remote and terrifying as gods of old Aiguptos come to life. I felt helpless before them.

The older and taller one called himself Eleazar. To me he was Horus, because of his great hawk nose. He looked like an Aiguptian and he was wearing the white linen robe of an Aiguptian. The other, squat and heavily muscled, with a baboon face worthy of Thoth, told me he was Leonardo di Filippo, which is of course a Roman name, and he had an oily Roman look about him. But I knew he was no more Roman than I am. Nor the other, Aiguptian. Both of them spoke in Hebrew, and with an ease that no outsider could ever attain. These were two Israelites, men of my own obscure tribe. Perhaps di Filippo had been born to a father not of the faith, or perhaps he simply liked to pretend that he was one of the world's masters and not one of God's forgotten people. I will never know.

Eleazar stared at me, at the photograph of me on the jacket of my account of the Wars of the Reunification, and at me again, as though trying to satisfy himself that I really was Nathan ben-Simeon. The picture was fifteen years old. My beard had been black then. He tapped the book and pointed questioningly to me and I nodded. 'Good,' he said. He told me to pack a suitcase, fast, as though I were going down to Alexandria for a weekend holiday. 'Moshe sent us to get you,' he said. 'Moshe wants you. Moshe needs you. He has important work for you.'

'Moshe?'

'The Leader,' Eleazar said, in tones that you would ordinarily reserve for Pharaoh, or perhaps the First Consul. 'You don't know anything about him yet, but you will. All of Aiguptos will know him soon. The whole world.'

'What does your Moshe want with me?'

'You're going to write an account of the Exodus for him,' said di Filippo.

'Ancient history isn't my field,' I told him.

'We're not talking about ancient history.'

'The Exodus was three thousand years ago, and what can you say about it at this late date except that it's a damned shame that it didn't work out?'

Di Filippo looked blank for a moment. Then he said, 'We're not talking about that one. The Exodus is now. It's about to happen, the new one, the real one. That other one long ago was a mistake, a false try.'

'And this new Moshe of yours wants to do it all over again? Why? Can't he be satisfied with the first fiasco? Do we need another? Where could we possibly go that would be any better than Aiguptos?'

'You'll see. What Moshe is doing will be the biggest news since the burning bush.'

'Enough,' Eleazar said. 'We ought to be hitting the road. Get your things together, Dr Ben-Simeon.'

So they really meant to take me away. I felt fear and disbelief. Was this actually happening? Could I resist them? I would not let it happen. Time for some show of firmness, I thought. The scholar standing on his authority. Surely they wouldn't attempt force. Whatever else they might be, they were Hebrews. They would respect a scholar. Brusque, crisp,

fatherly, the *melamed*, the man of learning. I shook my head.
'I'm afraid not. It's simply not possible.'

Eleazar made a small gesture with one hand. Di Filippo
moved ominously close to me and his stocky body seemed to
expand in a frightening way. 'Come on,' he said quietly. 'We've
got a car waiting right outside. It's a four-hour drive, and
Moshe said to get you there before sundown.'

My sense of helplessness came sweeping back. 'Please. I have
work to do, and – '

'Screw your work, Professor. Start packing, or we'll take you
just as you are.'

The street was silent and empty, with that forlorn midday look
that makes Menfe seem like an abandoned city when the sun
is at its height. I walked between them, a prisoner, trying to
remain calm. When I glanced back at the battered old grey
façades of the Hebrew Quarter where I had lived all my life,
I wondered if I would ever see them again, what would happen
to my books, who would preserve my papers. It was like a
dream.

A sharp dusty wind was blowing out of the west, reddening
the sky so that it seemed that the whole Delta must be aflame,
and the noontime heat was enough to kosher a pig. The air
smelled of cooking oil, of orange blossoms, of camel dung, of
smoke. They had parked on the far side of Amenhotep Plaza
just behind the vast ruined statue of Pharaoh, probably in hope
of catching the shadows, but at this hour there were no shadows
and the car was like an oven. Di Filippo drove, Eleazar sat in
back with me. I kept myself completely still, hardly breathing,
as though I could construct a sphere of invulnerability around
me by remaining motionless. But when Eleazar offered me a
cigarette I snatched it from him with such sudden ferocity that
he looked at me in amazement.

We circled the Hippodrome and the Great Basilica where
the judges of the Republic hold court, and joined the sparse
flow of traffic that was entering the Sacred Way. So our route
lay eastward out of the city, across the river and into the desert.

I asked no questions. I was frightened, numbed, angry, and – I suppose – to some degree curious. It was a paralysing combination of emotions. So I sat quietly, praying only that these men and their Leader would be done with me in short order and return me to my home and my studies.

'This filthy city,' Eleazar muttered. 'How I despise it!'

In fact it had always seemed grand and beautiful to me: a measure of my assimilation, some might say, though inwardly I feel very much the Israelite, not in the least Aiguptian. Even a Hebrew must concede that Menfe is one of the world's great cities. It is the most majestic city this side of Roma, so everyone says, and so I am willing to believe, though I have never been beyond the borders of the province of Aiguptos in my life.

The splendid old temples of the Sacred Way went by on both sides, the Temple of Isis and the Temple of Sarapis and the Temple of Jupiter Ammon and all the rest, fifty or a hundred of them on that great boulevard whose pavements are lined with sphinxes and bulls: Dagon's temple, Mithra's and Cybele's, Baal's, Marduk's, Zarathustra's, a temple for every god and goddess anyone had ever imagined, except, of course, the One True God, whom we few Hebrews prefer to worship in our private way behind the walls of our own Quarter. The gods of all the Earth have washed up here in Menfe like so much Nile mud. Of course hardly anyone takes them very seriously these days, even the supposed faithful. It would be folly to pretend that this is a religious age. Mithra's shrine still gets some worshippers, and of course that of Jupiter Ammon. People go to those to do business, to see their friends, maybe to ask favours on high. The rest of the temples might as well be museums. No one gets into them except Roman and Japanese tourists. Yet here they still stand, many of them thousands of years old. Nothing is ever thrown away in the land of Misr.

'Look at them,' Eleazar said scornfully, as we passed the huge half-ruined Sarapion. 'I hate the sight of them. The foolishness! The waste! And all of them built with our forefathers' sweat.'

In fact there was little truth in that. Perhaps in the time of the first Moshe we did indeed labour to build the Great Pyramids for Pharaoh, as it says in Scripture. But there could never have been enough of us to add up to much of a work force. Even now, after a sojourn along the Nile that has lasted some four thousand years, there are only about twenty thousand of us. Lost in a sea of ten million Aiguptians, we are, and the Aiguptians themselves are lost in an ocean of Romans and imitation Romans, so we are a minority within a minority, an ethnographic curiosity, a drop in the vast ocean of humanity, an odd and trivial sect, insignificant except to ourselves.

The temple district dropped away behind us and we moved out across the long slim shining arch of the Caesar Augustus Bridge, and into the teeming suburb of Hikuptah on the eastern bank of the river, with its leather and gold bazaars, its myriad coffeehouses, its tangle of medieval alleys. Then Hikuptah dissolved into a wilderness of fig trees and canebrake, and we entered a transitional zone of olive orchards and date palms; and then abruptly we came to the place where the land changes from black to red and nothing grows. At once the awful barrenness and solitude of the place struck me like a tangible force. It was a fearful land, stark and empty, a dead place full of terrible ghosts. The sun was a scourge above us. I thought we would bake; and when the car's engine once or twice began to cough and sputter, I knew from the grim look on Eleazar's face that we would surely perish if we suffered a breakdown. Di Filippo drove in a hunched, intense way, saying nothing, gripping the steering stick with an unbending rigidity that spoke of great uneasiness. Eleazar too was quiet. Neither of them had said much since our departure from Menfe, nor I, but now in that hot harsh land they fell utterly silent, and the three of us neither spoke nor moved, as though the car had become our tomb. We laboured onwards, slowly, uncertain of engine, with windborne sand whistling all about us out of the west. In the great heat every breath was a struggle. My clothing clung to my skin. The road was fine for a while, broad and straight and well paved, but then it narrowed, and finally it was nothing more than a potholed white ribbon half covered with drifts.

They were better at highway maintenance in the days of Imperial Roma. But that was long ago. This is the era of the Consuls, and things go to hell in the hinterlands and no one cares.

'Do you know what route we're taking, Doctor?' Eleazar asked, breaking the taut silence at last when we were an hour or so into that bleak and miserable desert.

My throat was dry as strips of leather that have been hanging in the sun a thousand years, and I had trouble getting words out. 'I think we're heading east,' I said finally.

'East, yes. It happens that we're travelling the same route that the first Moshe took when he tried to lead our people out of bondage. Towards the Bitter Lakes, and the Reed Sea. Where Pharaoh's army caught up with us and ten thousand innocent people drowned.'

There was crackling fury in his voice, as though that were something that had happened just the other day, as though he had learned of it not from the Book of Aaron but from this morning's newspaper. And he gave me a fiery glance, as if I had had some complicity in our people's long captivity among the Aiguptians and some responsibility for the ghastly failure of that ancient attempt to escape. I flinched before that fierce gaze of his and looked away.

'Do you care, Dr Ben-Simeon? That they followed us and drove us into the sea? That half our nation, or more, perished in a single day in horrible fear and panic? That young mothers with babies in their arms were crushed beneath the wheels of Pharaoh's chariots?'

'It was all so long ago,' I said lamely.

As the words left my lips I knew how foolish they were. It had not been my intent to minimize the débâcle of the Exodus. I had meant only that the great disaster to our people was sealed over by thousands of years of healing, that although crushed and dispirited and horribly reduced in numbers we had somehow gone on from that point, we had survived, we had endured, the survivors of the catastrophe had made new lives for themselves along the Nile under the rule of Pharaoh and under the Greeks who had conquered Pharaoh and the Romans who had conquered the Greeks. We still survived, did we not, here in the long sleepy decadence of the Imperium, the Pax Romana, when even the everlasting Empire had crumbled and the absurd and pathetic Second Republic ruled the world?

But to Eleazar it was as if I had spat upon the scrolls of the Law. '*It was all so long ago*,' he repeated, savagely mocking me. 'And therefore we should forget? Shall we forget the Patriarchs too? Shall we forget the Covenant? Is Aiguptos the land that the Lord meant us to inhabit? Were we chosen by Him to be set above all the peoples of the Earth, or were we meant to be the slaves of Pharaoh forever?'

'I was trying only to say – '

What I had been trying to say didn't interest him. His eyes were shining, his face was flushed, a vein stood out astonishingly on his broad forehead. 'We were meant for greatness. The Lord God gave His blessing to Abraham, and said that He would multiply Abraham's seed as the stars of the heaven, and as the sand which is upon the seashore. And the seed of Abraham shall possess the gate of his enemies. And in his seed shall all the nations of the Earth be blessed. Have you ever heard those words before, Dr Ben-Simeon? And do you think they signified anything, or were they only the boasting of noisy little desert chieftains? No, I tell you we were meant for greatness, we were meant to shake the world: and we have been too long in recovering from the catastrophe at the Reed Sea. An hour, two hours later and all of history would have been different. We would have crossed into Sinai and the fertile lands beyond; we would have built our kingdom there as the Covenant decreed; we would have made the world listen to the thunder of our God's voice; and today the entire world would look up to us as it has looked to the Romans these past twenty centuries. But it is not too late, even now. A new Moshe is in the land and he will succeed where the first one failed. And we *will* come forth from Aiguptos, Dr Ben-Simeon, and we *will* have what is rightfully ours. At last, Dr Ben-Simeon. At long last.'

He sat back, sweating, trembling, ashen, seemingly exhausted by his own eloquence. I didn't attempt to reply. Against such force of conviction there is no victory; and what could I possibly have gained, in any case, by contesting his vision of Israel triumphant? Let him have his faith; let him have his new Moshe; let him have his dream of Israel triumphant. I myself had a different vision, less romantic, more cynical. I could easily imagine, yes, the children of Israel escaping from their bondage under Pharaoh long ago and crossing into Sinai, and going on beyond it into sweet and fertile Palestina. But what then? Global dominion? What was there in our history, in our character, our national temperament, that would lead us on to that? Preaching Jehovah to the Gentiles? Yes, but would they listen, would they understand? No. No. We would always have been a special people, I suspected, a small and stubborn tribe, clinging to our knowledge of the One God amidst the hordes who needed to believe in many. We might have conquered Palestina, we might have taken Syria too, even spread out a little further around the perimeter of the Great Sea; but still there would have been the Assyrians to contend with, and the Babylonians, and the Persians, and Alexander's Greeks, and the Romans, especially the stolid dull invincible Romans, whose destiny it was to engulf every corner of the planet and carve it into Roman provinces full of Roman highways and Roman bridges and Roman whorehouses. Instead of living in Aiguptos under the modern Pharaoh, who is the puppet of the First Consul who has replaced the Emperor of Roma, we would be living in Palestina under the rule of some minor procurator or proconsul or prefect, and we would speak some sort of Greek or Latin to our masters instead of Aiguptian, and everything else would be the same. But I said none of this to Eleazar. He and I were different sorts of men. His soul and his vision were greater and grander than mine. Also his strength was superior and his temper was shorter. I might take issue with his theories of history, and he might hit me in his rage; and which of us then would be the wiser?

* * *

The sun slipped away behind us and the wind shifted, hurling sand now against our front windows instead of the rear. I saw the dark shadows of mountains to the south and ahead of us, far across the strait that separates Aiguptos from the Sinai wilderness. It was late afternoon, almost evening. Suddenly there was a village ahead of us, springing up out of nowhere in the nothingness.

It was more a camp, really, than a village. I saw a few dozen lopsided tin huts and some buildings that were even more modest, strung together of reed latticework. Carbide lamps glowed here and there. There were three or four dilapidated trucks and a handful of battered old cars scattered haphazardly about. A well had been driven in the centre of things and a crazy network of above-ground conduits ran off in all directions. In back of the central area I saw one building much larger than the others, a big tin-roofed shed or lean-to with other trucks parked in front of it.

I had arrived at the secret headquarters of some underground movement, yet no attempt had been made to disguise or defend it. Situating it in this forlorn zone was defence enough: no one in his right mind would come out here without good reason. The patrols of the Pharaonic police did not extend beyond the cities, and the civic officers of the Republic certainly had no cause to go sniffing around in these remote and distasteful parts. We live in a decadent era but a placid and trusting one.

Eleazar, jumping out of the car, beckoned to me, and I hobbled after him. After hours without a break in the close quarters of the car I was creaky and wilted and the reek of gasoline fumes had left me nauseated. My clothes were acrid and stiff from my own dried sweat. The evening coolness had not yet descended on the desert and the air was hot and close. To my nostrils it had a strange vacant quality, the myriad stinks of the city being absent. There was something almost frightening about that. It was like the sort of air the Moon might have, if the Moon had air.

'This place is called Beth Israel,' Eleazar said. 'It is the capital of our nation.'

Not only was I among fanatics; I had fallen in with madmen who suffered the delusion of grandeur. Or does one quality go automatically with the other?

A woman wearing man's clothing came trotting up to us. She was young and very tall, with broad shoulders and a great mass of dark thick hair tumbling to her shoulders and eyes as bright as Eleazar's. She had Eleazar's hawk's nose, too, but somehow it made her look all the more striking. 'My sister Miriam,' he said. 'She'll see that you get settled. In the morning I'll show you around and explain your duties to you.'

And he walked away, leaving me with her.

She was formidable. I would have carried my bag, but she insisted, and set out at such a brisk pace towards the perimeter of the settlement that I was hard put to keep up with her. A hut all my own was ready for me, somewhat apart from everything else. It had a cot, a desk and typewriter, a washbasin, and a single dangling lamp. There was a cupboard for my things. Miriam unpacked for me, setting my little stock of fresh clothing on the shelves and putting the few books I had brought with me beside the cot. Then she filled the basin with water and told me to get undressed. I stared at her, astounded. 'You can't wear what you've got on now,' she said. 'While you're having a bath I'll take your things to be washed.' She might have waited outside, but no. She stood there, arms folded, looking impatient. I shrugged and gave her my shirt, but she wanted everything else, too. This was new to me, her straightforwardness, her absolute indifference to modesty. There have been few women in my life and none since the death of my wife; how could I strip myself before this one, who was young enough to be my daughter? But she insisted. In the end I gave her every stitch – my nakedness did not seem to matter to her at all – and while she was gone I sponged myself clean and hastily put on fresh clothing, so she would not see me naked again. But she was gone a long time. When she returned, she brought with her a tray, my dinner, a bowl of porridge, some stewed lamb, a little flask of pale red wine. Then I was left alone. Night had fallen now, desert night, awesomely black with the stars burning like beacons. When I had eaten I stepped outside my hut and stood in the darkness. It scarcely seemed real to me, that I had been snatched away like this, that I was in this alien place rather than in my familiar cluttered little flat in the Hebrew Quarter of Menfe. But it was peaceful here. Lights glimmered in the distance. I heard laughter, the pleasant sound of a kithara, someone singing an old Hebrew song in a deep, rich voice. Even in my bewildering captivity I felt a strange tranquillity descending on me. I knew that I was in the presence of a true community, albeit one dedicated to some bizarre goal beyond my comprehension. If I had dared, I would have gone out among them and made myself known to them; but I was a stranger, and afraid. For a long while I stood in the darkness, listening, wondering. When the night grew cold I went inside. I lay awake until dawn, or so it seemed, gripped by that icy clarity that will not admit sleep; and yet I must have slept at least a little while, for there were fragments of dreams drifting in my mind in the morning, images of horsemen and chariots, of men with spears, of a great black-bearded angry Moshe holding aloft the tablets of the Law.

A small girl shyly brought me breakfast. Afterwards Eleazar came to me. In the confusion of yesterday I had not taken note of how overwhelming his physical presence was: he had seemed merely big, but now I realized that he was a giant, taller than I by a span or more, and probably sixty minas heavier. His features were ruddy and a vast tangle of dark thick curls spilled down to his shoulders. He had put aside his Aiguptian robes this morning and was dressed Roman style, an open-throated white shirt, a pair of khaki trousers.

'You know,' he said, 'we don't have any doubt at all that you're the right man for this job. Moshe and I have discussed your books many times. We agree that no one has a firmer grasp of the logic of history, of the inevitability of the processes that flow from the nature of human beings.'

To this I offered no response.

'I know how annoyed you must be at being grabbed like this.

But you are essential to us; and we knew you'd never have come of your own free will.'

'Essential?'

'Great movements need great chroniclers.'

'And the nature of your movement – '

'Come,' he said.

He led me through the village. But it was a remarkably uninformative walk. His manner was mechanical and aloof, as if he were following a pre-programmed route, and whenever I asked a direct question he was vague or even evasive. The big tin-roofed building in the centre of things was the factory where the work of the Exodus was being carried out, he said, but my request for further explanation went unanswered. He showed me the house of Moshe, a crude shack like all the others. Of Moshe himself, though, I saw nothing. 'You will meet him at a later time,' Eleazar said. He pointed out another shack that was the synagogue, another that was the library, another that housed the electrical generator. When I asked to visit the library he merely shrugged and kept walking. On the far side of it I saw a second group of crude houses on the lower slope of a fair-sized hill that I had not noticed the night before. 'We have a population of five hundred,' Eleazar told me. More than I had imagined.

'All Hebrews?' I asked.

'What do you think?'

It surprised me that so many of us could have migrated to this desert settlement without my hearing about it. Of course, I have led a secluded scholarly life, but still, five hundred Israelites is one out of every forty of us. That is a major movement of population, for us. And not one of them someone of my acquaintance, or even a friend of a friend? Apparently not. Well, perhaps most of the settlers of Beth Israel had come from the Hebrew community in Alexandria, which has relatively little contact with those of us who live in Menfe. Certainly I recognized no one as I walked through the village.

From time to time Eleazar made veiled references to the Exodus that was soon to come, but there was no real information in anything he said; it was as if the Exodus were merely some bright toy that he enjoyed cupping in his hands, and I was allowed from time to time to see its gleam but not its form. There was no use in questioning him. He simply walked along, looming high above me, telling me only what he wished to tell. There was an unstated grandiosity to the whole mysterious project that puzzled and irritated me. If they wanted to leave Aiguptos, why not simply leave? The borders weren't guarded. We had ceased to be the slaves of Pharaoh two thousand years ago. Eleazar and his friends could settle in Palestina or Syria or anyplace else they liked, even Gallia, even Hispania, even Nuova Roma far across the ocean, where they could try to convert the redskinned men to Israel. The Republic wouldn't care where a few wild-eyed Hebrews chose to go. So why all this pomp and mystery, why such an air of conspiratorial secrecy? Were these people up to something truly extraordinary? Or, I wondered, were they simply crazy?

That afternoon Miriam brought back my clothes, washed and ironed, and offered to introduce me to some of her friends. We went down into the village, which was quiet. Almost everyone is at work, Miriam explained. But there were a few young men and women on the porch of one of the buildings: this is Deborah, she said, and this is Ruth, and Reuben, and Isaac, and Joseph, and Saul. They greeted me with great respect, even reverence, but almost immediately went back to their animated conversation as if they had forgotten I was there. Joseph, who was dark and sleek and slim, treated Miriam with an ease bordering on intimacy, finishing her sentences for her, once or twice touching her lightly on the arm to underscore some point he was making. I found that unexpectedly disturbing. Was he her husband? Her lover? Why did it matter to me? They were both young enough to be my children. Great God, why did it matter?

Unexpectedly and with amazing swiftness my attitude towards my captors began to change. Certainly I had had a troublesome introduction to them – the lofty pomposity of Eleazar, the brutal directness of di Filippo, the ruthless way I had been seized and taken to this place – but as I met others I found them generally charming, graceful, courteous, appealing. Prisoner though I might be, I felt myself quickly being drawn into sympathy with them.

In the first two days I was allowed to discover nothing except that these were busy, determined folk, most of them young and evidently all of them intelligent, working with tremendous zeal on some colossal undertaking that they were convinced would shake the world. They were passionate in the way that I imagined the Hebrews of that first and ill-starred Exodus had been: contemptuous of the sterile and alien society within which they were confined, striving towards freedom and the light, struggling to bring a new world into being. But how? By what means? I was sure that they would tell me more in their own good time; and I knew also that that time had not yet come. They were watching me, testing me, making certain I could be trusted with their secret.

Whatever it was, that immense surprise which they meant to spring upon the Republic, I hoped there was substance to it, and I wished them well with it. I am old and perhaps timid but far from conservative: change is the way of growth, and the Empire, with which I include the Republic that ostensibly has replaced it, is the enemy of change. For twenty centuries it had strangled mankind in its benign grip. The civilization that it had constructed was hollow, the life that most of us led was a meaningless trek that had neither values nor purpose. By its shrewd acceptance and absorption of the alien gods and alien ways of the peoples it had conquered, the Empire had flattened everything into shapelessness. The grand and useless temples of the Sacred Way, where all gods were equal and equally insignificant, were the best symbol of that. By worshipping everyone indiscriminately, the rulers of the Imperium had turned the sacred into a mere instrument of governance. And ultimately their cynicism had come to pervade everything: the relationship between man and the Divine was destroyed, so that we had nothing left to venerate except the status quo itself, the holy stability of the world government. I had felt for years that the time was long overdue for some great revolution, in which all fixed, fast-frozen relationships, with their train of ancient and venerable prejudices and opinions, would be swept away – a time when all that is solid melts into air, all that is holy is profaned, and man is at last compelled to face with sober senses his real conditions of life. Was that what the Exodus somehow would bring? Profoundly did I hope so. For the Empire was defunct and didn't know it. Like some immense dead beast it lay upon the soul of humanity, smothering it beneath itself: a beast so huge that its limbs hadn't yet heard the news of its own death.

On the third day di Filippo knocked on my door and said, 'The leader will see you now.'

The interior of Moshe's dwelling was not very different from mine: a simple cot, one stark lamp, a basin, a cupboard. But he had shelf upon shelf overflowing with books. Moshe himself was smaller than I expected, a short, compact man who nevertheless radiated tremendous, even invincible, force. I hardly needed to be told that he was Eleazar's older brother. He had Eleazar's wild mop of curly hair and his ferocious eyes and his savage beak of a nose; but because he was so much shorter than Eleazar his power was more tightly compressed, and seemed to be in peril of immediate eruption. He seemed poised, controlled, an austere and frightening figure.

But he greeted me warmly and apologized for the rudeness of my capture. Then he indicated a well-worn row of my books on his shelves. 'You understand the Republic better than anyone, Dr Ben-Simeon,' he said. 'How corrupt and weak it is behind its façade of universal love and brotherhood. How deleterious its influence has been. How feeble its power. The world is waiting now for something completely new: but what will it be? Is that not the question, Dr Ben-Simeon? *What will it be*?'

It was a pat, obviously preconceived speech, which no doubt he had carefully constructed for the sake of impressing me and enlisting me in his cause, whatever that cause might be. Yet he did impress me with his passion and his conviction. He spoke for some time, rehearsing themes and arguments that were long familiar to me. He saw the Roman Imperium, as I did, as something dead and beyond revival, though still moving with eerie momentum. Call it an Empire, call it a Republic, it was still a world state, and that was an unsustainable concept in the modern era. The revival of local nationalisms that had been thought extinct for thousands of years was impossible to ignore. Roman tolerance for local customs, religions, languages, and rulers had been a shrewd policy for centuries, but it carried with it the seeds of destruction for the Imperium. Too much of the world now had only the barest knowledge of the two official languages of Latin and Greek, and transacted its business in a hodgepodge of other tongues. In the old Imperial heartland itself Latin had been allowed to break down into regional dialects that were in fact separate languages – Gallian, Hispanian, Lusitanian, and all the rest. Even the Romans at Roma no longer spoke true Latin, Moshe pointed out, but rather the simple, melodic, lazy thing called Roman, which might be suitable for singing opera but lacked the precision that was needed for government. As for the religious diversity that the Romans in their easy way had encouraged, it had led not to the perpetuation of faiths but to the erosion of them. Scarcely anyone except the most primitive peoples and a few unimportant encapsulated minorities like us believed anything at all; nearly everyone gave lip-service instead to the local version of the official Roman pantheon and any other gods that struck their fancy, but a society that tolerates all gods really has no faith in any. And a society without faith is one without a rudder: without even a course.

These things Moshe saw, as I did, not as signs of vitality and diversity but as confirmation of the imminence of the end. This time there would be no Reunification. When the Empire had fallen, conservative forces had been able to erect the Republic

219

in its place, but that was a trick that could be managed only once. Now a period of flames unmatched in history was surely coming as the sundered segments of the old Imperium warred against one another.

'And this Exodus of yours?' I said finally, when I dared to break his flow. 'What is that, and what does it have to do with what we've been talking about?'

'The end is near,' Moshe said. 'We must not allow ourselves to be destroyed in the chaos that will follow the fall of the Republic, for we are the instruments of God's great plan, and it is essential that we survive. Come: let me show you something.'

We stepped outside. Immediately an antiquated and unreliable-looking car pulled up, with the dark slender boy Joseph at the stick. Moshe indicated that I should get in, and we set out on a rough track that skirted the village and entered the open desert just behind the hill that cut the settlement in half. For perhaps ten minutes we drove north through a district of low rocky dunes. Then we circled another steep hill and on its farther side, where the land flattened out into a broad plain, I was astonished to see a weird tubular thing of gleaming silvery metal rising on half a dozen frail spidery legs to a height of some thirty cubits in the midst of a hubbub of machinery, wires, and busy workers.

My first thought was that it was an idol of some sort, a Moloch, a Baal, and I had a sudden vision of the people of Beth Israel coating their bodies in pigs' grease and dancing naked around it to the sound of drums and tambourines. But that was foolishness.

'What is it?' I asked. 'A sculpture of some sort?'

Moshe looked disgusted. 'Is that what you think? It is a vessel, a holy ark.'

I stared at him.

'It is the prototype for our starship,' Moshe said, and his voice took on an intensity that cut me like a blade. 'Into the heavens is where we will go, in ships like these – towards God, towards His brightness – and there we will settle, in the new

Eden that awaits us on another world, until it is time for us to return to Earth.'

'The new Eden – on another world – ' My voice was faint with disbelief. A ship to sail between the stars, as the Roman skyships travel between continents? Was such a thing possible? Hadn't the Romans themselves, those most able of engineers, discussed the question of space travel years ago and concluded that there was no practical way of achieving it and nothing to gain from it even if there was? Space was inhospitable and unattainable: everyone knew that. I shook my head. 'What other world? Where?'

Grandly he ignored my question. 'Our finest minds have been at work for five years on what you see here. Now the time to test it has come. First a short journey, only to the Moon and back – and then deeper into the heavens, to the new world that the Lord has pledged to reveal to me, so that the pioneers may plant the settlement. And after that – ship after ship, one shining ark after another, until every Israelite in the land of Aiguptos has crossed over into the promised land – ' His eyes were glowing. 'Here is our Exodus at last! What do you think, Dr Ben-Simeon? What do you think?'

I thought it was madness of the most terrifying kind, and Moshe a lunatic who was leading his people – and mine – into cataclysmic disaster. It was a dream, a wild feverish fantasy. I would have preferred it if he had said they were going to worship this thing with incense and cymbals, than that they were going to ride it into the darkness of space. But Moshe stood before me so hot with blazing fervour that to say anything like that to him was unthinkable. He took me by the arm and led me, virtually dragged me, down the slope into the work area. Close up, the starship seemed huge and yet at the same time painfully flimsy. He slapped its flank and I heard a hollow ring. Thick grey cables ran everywhere, and subordinate machines of a nature that I could not even begin to comprehend. Fierce-eyed young men and women raced to and fro, carrying pieces of equipment and shouting instructions to one another as if striving to outdo one another in their dedication to their tasks. Moshe scrambled up a narrow ladder, gesturing for me to follow him. We entered a kind of cabin at the starship's narrow tip; in that cramped and all but airless room I saw screens, dials, more cables, things beyond my understanding. Below the cabin a spiral staircase led to a chamber where the crew could sleep, and below that, said Moshe, were the rockets that would send the ark of the Exodus into the heavens.

'And will it work?' I managed finally to ask.

'There is no doubt of it,' Moshe said. 'Our finest minds have produced what you see here.'

He introduced me to some of them. The oldest appeared to be about twenty-five. Curiously, none of them had Moshe's radiant look of fanatic zeal; they were calm, even businesslike, imbued with a deep and quiet confidence. Three or four of them took turns explaining the theory of the vessel to me, its means of propulsion, its scheme of guidance, its method of escaping the pull of the Earth's inner force. My head began to ache. But yet I was swept under by the power of their conviction. They spoke of 'combustion', of 'acceleration', of 'neutralizing the planet-force'. They talked of 'mass' and 'thrust' and 'freedom velocity'. I barely understood a tenth of what they were saying, or a hundredth; but I formed the image of a giant bursting his bonds and leaping triumphantly from the ground to soar joyously into unknown realms. Why not? Why not? All it took was the right fuel and a controlled explosion, they said. Kick the Earth hard enough and you must go upwards with equal force. Yes. Why not? Within minutes I began to think that this insane starship might well be able to rise on a burst of flame and fly off into the darkness of the heavens. By the time Moshe ushered me out of the ship, nearly an hour later, I did not question that at all.

Joseph drove me back to the settlement alone. The last I saw of Moshe he was standing at the hatch of his starship, peering impatiently towards the fierce midday sky.

My task, I already knew, but which Eleazar told me again later that dazzling and bewildering day, was to write a chronicle of all that had been accomplished thus far in this hidden outpost of Israel and all that would be achieved in the apocalyptic days to come. I protested mildly that they would be better off finding some journalist, preferably with a background in science; but no, they didn't want a journalist, Eleazar said, they wanted someone with a deep understanding of the long currents of history. What they wanted from me, I realized, was a work that was not merely journalism and not merely history, but one that had the profundity and eternal power of Scripture. What they wanted from me was the Book of the Exodus, that is, the Book of the Second Moshe.

They gave me a little office in their library building and opened their archive to me. I was shown Moshe's early visionary essays, his letters to intimate friends, his sketches and manifestos insisting on the need for an Exodus far more ambitious than anything his ancient namesake could have imagined. I saw how he had assembled – secretly and with some uneasiness, for he knew that what he was doing was profoundly subversive and would bring the fullest wrath of the Republic down on him if he should be discovered – his cadre of young revolutionary scientists. I read furious memoranda from Eleazar, taking issue with his older brother's fantastic scheme; and then I saw Eleazar gradually converting himself to the cause in letter after letter until he became more of a zealot than Moshe himself. I studied technical papers until my eyes grew bleary, not only those of Moshe and his associates but some by Romans nearly a century old, and even one by a Teuton, arguing for the historical necessity of space exploration and for its technical feasibility. I learned something more of the theory of the starship's design and functioning.

My guide to all those documents was Miriam. We worked side by side, together in one small room. Her youth, her beauty, the dark glint of her eyes, made me tremble. Often I longed to reach towards her, to touch her arm, her shoulder, her cheek. But I was too timid. I feared that she would react with laughter, with anger, with disdain, even with revulsion.

Certainly it was an ageing man's fear of rejection that inspired such caution. But also I reminded myself that she was the sister of those two fiery prophets, and that the blood that flowed in her veins must be as hot as theirs. What I feared was being scalded by her touch.

The day Moshe chose for the starship's flight was the twenty-third of Tishri, the joyful holiday of Simchat Torah in the year 5730 by our calendar, that is, 2723 of the Roman reckoning. It was a brilliant early autumn day, very dry, the sky cloudless, the sun still in its fullest blaze of heat. For three days preparations had been going on around the clock at the launch site and it had been closed to all but the inner circle of scientists; but now, at dawn, the whole village went out by truck and car and some even on foot to attend the great event.

The cables and support machinery had been cleared away. The starship stood by itself, solitary and somehow vulnerable-looking, in the centre of the sandy clearing, a shining upright needle, slender, fragile. The area was roped off; we would watch from a distance, so that the searing flames of the engines would not harm us.

A crew of three men and two women had been selected: Judith, who was one of the rocket scientists, and Leonardo di Filippo, and Miriam's friend Joseph, and a woman named Sarah whom I had never seen before. The fifth, of course, was Moshe. This was his chariot; this was his adventure, his dream; he must surely be the one to ride at the helm as the *Exodus* made its first leap towards the stars.

One by one they emerged from the blockhouse that was the control centre for the flight. Moshe was the last. We watched in total silence, not a murmur, barely daring to draw breath. The five of them wore uniforms of white satin, brilliant in the morning sun, and curious glass helmets like divers' bowls over their faces. They walked towards the ship, mounted the ladder, turned one by one to look back at us, and went up inside. Moshe hesitated for a moment before entering, as if in prayer, or perhaps simply to savour the fullness of his joy.

Then there was a long wait, interminable, unendurable. It might have been twenty minutes; it might have been an hour. No doubt there was some last-minute checking to do, or perhaps even some technical hitch. Still we maintained our silence. We could have been statues. After a time I saw Eleazar turn worriedly towards Miriam, and they conferred in whispers. Then he trotted across to the blockhouse and went inside. Five minutes went by, ten; then he emerged, smiling, nodding, and returned to Miriam's side. Still nothing happened. We continued to wait.

Suddenly there was a sound like a thundercrack and a noise like the roaring of a thousand great bulls, and black smoke billowed from the ground around the ship, and there were flashes of dazzling red flame. The *Exodus* rose a few feet from the ground. There it hovered as though magically suspended, for what seemed to be forever.

And then it rose, jerkily at first, more smoothly then, and soared on a stunningly swift ascent towards the dazzling blue vault of the sky. I gasped; I grunted as though I had been struck; and I began to cheer. Tears of wonder and excitement flowed freely along my cheeks. All about me, people were cheering also, and weeping, and waving their arms, and the rocket, roaring, rose and rose, so high now that we could scarcely see it against the brilliance of the sky.

We were still cheering when a white flare of unbearable light, like a second sun more brilliant than the first, burst into the air high above us and struck us with overmastering force, making us drop to our knees in pain and terror, crying out, covering our faces with our hands.

When I dared look again, finally, that terrible point of ferocious illumination was gone, and in its place was a ghastly streak of black smoke that smeared halfway across the sky, trickling away in a dying trail somewhere to the north. I could not see the rocket. I could not hear the rocket.

'It's gone!' someone cried.

'Moshe! Moshe!'

'It blew up! I saw it!'

'Moshe!'

'Judith – ' said a quieter voice behind me.

I was too stunned to cry out. But all around me there was a steadily rising sound of horror and despair, which began as a low choking wail and mounted until it was a shriek of the greatest intensity coming from hundreds of throats at once. There was fearful panic, universal hysteria. People were running about as if they had gone mad. Some were rolling on the ground, some were beating their hands against the sand. 'Moshe!' they were screaming. 'Moshe! Moshe! Moshe!'

I looked towards Eleazar. He was white-faced and his eyes seemed wild. Yet even as I looked towards him I saw him draw in his breath, raise his hands, step forward to call for attention. Immediately all eyes turned towards him. He swelled until he appeared to be five cubits high.

'Where's the ship?' someone cried. 'Where's Moshe?'

And Eleazar said, in a voice like the trumpet of the Lord, 'He was the Son of God, and God has called him home.'

Screams. Wails. Hysterical shrieks.

'Dead!' came the cry. 'Moshe is dead!'

'He will live forever,' Eleazar boomed.

'The Son of God!' came the cry, from three voices, five, a dozen. 'The Son of God!'

I was aware of Miriam at my side, warm, pressing close, her arm through mine, her soft breast against my ribs, her lips at my ear. 'You must write the book,' she whispered, and her voice held a terrible urgency. '*His* book, you must write. So that this day will never be forgotten. So that he will live forever.'

'Yes,' I heard myself saying. 'Yes.'

In that moment of frenzy and terror I felt myself sway like a tree of the shore that has been assailed by the flooding of the Nile; and I was uprooted and swept away. The fireball of the *Exodus* blazed in my soul like a second sun indeed, with a brightness that could never fade. And I knew that I was engulfed, that I was conquered, that I would remain here to write and preach, that I would forge the gospel of the new

Moshe in the smithy of my soul and send the word to all the lands. Out of these five today would come rebirth; and to the peoples of the Republic we would bring the message for which they had waited so long in their barrenness and their confusion, and when it came they would throw off the shackles of their masters; and out of the death of the Imperium would come a new order of things. Were there other worlds, and could we dwell upon them? Who could say? But there was a new truth that we could teach, which was the truth of the second Moshe who had given his life so that we might go to the stars, and I would not let that new truth die. I would write, and others of my people would go forth and carry the word that I had written to all the lands, and the lands would be changed. And some day, who knew how soon, we would build a new ship, and another, and another, and they would carry us from this world of woe. God had sent His Son, and God had called him home, and one day we would all follow him on wings of flame, up from the land of bondage into the heavens where he dwells eternally.

The Asenion Solution

This one was done basically as a lark. But there was a gesture of reconciliation buried in it, putting to an end a strange episode of unpleasantness between two basically even-tempered and good-natured people who happen to be very old friends.

The year 1989 marked Isaac Asimov's fiftieth anniversary as a professional writer. One day in the summer of 1988 I got a letter from the anthologist Martin H. Greenberg, who regards Isaac virtually as his second father. Very quietly Marty was going to assemble an anthology called *Foundation's Friends*, made up of original stories based on themes made famous by Isaac; it would be presented to Isaac in October of 1989 during the course of the festivities commemorating his dazzling fifty-year career. Did I want to take part? Marty asked. Don't be silly, I said.

And sat down and wrote 'The Asenion Solution' in September of 1988 – coincidentally, the same month when I had agreed to collaborate with Isaac on novel-length versions of his famous story 'Nightfall' and two other classic novelettes.

The character I call 'Ichabod Asenion' is only partially based on the real-world individual known as Isaac Asimov. Asenion is brilliant, yes, and lives in a Manhattan penthouse. True of Asimov on both counts. But Asenion is described as ascetic and reclusive, two words that I suspect have never been applied, even in jest, to Isaac Asimov. Asenion is a physicist; Isaac's scientific field was biochemistry before he deviated into writing books. And Asenion is a fanatic horticulturist. Asimov – I'm only guessing here, but with some confidence – probably doesn't know one plant from the next, living as he does high above the streets of Manhattan, and he certainly doesn't have time to tend to a greenhouse, writing as he does three

228

or four books a week. Asenion, then, is a kind of fantasy-Asimov, a figure made up of equal parts of the real thing and of pure fiction.

The odd surname, though, is Asimovian, as a few insiders know. 'Asenion' was a famous typographical error for 'Asimov', going back close to fifty years when he was still writing fan letters to science-fiction magazines. He took a lot of kidding about it, but remained genial enough to use the name himself in his Robot series. I figured it was good for one more go-round here.

And the gesture of reconciliation I was talking about a few paragraphs back?

It has to do with the plutonium-186 plot thread.

I've known Isaac Asimov since 1955 or so, and in all that time there's been only one disharmonious moment in what has otherwise been a relationship of affection and mutual respect. It occurred when, at a science-fiction convention in New York about 1970, I made a joking reference to the imaginary isotope plutonium-186 during a panel discussion where Isaac was in the audience. I knew, of course, that a heavy element like plutonium couldn't have so light an isotope as that – that was the whole point of my remark. Isaac guffawed when he heard me speak of it. And went home and started writing a short story for an anthology I was editing, a story in which he intended to come up with some plausible situation in which plutonium-186 could actually exist.

And so he did; but one thing led to another and the 'story' turned into his first science-fiction novel in a decade and a half, *The Gods Themselves*. Well and good: I had inspired his return to the field with a remarkable work. The only trouble was that Isaac thought I was *serious* about plutonium-186, and took an extremely public, though gentle and loving, way of berating me for my scientific ignorance: he dedicated the book to me with a long introduction thanking me because my demonstration of scientific illiteracy at that convention had unwittingly inspired his novel.

I wasn't amused. I told him so. He was surprised by my irritation, and told me so. We went around and around on it for a little while, and then each of us came to understand the other one's point. The offending dedication was removed from future editions of the book, and the whole squabble was dropped. And we went back to being good friends and high admirers of each other's work and intelligence, and eventually, through a set of circumstances nobody could have predicted, we even wound up becoming collaborators. But all these years I continued to suspect that Isaac still felt guilty/defensive/touchy/uneasy/wronged by our plutonium-186 contretemps.

So when the time came for me to write a story for a *festschrift* commemorating his fifty years as a professional author, I thought I'd send Isaac a signal that I carried no lingering bitterness over the misunderstanding, that in fact the whole thing now seemed to me a trifle that could be chuckled over. Thus I wrote 'The Asenion Solution', yoking together Isaac's celebrated 1948 'thiotimoline' article with good old PU-186, by way of telling him that I bore no lasting resentment. It was fun to do, and, I hope, forever obliterated the one blemish on our long and harmonious friendship.

Foundation's Friends duly appeared on the anniversary of the beginning of Isaac's career and – though I wasn't at the publication party, 3000 miles from where I live – I hear that Isaac was greatly delighted by the book. Ray Bradbury did a preface for the book and the contributors included Frederik Pohl, Robert Sheckley, Harry Harrison, Hal Clement, and a lot of other fine writers who had terrific fun running their own variations on Isaac's classic themes. The clever jacket painting shows the various writers in the guise of robots – I'm the world-weary one in the middle, leaning on the bar, and that's Isaac himself in the samurai helmet down at lower right.

One thing I didn't expect, for a story that was just a prank. David Garnett chose it as one of the best science-fiction stories of 1989 for *The Orbit Science Fiction Yearbook*, the new British anthology that he edits. You never can tell about such things.

Fletcher stared bleakly at the small mounds of grey metal that were visible behind the thick window of the storage chamber.

'Plutonium-186,' he muttered. 'Nonsense! Absolute nonsense!'

'Dangerous nonsense, Lew,' said Jesse Hammond, standing behind him. 'Catastrophic nonsense.'

Fletcher nodded. The very phrase, 'plutonium-186', sounded

like gibberish to him. There wasn't supposed to be any such substance. Plutonium-186 was an impossible isotope, too light by a good fifty neutrons. Or a bad fifty neutrons, considering the risks the stuff was creating as it piled up here and there around the world. But the fact that it was theoretically imposs-ible for plutonium-186 to exist did not change the other, and uglier, fact that he was looking at three kilograms of it right this minute. Or that as the quantity of plutonium-186 in the world continued to increase, so did the chance of an uncontrol-lable nuclear reaction leading to an atomic holocaust.

'Look at the morning reports,' Fletcher said, waving a sheaf of faxprints at Hammond. 'Thirteen grams more turned up at the nucleonics lab of Accra University. Fifty grams in Geneva. Twenty milligrams in – well, that little doesn't matter. But Chicago, Jesse, Chicago – three hundred grams in a single chunk!'

'Christmas presents from the Devil,' Hammond muttered.

'Not the Devil, no. Just decent serious-minded scientific folk who happen to live in another universe where plutonium-186 is not only possible but also perfectly harmless. And who are so fascinated by the idea that *we're* fascinated by it that they keep on shipping the stuff to us in wholesale lots! What are we going to do with it all, Jesse? What in God's name are we going to do with it all?'

Raymond Niklaus looked up from his desk at the far side of the room.

'Wrap it up in shiny red-and-green paper and ship it right back to them?' he suggested.

Fletcher laughed hollowly. 'Very funny, Raymond. Very very funny.'

He began to pace the room. In the silence the clicking of his shoes against the flagstone floor seemed to him like the ticking of a detonating device, growing louder, louder, louder . . .

He – they, all of them – had been wrestling with the problem all year, with an increasing sense of futility. The plutonium-186 had begun mysteriously to appear in laboratories all over the world – wherever supplies of one of the two elements with equivalent atomic weights existed. Gram for gram, atom for atom, the matching elements disappeared just as mysteriously: equal quantities of tungsten-186 or osmium-186.

Where was the tungsten and osmium going? Where was the plutonium coming from? Above all, how was it possible for a plutonium isotope whose atoms had only ninety-two neutrons in its nucleus to exist even for a fraction of a fraction of an instant? Plutonium was one of the heavier chemical elements, with a whopping ninety-four protons in the nucleus of each of its atoms. The closest thing to a stable isotope of plutonium was plutonium-244, in which 150 neutrons held those ninety-four protons together; and even at that, plutonium-244 had an inevitable habit of breaking down in radioactive decay, with a half-life of some seventy-six million years. Atoms of plutonium-186, if they could exist at all, would come dramatically apart in very much less than one seventy-six-millionth of a second.

But the stuff that was turning up in the chemistry labs to replace the tungsten-186 and the osmium-186 had an atomic number of ninety-four, no question about that. And element ninety-four was plutonium. That couldn't be disputed either. The defining characteristic of plutonium was the presence of ninety-four protons in its nucleus. If that was the count, plutonium was what that element had to be.

This impossibly light isotope of plutonium, this plutonium-186, had another impossible characteristic about it: not only was it stable, it was so completely stable that it wasn't even radioactive. It just sat there, looking exceedingly unmysterious, not even deigning to emit a smidgen of energy. At least, not when first tested. But a second test revealed positron emission, which a third baffled look confirmed. The trouble was that the third measurement showed an even higher level of radioactivity than the second one. The fourth was higher than the third. And so on and so on.

Nobody had ever heard of any element, of whatever atomic number or weight, that started off stable and then began to demonstrate a steadily increasing intensity of radioactivity. No one knew what was likely to happen, either, if the process continued unchecked, but the possibilities seemed pretty explosive. The best suggestion anyone had was to turn it to powder and mix it with radioactive tungsten. That worked for a little while, until the tungsten turned radioactive too. After that graphite was used, with somewhat better results, to damp down the strange element's output of energy. There were no explosions. But more and more plutonium-186 kept arriving.

The only explanation that made any sense – and it did not make *very* much sense – was that it was coming from some unknown and perhaps even unknowable place, some sort of parallel universe, where the laws of nature were different and the binding forces of the atom were so much more powerful that plutonium-186 could be a stable isotope.

Why they were sending odd lumps of plutonium-186 here was something that no one could begin to guess. An even more important question was how they could be made to stop doing it. The radioactive breakdown of the plutonium-186 would eventually transform it into ordinary osmium or tungsten, but the twenty positrons that each plutonium nucleus emitted in the course of that process encountered and annihilated an equal number of electrons. Our universe could afford to lose twenty electrons here and there, no doubt. It could probably afford to go on losing electrons at a constant rate for an astonishingly long time without noticing much difference. But sooner or later the shift towards an overall positive charge that this electron loss created would give rise to grave and perhaps incalculable problems of symmetry and energy conservation. Would the equilibrium of the universe break down? Would nuclear interactions begin to intensify? Would the stars – even the Sun – erupt into supernovas?

'This can't go on,' Fletcher said gloomily.

Hammond gave him a sour look. 'So? We've been saying that for six months now.'

'It's time to do something. They keep shipping us more and

more and more, and we don't have any idea how to go about telling them to cut it out.'

'We don't even have any idea whether they really exist,' Raymond Niklaus put in.

'Right now that doesn't matter. What matters is that the stuff is arriving constantly, and the more of it we have, the more dangerous it is. We don't have the foggiest idea of how to shut off the shipments. So we've got to find some way to get rid of it as it comes in.'

'And what do you have in mind, pray tell?' Hammond asked.

Fletcher said, glaring at his colleague in a way that conveyed the fact that he would brook no opposition, 'I'm going to talk to Asenion.'

Hammond guffawed. 'Asenion? You're crazy!'

'No. *He* is. But he's the only person who can help us.'

It was a sad case, the Asenion story, poignant and almost incomprehensible. One of the finest minds atomic physics had ever known, a man to rank with Rutherford, Bohr, Heisenberg, Fermi, Meitner. A Harvard degree at twelve, his doctorate from MIT five years later, after which he had poured forth a dazzling flow of technical papers that probed the deepest mysteries of the nuclear binding forces. As the twenty-first century entered its closing decades he had seemed poised to solve once and for all the eternal riddles of the universe. And then, at the age of twenty-eight, without having given the slightest warning, he walked away from the whole thing.

'I have lost interest,' he declared. 'Physics is no longer of any importance to me. Why should I concern myself with these issues of the way in which matter is constructed? How tiresome it all is! When one looks at the Parthenon, does one care what the columns are made of, or what sort of scaffolding was needed to put them in place? That the Parthenon exists, and is sublimely beautiful, is all that should interest us. So too with the universe. I see the universe, and it is beautiful and perfect. Why should I pry into the nature of its scaffolding? Why should anyone?'

And with that he resigned his professorship, burned his papers, and retreated to the thirty-third floor of an apartment building on Manhattan's West Side, where he built an elaborate laboratory-greenhouse in which he intended to conduct experiments in advanced horticulture.

'Bromeliads,' said Asenion. 'I will create hybrid bromeliads. Bromeliads will be the essence and centre of my life from now on.'

Romelmeyer, who had been Asenion's mentor at Harvard, attributed his apparent breakdown to overwork, and thought that he would snap back in six or eight months. Jantzen, who had had the rare privilege of being the first to read his astonishing dissertation at MIT, took an equally sympathetic position, arguing that Asenion must have come to some terrifying impasse in his work that had compelled him to retreat dramatically from the brink of madness. 'Perhaps he found himself looking right into an abyss of inconsistencies when he thought he was about to find the ultimate answers,' Jantzen suggested. 'What else could he do but run? But he won't run for long. It isn't in his nature.'

Burkhardt, of Cal Tech, whose own work had been carried out in the sphere that Asenion was later to make his own, agreed with Jantzen's analysis. 'He must have hit something really dark and hairy. But he'll wake up one morning with the solution in his head, and it'll be goodbye horticulture for him. He'll turn out a paper by noon that will revolutionize everything we think we know about nuclear physics, and that'll be that.'

But Jesse Hammond, who had played tennis with Asenion every morning for the last two years of his career as a physicist, took a less charitable position. 'He's gone nuts,' Hammond said. 'He's flipped out altogether, and he's never going to get himself together again.'

'You think?' said Lew Fletcher, who had been almost as close to Asenion as Hammond, but who was no tennis player.

Hammond smiled. 'No doubt of it. I began noticing a weird look in his eyes starting just about two years back. And then his playing started to turn weird too. He'd serve and not even look where he was serving. He'd double-fault without even caring. And you know what else? He didn't challenge me on a single out-of-bounds call the whole year. That was the key thing. Used to be, he'd fight me every call. Now he just didn't seem to care. He just let everything go by. He was completely indifferent. I said to myself, This guy must be flipping out.'

'Or working on some problem that seems more important to him than tennis.'

'Same thing,' said Hammond. 'No, Lew, I tell you – he's gone completely unglued. And nothing's going to glue him again.'

That conversation had taken place almost a year ago. Nothing had happened in the interim to change anyone's opinion. The astounding arrival of plutonium-186 in the world had not brought forth any comment from Asenion's Manhattan penthouse. The sudden solemn discussions of fantastic things like parallel universes by otherwise reputable physicists had apparently not aroused him either. He remained closeted with his bromeliads, high above the streets of Manhattan.

Well, maybe he *is* crazy, Fletcher thought. But his mind can't have shorted out entirely. And he might just have an idea or two left in him –

Asenion said, 'Well, you don't look a whole lot older, do you?'

Fletcher felt himself reddening. 'Jesus, Ike, it's only been eighteen months since we last saw each other!'

'Is that all?' Asenion said indifferently. 'It feels like a lot more to me.'

He managed a thin, remote smile. He didn't look very interested in Fletcher or in whatever it was that had brought Fletcher to his secluded eyrie.

Asenion had always been an odd one, of course – aloof, mysterious, with a faint but unmistakable air of superiority about him that nearly everyone found instantly irritating. Of course, he *was* superior. But he had made sure that he let you know it, and never seemed to care that others found the trait less than endearing.

He appeared more remote than ever, now, stranger and more alien. Outwardly he had not changed at all: the same slender, debonair figure, surprisingly handsome, even striking. Though rumour had it that he had not left his penthouse in more than a year, there was no trace of indoor pallor about him. His skin still had its rich deep olive colouring, almost swarthy, a Mediterranean tone. His hair, thick and dark, tumbled down rakishly over his broad forehead. But there was something different about his dark, gleaming eyes. The old Asenion, however preoccupied he might have been with some abstruse problem of advanced physics, had nearly always had a playful sparkle in his eyes, a kind of amiable devilish glint. This man, this horticultural recluse, wore a different expression altogether – ascetic, mist-shrouded, *absent*. His gaze was as bright as ever, but the brightness was a cold one that seemed to come from some far-off star.

Fletcher said, 'The reason I've come here – '

'We can go into all that later, can't we, Lew? First come into the greenhouse with me. There's something I want to show you. Nobody else has seen it yet, in fact.'

'Well, if you – '

'Insist, yes. Come. I promise you, it's extraordinary.'

He turned and led the way through the intricate pathways of the apartment. The sprawling many-roomed penthouse was furnished in the most offhand way, cheap student furniture badly cared for. Cats wandered everywhere, five, six, eight of them, sharpening their claws on the upholstery, prowling in empty closets whose doors stood ajar, peering down from the tops of bookcases containing jumbled heaps of coverless volumes. There was a rank smell of cat urine in the air.

But then suddenly Asenion turned a corridor and Fletcher, following just behind, found himself staring into what could have been an altogether different world. They had reached the entrance to the spectacular glass-walled extension that had been wrapped like an observation deck around the entire summit of the building. Beyond, dimly visible inside, Fletcher could see hundreds or perhaps thousands of strange-looking plants, some hanging from the ceiling, some mounted along the sides of wooden pillars, some rising in stepped array on benches, some growing out of beds set in the floor.

Asenion briskly tapped out the security-combination code on a diamond-shaped keyboard mounted in the wall, and the glass door slid silently back. A blast of warm humid air came forth.

'Quickly!' he said. 'Inside!'

It was like stepping straight into the Amazon jungle. In place of the harsh, dry atmosphere of a Manhattan apartment in midwinter there was, abruptly, the dense moist sweet closeness of the tropics, enfolding them like folds of wet fabric. Fletcher almost expected to hear parrots screeching overhead.

And the plants! The bizarre plants, clinging to every surface, filling every available square inch!

Most of them followed the same general pattern, rosettes of broad shining strap-shaped leaves radiating outward from a central cup-shaped structure deep enough to hold several ounces of water. But beyond that basic area of similarity they differed wildly from one another. Some were tiny, some were colossal. Some were marked with blazing stripes of yellow and red and purple that ran the length of their thick, succulent leaves. Some were mottled with fierce blotches of shimmering, assertive, bewilderingly complicated combinations of colour. Some, whose leaves were green, were a fiery scarlet or crimson, or a sombre, mysterious blue, at the place where the leaves came together to form the cup. Some were armed with formidable teeth and looked ready to feed on unwary visitors. Some were topped with gaudy spikes of strangely shaped brilliant-hued flowers taller than a man, which sprang like radiant spears from their centres.

Everything glistened. Everything seemed poised for violent, explosive growth. The scene was alien and terrifying. It was like looking into a vast congregation of hungry monsters. Fletcher had to remind himself that these were merely plants, hothouse specimens that probably wouldn't last half an hour in the urban environment outside.

'These are bromeliads,' Asenion said, shaping the word sensuously in his throat as though it were the finest word any language had ever produced. 'Tropical plants, mainly. South and Central America is where most of them live. They tend to cling to trees, growing high up in the forks of branches, mainly. Some live at ground level, though. Such as the bromeliad you know best, which is the pineapple. But there are hundreds of others in this room. Thousands. And this is the humid room, where I keep the guzmanias and the vrieseas and some of the aechmeas. As we go around, I'll show you the tillandsias – they like it a lot drier – and the terrestrial ones, the hechtias and the dyckias, and then over on the far side – '

'Ike,' Fletcher said quietly.

'You know I've never liked that name.'

'I'm sorry. I forgot.' That was a lie. Asenion's given name was Ichabod. Neither Fletcher nor anyone Fletcher knew had ever been able to bring himself to call him that. 'Look, I think what you've got here is wonderful. Absolutely wonderful. But I don't want to intrude on your time, and there's a very serious problem I need to discuss with – '

'First the plants,' Asenion said. 'Indulge me.' His eyes were glowing. In the half-light of the greenhouse he looked like a jungle creature himself, exotic, weird. Without a moment's hesitation, he pranced off down the aisle towards a group of oversized bromeliads near the outer wall. Willy-nilly, Fletcher followed.

Asenion gestured grandly.

'Here it is! Do you see? *Aechmea asenionii*! Discovered in north-western Brazil two years ago – I sponsored the expedition myself – of course, I never expected them to name it for me, but you know how these things sometimes happen – '

Fletcher stared. The plant was a giant among giants, easily two metres across from leaf-tip to leaf-tip. Its dark green leaves were banded with jagged pale scrawls that looked like the hieroglyphs of some lost race. Out of the central cup, which was the size of a man's head and deep enough to drown rabbits in, rose the strangest flower Fletcher ever hoped to see, a thick yellow stalk of immense length from which sprang something like a cluster of black thunderbolts tipped with ominous red globes like dangling moons. A pervasive odour of rotting flesh came from it.

'The only specimen in North America!' Asenion cried. 'Perhaps one of six or seven in the world. And I've succeeded in inducing it to bloom. There'll be seed, Lew, and perhaps there'll be offsets as well – I'll be able to propagate it, and cross it with others – can you imagine it crossed with *Aechmea chantinii*, Fletcher? Or perhaps an interspecific hybrid? With *Neoregelia carcharadon*, say? No. Of course you can't imagine it. What am I saying? But it would be spectacular beyond belief. Take my word for it.'

'I have no doubt.'

'It's a privilege, seeing this plant in bloom. But there are others here you must see too. The puyas – the pitcairnias – there's a clump of *Dyckia marnier-lapostollei* in the next room that you wouldn't believe – '

He bubbled with boyish enthusiasm. Fletcher forced himself to be patient. There was no help for it: he would simply have to take the complete tour.

It went on for what seemed like hours, as Asenion led him frantically from one peculiar plant to another, in room after room. Some were actually quite beautiful, Fletcher had to admit. Others seemed excessively flamboyant, or incomprehensibly ordinary to his untutored eye, or downright grotesque. What struck him most forcefully of all was the depth of Asenion's obsession. Nothing in the universe seemed to matter to him except this horde of exotic plants. He had given himself up totally to the strange world he had created here.

But at last even Asenion's manic energies seemed to flag. The pace had been merciless, and both he and Fletcher, drenched with sweat and gasping in the heat, paused for breath in a section of the greenhouse occupied by small grey gnarly plants that seemed to have no roots, and were held to the wall by barely visible wires.

Abruptly Asenion said, 'All right. You aren't interested anyway. Tell me what you came here to ask me, and then get on your way. I have all sorts of things to do this after-noon.'

'It's about plutonium-186,' Fletcher began.

'Don't be idiotic. That's not a legitimate isotope. It can't possibly exist.'

'I know,' Fletcher said. 'But it does.'

Quickly, almost desperately, he outlined the whole fantastic story for the young physicist-turned-botanist. The mysterious substitution of a strange element for tungsten or osmium in various laboratories, the tests indicating that its atomic number was that of plutonium but its atomic weight was far too low, the absurd but necessary theory that the stuff was a gift from some parallel universe and – finally – the fact that the new element, stable when it first arrived, rapidly began to undergo radioactive decay in a startlingly accelerative way.

Asenion's saturnine face was a study in changing emotions as Fletcher spoke. He seemed bored and irritated at first, then scornful, then, perhaps, furious; but not a word did he utter, and gradually the fury ebbed, turning to distant curiosity and then, finally, a kind of fascination. Or so Fletcher thought. He realized that he might be altogether wrong in his interpretations of what was going on in the unique, mercurial mind of the other man.

When Fletcher fell silent Asenion said, 'What are you most afraid of? Critical mass? Or cumulative electron loss?'

'We've dealt with the critical mass problem by powdering the stuff, shielding it in graphite, and scattering it in low con-centrations to fifty different storage points. But it keeps on coming in – they love to send it to us, it seems. And the thought that every atom of it is giving off positrons that go around looking for electrons to annihilate – ' Fletcher shrugged. 'On a small scale it's a useful energy pump, I suppose, tungsten swapped for plutonium with energy gained in each cycle. But on a large scale, as we continue to transfer electrons from our universe to theirs – '

'Yes,' Asenion said.

'So we need a way to dispose of – '

241

'Yes.' He looked at his watch. 'Where are you staying while you're in town, Fletcher?'

'The Faculty Club, as usual.'

'Good. I've got some crosses to make and I don't want to wait any longer, on account of possible pollen contamination. Go over to the Club and keep yourself amused for a few hours. Take a shower. God knows you need one: you smell like something out of the jungle. Relax, have a drink, come back at five o'clock. We can talk about this again then.' He shook his head. 'Plutonium-186! What lunacy! It offends me just to say it out loud. It's like saying – saying – well, *Billbergia yukonensis*, or *Tillandsia bostoniae*. Do you know what I mean? No. No. Of course you don't.' He waved his hands. 'Out! Come back at five!'

It was a long afternoon for Fletcher. He phoned his wife, he phoned Jesse Hammond at the laboratory, he phoned an old friend and made a date for dinner. He showered and changed. He had a drink in the ornate lounge on the Fifth Avenue side of the Club.

But his mood was grim, and not merely because Hammond had told him that another four kilograms of plutonium-186 had been reported from various regions that morning. Asenion's madness oppressed him.

There was nothing wrong with an interest in plants, of course. Fletcher kept a philodendron and something else, whose name he could never remember, in his own office. But to immerse yourself in one highly specialized field of botany with such intensity – it seemed sheer lunacy. No, Fletcher decided, even that was all right, difficult as it was for him to understand why anyone would want to spend his whole life cloistered with a bunch of eerie plants. What was hard for him to forgive was Asenion's renunciation of physics. A mind like that – the breadth of its vision – the insight Asenion had had into the greatest of mysteries – damn it, Fletcher thought, he had owed it to the world to stick to it! And instead, to walk away from everything, to hole himself up in a cage of glass –

Hammond's right, Fletcher told himself. Asenion really is crazy.

But it was useless to fret about it. Asenion was not the first supergenius to snap under contemplation of the Ultimate. His withdrawal from physics, Fletcher said sternly to himself, was a matter between Asenion and the universe. All that concerned Fletcher was getting Asenion's solution to the plutonium-186 problem; and then the poor man could be left with his bromeliads in peace.

About half past four Fletcher set out by cab to battle the traffic the short distance uptown to Asenion's place.

Luck was with him. He arrived at ten to five. Asenion's house-robot greeted him solemnly and invited him to wait. 'The master is in the greenhouse,' the robot declared. 'He will be with you when he has completed the pollination.'

Fletcher waited. And waited and waited.

Geniuses, he thought bitterly. Pains in the neck, all of them. Pains in the –

Just then the robot reappeared. It was half past six. All was blackness outside the window. Fletcher's dinner date was for seven. He would never make it.

'The master will see you now,' said the robot.

Asenion looked limp and weary, as though he had spent the entire afternoon smashing up boulders. But the formidable edge seemed gone from him, too. He greeted Fletcher with a pleasant enough smile, offered a word or two of almost-apology for his tardiness, and even had the robot bring Fletcher a sherry. It wasn't very good sherry, but to get anything at all to drink in a teetotaller's house was a blessing, Fletcher figured.

Asenion waited until Fletcher had had a few sips. Then he said, 'I have your answer.'

'I knew you would.'

There was a long silence.

'Thiotimoline,' said Asenion finally.

'Thiotimoline?'

243

'Absolutely. Endochronic disposal. It's the only way. And, as you'll see, it's a *necessary* way.'

Fletcher took a hasty gulp of the sherry. Even when he was in a relatively mellow mood, it appeared, Asenion was maddening. And mad. What was this new craziness now? Thiotimoline? How could that preposterous substance, as insane in its way as plutonium-186, have any bearing on the problem?

Asenion said, 'I take it you know the special properties of thiotimoline?'

'Of course. Its molecule is distorted into adjacent temporal dimensions. Extends into the future, and, I think, into the past. Thiotimoline powder will dissolve in water one second *before* the water is added.'

'Exactly,' Asenion said. 'And if the water isn't added, it'll go looking for it. In the future.'

'What does this have to do with – '

'Look here,' said Asenion. He drew a scrap of paper from his shirt pocket. 'You want to get rid of something. You put it in this container here. You surround the container with a shell made of polymerized thiotimoline. You surround the shell with a water tank that will deliver water to the thiotimoline on a timed basis, and you set your timer so that the water is due to arrive a few seconds from now. But at the last moment the timing device withholds the water.'

Fletcher stared at the younger man in awe.

Asenion said, 'The water is always about to arrive, but never quite does. The thiotimoline making up the plastic shell is pulled forward one second into the future to encounter the water. The water has a high probability of being there, but not quite high enough. It's actually another second away from delivery, and always will be. The thiotimoline gets dragged farther and farther into the future. The world goes forward into the future at a rate of one second per second, but the thiotimoline's velocity is essentially infinite. And of course it carries with it the inner container, too.'

'In which we have put our surplus plutonium-186.'

'Or anything else you want to dispose of,' said Asenion.

Fletcher felt dizzy. 'Which will travel on into the future at an infinite rate – '

'Yes. And because the rate is infinite, the problem of the breakdown of thiotimoline into its stable isochronic form, which has hampered most time-transport experiments, isn't an issue. Something travelling through time at an infinite velocity isn't subject to little limitations of that kind. It'll simply keep going until it can't go any farther.'

'But how does sending it into the future solve the problem?' Fletcher asked. 'The plutonium-186 still stays in our universe, even if we've bumped it away from our immediate temporal vicinity. The electron loss continues. Maybe even gets worse, under temporal acceleration. We still haven't dealt with the fundamental – '

'You never were much of a thinker, were you, Fletcher?' said Asenion quietly, almost gently. But the savage contempt in his eyes had the force of a sun going nova.

'I do my best. But I don't see – '

Asenion sighed. 'The thiotimoline will chase the water in the outer container to the end of time, carrying with it the plutonium in the inner container. To the end of time. *Literally*.'

'And?'

'What happens at the end of time, Fletcher?'

'Why – absolute entropy – the heat-death of the universe – '

'Precisely. The Final Entropic Solution. All molecules equally distributed throughout space. There will be no further place for the water-seeking thiotimoline to go. The end of the line is the end of the line. It, and the plutonium it's hauling with it, and the water it's trying to catch up with, will all plunge together over the entropic brink into anti-time.'

'Anti-time,' said Fletcher in a leaden voice. 'Anti-time?'

'Naturally. Into the moment before the creation of the universe. Everything is in stasis. Zero time, infinite temperature. All the universal mass contained in a single incomprehensible body. Then the thiotimoline and the plutonium and the water arrive.' Asenion's eyes were radiant. His face was flushed. He waved his scrap of paper around as though it were the scripture of some new creed. 'There will be a tremendous explosion. A Big Bang, so to speak. The beginning of all things. You – or should I say I? – will be responsible for the birth of the universe.'

Fletcher, stunned, said after a moment, 'Are you serious?'

'I am never anything but serious. You have your solution. Pack up your plutonium and send it on its way. No matter how many shipments you make, they'll all arrive at the same instant. And with the same effect. You have no choice, you know. The plutonium *must* be disposed of. And – ' His eyes twinkled with some of the old Asenion playfulness. 'The universe *must* be created, or else how will any of us get to be where we are? And this is how it was done. *Will* be done. Inevitable, ineluctable, unavoidable, mandatory. Yes? You see?'

'Well, no. Yes. Maybe. That is, I think I do,' said Fletcher, as if in a daze.

'Good. Even if you don't, you will.'

'I'll need – to talk to the others – '

'Of course you will. That's how you people do things. That's why I'm here and you're there.' Asenion shrugged. 'Well, no hurry about it. Create the universe tomorrow, create it the week after next, what's the difference? It'll get done sooner or later. It has to, because it already has been done. You see?'

'Yes. Of course. Of – course. And now – if you'll excuse me – ' Fletcher murmured. 'I – ah – have a dinner appointment in a little while – '

'That can wait too, can't it?' said Asenion, smiling with sudden surprising amiability. He seemed genuinely glad to have been of assistance. 'There's something I forgot to show you this afternoon. A remarkable plant, possibly unique – a nidularium, it is, Brazilian, not even named yet, as a matter of fact – just coming into bloom. And this one – wait till you see it, Fletcher, wait till you see it – '

A Sleep and a Forgetting

The Benford-Greenberg alternate-universe anthology, *What Might Have Been*, was followed by a second volume of similar stories. The first had concentrated on alterations of a single historical event; this one dealt with changes in the lives of great history-making individuals. Again I was invited to contribute; and the individual I chose to write about was Genghis Khan.

His name, of course, has come to be used as an archetype of the monstrous looting-and-plundering barbarian chieftain. Indeed he probably wasn't a nice sort of person, and it's certainly all right with me that the twentieth century, amidst its Hitlers and Stalins and Khomeinis and such, hasn't had to deal with Genghis Khan as well. But the historical truth is that he was not merely an invincible conqueror but a complex and intelligent leader, an empire-builder who followed a distinctive plan of conquest which not only created a vast realm but also brought governmental order where only chaos had been. I'd like to think that he had more in common with Augustus Caesar or Alexander the Great than he did with the classic butchers of history.

But the Mongol Empire's limitations – the limitations inherent in having a family-controlled élite of nomadic horsemen trying to rule vast bureaucratic states – eventually set bounds on the ambitions of Genghis and his descendants. What, I asked myself, would the world have been like if Genghis Khan, that singular man of formidable drive and energy, hadn't been raised as a Mongol nomad at all, but as a civilized city-dweller – as a Byzantine Christian, say? That was the point from which this story appeared. Alice Turner bought it for *Playboy*, and Don Wollheim chose it for his

247

best-of-the-year anthology, an honour in which, as I've already pointed out, I always take special pleasure.

'Channelling?' I said. 'For Christ's sake, Joe! You brought me all the way down here for dumb bullshit like that?'

'This isn't channelling,' Joe said.

'The kid who drove me from the airport said you've got a machine that can talk with dead people.'

A slow, angry flush spread across Joe's face. He's a small, compact man with very glossy skin and very sharp features, and when he's annoyed he inflates like a puff-adder.

'He shouldn't have said that.'

'Is that what you're doing here?' I asked. 'Some sort of channelling experiments?'

'Forget that shithead word, will you, Mike?' Joe sounded impatient and irritable. But there was an odd fluttery look in his eye, conveying – what? Uncertainty? Vulnerability? Those were traits I hadn't ever associated with Joe Hedley, not in the thirty years we'd known each other. 'We aren't sure what the fuck we're doing here,' he said. 'We thought maybe you could tell us.'

'Me?'

'You, yes. Here, put the helmet on. Come on, put it on, Mike. Put it on. Please.'

I stared. Nothing ever changes. Ever since we were kids Joe's been using me for one cockeyed thing or another, because he knows he can count on me to give him a sober-minded common-sense opinion. Always bouncing this bizarre scheme or that off me, so he can measure the caroms.

The helmet was a golden strip of wire mesh studded with a row of microwave pickups the size of a dime and flanked by a pair of suction electrodes that fit over the temples. It looked like some vagrant piece of death-house equipment.

I ran my fingers over it. 'How much current is this thing capable of sending through my head?'

He looked even angrier. 'Oh, fuck you, you hypercautious

bastard! Would I ever ask you to do anything that could harm you?'

With a patient little sigh I said, 'Okay. How do I do this?'

'Ear to ear, over the top of your head. I'll adjust the electrodes for you.'

'You won't tell me what any of this is all about?'

'I want an uncontaminated response. That's science talk, Mike. I'm a scientist. You know that, don't you?'

'So that's what you are. I wondered.'

Joe bustled about above me, moving the helmet around, pressing the electrodes against my skull.

'How does it fit?'

'Like a glove.'

'You always wear your gloves on your head?' he asked.

'You must be goddamn nervous if you think that's funny.'

'I am,' he said. 'You must be too, if you take a line like that seriously. But I tell you that you won't get hurt. I promise you that, Mike.'

'All right.'

'Just sit down here. We need to check the impedances, and then we can get going.'

'I wish I understood at least a little bit about – '

'Please,' he said. He gestured through a glass partition at a technician in the adjoining room, and she began to do things with dials and switches. This was turning into a movie, a very silly one, full of mad doctors in white jackets and sputtering electrical gadgets. The tinkering went on and on, and I felt myself passing beyond apprehension and annoyance into a kind of grey realm of Zen serenity, the way I sometimes do while sitting in the dentist's chair waiting for the scraping and poking to begin.

On the hillside visible from the laboratory window yellow hibiscus was blooming against a background of billowing scarlet bougainvillaea in brilliant California sunshine. It had been cold and raining, this February morning, when I drove to Sea-Tac Airport thirteen hundred miles to the north. Hedley's lab is just outside La Jolla, on a sandy bluff high up over the blue

Pacific. When Joe and I were kids growing up in Santa Monica we took this kind of luminous winter day for granted, but I had lived in the Northwest for twenty years now, and I couldn't help thinking I'd gone on a day-trip to Eden. I studied the colours on the hillside until my eyes began to get blurry.

'Here we go, now,' Joe said, from a point somewhere far away behind my left shoulder.

It was like stepping into a big cage full of parakeets and mynahs and crazed macaws. I heard scratchy screeching sounds, and a harsh loony almost-laughter that soared through three or four octaves, and a low ominous burbling noise, as if some hydraulic device was about to blow a gasket. I heard weird wire-edged shrieks that went tumbling away as though the sound was falling through an infinite abyss. I heard queeblings. I heard hissings.

Then came a sudden burst of clearly enunciated syllables, floating in isolation above the noise:

– *Onoodor* –

That startled me.

A nonsense word? No, no, a real one, one that had meaning for me, a word in an obscure language that I just happen to understand.

'Today,' that's what it means. In Khalkha. My speciality. But it was crazy that this machine would be speaking Khalkha to me. This had to be some sort of coincidence. What I'd heard was a random clumping of sounds that I must automatically have arranged into a meaningful pattern. I was kidding myself. Or else Joe was playing an elaborate practical joke. Only he seemed very serious.

I strained to hear more. But everything was babble again.

Then, out of the chaos:

– *Usan deer* –

Khalkha, again: 'On the water.' It couldn't be a coincidence. More noise. Skwkaark skreek yubble gobble.

– *Aawa namaig yawuulawa* –

'Father sent me.'

Skwkaark. Yabble. Eeeeesh.

'Go on,' I said. I felt sweat rolling down my back. 'Your father sent you where? Where? *Khaana*. Tell me where.'

– *Usan deer* –

'On the water, yes.'

Yarkhh. Skreek. Tshhhhhhh.

– *Akhanartan* –

'To his elder brother. Yes.'

I closed my eyes and let my mind rove out into the darkness. It drifted on a sea of scratchy noise. Now and again I caught an actual syllable, half a syllable, a slice of a word, a clipped fragment of meaning. The voice was brusque, forceful, a drill-sergeant voice, carrying an undertone of barely suppressed rage.

Somebody very angry was speaking to me across a great distance, over a channel clotted with interference, in a language that hardly anyone in the United States knew anything about: Khalkha. Spoken a little oddly, with an unfamiliar intonation, but plainly recognizable.

I said, speaking very slowly and carefully and trying to match the odd intonation of the voice at the other end, 'I can hear you and I can understand you. But there's a lot of interference. Say everything three times and I'll try to follow.'

I waited. But now there was only a roaring silence in my ears. Not even the shrieking, not even the babble.

I looked up at Hedley like someone coming out of a trance. 'It's gone dead.'

'You sure?'

'I don't hear anything, Joe.'

He snatched the helmet from me and put it on, fiddling with the electrodes in that edgy, compulsively precise way of his. He listened for a moment, scowled, nodded. 'The relay satellite must have passed around the far side of the sun. We won't get anything more for hours if it has.'

'The relay satellite? Where the hell was that broadcast coming from?'

'In a minute,' he said. He reached around and took the helmet off. His eyes had a brassy gleam and his mouth was

251

twisted off to the corner of his face, almost as if he'd had a stroke. 'You were actually able to understand what he was saying, weren't you?'

I nodded.

'I knew you would. And was he speaking Mongolian?'

'Khalkha, yes. The main Mongolian dialect.'

The tension left his face. He gave me a warm, loving grin. 'I was sure you'd know. We had a man in from the university here, the comparative linguistics department – you probably know him, Malmstrom's his name – and he said it sounded to him like an Altaic language, maybe Turkic – is that right, Turkic? – but more likely one of the Mongolian languages, and the moment he said Mongolian I thought, That's it, get Mike down here right away – ' He paused. 'So it's the language that they speak in Mongolia right this very day, would you say?'

'Not quite. His accent was a little strange. Something stiff about it, almost archaic.'

'Archaic.'

'It had that feel, yes. I can't tell you why. There's just something formal and old-fashioned about it, something, well – '

'Archaic,' Hedley said again. Suddenly there were tears in his eyes. I couldn't remember ever having seen him crying before.

What they have, the kid who picked me up at the airport had said, *is a machine that lets them talk with the dead.*

'Joe?' I said. 'Joe, what in God's name is this all about?'

We had dinner that night in a sleek restaurant on a sleek, quiet La Jolla street of elegant shops and glossy-leaved trees, just the two of us, the first time in a long while that we'd gone out alone like that. Lately we tended to see each other once or twice a year at most, and Joe, who is almost always between marriages, would usually bring along his latest squeeze, the one who was finally going to bring order and stability and other such things to his tempestuous private life. And since he always needs to show the new one what a remarkable human being he is, he's forever putting on a performance, for the woman, for me, for the waiters, for the people at the nearby tables. Generally the fun's at my expense, for compared with Hedley I'm very staid and proper and I'm eighteen years into my one and only marriage so far, and Joe often seems to enjoy making me feel that there's something wrong with that. I never see him with the same woman twice, except when he happens to marry one of them. But tonight it was all different. He was alone, and the conversation was subdued and gentle and rueful, mostly about the years we'd put in knowing each other, the fun we'd had, the regret Joe felt during the occasional long periods when we didn't see much of each other. He did most of the talking. There was nothing new about that. But mostly it was just chatter. We were three quarters of the way down the bottle of silky Cabernet before Joe brought himself around to the topic of the experiment. I hadn't wanted to push.

'It was pure serendipity,' he said. 'You know, the art of finding what you're not looking for. We were trying to clean up some problems in radio transmission from the Icarus relay station – that's the one that the Japs and the French hung around the Sun inside the orbit of Mercury – and we were fiddling with this and fiddling with that, sending out an assortment of test signals at a lot of different frequencies, when out of nowhere we got a voice coming back at us. A man's voice. Speaking a strange language. Which turned out to be Chaucerian English.'

'Some kind of academic prank?' I suggested.

He looked annoyed. 'I don't think so. But let me tell it, Mike, okay? Okay?' He cracked his knuckles and rearranged the knot of his tie. 'We listened to this guy and gradually we figured out a little of what he was saying and we called in a grad student from UCSD who confirmed it – thirteenth-century English – and it absolutely knocked us on our asses.' He tugged at his earlobes and rearranged his tie again. A sort of manic sheen was coming into his eyes. 'Before we could even begin to comprehend what we were dealing with, the Englishman was gone and we were picking up some woman making a speech in medieval French. Like we were getting a broadcast from

Joan of Arc, do you see? Not that I'm arguing that that's who she was. We had her for half an hour, a minute here and a minute there with a shitload of interference, and then came a solar flare that disrupted communications, and when we had things tuned again we got a quick burst of what turned out to be Arabic, and then someone else talking in Middle English, and then, last week, this absolutely incomprehensible stuff, which Malmstrom guessed was Mongolian and you have now confirmed. The Mongol has stayed on the line longer than all the others put together.'

'Give me some more wine,' I said.

'I don't blame you. It's made us all crazy too. The best we can explain it to ourselves, it's that our beam passes through the Sun, which as I think you know, even though your speciality happens to be Chinese history and not physics, is a place where the extreme concentration of mass creates some unusual stresses on the fabric of the continuum, and some kind of relativistic force warps the hell out of it, so that the solar field sends our signal kinking off into God knows where, and the effect is to give us a telephone line to the Middle Ages. If that sounds like gibberish to you, imagine how it sounds to us.' Hedley spoke without raising his head, while moving his silverware around busily from one side of his plate to the other. 'You see now about channelling? It's no fucking joke. Shit, we *are* channelling, only looks like it might actually be real, doesn't it?'

'I see,' I said. 'So at some point you're going to have to call up the Secretary of Defence and say, Guess what, we've been getting telephone calls on the Icarus beam from Joan of Arc. And then they'll shut down your lab here and send you off to get your heads replumbed.'

He stared at me. His nostrils flickered contemptuously.

'Wrong. Completely wrong. You never had any notion of flair, did you? The sensational gesture that knocks everybody out? No. Of course not. Not *you*. Look, Mike, if I can go in there and say, We can talk to the dead, and we can *prove* it, they'll kiss our asses for us. Don't you see how fucking sensational it would be, something coming out of these government labs that ordinary people can actually understand and cheer and yell about? Telephone line to the past! George Washington himself, talking to Mr and Mrs America! Abe Lincoln! Something straight out of the *National Enquirer*, right, only *real*? We'd all be heroes. But it's got to be real, that's the kicker. We don't need a rational explanation for it, at least not right away. All it has to do is work. Christ, ninety-nine per cent of the people don't even know why electric lights light up when you flip the switch. We have to find out what we really have and get to understand it at least a little and be two hundred per cent sure of ourselves. And then we present it to Washington and we say, Here, this is what we did and this is what happens, and don't blame us if it seems crazy. But we have to keep it absolutely to ourselves until we understand enough of what we've stumbled on to be able to explain it to them with confidence. If we do it right we're goddamned kings of the world. A Nobel would be just the beginning. You understand now?'

'Maybe we should get another bottle of wine,' I said.

We were back in the lab by midnight. I followed Hedley through a maze of darkened rooms, ominous with mysterious equipment glowing in the night.

A dozen or so staffers were on duty. They smiled wanly at Hedley as if there was nothing unusual about his coming back to work at this hour.

'Doesn't anyone sleep around here?' I asked.

'It's a twenty-four-hour information world,' Joe said. 'We'll be recapturing the Icarus beam in forty-three minutes. You want to hear some of the earlier tapes?'

He touched a switch and from an unseen speaker came crackles and bleebles and then a young woman's voice, strong and a little harsh, uttering brief blurts of something that sounded like strange singsong French, to me not at all understandable.

'Her accent's terrible,' I said. 'What's she saying?'

'It's too fragmentary to add up to anything much. She's

255

praying, mostly. May the king live, may God strengthen his arm, something like that. For all we know it *is* Joan of Arc. We haven't got more than a few minutes' total coherent verbal output out of any of them, usually a lot less. Except for the Mongol. He goes on and on. It's like he doesn't want to let go of the phone.'

'And it really is a phone?' I asked. 'What we say here, they can hear there?'

'We don't know that, because we haven't been able to make much sense out of what they say, and by the time we get it deciphered we've lost contact. But it's got to be a two-way contact. They must be getting *something* from us, because we're able to get their attention somehow and they talk back to us.'

'They receive your signal without a helmet?'

'The helmet's just for your benefit. The actual Icarus signal comes in digitally. The helmet's the interface between our computer and your ears.'

'Medieval people don't have digital computers either, Joe.'

A muscle started popping in one of his cheeks. 'No, they don't,' he said. 'It must come like a voice out of the sky. Or right inside their heads. But they hear us.'

'How?'

'Do I know? You want this to make sense, Mike? *Nothing* about this makes sense. Let me give you an example. You were talking with that Mongol, weren't you? You asked him something and he answered you?'

'Yes. But – '

'Let me finish. What did you ask him?'

'He said his father sent him somewhere. I asked him where, and he said, On the water. To visit his elder brother.'

'He answered you right away?'

'Yes,' I said.

'Well, that's actually impossible. The Icarus is ninety-three million miles from here. There has to be something like an eight-minute time-lag in radio transmission. You follow? You ask him something and it's eight minutes before the beam reaches Icarus, and eight minutes more for his answer to come back. He sure as hell can't hold a real-time conversation with you. But you say he was.'

'It may only have seemed that way. It could just have been coincidence that what I asked and what he happened to say next fit together like question and response.'

'Maybe. Or maybe whatever kink in time we're operating across eats up the lag for us, too. I tell you, nothing makes sense about this. But one way or another the beam is reaching them and it carries coherent information. I don't know why that is. It just is. Once you start dealing in impossible stuff, anything might be true. So why can't our voices come out of thin air to them?' Hedley laughed nervously. Or perhaps it was a cough, I thought. 'The thing is,' he went on, 'this Mongol is staying on line longer than any of the others, so with you here we have a chance to have some real communication with him. You speak his language. You can validate this whole goddamn, grotesque event for us, do you see? You can have an honest-to-God chat with some guy who lived six hundred years ago, and find out where he really is and what he thinks is going on, and tell us all about it.'

I stole a glance at the wall clock. Half past twelve. I couldn't remember the last time I'd been up this late. I lead a nice quiet tenured life, full professor thirteen years now, University of Washington Department of Sinological Studies.

'We're about ready to acquire signal again,' Hedley said. 'Put the helmet on.'

I slipped it into place. I thought about that little communications satellite chugging around the Sun, swimming through inconceivable heat and unthinkable waves of hard radiation and somehow surviving, coming around the far side now, beaming electromagnetic improbabilities out of the distant past at my head.

The squawking and screeching began.

Then, emerging from the noise and murk and sonic darkness, came the Mongol's voice, clear and steady:

'Where are you, you voice, you? Speak to me.'

'Here,' I said. 'Can you hear me?'

Aark. Yaaarp. Tshhhhhhh.

The Mongol said, 'Voice, what are you? Are you mortal or are you a prince of the Master?'

I wrestled with the puzzling words. I'm fluent enough in Khalkha, though I don't get many opportunities for speaking it, but there was a problem of context here.

'Which master?' I asked finally. 'What prince?'

'There is only one Master,' said the Mongol. He said this with tremendous force and assurance, putting terrific spin on every syllable, and the capital letter was apparent in his tone. 'I am his servant. The *angeloi* are his princes. Are you an *angelos*, voice?'

Angeloi? That was Greek. A Mongol, asking me if I was an angel of God?

'Not an angel, no,' I said.

'Then how can you speak to me this way?'

'It's a kind of – ' I paused. I couldn't come up with the Khalka for 'miracle'. After a moment I said, 'It's by the grace of heaven on high. I'm speaking to you from far away.'

'How far?'

'Tell me where you are.'

Skrawwwwk. Tshhhhhh.

'Again. Where are you?'

'Nova Roma. Constantinopolis.'

I blinked. 'Byzantium?'

'Byzantium, yes.'

'I am very far from there.'

'*How* far?' the Mongol said fiercely.

'Many many days' ride. Many many.' I hesitated. 'Tell me what year it is, where you are.'

Vzsqkk. Blzzp. Yiiiiiik.

'What's he saying to you?' Hedley asked. I waved at him furiously to be quiet.

'The year,' I said again. 'Tell me what year it is.'

The Mongol said scornfully, 'Everyone knows the year, voice.'

'Tell me.'

'It is the year 1187 of our Saviour.'

I began to shiver. Our Saviour? Weirder and weirder, I thought. A Christian Mongol? Living in Byzantium? Talking to me on the space telephone out of the twelfth century? The room around me took on a smoky, insubstantial look. My elbows were aching, and something was throbbing just above my left cheekbone. This had been a long day for me. I was very tired. I was heading into that sort of weariness where walls melted and bones turned soft. Joe was dancing around in front of me like someone with tertiary St Vitus's.

'And your name?' I said.

'I am Petros Alexios.'

'Why do you speak Khalkha if you are Greek?'

A long silence, unbroken even by the hellish static.

'I am not Greek,' came the reply finally. 'I am by birth Khalkha Mongol, but raised Christian among the Christians from age eleven, when my father sent me on the water and I was taken. My name was Temujin. Now I am twenty and I know the Saviour.'

I gasped and put my hand to my throat as though it had been skewered out of the darkness by a spear.

'Temujin,' I said, barely getting the word out.

'My father was Yesugei the chieftain.'

'Temujin,' I said again. 'Son of Yesugei.' I shook my head. Aaark. Blzzzp. Tshhhhhh.

Then no static, no voice, only the hushed hiss of silence.

'Are you okay?' Hedley asked.

'We've lost contact, I think.'

'Right. It just broke. You look like your brain has shorted out.'

I slipped the helmet off. My hands were shaking.

'You know,' I said, 'maybe that French woman really was Joan of Arc.'

'What?'

I shrugged. 'She really might have been,' I said wearily. 'Anything's possible, isn't it?'

'What the hell are you trying to tell me, Mike?'

'Why shouldn't she have been Joan of Arc?' I asked. 'Listen, Joe. This is making me just as nutty as you are. You know what I've just been doing? I've been talking to Genghis Khan on this fucking telephone of yours.'

I managed to get a few hours of sleep by simply refusing to tell Hedley anything else until I'd had a chance to rest. The way I said it, I left him no options, and he seemed to grasp that right away. At the hotel, I sank from consciousness like a leaden whale, hoping I wouldn't surface again before noon, but old habit seized me and pushed me up out of the tepid depths at seven, irreversibly awake and not a bit less depleted. I put in a quick call to Seattle to tell Elaine that I was going to stay down in La Jolla a little longer than expected. She seemed worried – not that I might be up to any funny business, not me, but only that I sounded so groggy. 'You know Joe,' I said. 'For him it's a twenty-four-hour information world.' I told her nothing else. When I stepped out on the breakfast patio half an hour later, I could see the lab's blue van already waiting in the hotel lot to pick me up.

Hedley seemed to have slept at the lab. He was rumpled and red-eyed but somehow he was at normal functioning level, scurrying around the place like a yappy little dog. 'Here's a printout of last night's contact,' he said, the moment I came in. 'I'm sorry if the transcript looks cockeyed. The computer doesn't know how to spell in Mongolian.' He shoved it into my hands. 'Take a squint at it and see if you really heard all the things you thought you heard.'

I peered at the single long sheet. It seemed to be full of jabberwocky, but once I figured out the computer's system of phonetic equivalents I could read it readily enough. I looked up after a moment, feeling very badly shaken.

'I was hoping I dreamed all this. I didn't.'

'You want to explain it to me?'

'I can't.'

Joe scowled. 'I'm not asking for fundamental existential analysis. Just give me a goddamned translation, all right?'

'Sure,' I said.

He listened with a kind of taut, explosive attention that seemed to me to be masking a mixture of uneasiness and bubbling excitement. When I was done he said, 'Okay. What's this Genghis Khan stuff?'

'Temujin was Genghis Khan's real name. He was born around 1167 and his father Yesugei was a minor chief somewhere in north-eastern Mongolia. When Temujin was still a boy, his father was poisoned by enemies, and he became a fugitive, but by the time he was fifteen he started putting together a confederacy of Mongol tribes, hundreds of them, and eventually he conquered everything in sight. Genghis Khan means "Ruler of the Universe".'

'So? Our Mongol lives in Constantinople, you say. He's a Christian and he uses a Greek name.'

'He's Temujin, son of Yesugei. He's twenty years old in the year when Genghis Khan was twenty years old.'

Hedley looked belligerent. 'Some other Temujin. Some other Yesugei.'

'Listen to the way he speaks. He's scary. Even if you can't understand a word of what he's saying, can't you feel the power in him? The coiled-up anger? That's the voice of somebody capable of conquering whole continents.'

'Genghis Khan wasn't a Christian. Genghis Khan wasn't kidnapped by strangers and taken to live in Constantinople.'

'I know,' I said. To my own amazement I added, 'But maybe this one was.'

'Jesus God Almighty. What's that supposed to mean?'

'I'm not certain.'

Hedley's eyes took on a glaze. 'I hoped you were going to be part of the solution, Mike. Not part of the problem.'

'Just let me think this through,' I said, waving my hands above his face as if trying to conjure some patience into him. Joe was peering at me in a stunned, astounded way. My eyeballs throbbed. Things were jangling up and down along my spinal column. Lack of sleep had coated my brain with a hard crust of adrenaline. Bewilderingly strange ideas were rising like sewer gases in my mind and making weird bubbles. 'All right, try this,' I said at last. 'Say that there are all sorts of possible worlds. A world in which you're King of England, a world in which I played third base for the Yankees, a world in which the dinosaurs never died out and Los Angeles gets invaded every summer by hungry tyrannosaurs. And one world where Yesugei's son Temujin wound up in twelfth-century Byzantium as a Christian instead of founding the Mongol Empire. And that's the Temujin I've been talking to. This cockeyed beam of yours not only crosses time-lines, somehow it crosses probability-lines too, and we've fished up some alternate reality that – '

'I don't believe this,' Hedley said.

'Neither do I, really. Not seriously. I'm just putting forth one possible hypothesis that might explain – '

'I don't mean your fucking hypothesis. I mean I find it hard to believe that you of all people, my old pal Mike Michaelson, can be standing here running off at the mouth this way, working hard at turning a mystifying event into a goddamned nonsensical one – you, good old sensible steady Mike, telling me some shit about tyrannosaurs amok in Los Angeles – '

'It was only an example of – '

'Oh, fuck your example,' Hedley said. His face darkened with exasperation bordering on fury. He looked ready to cry. 'Your example is absolute crap. Your example is garbage. You know, man, if I wanted someone to feed me a lot of New Age crap I didn't have to go all the way to Seattle to find one. Alternate realities! Third base for the Yankees!'

A girl in a lab coat appeared out of nowhere and said, 'We have signal acquisition, Dr Hedley.'

I said, 'I'll catch the next plane north, okay?'

Joe's face was red and starting to do its puff-adder trick and his Adam's apple bobbed as if trying to find the way out.

'I wasn't trying to mess up your head,' I said. 'I'm sorry if I did. Forget everything I was just saying. I hope I was at least of some help, anyway.'

Something softened in Joe's eyes.

'I'm so goddamned tired, Mike.'

'I know.'

'I didn't mean to yell at you like that.'

'No offence taken, Joe.'

'But I have trouble with this alternate-reality thing of yours. You think it was easy for me to believe that what we were doing here was talking to people in the past? But I brought myself around to it, weird though it was. Now you give it an even weirder twist, and it's too much. It's too fucking much. It violates my sense of what's right and proper and fitting. You know what Occam's Razor is, Mike? The old medieval axiom, *Never multiply hypotheses needlessly*? Take the simplest one. Here even the simplest one is crazy. You push it too far.'

'Listen,' I said, 'if you'll just have someone drive me over to the hotel – '

'No.'

'No?'

'Let me think a minute,' he said. 'Just because it doesn't make sense doesn't mean that it's impossible, right? And if we get one impossible thing, we can have two, or six, or sixteen. Right? Right?' His eyes were like two black holes with cold stars blazing at their bottoms. 'Hell, we aren't at the point where we need to worry about explanations. We have to find out the basic stuff first. Mike, I don't want you to leave. I want you to stay here.'

'What?'

'Don't go. Please. I still need somebody to talk to the Mongol for me. Don't go. Please, Mike? Please?'

The times, Temujin said, were very bad. The infidels under Saladin had smashed the Crusader forces in the Holy Land and Jerusalem itself had fallen to the Moslems. Christians everywhere mourn the loss, said Temujin. In Byzantium – where Temujin was captain of the guards in the private army of a prince named Theodore Lascaris – God's grace seemed also to have been withdrawn. The great empire was in heavy weather. Insurrections had brought down two emperors in the past four years and the current man was weak and timid. The provinces of Hungary, Cyprus, Serbia, and Bulgaria were all in revolt. The Normans of Sicily were chopping up Byzantine Greece and on the other side of the empire the Seljuk Turks were chewing their way through Asia Minor. 'It is the time of the wolf,' said Temujin. 'But the sword of the Lord will prevail.'

The sheer force of him was astounding. It lay not so much in what he said, although that was sharp and fierce, as in the way he said it. I could feel the strength of the man in the velocity and impact of each syllable. Temujin hurled his words as if from a catapult. They arrived carrying a crackling electrical charge. Talking with him was like holding live cables in my hands.

Hedley, jigging and fidgeting around the lab, paused now and then to stare at me with what looked like awe and wonder in his eyes, as if to say, *You really can make sense of this stuff*? I smiled at him. I felt bizarrely cool and unflustered. Sitting there with some electronic thing on my head, letting that terrific force go hurtling through my brain. Discussing twelfth-century politics with an invisible Byzantine Mongol. Making small talk with Genghis Khan. All right. I could handle it.

I beckoned for notepaper. *Need printout of world historical background late twelfth century*, I scrawled, without interrupting my conversation with Temujin. *Esp. Byzantine history, Crusades, etc.*

The kings of England and France, said Temujin, were talking about launching a new Crusade. But at the moment they happened to be at war with each other, which made cooperation difficult. The powerful Emperor Frederick Barbarossa of Germany was also supposed to be getting up a Crusade, but that, he said, might mean more trouble for Byzantium than for the Saracens, because Frederick was the friend of Byzantium's enemies in the rebellious provinces, and he'd have to march through those provinces on the way to the Holy Land.

'It is a perilous time,' I agreed.

Then suddenly I was feeling the strain. Temujin's rapid-fire delivery was exhausting to follow, he spoke Mongolian with what I took to be a Byzantine accent, and he sprinkled his statements with the names of emperors, princes, and even nations that meant nothing to me. Also there was that powerful force of him to contend with – it hit you like an avalanche – and beyond that his anger: the whipcrack inflection that seemed the thinnest of bulwarks against some unstated inner rage, fury, frustration. It's hard to feel at ease with anyone who seethes that way. Suddenly I just wanted to go somewhere and lie down.

But someone put printout sheets in front of me, closely packed columns of stuff from the *Britannica*. Names swam before my eyes: Henry II, Barbarossa, Stephan Nemanya, Isaac II Angelos, Guy of Jerusalem, Richard the Lion-Hearted. Antioch, Tripoli, Thessalonica, Venice. I nodded my thanks and pushed the sheets aside.

Cautiously I asked Temujin about Mongolia. It turned out that he knew almost nothing about Mongolia. He'd had no contact at all with his native land since his abduction at the age of eleven by Byzantine traders who carried him off to Constantinople. His country, his father, his brothers, the girl to whom he had been betrothed when he was still a child – they were all just phantoms to him now, far away, forgotten. But in the privacy of his own soul he still spoke Khalkha. That was all that was left.

By 1187, I knew, the Temujin who would become Genghis Khan had already made himself the ruler of half of Mongolia. His fame would surely have spread to cosmopolitan Byzantium. How could this Temujin be unaware of him? Well, I saw one way. But Joe had already shot it down. And it sounded pretty nutty even to me.

'Do you want a drink?' Hedley asked. 'Tranks? Aspirin?'

I shook my head. 'I'm okay,' I murmured.

To Temujin I said, 'Do you have a wife? Children?'

'I have vowed not to marry until Jesus rules again in His own land.'

'So you're going to go on the next Crusade?' I asked.

Whatever answer Temujin made was smothered by static.

Awkkk. Skrrkkk. Tsssshhhhhhh.

Then silence, lengthening into endlessness.

'Signal's gone,' someone said.

'I could use that drink now,' I said. 'Scotch.'

The lab clock said it was ten in the morning. To me it felt like the middle of the night.

An hour had passed. The signal hadn't returned.

Hedley said, 'You really think he's Genghis Khan?'

'I really think he *could* have been.'

'In some other probability world.'

Carefully I said, 'I don't want to get you all upset again, Joe.'

'You won't. Why the hell *not* believe we're tuned into an alternate reality? It's no more goofy than any of the rest of this. But tell me this: is what he says consistent with being Genghis Khan?'

'His name's the same. His age. His childhood, up to the point when he wandered into some Byzantine trading caravan and they took him away to Constantinople with them. I can imagine the sort of fight he put up, too. But his life-line must have diverged completely from that point on. A whole new world-line split off from ours. And in that world, instead of turning into Genghis Khan, ruler of all Mongolia, he grew up to be Petros Alexios of Prince Theodore Lascaris's private guards.'

'And he has no idea of who he could have been?' Joe asked.

'How could he? It isn't even a dream to him. He was born into another world that wasn't ever destined to have a Genghis Khan. You know the poem:

> ' "*Our birth is but a sleep and a forgetting.*
> *The soul that rises with us, our life's star,*
> *Hath had elsewhere its setting,*
> *And cometh from afar.*" '

'Very pretty. Is that Yeats?' Hedley said.

266

'Wordsworth,' I said. 'When's the signal coming back?'

'An hour, two, three. It's hard to say. You want to take a nap, and we'll wake you when we have acquisition?'

'I'm not sleepy.'

'You look pretty ragged,' Joe said.

I wouldn't give him the satisfaction.

'I'm okay. I'll sleep for a week, later on. What if you can't raise him again?'

'There's always that chance, I suppose. We've already had him on the line five times as long as all the rest put together.'

'He's a very determined man,' I said.

'He ought to be. He's Genghis fucking Khan.'

'Get him back,' I said. 'I don't want you to lose him. I want to talk to him some more.'

Morning ticked on into afternoon. I phoned Elaine twice while we waited, and I stood for a long time at the window watching the shadows of the oncoming winter evening fall across the hibiscus and the bougainvillaea, and I hunched my shoulders up and tried to pull in the signal by sheer body English. Contemplating the possibility that they might never pick up Temujin again left me feeling weirdly forlorn. I was beginning to feel that I had a real relationship with that eerie disembodied angry voice coming out of the crackling night. Towards mid-afternoon I thought I was starting to understand what was making Temujin so angry, and I had some things I wanted to say to him about that.

Maybe you ought to get some sleep, I told myself.

At half past four someone came to me and said the Mongol was on the line again.

The static was very bad. But then came the full force of Temujin soaring over it. I heard him saying, 'The Holy Land must be redeemed. I cannot sleep so long as the infidels possess it.'

I took a deep breath.

In wonder I watched myself set out to do something unlike anything I had ever done before.

267

'Then you must redeem it yourself,' I said firmly.

'I?'

'Listen to me, Temujin. Think of another world far from yours. There is a Temujin in that world too, son of Yesugei, husband to Bortei who is daughter of Dai the Wise.'

'Another world? What are you saying?'

'Listen. Listen. He is a great warrior, that other Temujin. No one can withstand him. His own brothers bow before him. All Mongols everywhere bow before him. His sons are like wolves, and they ride into every land and no one can withstand them. This Temujin is master of all Mongolia. He is the Great Khan, the Genghis Khan, the ruler of the universe.'

There was silence. Then Temujin said, 'What is this to me?'

'He is you, Temujin. You are the Genghis Khan.'

Silence again, longer, broken by hideous shrieks of interplanetary noise.

'I have no sons and I have not seen Mongolia in years, or even thought of it. What are you saying?'

'That you can be as great in your world as this other Temujin is in his.'

'I am Byzantine. I am Christian. Mongolia is nothing to me. Why would I want to be master in that savage place?'

'I'm not talking about Mongolia. You are Byzantine, yes. You are Christian. But you were born to lead and fight and conquer,' I said. 'What are you doing as a captain of another man's palace guards? You waste your life that way, and you know it, and it maddens you. You should have armies of your own. You should carry the Cross into Jerusalem.'

'The leaders of the new Crusade are quarrelsome fools. It will end in disaster.'

'Perhaps not. Frederick Barbarossa's Crusade will be unstoppable.'

'Barbarossa will attack Byzantium instead of the Moslems. Everyone knows that.'

'No,' I said. That inner force of Temujin was rising and rising in intensity, like a gale climbing towards being a hurricane. I was awash in sweat, now, and I was dimly aware of the others staring at me as though I had lost my senses. A strange exhilaration gripped me. I went plunging joyously ahead. 'Emperor Isaac Angelos will come to terms with Barbarossa. The Germans will march through Byzantium and go on towards the Holy Land. But there Barbarossa will die and his army will scatter – unless you are there, at his right hand, taking command in his place when he falls, leading them onwards to Jerusalem. You, the invincible, the Genghis Khan.'

There was silence once more, this time so prolonged that I was afraid the contact had been broken for good.

Then Temujin returned. 'Will you send soldiers to fight by my side?' he asked.

'That I cannot do.'

'You have the power to send them, I know,' said Temujin. 'You speak to me out of the air. I know you are an angel, or else you are a demon. If you are a demon, I invoke the name of Christos Pantokrator upon you, and begone. But if you are an angel, you can send me help. Send it, then, and I will lead your troops to victory. I will take the Holy Land from the infidel. I will create the Empire of Jesus in the world and bring all things to fulfilment. Help me. Help me.'

'I've done all I can,' I said. 'The rest is for you to achieve.'

There was another spell of silence.

'Yes,' Temujin said finally. 'I understand. Yes. Yes. The rest is for me.'

'Christ, you look peculiar,' Joe Hedley said, staring at me almost fearfully. 'I've never seen you looking like this before. You look like a wild man.'

'Do I?' I said.

'You must be dead tired, Mike. You must be asleep on your feet. Listen, go over to the hotel and get some rest. We'll have a late dinner, okay? You can fill me in then on whatever you've just been jabbering about. But relax now. The Mongol's gone and we may not get him back till tomorrow.'

'You won't get him back at all,' I said.

'You think?' He peered close. 'Hey, are you okay? Your

eyes – your face – ' Something quivered in his cheek. 'If I didn't know better I'd say you were stoned.'

'I've been changing the world. It's hard work.'

'Changing the world?'

'Not this world. The other one. Look,' I said hoarsely, 'they never had a Genghis Khan, so they never had a Mongol Empire, and the whole history of China and Russia and the Near East and a lot of other places was very different. But I've got this Temujin all fired up now to be a Christian Genghis Khan. He got so Christian in Byzantium that he forgot what was really inside him, but I've reminded him, I've told him how he can still do the thing that he was designed to do, and he understands. He's found his true self again. He'll go out to fight in the name of Jesus and he'll build an empire that'll eat the Moslem powers for breakfast and then blow away Byzantium and Venice and go on from there to do God knows what. He'll probably conquer all of Europe before he's finished. And I did it. I set it all in motion. He was sending me all this energy, this Genghis Khan zap that he has inside him, and I figured the least I could do for him was turn some of it around and send it back to him, and say, Here, go, be what you were supposed to be.'

'Mike – '

I stood close against him, looming over him. He gave me a bewildered look.

'You really didn't think I had it in me, did you?' I said. 'You son of a bitch. You've always thought I'm as timid as a turtle. Your good old sober stick-in-the-mud pal Mike. What do you know? What the hell do you know?' Then I laughed. He looked so stunned that I had to soften it for him a little. Gently I touched his shoulder. 'I need a shower and a drink. And then let's think about dinner.'

Joe gawked at me. 'What if it wasn't some other world you changed, though? Suppose it was this one.'

'Suppose it was,' I said. 'Let's worry about that later. I still need that shower.'

Enter a Soldier. Later: Enter Another

A curious phenomenon of American science-fiction publishing in the late 1980s, which will probably not be dealt with in a kindly way by future historians of the field, was the 'shared-world' anthology. I use the past tense for it because the notion of gathering a bunch of writers together to set stories against a common background defined by someone else appears, as I write this, to be losing its popularity. But for a time in 1987 and 1988 it began to seem as though *everything* in science fiction was becoming part of some shared-world project.

In truth both good and bad fiction came out of the various shared-world enterprises. The idea itself was far from new; I can't tell you, without burrowing deep into the archives, which was the first of the species, though I think it was the round-robin novel *Cosmos* that assorted well-known writers did for fun in the early 1930s. Certainly one distinguished example of the modern sort of shared-world project appeared as far back as 1952 – *The Petrified Planet*, a book in which the scientist John D. Clark devised specifications for an unusual planet and the writers Fletcher Pratt, H. Beam Piper, and Judith Merril produced fine novellas set on that world. A similar book a year or two later was made up of stories by Isaac Asimov, Poul Anderson, and a third writer whose name I don't recall; for some reason the book itself never was published, but the Asimov and Anderson stories appeared individually, and they were fine ones.

Fifteen years later I revised the 'triplet' idea with a book called *Three for Tomorrow* – fiction by James Blish, Roger Zelazny, and myself, based on a theme proposed by Arthur C. Clarke – and I edited several others in the years following. In 1975 came Harlan Ellison's *Medea*, an elaborate and brilliantly conceived colossus of a book that made use of the talents of Frank Herbert, Theodore Sturgeon, Frederik Pohl, Larry Niven, Hal Clement, and a whole galaxy of other writers of their stature. But the real deluge of shared-world projects began a few years afterwards, in the wake of the vast success of Robert Asprin's fantasy series, *Thieves' World*. Suddenly every publisher in the business wanted to duplicate the *Thieves' World* bonanza, and from all sides appeared one hastily conceived imitator and another.

I dabbled in a couple of these books myself – a story that I wrote for one of them won a Hugo, in fact – but my enthusiasm for the shared-world whirl cooled quickly once I saw how shapeless and incoherent most of the books were. The writers tended not to pay much attention to the specifications, and simply went off in their own directions; the editors, generally, were too lazy or too cynical or simply too incompetent to do anything about it; and the books became formless jumbles of incompatible work.

Before I became fully aware of that, though, I let myself be seduced into editing one shared-world series myself. The initiator of this was Jim Baen, the publisher of Baen Books, whose idea centred around setting computer-generated simulacra of historical figures against each other in intellectual conflict. That appealed to me considerably; and when I was told that book-packager Bill Fawcett would work with me on the production end of things, I agreed to work out the conception in detail and serve as general editor.

So I produced an elaborate prospectus outlining the historical background of the near-future world in which these simulacra would hold forth; I rounded up a compatible group of writers (Poul Anderson, Robert Sheckley, Gregory Benford, and Pat Murphy); and to ensure that the book would unfold with consistency to my underlying vision, I wrote the first story myself, a 15,000-word opus for which I chose the characters of Socrates and Francisco Pizarro as my protagonists.

It was all, I have to admit, a matter of commerce rather than art: just a job of work, to fill somebody's current publishing need. But a writer's intentions and the ultimate result of his work don't bear any necessary relationship. In this case I was surprised and delighted to find the story taking on unanticipated life as I wrote, and what might have been a routine job of word-spinning turned out, unexpectedly, to be rather more than that when I was done with it.

It led off the shared-world anthology, which we called *Time Gate*, and was published in *Isaac Asimov's Science Fiction Magazine*. Gardner Dozois used it in his 1989 *Year's Best* collection, and in 1990 it was a finalist on both the Nebula and Hugo ballots – one of my most widely liked stories in a long while. The Nebula eluded me that year, but at the World Science Fiction Convention in Holland in August 1990 'Enter a Soldier' earned me a Hugo award, the fourth I have won, as the year's best novelette.

Time Gate itself turned out pretty well too, as such projects go. Readers liked it and Bill Fawcett and I went on to put together a second volume for Jim Baen, and then we were asked to do a third. But at that point I balked. The individual stories were fine ones, in the main, but the writers, as writers usually do, weren't paying much attention to the development of the overall concept I had devised for the book, and it seemed to me as volume two took shape that the result was an increasingly static and repetitive affair. Perhaps it's unrealistic to think that a team of gifted, independent-minded writers can ever produce what is in essence a collaborative novel that has been designed by someone else. In any case, the series wasn't taking the direction I had hoped for, and after the second volume I resigned from it, nor have I had much to do with shared-world collections ever since. But my involvement with this one did, at least, produce a story with which I'm more than a little pleased.

It might be heaven. Certainly it wasn't Spain and he doubted it could be Peru. He seemed to be floating, suspended midway between nothing and nothing. There was a shimmering golden sky far above him and a misty, turbulent sea of white clouds boiling far below. When he looked down he saw his legs and his feet dangling like child's toys above an unfathomable abyss, and the sight of it made him want to puke, but there was nothing in him for the puking. He was hollow. He was made of air. Even the old ache in his knee was gone, and so was the everlasting dull burning in the fleshy part of his arm where the

Indian's little arrow had taken him, long ago on the shore of that island of pearls, up by Panama.

It was as if he had been born again, sixty years old but freed of all the harm that his body had experienced and all its myriad accumulated injuries: freed, one might almost say, of his body itself.

'Gonzalo?' he called. 'Hernando?'

Blurred dreamy echoes answered him. And then silence.

'Mother of God, am I dead?'

No. No. He had never been able to imagine death. An end to all striving? A place where nothing moved? A great emptiness, a pit without a bottom? Was this place the place of death, then? He had no way of knowing. He needed to ask the holy fathers about this.

'Boy, where are my priests? Boy?'

He looked about for his page. But all he saw was blinding whorls of light coiling off to infinity on all sides. The sight was beautiful but troublesome. It was hard for him to deny that he had died, seeing himself afloat like this in a realm of air and light. Died and gone to heaven. This is heaven, yes, surely, surely. What else could it be?

So it was true, that if you took the Mass and took the Christ faithfully into yourself and served Him well you would be saved from your sins, you would be forgiven, you would be cleansed. He had wondered about that. But he wasn't ready yet to be dead, all the same. The thought of it was sickening and infuriating. There was so much yet to be done. And he had no memory even of being ill. He searched his body for wounds. No, no wounds. Not anywhere. Strange. Again he looked around. He was alone here. No one to be seen, not his page, nor his brother, nor De Soto, nor the priests, nor anyone. 'Fray Marcos! Fray Vicente! Can't you hear me? Damn you, where are you? Mother of God! Holy Mother, blessed among women! Damn you, Fray Vicente, tell me – tell me – '

His voice sounded all wrong: too thick, too deep, a stranger's voice. The words fought with his tongue and came from his lips malformed and lame, not the good crisp Spanish of Estremadura but something shameful and odd. What he heard was like the spluttering foppishness of Madrid or even the furry babble that they spoke in Barcelona; why, he might almost be a Portuguese, so coarse and clownish was his way of shaping his speech.

He said carefully and slowly, 'I am the Governor and Captain-General of New Castile.'

That came out no better, a laughable noise.

'Adelantado – Alguacil Mayor – Marques de la Conquista – '

The strangeness of his new way of speech made insults of his own titles. It was like being tongue-tied. He felt streams of hot sweat breaking out on his skin from the effort of trying to frame his words properly; but when he put his hand to his forehead to brush the sweat away before it could run into his eyes he seemed dry to the touch, and he was not entirely sure he could feel himself at all.

He took a deep breath. 'I am Francisco Pizarro!' he roared, letting the name burst desperately from him like water breaching a rotten dam.

The echo came back, deep, rumbling, mocking. *Frantheethco. Peetharro*.

That too. Even his own name, idiotically garbled.

'O great God!' he cried. 'Saints and angels!'

More garbled noises. Nothing would come out as it should. He had never known the arts of reading or writing; now it seemed that true speech itself was being taken from him. He began to wonder whether he had been right about this being heaven, supernal radiance or no. There was a curse on his tongue; a demon, perhaps, held it pinched in his claws. Was this hell, then? A very beautiful place, but hell nevertheless?

He shrugged. Heaven or hell, it made no difference. He was beginning to grow more calm, beginning to accept and take stock. He knew – had learned, long ago – that there was nothing to gain from raging against that which could not be helped, even less from panic in the face of the unknown. He was here, that was all there was to it – wherever *here* was – and he must find a place for himself, and not this place, floating here between nothing and nothing. He had been in hells before, small hells, hells on Earth. That barren isle called Gallo, where the sun cooked you in your own skin and there was nothing to eat but crabs that had the taste of dog-dung. And that dismal swamp at the mouth of the Rio Biru, where the rain fell in rivers and the trees reached down to cut you like swords. And the mountains he had crossed with his army, where the snow was so cold that it burned, and the air went into your throat like a dagger at every breath. He had come forth from those, and they had been worse than this. Here there was no pain and no danger; here there was only soothing light and a strange absence of all discomfort. He began to move forwards. He was walking on air. Look, look, he thought, I am walking on air! Then he said it out loud. 'I am walking on air,' he announced, and laughed at the way the words emerged from him. 'Santiago! Walking on air! But why not? I am Pizarro!' He shouted it with all his might, 'Pizarro! Pizarro!' and waited for it to come back to him.

Peetharro. Peetharro.

He laughed. He kept on walking.

Tanner sat hunched forward in the vast sparkling sphere that was the ninth-floor imaging lab, watching the little figure at the distant centre of the holotank strut and preen. Lew Richardson, crouching beside him with both hands thrust into the data gloves so that he could feed instructions to the permutation network, seemed almost not to be breathing – seemed to be just one more part of the network, in fact.

But that was Richardson's way, Tanner thought: total absorption in the task at hand. Tanner envied him that. They were very different sorts of men. Richardson lived for his programming and nothing but his programming. It was his grand passion. Tanner had never quite been able to understand people who were driven by grand passions. Richardson was like some throwback to an earlier age, an age when things had really mattered, an age when you were able to have some faith in the significance of your own endeavours.

'How do you like the armour?' Richardson asked. 'The armour's very fine, I think. We got it from old engravings. It has real flair.'

'Just the thing for tropical climates,' said Tanner. 'A nice tin suit with matching helmet.'

He coughed and shifted about irritably in his seat. The demonstration had been going on for half an hour without anything that seemed to be of any importance happening – just the minuscule image of the bearded man in Spanish armour tramping back and forth across the glowing field – and he was beginning to get impatient.

Richardson didn't seem to notice the harshness in Tanner's voice or the restlessness of his movements. He went on making small adjustments. He was a small man himself, neat and precise in dress and appearance, with faded blond hair and pale blue eyes and a thin, straight mouth. Tanner felt huge and shambling beside him. In theory Tanner had authority over Richardson's research projects, but in fact he always had simply permitted Richardson to do as he pleased. This time, though, it might be necessary finally to rein him in a little.

This was the twelfth or thirteenth demonstration that Richardson had subjected him to since he had begun fooling around with this historical-simulation business. The others all had been disasters of one kind or another, and Tanner expected that this one would finish the same way. And basically Tanner was growing uneasy about the project that he once had given his stamp of approval to, so long ago. It was getting harder and harder to go on believing that all this work served any useful purpose. Why had it been allowed to absorb so much of Richardson's group's time and so much of the lab's research budget for so many months? What possible value was it going to have for anybody? What possible use?

It's just a game, Tanner thought. One more desperate meaningless technological stunt, one more pointless pirouette in a meaningless ballet. The expenditure of vast resources on a display of ingenuity for ingenuity's sake and nothing else: now *there's* decadence for you.

The tiny image in the holotank suddenly began to lose colour and definition.

'Uh-oh,' Tanner said. 'There it goes. Like all the others.'

But Richardson shook his head. 'This time it's different, Harry.'

'You think?'

'We aren't losing him. He's simply moving around in there of his own volition, getting beyond our tracking parameters. Which means that we've achieved the high level of autonomy that we were shooting for.'

'Volition, Lew? Autonomy?'

'You know that those are our goals.'

'Yes, I know what our goals are supposed to be,' said Tanner, with some annoyance. 'I'm simply not convinced that a loss of focus is a proof that you've got volition.'

'Here,' Richardson said. 'I'll cut in the stochastic tracking program. He moves freely, we freely follow him.' Into the computer ear in his lapel he said, 'Give me a gain boost, will you?' He made a quick flicking gesture with his left middle finger to indicate the quantitative level.

The little figure in ornate armour and pointed boots grew sharp again. Tanner could see fine details on the armour, the plumed helmet, the tapering shoulder-pieces, the joints at the elbows, the intricate pommel of his sword. He was marching from left to right in a steady hip-rolling way, like a man who was climbing the tallest mountain in the world and didn't mean to break his stride until he was across the summit. The fact that he was walking in what appeared to be mid-air seemed not to trouble him at all.

'There he is,' Richardson said grandly. 'We've got him back, all right? The conqueror of Peru, before your very eyes, in the flesh. So to speak.'

Tanner nodded. Pizarro, yes, before his very eyes. And he had to admit that what he saw was impressive and even, some-how, moving. Something about the dogged way with which that small armoured figure was moving across the gleaming pearly field of the holotank aroused a kind of sympathy in him. That little man was entirely imaginary, but *he* didn't seem to know that, or if he did he wasn't letting it stop him for a moment: he went plugging on, and on and on, as if he intended actually to get somewhere. Watching that, Tanner was oddly captivated by it, and found himself surprised suddenly to discover that his interest in the entire project was beginning to rekindle.

'Can you make him any bigger?' he asked. 'I want to see his face.'

'I can make him big as life,' Richardson said. 'Bigger. Any size you like. Here.'

He flicked a finger and the hologram of Pizarro expanded instantaneously to a height of about two metres. The Spaniard halted in mid-stride as though he might actually be aware of the imaging change.

That can't be possible, Tanner thought. That isn't a living consciousness out there. Or is it?

Pizarro stood poised easily in mid-air, glowering, shading his eyes as if staring into a dazzling glow. There were brilliant streaks of colour in the air all around him, like an aurora. He was a tall, lean man in late middle age with a grizzled beard and a hard, angular face. His lips were thin, his nose was sharp, his eyes were cold, shrewd, keen. It seemed to Tanner that those eyes had come to rest on him, and he felt a chill.

My God, Tanner thought, he's *real*.

It had been a French program to begin with, something developed at the Centre Mondial de la Computation in Lyons about the year 2119. The French had some truly splendid minds working in software in those days. They worked up astounding programs, and then nobody did anything with them. That was *their* version of Century Twenty-Two Malaise.

The French programmers' idea was to use holograms of actual historical personages to dress up the *son et lumière* tourist events at the great monuments of their national history. Not just pre-programmed robot mockups of the old Disneyland kind, which would stand around in front of Notre Dame or the Arc de Triomphe or the Eiffel Tower and deliver canned spiels, but apparent reincarnations of the genuine great ones, who could freely walk and talk and answer questions and make little quips. Imagine Louis XIV demonstrating the fountains of Versailles, they said, or Picasso leading a tour of Paris museums, or Sartre sitting in his Left Bank café exchanging existential *bons mots* with passersby! Napoleon! Joan of Arc! Alexandre Dumas! Perhaps the simulations could do even more than that: perhaps they could be designed so well that they would be able to extend and embellish the achievements of their original lifetimes with new accomplishments, a fresh spate of paintings and novels and works of philosophy and great architectural visions by vanished masters.

The concept was simple enough in essence. Write an intelligencing program that could absorb data, digest it, correlate it, and generate further programs based on what you had given it. No real difficulty there. Then start feeding your program with the collected written works – if any – of the person to be simulated: that would provide not only a general sense of his ideas and positions but also of his underlying pattern of approach to situations, his style of thinking – for *le style*, after all, *est l'homme même*. If no collected works happened to be available, why, find works *about* the subject by his contemporaries, and use those. Next, toss in the totality of the historical record of the subject's deeds, including all significant subsequent scholarly analyses, making appropriate allowances for conflicts in interpretation – indeed, taking advantage of such conflicts to generate a richer portrait, full of the ambiguities and contradictions that are the inescapable hallmarks of any human being. Now build in substrata of general cultural data of the proper period so that the subject has a loam of references and vocabulary out of which to create thoughts that are appropriate to his place in time and space. Stir. *Et voilà!* Apply a little sophisticated imaging technology and you had a simulation capable of thinking and conversing and behaving as though it is the actual self after which it was patterned.

Of course, this would require a significant chunk of computer power. But that was no problem, in a world where 150-gigaflops networks were standard laboratory items and ten-year-olds carried pencil-sized computers with capacities far beyond the ponderous mainframes of their great-great-grandparents' day. No, there was no theoretical reason why the French project could not have succeeded. Once the Lyons programmers had worked out the basic intelligencing scheme that was needed to write the rest of the programs, it all should have followed smoothly enough.

Two things went wrong: one rooted in an excess of ambition that may have been a product of the peculiarly French personalities of the original programmers, and the other having to do with an abhorrence of failure typical of the major nations of the mid-twenty-second century, of which France was one.

The first was a fatal change of direction that the project underwent in its early phases. The King of Spain was coming to Paris on a visit of state; and the programmers decided that in his honour they would synthesize Don Quixote for him as their initial project. Though the intelligencing program had been designed to simulate only individuals who had actually existed, there seemed no inherent reason why a fictional character as well documented as Don Quixote could not be produced instead. There was Cervantes' lengthy novel; there was ample background data available on the milieu in which Don Quixote supposedly had lived; there was a vast library of critical analysis of the book and of the Don's distinctive and flamboyant personality. Why should bringing Don Quixote to life out of a computer be any different from simulating Louis XIV, say, or Molière, or Cardinal Richelieu? True, they had all existed once, and the knight of La Mancha was a mere figment; but had Cervantes not provided far more detail about Don Quixote's mind and soul than was known of Richelieu, or Molière, or Louis XIV?

Indeed he had. The Don – like Oedipus, like Odysseus, like Othello, like David Copperfield – had come to have a reality far more profound and tangible than that of most people who had indeed actually lived. Such characters as those had transcended their fictional origins. But not so far as the computer was concerned. It was able to produce a convincing fabrication of Don Quixote, all right – a gaunt, bizarre holographic figure that had all the right mannerisms, that ranted and raved in the expectable way, that referred knowledgeably to Dulcinea and Rosinante and Mambrino's helmet. The Spanish king was amused and impressed. But to the French the experiment was a failure. They had produced a Don Quixote who was hopelessly locked to the Spain of the late sixteenth century and to the book from which he had sprung. He had no capacity for independent life and thought – no way to perceive the world that had brought him into being, or to comment on it, or to interact with it. There was nothing new or interesting about that. Any actor could dress up in armour and put on a scraggly beard and recite snatches of Cervantes. What had come forth from the computer, after three years of work, was no more than a predictable reprocessing of what had gone into it, sterile, stale.

Which led the Centre Mondial de la Computation to its next fatal step: abandoning the whole thing. *Zut*! And the project was cancelled without any further attempts. No simulated Picassos, no simulated Napoleons, no Joans of Arc. The Quixote event had soured everyone and no one had the heart to proceed with the work from there. Suddenly it had the taint of failure about it, and France – like Germany, like Australia, like the Han Commercial Sphere, like Brazil, like any of the dynamic centres of the modern world – had a horror of failure. Failure was something to be left to the backward nations or the decadent ones – to the Islamic Socialist Union, say, or the Soviet People's Republic, or to that slumbering giant, the United States of America. So the historic-personage simulation scheme was put aside.

The French thought so little of it, as a matter of fact, that after letting it lie fallow for a few years they licensed it to a bunch of Americans, who had heard about it somehow and felt it might be amusing to play with.

'You may really have done it this time,' Tanner said.

'Yes. I think we have. After all those false starts.'

Tanner nodded. How often had he come into this room with hopes high, only to see some botch, some inanity, some depressing bungle? Richardson had always had an explanation. Sherlock Holmes hadn't worked because he was fictional: that was a necessary recheck of the French Quixote project, demonstrating that fictional characters didn't have the right sort of reality texture to take proper advantage of the program, not enough ambiguity, not enough contradiction. King Arthur had failed for the same reason. Julius Caesar? Too far in the past, maybe: unreliable data, bordering on fiction. Moses? Ditto. Einstein? Too complex, perhaps, for the project in its present level of development: they needed more experience first. Queen Elizabeth I? George Washington? Mozart? We're learning more each time, Richardson insisted after each failure. This isn't black magic we're doing, you know. We aren't necromancers, we're programmers, and we have to figure out how to give the program what it needs.

And now Pizarro?

'Why do you want to work with *him*?' Tanner had asked, five or six months earlier. 'A ruthless medieval Spanish imperialist, is what I remember from school. A bloodthirsty despoiler of a great culture. A man without morals, honour, faith – '

'You may be doing him an injustice,' said Richardson. 'He's had a bad press for centuries. And there are things about him that fascinate me.'

'Such as?'

'His drive. His courage. His absolute confidence. The other side of ruthlessness, the good side of it, is a total concentration on your task, an utter unwillingness to be stopped by any obstacle. Whether or not you approve of the things he accomplished, you have to admire a man who – '

'All right,' Tanner said, abruptly growing weary of the whole enterprise. 'Do Pizarro. Whatever you want.'

The months had passed. Richardson gave him vague progress reports, nothing to arouse much hope. But now Tanner stared at the tiny strutting figure in the holotank and the conviction began to grow in him that Richardson finally had figured out how to use the simulation program as it was meant to be used.

'So you've actually recreated him, you think? Someone who lived – what, five hundred years ago?'

'He died in 1541,' said Richardson.

'Almost six hundred, then.'

'And he's not like the others – not simply a recreation of a great figure out of the past who can run through a set of pre-programmed speeches. What we've got here, if I'm right, is an artificially generated intelligence which can think for itself in modes other than the ones its programmers think in. Which has more information available to itself, in other words, than we've provided it with. That would be the real accomplishment. That's the fundamental philosophical leap that we were going for when we first got involved with this project. To use the program to give us new programs that are capable of true autonomous thought – a program that can think like Pizarro, instead of like Lew Richardson's idea of some historian's idea of how Pizarro might have thought.'

'Yes,' Tanner said.

'Which means we won't just get back the expectable, the predictable. There'll be surprises. There's no way to learn any-thing, you know, except through surprises. The sudden combi-nation of known components into something brand new. And that's what I think we've managed to bring off here, at long last. Harry, it may be the biggest artificial-intelligence breakthrough ever achieved.'

Tanner pondered that. Was it so? Had they truly done it?

And if they had–

Something new and troubling was beginning to occur to him, much later in the game than it should have. Tanner stared at the holographic figure floating in the centre of the tank, that fierce old man with the harsh face and the cold, cruel eyes. He thought about what sort of man he must have been – the man after whom this image had been modelled. A man who was willing to land in South America at age fifty or sixty or whatever he had been, an ignorant illiterate Spanish peasant wearing a suit of ill-fitting armour and waving a rusty sword, and set out to conquer a great empire of millions of people spreading over thousands of miles. Tanner wondered what sort of man would be capable of carrying out a thing like that. Now that man's eyes were staring into his own and it was a struggle to meet so implacable a gaze.

After a moment he looked away. His left leg began to quiver. He glanced uneasily at Richardson.

'Look at those eyes, Lew. Christ, they're scary!'

'I know. I designed them myself, from the old prints.'

'Do you think he's seeing us right now? Can he do that?'

'All he is is software, Harry.'

'He seemed to know it when you expanded the image.'

Richardson shrugged. 'He's very good software. I tell you, he's got autonomy, he's got volition. He's got an electronic *mind*, is what I'm saying. He may have perceived a transient voltage kick. But there are limits to his perceptions, all the same. I don't think there's any way that he can see anything that's outside the holotank unless it's fed to him in the form of data he can process, which hasn't been done.'

'You don't *think*? You aren't sure?'

'Harry. Please.'

'This man conquered the entire enormous Incan Empire with fifty soldiers, didn't he?'

'In fact I believe it was more like a hundred and fifty.'

'Fifty, a hundred fifty, what's the difference? Who knows what you've actually got here? What if you did an even better job than you suspect?'

'What are you saying?'

'What I'm saying is, I'm uneasy all of a sudden. For a long time I didn't think this project was going to produce anything at all. Suddenly I'm starting to think that maybe it's going to produce more than we can handle. I don't want any of your goddamned simulations walking out of the tank and conquering *us*.'

Richardson turned to him. His face was flushed, but he was grinning. 'Harry, Harry! For God's sake! Five minutes ago you didn't think we had anything at all here except a tiny picture that wasn't even in focus. Now you've gone so far the other way that you're imagining the worst kind of – '

'I see his eyes, Lew. I'm worried that his eyes see me.'

'Those aren't real eyes you're looking at. What you see is nothing but a graphics program projected into a holotank. There's no visual capacity there as you understand the concept. His eyes will see you only if I want them to. Right now they don't.'

'But you can make them see me?'

'I can make them see anything I want them to see. I created him, Harry.'

'With volition. With autonomy.'

'After all this time you start worrying *now* about these things?'

'It's my neck on the line if something that you guys on the technical side make runs amok. This autonomy thing suddenly troubles me.'

'I'm still the one with the data gloves,' Richardson said. 'I twitch my fingers and he dances. That's not really Pizarro down there, remember. And that's no Frankenstein monster either. It's just a simulation. It's just so much data, just a bunch of electromagnetic impulses that I can shut off with one movement of my pinkie.'

'Do it, then.'

'Shut him off? But I haven't begun to show you – '

'Shut him off, and then turn him on,' Tanner said.

Richardson looked bothered. 'If you say so, Harry.'

He moved a finger. The image of Pizarro vanished from the holotank. Swirling grey mists moved in it for a moment, and then all was white wool. Tanner felt a quick jolt of guilt, as though he had just ordered the execution of the man in the medieval armour. Richardson gestured again, and colour flashed across the tank, and then Pizarro reappeared.

'I just wanted to see how much autonomy your little guy really has,' said Tanner. 'Whether he was quick enough to head you off and escape into some other channel before you could cut his power.'

'You really don't understand how this works at all, do you, Harry?'

'I just wanted to see,' said Tanner again, sullenly. After a moment's silence he said, 'Do you ever feel like God?'

'Like God?'

'You breathed life in. Life of a sort, anyway. But you breathed free will in, too. That's what this experiment is all about, isn't it? All your talk about volition and autonomy? You're trying to recreate a human mind – which means to create it all over again – a mind that can think in its own special way, and come up with its own unique responses to situations, which will not necessarily be the responses that its programmers might anticipate, in fact almost certainly will not be, and which might not be all that desirable or beneficial, either, and you simply have to allow for that risk, just as God, once He gave free will to mankind, knew that He was likely to see all manner of evil deeds being performed by His creations as they exercised that free will – '

'Please, Harry – '

'Listen, is it possible for me to talk with your Pizarro?'

'Why?'

'By way of finding out what you've got there. To get some first-hand knowledge of what the project has accomplished. Or you could say I just want to test the quality of the simulation. Whatever. I'd feel more a part of this thing, more aware of what it's all about in here, if I could have some direct contact with him. Would it be all right if I did that?'

'Yes. Of course.'

'Do I have to talk to him in Spanish?'

'In any language you like. There's an interface, after all. He'll think it's his own language coming in, no matter what, sixteenth-century Spanish. And he'll answer you in what seems like Spanish to him, but you'll hear it in English.'

'Are you sure?'

'Of course.'

'And you don't mind if I make contact with him?'

'Whatever you like.'

'It won't upset his calibration, or anything?'

'It won't do any harm at all, Harry.'

'Fine. Let me talk to him, then.'

There was a disturbance in the air ahead, a shifting, a swirling, like a little whirlwind. Pizarro halted and watched it for a moment, wondering what was coming next. A demon arriving to torment him, maybe. Or an angel. Whatever it was, he was ready for it.

Then a voice out of the whirlwind said, in that same comically exaggerated Castilian Spanish that Pizarro himself had found himself speaking a little while before, 'Can you hear me?'

'I hear you, yes. I don't see you. Where are you?'

'Right in front of you. Wait a second. I'll show you.' Out of the whirlwind came a strange face that hovered in the middle of nowhere, a face without a body, a lean face, close-shaven, no beard at all, no moustache, the hair cut very short, dark eyes set close together. He had never seen a face like that before.

'What are you?' Pizarro asked. 'A demon or an angel?'

'Neither one.' Indeed he didn't sound very demonic. 'A man just like you.'

'Not much like me, I think. Is a face all there is to you, or do you have a body too?'

'All you see of me is a face?'

'Yes.'

'Wait a second.'

'I will wait as long as I have to. I have plenty of time.'

The face disappeared. Then it returned, attached to the body of a big, wide-shouldered man who was wearing a long loose grey robe, something like a priest's cassock, but much more ornate, with points of glowing light gleaming on it everywhere. Then the body vanished and Pizarro could see only the face again. He could make no sense out of any of this. He began to understand how the Indians must have felt when the first

Spaniards came over the horizon, riding horses, carrying guns, wearing armour.

'You are very strange. Are you an Englishman, maybe?'

'American.'

'Ah,' Pizarro said, as though that made things better. 'An American. And what is that?'

The face wavered and blurred for a moment. There was mysterious new agitation in the thick white clouds surrounding it. Then the face grew steady and said, 'America is a country north of Peru. A very large country, where many people live.'

'You mean New Spain, which was Mexico, where my kinsman Cortes is Captain-General?'

'North of Mexico. Far to the north of it.'

Pizarro shrugged. 'I know nothing of those places. Or not very much. There is an island called Florida, yes? And stories of cities of gold, but I think they are only stories. I found the gold, in Peru. Enough to choke on, I found. Tell me this, am I in heaven now?'

'No.'

'Then this is hell?'

'Not that, either. Where you are – it's very difficult to explain, actually – '

'I am in America.'

'Yes. In America, yes.'

'And am I dead?'

There was silence for a moment.

'No, not dead,' the voice said uneasily.

'You are lying to me, I think.'

'How could we be speaking with each other, if you were dead?'

Pizarro laughed hoarsely. 'Are you asking *me*? I understand nothing of what is happening to me in this place. Where are my priests? Where is my page? Send me my brother!' He glared. 'Well? Why don't you get them for me?'

'They aren't here. You're here all by yourself, Don Francisco.'

'In America. All by myself in your America. Show me your

289

America, then. Is there such a place? Is America all clouds and whorls of light? Where is America? Let me see America. Prove to me that I am in America.'

There was another silence, longer than the last. Then the face disappeared and the wall of white cloud began to boil and churn more fiercely than before. Pizarro stared into the midst of it, feeling a mingled sense of curiosity and annoyance. The face did not reappear. He saw nothing at all. He was being toyed with. He was a prisoner in some strange place and they were treating him like a child, like a dog, like – like an Indian. Perhaps this was the retribution for what he had done to King Atahuallpa, then, that fine noble foolish man who had given himself up to him in all innocence, and whom he had put to death so that he might have the gold of Atahuallpa's kingdom.

Well, so be it, Pizarro thought. Atahuallpa accepted all that befell him without complaint and without fear, and so will I. Christ will be my guardian, and if there is no Christ, well, then I will have no guardian, and so be it. So be it.

The voice out of the whirlwind said suddenly, 'Look, Don Francisco. This is America.'

A picture appeared on the wall of cloud. It was a kind of picture Pizarro had never before encountered or even imagined, one that seemed to open before him like a gate and sweep him in and carry him along through a vista of changing scenes depicted in brilliant, vivid bursts of colour. It was like flying high above the land, looking down on an infinite scroll of miracles. He saw vast cities without walls, roadways that unrolled like endless skeins of white ribbon, huge lakes, mighty rivers, gigantic mountains, everything speeding past him so swiftly that he could scarcely absorb any of it. In moments it all became chaotic in his mind: the buildings taller than the highest cathedral spire, the swarming masses of people, the shining metal chariots without beasts to draw them, the stupendous landscapes, the close-packed complexity of it all. Watching all this, he felt the fine old hunger taking possession of him again: he wanted to grasp this strange vast place, and seize it, and clutch it close, and ransack it for all it was worth.

But the thought of that was overwhelming. His eyes grew glassy and his heart began to pound so terrifyingly that he supposed he would be able to feel it thumping if he put his hand to the front of his armour. He turned away, muttering, 'Enough. Enough.'

The terrifying picture vanished. Gradually the clamour of his heart subsided.

Then he began to laugh.

'Peru!' he cried. 'Peru was nothing, next to your America! Peru was a hole! Peru was mud! How ignorant I was! I went to Peru, when there was America, ten thousand times as grand! I wonder what I could find, in America.' He smacked his lips and winked. Then, chuckling, he said, 'But don't be afraid. I won't try to conquer your America. I'm too old for that now. And perhaps America would have been too much for me, even before. Perhaps.' He grinned savagely at the troubled staring face of the short-haired beardless man, the American. 'I really am dead, is this not so? I feel no hunger, I feel no pain, no thirst, when I put my hand to my body I do not feel even my body. I am like one who lies dreaming. But this is no dream. Am I a ghost?'

'Not – exactly.'

'Not exactly a ghost! Not exactly! No one with half the brains of a pig would talk like that. What is that supposed to mean?'

'It's not easy explaining it in words you would understand, Don Francisco.'

'No, of course not. I am very stupid, as everyone knows, and that is why I conquered Peru, because I was so very stupid. But let it pass. I am not exactly a ghost, but I am dead all the same, right?'

'Well – '

'I am dead, yes. But somehow I have not gone to hell or even to purgatory but I am still in the world, only it is much later now. I have slept as the dead sleep, and now I have awakened in some year that is far beyond my time, and it is the time of America. Is this not so? Who is king now? Who is pope? What year is this? 1750? 1800?'

'The year 2130,' the face said, after some hesitation.

'Ah.' Pizarro tugged thoughtfully at his lower lip. 'And the king? Who is king?'

A long pause. 'Alfonso is his name,' said the face.

'Alfonso? The kings of Aragon were called Alfonso. The father of Ferdinand, he was Alfonso. Alfonso V, he was.'

'Alfonso XIX is King of Spain now.'

'Ah. Ah. And the pope? Who is pope?'

A pause again. Not to know the name of the pope, immediately upon being asked? How strange. Demon or no, this was a fool.

'Pius,' said the voice, when some time had passed. 'Pius XVI.'

'The sixteenth Pius,' said Pizarro sombrely. 'Jesus and Mary, the sixteenth Pius! What has become of me? Long dead, is what I am. Still unwashed of all my sins. I can feel them clinging to my skin like mud, still. And you are a sorcerer, you American, and you have brought me to life again. Eh? Eh? Is that not so?'

'It is something like that, Don Francisco,' the face admitted.

'So you speak your Spanish strangely because you no longer understand the right way of speaking it. Eh? Even I speak Spanish in a strange way, and I speak it in a voice that does not sound like my own. No one speaks Spanish any more, eh? Eh? Only American, they speak. Eh? But you try to speak Spanish, only it comes out stupidly. And you have caused me to speak the same way, thinking it is the way I spoke, though you are wrong. Well, you can do miracles, but I suppose you can't do everything perfectly, even in this land of miracles of the year 2130. Eh? Eh?' Pizarro leaned forward intently. 'What do you say? You thought I was a fool, because I don't have reading and writing? I am not so ignorant, eh? I understand things quickly.'

'You understand very quickly indeed.'

'But you have knowledge of many things that are unknown to me. You must know the manner of my death, for example. How strange that is, talking to you of the manner of my death, but you must know it, eh? When did it come to me? And how? Did it come in my sleep? No, no, how could that be? They die in their sleep in Spain, but not in Peru. How was it, then? I was set upon by cowards, was I? Some brother of Atahuallpa, falling upon me as I stepped out of my house? A slave sent by the Inca Manco, or one of those others? No. No. The Indians would not harm me, for all that I did to them. It was the young Almagro who took me down, was it not, in vengeance for his father, or Juan de Herrada, eh? Or perhaps even Picado, my own secretary – no, not Picado, he was my man, always – but maybe Alvarado, the young one, Diego – well, one of those, and it would have been sudden, very sudden or I would have been able to stop them – am I right, am I speaking the truth? Tell me. You know these things. Tell me of the manner of my dying.' There was no answer. Pizarro shaded his eyes and peered into the dazzling pearly whiteness. He was no longer able to see the face of the American. 'Are you there?' Pizarro said. 'Where have you gone? Were you only a dream? American! American! Where have you gone?'

The break in contact was jolting. Tanner sat rigid, hands trembling, lips tightly clamped. Pizarro, in the holotank, was no more than a distant little streak of colour now, no larger than his thumb, gesticulating amid the swirling clouds. The vitality of him, the arrogance, the fierce probing curiosity, the powerful hatreds and jealousies, the strength that had come from vast ventures recklessly conceived and desperately seen through to triumph, all the things that were Francisco Pizarro, all that Tanner had felt an instant before – all that had vanished at the flick of a finger.

After a moment or two Tanner felt the shock beginning to ease. He turned towards Richardson.

'What happened?'

'I had to pull you out of there. I didn't want you telling him anything about how he died.'

'I don't know how he died.'

'Well, neither does he, and I didn't want to chance it that

you did. There's no predicting what sort of psychological impact that kind of knowledge might have on him.'

'You talk about him as though he's alive.'

'Isn't he?' Richardson said.

'If I said a thing like that, you'd tell me that I was being ignorant and unscientific.'

Richardson smiled faintly. 'You're right. But somehow I trust myself to know what I'm saying when I say that he's alive. I know I don't mean it literally and I'm not sure about you. What did you think of him, anyway?'

'He's amazing,' Tanner said. 'Really amazing. The strength of him – I could feel it pouring out at me in waves. And his mind! So quick, the way he picked up on everything. Guessing that he must be in the future. Wanting to know what number pope was in office. Wanting to see what America looked like. And the cockiness of him! Telling me that he's not up to the conquest of America, that he might have tried for it instead of Peru a few years earlier, but not now, now he's a little too old for that. Incredible! Nothing could faze him for long, even when he realized that he must have been dead for a long time. Wanting to know how he died, even!' Tanner frowned. 'What age did you make him, anyway, when you put this program together?'

'About sixty. Five or six years after the conquest, and a year or two before he died. At the height of his power, that is.'

'I suppose you couldn't have let him have any knowledge of his actual death. That way he'd be too much like some kind of a ghost.'

'That's what we thought. We set the cutoff at a time when he had done everything that he had set out to do, when he was the complete Pizarro. But before the end. He didn't need to know about that. Nobody does. That's why I had to yank you, you see? In case you knew. And started to tell him.'

Tanner shook his head. 'If I ever knew, I've forgotten it. How did it happen?'

'Exactly as he guessed: at the hands of his own comrades.'

'So he saw it coming.'

'At the age we made him, he already knew that a civil war had started in South America, that the conquistadores were quarrelling over the division of the spoils. We built that much into him. He knows that his partner Almagro has turned against him and been beaten in battle, and that they've executed him. What he doesn't know, but obviously can expect, is that Almagro's friends are going to break into his house and try to kill him. He's got it all figured out pretty much as it's going to happen. As it *did* happen, I should say.'

'Incredible. To be that shrewd.'

'He was a son of a bitch, yes. But he was a genius too.'

'Was he, really? Or is it that you made him one when you set up the program for him?'

'All we put in were the objective details of his life, patterns of event and response. Plus an overlay of commentary by others, his contemporaries and later historians familiar with the record, providing an extra dimension of character density. Put in enough of that kind of stuff and apparently they add up to the whole personality. It isn't *my* personality or that of anybody else who worked on this project, Harry. When you put in Pizarro's set of events and responses you wind up getting Pizarro. You get the ruthlessness and you get the brilliance. Put in a different set, you get someone else. And what we've finally seen, this time, is that when we do our work right we get something out of the computer that's bigger than the sum of what we put in.'

'Are you sure?'

Richardson said, 'Did you notice that he complained about the Spanish that he thought you were speaking?'

'Yes. He said that it sounded strange, that nobody seemed to know how to speak proper Spanish any more. I didn't quite follow that. Does the interface you built speak lousy Spanish?'

'Evidently it speaks lousy sixteenth-century Spanish,' Richardson said. 'Nobody knows what sixteenth-century Spanish actually sounded like. We can only guess. Apparently we didn't guess very well.'

'But how would *he* know? You synthesized him in the first

place! If you don't know how Spanish sounded in his time, how would he? All he should know about Spanish, or about anything, is what you put into him.'

'Exactly,' Richardson said.

'But that doesn't make any sense, Lew!'

'He also said that the Spanish he heard himself speaking was no good, and that his own voice didn't sound right to him either. That we had *caused* him to speak this way, thinking that was how he actually spoke, but we were wrong.'

'How could he possibly know what his voice really sounded like, if all he is is a simulation put together by people who don't have the slightest notion of what his voice really – '

'I don't have any idea,' said Richardson quietly. 'But he *does* know.'

'Does he? Or is this just some diabolical Pizarro-like game that he's playing to unsettle us, because *that's* in his character as you devised it?'

'I think he does know,' Richardson said.

'Where's he finding it out, then?'

'It's there. We don't know where, but he does. It's somewhere in the data that we put through the permutation network, even if we don't know it and even though we couldn't find it now if we set out to look for it. *He* can find it. He can't manufacture that kind of knowledge by magic, but he can assemble what look to us like seemingly irrelevant bits and come up with new information leading to a conclusion which is meaningful to him. That's what we mean by artificial intelligence, Harry. We've finally got a program that works something like the human brain: by leaps of intuition so sudden and broad that they seem inexplicable and non-quantifiable, even if they really aren't. We've fed in enough stuff so that he can assimilate a whole stew of ostensibly unrelated data and come up with new information. We don't just have a ventriloquist's dummy in that tank. We've got something that thinks it's Pizarro and thinks like Pizarro and knows things that Pizarro knew and we don't. Which means we've accomplished the qualitative jump in artificial intelligence capacity that we set out to achieve with this project. It's awesome. I get shivers down my back when I think about it.'

'I do too,' Tanner said. 'But not so much from awe as fear.'

'Fear?'

'Knowing now that he has capabilities beyond those he was programmed for, how can you be so absolutely certain that he can't commandeer your network somehow and get himself loose?'

'It's technically impossible. All he is is electromagnetic impulses. I can pull the plug on him any time I like. There's nothing to panic over here. Believe me, Harry.'

'I'm trying to.'

'I can show you the schematics. We've got a phenomenal simulation in that computer, yes. But it's still only a simulation. It isn't a vampire, it isn't a werewolf, it isn't anything supernatural. It's just the best damned computer simulation anyone's ever made.'

'It makes me uneasy. *He* makes me uneasy.'

'He should. The power of the man, the indomitable nature of him – why do you think I summoned him up, Harry? He's got something that we don't understand in this country any more. I want us to study him. I want us to try to learn what that kind of drive and determination is really like. Now that you've talked to him, now that you've touched his spirit, of course you're shaken up by him. He radiates tremendous confidence. He radiates fantastic faith in himself. That kind of man can achieve anything he wants – even conquer the whole Inca Empire with a hundred fifty men, or however many it was. But I'm not frightened of what we've put together here. And you shouldn't be either. We should all be damned proud of it. You as well as the people on the technical side. And you will be, too.'

'I hope you're right,' Tanner said.

'You'll see.'

For a long moment Tanner stared in silence at the holotank, where the image of Pizarro had been.

'Okay,' said Tanner finally. 'Maybe I'm overreacting. Maybe

I'm sounding like the ignoramus layman that I am. I'll take it on faith that you'll be able to keep your phantoms in their boxes.'

'We will,' Richardson said.

'Let's hope so. All right,' said Tanner. 'So what's your next move?'

Richardson looked puzzled. 'My next move?'

'With this project? Where does it go from here?'

Hesitantly Richardson said, 'There's no formal proposal yet. We thought we'd wait until we had approval from you on the initial phase of the work, and then – '

'How does this sound?' Tanner asked. 'I'd like to see you start in on another simulation right away.'

'Well – yes, yes, of course – '

'And when you've got him worked up, Lew, would it be feasible for you to put him right there in the tank with Pizarro?'

Richardson looked startled. 'To have a sort of dialogue with him, you mean?'

'Yes.'

'I suppose we could do that,' Richardson said cautiously. '*Should* do that. Yes. Yes. A very interesting suggestion, as a matter of fact.' He ventured an uneasy smile. Up till now Tanner had kept in the background of this project, a mere management functionary, an observer, virtually an outsider. This was something new, his interjecting himself into the planning process, and plainly Richardson didn't know what to make of it. Tanner watched him fidget. After a little pause Richardson said, 'Was there anyone particular you had in mind for us to try next?'

'Is that new parallax thing of yours ready to try?' Tanner asked. 'The one that's supposed to compensate for time distortion and myth contamination?'

'Just about. But we haven't tested – '

'Good,' Tanner said. 'Here's your chance. What about trying for Socrates?'

There was billowing whiteness below him, and on every side,

as though all the world were made of fleece. He wondered if it might be snow. That was not something he was really familiar with. It snowed once in a great while in Athens, yes, but usually only a light dusting that melted in the morning sun. Of course he had seen snow aplenty when he had been up north in the war, at Potidaea, in the time of Pericles. But that had been long ago; and that stuff, as best he remembered it, had not been much like this. There was no quality of coldness about the whiteness that surrounded him now. It could just as readily be great banks of clouds.

But what would clouds be doing *below* him? Clouds, he thought, are mere vapour, air and water, no substance to them at all. Their natural place was overhead. Clouds that gathered at one's feet had no true quality of cloudness about them.

Snow that had no coldness? Clouds that had no buoyancy? Nothing in this place seemed to possess any quality that was proper to itself in this place, including himself. He seemed to be walking, but his feet touched nothing at all. It was more like moving through air. But how could one move in the air? Aristophanes, in that mercilessly mocking play of his, had sent him floating through the clouds suspended in a basket, and made him say things like, 'I am traversing the air and contemplating the sun.' That was Aristophanes' way of playing with him, and he had not been seriously upset, though his friends had been very hurt on his behalf. Still, that was only a play.

This felt real, insofar as it felt like anything at all.

Perhaps he was dreaming, and the nature of his dream was that he thought he was really doing the things he had done in Aristophanes' play. What was that lovely line? 'I have to suspend my brain and mingle the subtle essence of my mind with this air, which is of the same nature, in order clearly to penetrate the things of heaven.' Good old Aristophanes! Nothing was sacred to him! Except, of course, those things that were truly sacred, such as wisdom, truth, virtue. 'I would have discovered nothing if I had remained on the ground and pondered from below the things that are above: for the earth by its force

299

attracts the sap of the mind to itself. It's the same way with watercress.' And Socrates began to laugh.

He held his hands before him and studied them, the short sturdy fingers, the thick powerful wrists. His hands, yes. His old plain hands that had stood him in good stead all his life, when he had worked as a stonemason as his father had, when he had fought in his city's wars, when he had trained at the gymnasium. But now when he touched them to his face he felt nothing. There should be a chin here, a forehead, yes, a blunt stubby nose, thick lips; but there was nothing. He was touching air. He could put his hand right through the place where his face should be. He could put one hand against the other, and press with all his might, and feel nothing.

This is a very strange place indeed, he thought.

Perhaps it is that place of pure forms that young Plato liked to speculate about, where everything is perfect and nothing is quite real. Those are ideal clouds all around me, not real ones. This is ideal air upon which I walk. I myself am the ideal Socrates, liberated from my coarse ordinary body. Could it be? Well, maybe so. He stood for a while, considering that possibility. The thought came to him that this might be the life after life, in which case he might meet some of the gods, if there were any gods in the first place, and if he could manage to find them. I would like that, he thought. Perhaps they would be willing to speak with me. Athena would discourse with me on wisdom, or Hermes on speed, or Ares on the nature of courage, or Zeus on – well, whatever Zeus cared to speak on. Of course I would seem to be the merest fool to them, but that would be all right: anyone who expects to hold discourse with the gods as though he were their equal *is* a fool. I have no such illusion. If there are gods at all, surely they are far superior to me in all respects, for otherwise why would men regard them as gods?

Of course he had serious doubts that the gods existed at all. But if they did, it was reasonable to think that they might be found in a place such as this.

He looked up. The sky was radiant with brilliant golden

light. He took a deep breath and smiled and set out across the fleecy nothingness of this airy world to see if he could find the gods.

Tanner said, 'What do you think now? Still so pessimistic?'

'It's too early to say,' said Richardson, looking glum.

'He *looks* like Socrates, doesn't he?'

'That was the easy part. We've got plenty of descriptions of Socrates that came down from people who knew him, the flat wide nose, the bald head, the thick lips, the short neck. A standard Socrates face that everybody recognizes, just as they do Sherlock Holmes, or Don Quixote. So that's how we made him look. It doesn't signify anything important. It's what's going on inside his head that'll determine whether we really have Socrates.'

'He seems calm and good-humoured as he wanders around in there. The way a philosopher should.'

'Pizarro seemed just as much of a philosopher when we turned him loose in the tank.'

'Pizarro may *be* just as much of a philosopher,' Tanner said. 'Neither man's the sort who'd be likely to panic if he found himself in some mysterious place.' Richardson's negativism was beginning to bother him. It was as if the two men had exchanged places: Richardson now uncertain of the range and power of his own program, Tanner pushing the way on and on towards bigger and better things.

Bleakly Richardson said, 'I'm still pretty sceptical. We've tried the new parallax filters, yes. But I'm afraid we're going to run into the same problem the French did with Don Quixote, and that we did with Holmes and Moses and Caesar. There's too much contamination of the data by myth and fantasy. The Socrates who has come down to us is as much fictional as real, or maybe *all* fictional. For all we know, Plato made up everything we think we know about him, the same way Conan Doyle made up Holmes. And what we're going to get, I'm afraid, will be something second-hand, something lifeless, something lacking in the spark of self-directed intelligence that we're after.'

'But the new filters – '

'Perhaps. Perhaps.'

Tanner shook his head stubbornly. 'Holmes and Don Quixote are fiction through and through. They exist in only one dimension, constructed for us by their authors. You cut through the distortions and fantasies of later readers and commentators and all you find underneath is a made-up character. A lot of Socrates may have been invented by Plato for his own purposes, but a lot wasn't. He really existed. He took an actual part in civic activities in fifth-century Athens. He figures in books by a lot of other contemporaries of his besides Plato's dialogues. That gives us the parallax you're looking for, doesn't it – the view of him from more than one viewpoint?'

'Maybe it does. Maybe not. We got nowhere with Moses. Was *he* fictional?'

'Who can say? All you had to go by was the Bible. And a ton of Biblical commentary, for whatever that was worth. Not much, apparently.'

'And Caesar? You're not going to tell me that Caesar wasn't real,' said Richardson. 'But what we have of him is evidently contaminated with myth. When we synthesized him we got nothing but a caricature, and I don't have to remind you how fast even that broke down into sheer gibberish.'

'Not relevant,' Tanner said. 'Caesar was early in the project. You know much more about what you're doing now. I think this is going to work.'

Richardson's dogged pessimism, Tanner decided, must be a defence mechanism, designed to insulate himself against the possibility of a new failure. Socrates, after all, hadn't been Richardson's own choice. And this was the first time he had used these new enhancement methods, the parallax program that was the latest refinement of the process.

Tanner looked at him. Richardson remained silent.

'Go on,' Tanner said. 'Bring up Pizarro and let the two of

them talk to each other. Then we'll find out what sort of Socrates you've conjured up here.'

Once again there was a disturbance in the distance, a little dark blur on the pearly horizon, a blotch, a flaw in the gleaming whiteness. Another demon is arriving, Pizarro thought. Or perhaps it is the same one as before, the American, the one who liked to show himself only as a face, with short hair and no beard.

But as this one drew closer Pizarro saw that he was different from the last, short and stocky, with broad shoulders and a deep chest. He was nearly bald and his thick beard was coarse and unkempt. He looked old, at least sixty, maybe sixty-five. He looked very ugly, too, with bulging eyes and a flat nose that had wide, flaring nostrils, and a neck so short that his oversized head seemed to sprout straight from his trunk. All he wore was a thin, ragged brown robe. His feet were bare.

'You, there,' Pizarro called out. 'You! Demon! Are you also an American, demon?'

'Your pardon. An Athenian, did you say?'

'*American* is what I said. That's what the last one was. Is that where you come from too, demon? America?'

A shrug. 'No, I think not. I am of Athens.' There was a curious mocking twinkle in the demon's eyes.

'A Greek? This demon is a Greek?'

'I am of Athens,' the ugly one said again. 'My name is Socrates, the son of Sophroniscus. I could not tell you what a Greek is, so perhaps I may be one, but I think not, unless a Greek is what you call a man of Athens.' He spoke in a slow, plodding way, like one who was exceedingly stupid. Pizarro had sometimes met men like this before, and in his experience they were generally not as stupid as they wanted to be taken for. He felt caution rising in him. 'And I am no demon, but just a plain man: very plain, as you can easily see.'

Pizarro snorted. 'You like to chop words, do you?'

'It is not the worst of amusements, my friend,' said the

other, and put his hands together behind his back in the most casual way, and stood there calmly, smiling, looking off into the distance, rocking back and forth on the balls of his feet.

'Well?' Tanner said. 'Do we have Socrates or not? I say that's the genuine article there.'

Richardson looked up and nodded. He seemed relieved and quizzical both at once. 'So far so good, I have to say. He's coming through real and true.'

'Yes.'

'We may actually have worked past the problem of information contamination that ruined some of the earlier simulations. We're not getting any of the signal degradation we encountered then.'

'He's some character, isn't he?' Tanner said. 'I liked the way he just walked right up to Pizarro without the slightest sign of uneasiness. He's not at all afraid of him.'

'Why should he be?' Richardson asked.

'Wouldn't you? If you were walking along through God knows what kind of unearthly place, not knowing where you were or how you got there, and suddenly you saw a ferocious-looking bastard like Pizarro standing in front of you wearing full armour and carrying a sword – ' Tanner shook his head. 'Well, maybe not. He's Socrates, after all, and Socrates wasn't afraid of anything except boredom.'

'And Pizarro's just a simulation. Nothing but software.'

'So you've been telling me all along. But Socrates doesn't know that.'

'True,' Richardson said. He seemed lost in thought a moment. 'Perhaps there *is* some risk.'

'Huh?'

'If our Socrates is anything like the one in Plato, and he surely ought to be, then he's capable of making a considerable pest of himself. Pizarro may not care for Socrates' little verbal games. If he doesn't feel like playing, I suppose there's a theoretical possibility that he'll engage in some sort of aggressive response.'

That took Tanner by surprise. He swung around and said, 'Are you telling me that there's some way he can *harm* Socrates?'

'Who knows?' said Richardson. 'In the real world one program can certainly crash another one. Maybe one simulation can be dangerous to another one. This is all new territory for all of us, Harry. Including the people in the tank.'

The tall, grizzled-looking man said, scowling, 'You tell me you're an Athenian, but not a Greek. What sense am I supposed to make of that? I could ask Pedro de Candia, I guess, who is a Greek but not an Athenian. But he's not here. Perhaps you're just a fool, eh? Or you think I am.'

'I have no idea what you are. Could it be that you are a god?'

'A *god*?'

'Yes,' Socrates said. He studied the other impassively. His face was harsh, his gaze was cold. 'Perhaps you are Ares. You have a fierce warlike look about you, and you wear armour, but not such armour as I have ever seen. This place is so strange that it might well be the abode of the gods, and that could be a god's armour you wear, I suppose. If you are Ares, then I salute you with the respect that is due you. I am Socrates of Athens, the stonemason's son.'

'You talk a lot of nonsense. I don't know your Ares.'

'Why, the god of war, of course! Everyone knows that. Except barbarians, that is. Are you a barbarian, then? You sound like one, I must say – but then, I seem to sound like a barbarian myself, and I've spoken the tongue of Hellas all my life. There are many mysteries here, indeed.'

'Your language problem again,' Tanner said. 'Couldn't you even get classical Greek to come out right? Or are they both speaking Spanish to each other?'

'Pizarro thinks they're speaking Spanish. Socrates thinks they're speaking Greek. And of course the Greek is off. We

305

don't know how *anything* that was spoken before the age of recordings sounded. All we can do is guess.'

'But can't you – '

'Shhh,' Richardson said.

Pizarro said, 'I may be a bastard, but I'm no barbarian, fellow, so curb your tongue. And let's have no more blasphemy out of you either.'

'If I blaspheme, forgive me. It is in innocence. Tell me where I trespass, and I will not do it again.'

'This crazy talk of gods. Of my being a god. I'd expect a heathen to talk like that, but not a Greek. But maybe you're a heathen kind of Greek, and not to be blamed. It's heathens who see gods everywhere. Do I look like a god to you? I am Francisco Pizarro, of Trujillo in Estremadura, the son of the famous soldier Gonzalo Pizarro, colonel of infantry, who served in the wars of Gonzalo de Cordova whom men call the Great Captain. I have fought some wars myself.'

'Then you are not a god but simply a soldier? Good. I too have been a soldier. I am more at ease with soldiers than with gods, as most people are, I would think.'

'A soldier? You?' Pizarro smiled. This shabby ordinary little man, more bedraggled-looking than any self-respecting groom would be, a soldier? 'In which wars?'

'The wars of Athens. I fought at Potidaea, where the Corinthians were making trouble, and withholding the tribute that was due us. It was very cold there, and the siege was long and bleak, but we did our duty. I fought again some years later at Delium against the Boeotians. Laches was our general then, but it went badly for us, and we did our best fighting in retreat. And then,' Socrates said, 'when Brasidas was in Amphipolis, and they sent Cleon to drive him out, I – '

'Enough,' said Pizarro with an impatient wave of his hand. 'These wars are unknown to me.' A private soldier, a man of the ranks, no doubt. 'Well, then this is the place where they send dead soldiers, I suppose.'

'Are we dead, then?'

'Long ago. There's an Alfonso who's king, and Pius who's pope, and you wouldn't believe their numbers. Pius XVI, I think the demon said. And the American said also that it is the year 2130. The last year that I can remember was 1539. What about you?'

The one who called himself Socrates shrugged again. 'In Athens we use a different reckoning. But let us say, for argument's sake, that we are dead. I think that is very likely, considering what sort of place this seems to be, and how airy I find my body to be. So we have died, and this is the life after life. I wonder: is this a place where virtuous men are sent, or those who were not virtuous? Or do all men go to the same place after death, whether they were virtuous or not? What would you say?'

'I haven't figured that out yet,' said Pizarro.

'Well, were you virtuous in your life, or not?'

'Did I sin, you mean?'

'Yes, we could use that word.'

'Did I sin, he wants to know,' said Pizarro, amazed. 'He asks, Was I a sinner? Did I live a virtuous life? What business is that of his?'

'Humour me,' said Socrates. 'For the sake of the argument, if you will, allow me a few small questions – '

'So, it's starting,' Tanner said. 'You see? You really *did* do it! Socrates is drawing him into a dialogue!'

Richardson's eyes were glowing. 'He is, yes. How marvellous this is, Harry!'

'Socrates is going to talk rings around him.'

'I'm not so sure of that,' Richardson said.

'I gave as good as I got,' said Pizarro. 'If I was injured, I gave injury back. There's no sin in that. It's only common sense. A man does what is necessary to survive and to protect his place in the world. Sometimes I might forget a fast day, yes, or use the Lord's name in vain – those are sins, I suppose, Fray Vicente was always after me for things like that – but does that make me a sinner? I did my penances as soon as I could find time for them. It's a sinful world and I'm no different from anyone else, so why be harsh on me? Eh? God made me as I am. I'm done in His image. And I have faith in His Son.'

'So you are a virtuous man, then?'

'I'm not a sinner, at any rate. As I told you, if ever I sinned I did my contrition, which made it the same as if the sin hadn't ever happened.'

'Indeed,' said Socrates. 'Then you are a virtuous man and I have come to a good place. But I want to be absolutely sure. Tell me again: is your conscience completely clear?'

'What are you, a confessor?'

'Only an ignorant man seeking understanding. Which you can provide, by taking part with me in the exploration. If I have come to the place of virtuous men, then I must have been virtuous myself when I lived. Ease my mind, therefore, and let me know whether there is anything on your soul that you regret having done.'

Pizarro stirred uneasily. 'Well,' he said, 'I killed a king.'

'A wicked one? An enemy of your city?'

'No. He was wise and kind.'

'Then you have reason for regret indeed. For surely that is a sin, to kill a wise king.'

'But he was a heathen.'

'A what?'

'He denied God.'

'He denied his own god?' said Socrates. 'Then perhaps it was not so wrong to kill him.'

'No. He denied mine. He *preferred* his own. And so he was a heathen. And all his people were heathens, since they followed his way. That could not be. They were at risk of eternal damnation because they followed him. I killed him for the sake of his people's souls. I killed him out of the love of God.'

'But would you not say that all gods are the reflection of the one God?'

Pizarro considered that. 'In a way, that's true, I suppose.'

'And is the service of God not itself godly?'

'How could it be anything but godly, Socrates?'

'And you would say that one who serves his god faithfully according to the teachings of his god is behaving in a godly way?'

Frowning, Pizarro said, 'Well – if you look at it that way, yes – '

'Then I think the king you killed was a godly man, and by killing him you sinned against God.'

'Wait a minute!'

'But think of it: by serving his god he must also have served yours, for any servant of a god is a servant of the true God who encompasses all our imagined gods.'

'No,' said Pizarro sullenly. 'How could he have been a servant of God? He knew nothing of Jesus. He had no understanding of the Trinity. When the priest offered him the Bible, he threw it to the ground in scorn. He was a heathen, Socrates. And so are you. You don't know anything of these matters at all, if you think that Atahuallpa was godly. Or if you think you're going to get me to think so.'

'Indeed I have very little knowledge of anything. But you say he was a wise man, and kind?'

'In his heathen way.'

'And a good king to his people?'

'So it seemed. They were a thriving people when I found them.'

'Yet he was not godly.'

'I told you. He had never had the sacraments, and in fact he spurned them right up until the moment of his death, when he accepted baptism. *Then* he came to be godly. But by then the sentence of death was upon him and it was too late for anything to save him.'

'Baptism? Tell me what this is, Pizarro.'

'A sacrament.'

'And that is?'

'A holy rite. Done with holy water, by a priest. It admits one to Holy Mother Church, and brings forgiveness from sin both original and actual, and gives the gift of the Holy Spirit.'

'You must tell me more about these things another time. So

309

you made this good king godly by this baptism? And then you killed him?'

'Yes.'

'But he was godly when you killed him. Surely, then, to kill him was a sin.'

'He had to die, Socrates!'

'And why was that?' asked the Athenian.

'Socrates is closing in for the kill,' Tanner said. 'Watch this!'

'I'm watching. But there isn't going to be any kill,' said Richardson. 'Their basic assumptions are too far apart.'

'You'll see.'

'Will I?'

Pizarro said, 'I've already told you why he had to die. It was because his people followed him in all things. And so they worshipped the sun, because he said the sun was God. Their souls would have gone to hell if we had allowed them to continue that way.'

'But if they followed him in all things,' said Socrates, 'then surely they would have followed him into baptism, and become godly, and thus done that which was pleasing to you and to your god! Is that not so?'

'No,' said Pizarro, twisting his fingers in his beard.

'Why do you think that?'

'Because the king agreed to be baptized only after we had sentenced him to death. He was in the way, don't you see? He was an obstacle to our power! So we had to get rid of him. He would never have led his people to the truth of his own free will. That was why we had to kill him. But we didn't want to kill his soul as well as his body, so we said to him, Look, Atahuallpa, we're going to put you to death, but if you let us baptize you we'll strangle you quickly, and if you don't we'll burn you alive and it'll be very slow. So of course he agreed to be baptized, and we strangled him. What choice was there for anybody? He had to die. He still didn't believe the true faith, as we all well knew. Inside his head he was as big a

310

heathen as ever. But he died a Christian all the same.'

'A what?'

'A Christian! A Christian! One who believes in Jesus Christ the Son of God!'

'The *son* of God,' Socrates said, sounding puzzled. 'And do Christians believe in God too, or only His Son?'

'What a fool you are!'

'I would not deny that.'

'There is God the Father, and God the Son, and then there is the Holy Spirit.'

'Ah,' said Socrates. 'And which one did your Atahuallpa believe in, then, when the strangler came for him?'

'None of them.'

'And yet he died a Christian? Without believing in any of your three gods? How is that?'

'Because of the baptism,' said Pizarro in rising annoyance. 'What does it matter what he believed? The priest sprinkled the water on him! The priest said the words! If the rite is properly performed, the soul is saved regardless of what the man understands or believes! How else could you baptize an infant? An infant understands nothing and believes nothing – but he becomes a Christian when the water touches him!'

'Much of this is mysterious to me,' said Socrates. 'But I see that you regard the king you killed as godly as well as wise, because he was washed by the water your gods require, and so you killed a good king who now lives in the embrace of your gods because of the baptism. Which seems wicked to me; and so this cannot be the place where the virtuous are sent after death, so it must be that I too was not virtuous, or else that I have misunderstood everything about this place and why we are in it.'

'Damn you, are you trying to drive me crazy?' Pizarro roared, fumbling at the hilt of his sword. He drew it and waved it around in fury. 'If you don't shut your mouth I'll cut you in thirds!'

'Uh-oh,' Tanner said. 'So much for the dialectical method.'

* * *

311

Socrates said mildly, 'It isn't my intention to cause you any annoyance, my friend. I'm only trying to learn a few things.'

'You are a fool!'

'That is certainly true, as I have already acknowledged several times. Well, if you mean to strike me with your sword, go ahead. But I don't think it'll accomplish very much.'

'Damn you,' Pizarro muttered. He stared at his sword and shook his head. 'No. No, it won't do any good, will it? It would go through you like air. But you'd just stand there and let me try to cut you down, and not even blink, right? Right?' He shook his head. 'And yet you aren't stupid. You argue like the shrewdest priest I've ever known.'

'In truth I am stupid,' said Socrates. 'I know very little at all. But I strive constantly to attain some understanding of the world, or at least to understand something of myself.'

Pizarro glared at him. 'No,' he said. 'I won't buy this false pride of yours. I have a little understanding of people myself, old man. I'm on to your game.'

'What game is that, Pizarro?'

'I can see your arrogance. I see that you believe you're the wisest man in the world, and that it's your mission to go around educating poor sword-waving fools like me. And you pose as a fool to disarm your adversaries before you humiliate them.'

'Score one for Pizarro,' Richardson said. 'He's wise to Socrates' little tricks, all right.'

'Maybe he's read some Plato,' Tanner suggested.

'He was illiterate.'

'That was then. This is now.'

'Not guilty,' said Richardson. 'He's operating on peasant shrewdness alone, and you damned well know it.'

'I wasn't being serious,' Tanner said. He leaned forward, peering towards the holotank. 'God, what an astonishing thing this is, listening to them going at it. They seem absolutely real.'

'They are,' said Richardson.

'No, Pizarro, I am not wise at all,' Socrates said. 'But, stupid as I am, it may be that I am not the least wise man who ever lived.'

'You think you're wiser than I am, don't you?'

'How can I say? First tell me how wise you are.'

'Wise enough to begin my life as a bastard tending pigs and finish it as Captain-General of Peru.'

'Ah, then you must be very wise.'

'I think so, yes.'

'Yet you killed a wise king because he wasn't wise enough to worship God the way you wished him to. Was that so wise of you, Pizarro? How did his people take it, when they found out that their king had been killed?'

'They rose in rebellion against us. They destroyed their own temples and palaces, and hid their gold and silver from us, and burned their bridges, and fought us bitterly.'

'Perhaps you could have made some better use of him by *not* killing him, do you think?'

'In the long run we conquered them and made them Christians. It was what we intended to accomplish.'

'But the same thing might have been accomplished in a wiser way?'

'Perhaps,' said Pizarro grudgingly. 'Still, we accomplished it. That's the main thing, isn't it? We did what we set out to do. If there was a better way, so be it. Angels do things perfectly. We were no angels, but we achieved what we came for, and so be it, Socrates. So be it.'

'I'd call that one a draw,' said Tanner.

'Agreed.'

'It's a terrific game they're playing.'

'I wonder who we can use to play it next,' said Richardson.

'I wonder what we can do with this besides using it to play games,' said Tanner.

'Let me tell you a story,' said Socrates. 'The oracle at Delphi once said to a friend of mine, "There is no man wiser than Socrates," but I doubted that very much, and it troubled me to hear the oracle saying something that I knew was so far from the truth. So I decided to look for a man who was obviously wiser than I was. There was a politician in Athens who was famous for his wisdom, and I went to him and questioned him about many things. After I had listened to him for a time, I came to see that though many people, and most of all he himself, thought that he was wise, yet he was not wise. He only imagined that he was wise. So I realized that I must be wiser than he. Neither of us knew anything that was really worthwhile, but he knew nothing and thought that he knew, whereas I neither knew anything nor thought that I did. At least on one point, then, I was wiser than he: I didn't think that I knew what I didn't know.'

'Is this intended to mock me, Socrates?'

'I feel only the deepest respect for you, friend Pizarro. But let me continue. I went to other wise men, and they too, though sure of their wisdom, could never give me a clear answer to anything. Those whose reputations for wisdom were the highest seemed to have the least of it. I went to the great poets and playwrights. There was wisdom in their works, for the gods had inspired them, but that did not make *them* wise, though they thought that it had. I went to the stonemasons and potters and other craftsmen. They were wise in their own skills, but most of them seemed to think that that made them wise in everything, which did not appear to be the case. And so it went. I was unable to find anyone who showed true wisdom. So perhaps the oracle was right: that although I am an ignorant man, there is no man wiser than I am. But oracles often are right without there being much value in it, for I think that all she was saying was that no man is wise at all, that wisdom is reserved for the gods. What do you say, Pizarro?'

'I say that you are a great fool, and very ugly besides.'

'You speak the truth. So, then, you are wise after all. And honest.'

'Honest, you say? I won't lay claim to that. Honesty's a game for fools. I lied whenever I needed to. I cheated. I went back

314

on my word. I'm not proud of that, mind you. It's simply what you have to do to get on in the world. You think I wanted to tend pigs all my life? I wanted gold, Socrates! I wanted power over men! I wanted fame!'

'And did you get those things?'

'I got them all.'

'And were they gratifying, Pizarro?'

Pizarro gave Socrates a long look. Then he pursed his lips and spat.

'They were worthless.'

'Were they, do you think?'

'Worthless, yes. I have no illusions about that. But still it was better to have had them than not. In the long run nothing has any meaning, old man. In the long run we're all dead, the honest man and the villain, the king and the fool. Life's a cheat. They tell us to strive, to conquer, to gain – and for what? What? For a few years of strutting around. Then it's taken away, as if it had never been. A cheat, I say.' Pizarro paused. He stared at his hands as though he had never seen them before. 'Did I say all that just now? Did I mean it?' He laughed. 'Well, I suppose I did. Still, life is all there is, so you want as much of it as you can. Which means getting gold, and power, and fame.'

'Which you had. And apparently have no longer. Friend Pizarro, where are we now?'

'I wish I knew.'

'So do I,' said Socrates soberly.

'He's real,' Richardson said. 'They both are. The bugs are out of the system and we've got something spectacular here. Not only is this going to be of value to scholars, I think it's also going to be a tremendous entertainment gimmick, Harry.'

'It's going to be much more than that,' said Tanner in a strange voice.

'What do you mean by that?'

'I'm not sure yet,' Tanner said. 'But I'm definitely on to something big. It just began to hit me a couple of minutes ago, and it hasn't really taken shape yet. But it's something that might change the whole goddamned world.'

Richardson looked amazed and bewildered.

'What the hell are you talking about, Harry?'

Tanner said, 'A new way of settling political disputes, maybe. What would you say to a kind of combat-at-arms between one nation and another? Like a medieval tournament, so to speak. With each side using champions that we simulate for them – the greatest minds of all the past, brought back and placed in competition – ' He shook his head. 'Something like that. It needs a lot of working out, I know. But it's got possibilities.'

'A medieval tournament – combat-at-arms, using simulations? Is that what you're saying?'

'Verbal combat. Not actual jousts, for Christ's sake.'

'I don't see how – ' Richardson began.

'Neither do I, not yet. I wish I hadn't even spoken of it.'

'But – '

'Later, Lew. Later. Let me think about it a little while more.'

'You don't have any idea what this place is?' Pizarro said.

'Not at all. But I certainly think this is no longer the world where we once dwelled. Are we dead, then? How can we say? You look alive to me.'

'And you to me.'

'Yet I think we are living some other kind of life. Here, give me your hand. Can you feel mine against yours?'

'No. I can't feel anything.'

'Nor I. Yet I see two hands clasping. Two old men standing on a cloud, clasping hands.' Socrates laughed. 'What a great rogue you are, Pizarro!'

'Yes, of course. But do you know something, Socrates? You are too. A windy old rogue. I like you. There were moments when you were driving me crazy with all your chatter, but you amused me too. Were you really a soldier?'

'When my city asked me, yes.'

'For a soldier, you're damned innocent about the way the

316

world works, I have to say. But I guess I can teach you a thing or too.'

'Will you?'

'Gladly,' said Pizarro.

'I would be in your debt,' Socrates said.

'Take Atahuallpa,' Pizarro said. 'How can I make you understand why I had to kill him? There weren't even two hundred of us, and twenty-four millions of them, and his word was law, and once he was gone they'd have no one to command them. So of *course* we had to get rid of him if we wanted to conquer them. And so we did, and then they fell.'

'How simple you make it seem.'

'Simple is what it was. Listen, old man, he would have died sooner or later anyway, wouldn't he? This way I made his death useful: to God, to the Church, to Spain. And to Francisco Pizarro. Can you understand that?'

'I think so,' said Socrates. 'But do you think King Atahuallpa did?'

'Any king would understand such things.'

'Then he should have killed you the moment you set foot in his land.'

'Unless God meant us to conquer him, and allowed him to understand that. Yes. Yes, that must have been what happened.'

'Perhaps he is in this place too, and we could ask him,' said Socrates.

Pizarro's eyes brightened. 'Mother of God, yes! A good idea! And if he didn't understand, why, I'll try to explain it to him. Maybe you'll help me. You know how to talk, how to move words around and around. What do you say? Would you help me?'

'If we meet him, I would like to talk with him,' Socrates said. 'I would indeed like to know if he agrees with you on the subject of the usefulness of his being killed by you.'

Grinning, Pizarro said, 'Slippery, you are! But I like you. I like you very much. Come. Let's go look for Atahuallpa.'

317

We Are For the Dark

Where do story ideas come from? the non-writer often asks. And the writer's usual answer is a bemused shrug. But in this instance I can reply very precisely.

Karen and I were visiting London in September of 1987, and of course we were spending virtually every evening at the theatre and some afternoons besides. On the next to last day of our stay we were at the National Theatre, on the south side of the Thames, to see Anthony Hopkins and Judi Dench in *Antony and Cleopatra*, a wondrous, magical matinée performance. Act Five came around, Cleopatra's great catastrophe, and her serving-maid Iras signalled the beginning of the final act with lines long familiar to me:

> Finish, good lady; the bright day is done.
> And we are for the dark.

A mysterious shiver ran through me at those words, *we are for the dark*. I had seen the play half a dozen times or more over the years, and they had never seemed unusual to me before; but, hearing them now, I suddenly saw great vistas of black space opening before me. Later that splendid afternoon, strolling back across the bridge towards the heart of the city under brilliant summer sunshine, my mind continued to dwell on the vistas that Shakespeare's five words had evoked for me, and soon I was taking notes for a story that had absolutely nothing to do with the travails of Cleopatra or Antony.

That was the engendering point. The other details followed quickly enough, all but the mechanism of the matter-transmission system around which the interstellar venture of the story was to be built. That had to wait until late January of the following year. Now

318

I was in Los Angeles, resting and reading before going out for dinner, and suddenly I found myself scribbling down stuff about the spontaneous conversion of matter into antimatter and a necessary balancing conversion in the opposite direction. Whether any such thing is actually the case is beyond my own scientific expertise, but the idea seemed plausible enough to work with, and very quickly I had built an entire method of faster-than-light travel out of it, one which is probably utterly unfeasible in the real universe but serves well enough in mine, and at any rate is my very own. I wrote the story in March of 1988 and Gardner Dozois published it in *Isaac Asimov's Science Fiction Magazine*. For me it had some of the sweep and grandeur that first drew me to science fiction as a reader more than forty years ago, and it pleased me greatly on that account. I thought that it might attract some attention among readers, but, oddly, it seemed to pass almost unnoticed – no awards nominations, no year's-best selection. Which puzzled me; but eventually I put the matter out of mind. Stories of mine that I had thought of as quite minor indeed had gone on to gain not only awards nominations but, more than once, the awards themselves; stories that had seemed to me to be failures when I wrote them had been reprinted a dozen times over in later years; and, occasionally, a story that moved me profoundly as I composed it had gone straight from publication to oblivion almost as if it had never existed at all. 'We Are For the Dark' seems to have been one of those, though I still have hope for its rediscovery.

But the moral is clear, at least to me: write what satisfies you, and let the awards and anthologizations take care of themselves, because there's no sure way of predicting what kind of career a story will have. Strive always to do your best, and, when you believe that you have, allow yourself the pleasure of your own approval. If readers happen to share your delight in your own work, that's a bonus in which to rejoice, but it's folly ever to expect others to respond to your work in the same way that you do yourself.

Great warmth comes from him, golden cascades of bright, nurturing energy. The Master is often said to be like a sun, and so he is, a luminous creature, a saint, a sun indeed. But warmth is not the only thing that emanates from suns. They radiate at many frequencies of the spectrum, hissing and crackling and glaring like furnaces as they send forth the angry power that withers, the power that kills. The moment I enter the Master's presence I feel that other force, that terrible one, flowing from him. The air about him hums with it, though the warmth of him, the benevolence, is evident also. His power is frightful. And yet all he is is a man, a very old one at that, with a smooth round hairless head and pale, mysteriously gentle eyes. Why should I fear him? My faith is strong. I love the Master. We all love him.

This is only the fifth time I have met him. The last was seven years ago, at the time of the Altair launch. We of the other House rarely have reason to come to the Sanctuary, or they to us. But he recognizes me at once, and calls me by name, and pours cool clear golden wine for me with his own hand. As I expect, he says nothing at first about his reason for summoning me. He talks instead of his recent visit to the Capital, where great swarms of ragged hungry people trotted tirelessly alongside his palanquin as he was borne in procession, begging him to send them into the Dark. 'Soon, soon, my children,' is what he tells me now that he told them then. 'Soon we will all go to our new dwelling-places in the stars.' And he wept, he says, for sheer joy, feeling the intensity of their love for him, feeling their longing for the new worlds to which we alone hold the keys. It seems to me that he is quietly weeping now, telling me these things.

Behind his desk is a star-map of extraordinary vividness and detail, occupying the rear wall of his austere chamber. Indeed, it *is* the rear wall: a huge curving shield of some gleaming, dark substance blacker than night, within which I can see our galaxy depicted, its glittering core, its spiralling arms. Many of the high-magnitude stars shine forth clearly in their actual colours. Beyond, sinking into the depths of the dark matrix in a way that makes the map seem to stretch outwards to infinity, are the neighbouring galaxies, resting in clouds of shimmering dust.

More distant clusters and nebulae are visible still farther from the map's centre. As I stare, I feel myself carried on and on to the outermost ramparts of the universe. I compliment him on the ingenuity of the map, and on its startling realism.

But that seems to be a mistake. 'Realism? This map?' the Master cries, and the energies flickering around him grow fierce and sizzling once again. 'This map is nothing: a crazy hodge-podge. A lunacy. Look, this star sent us its light twelve billion years ago, and that one six billion years ago, and this other one twenty-three years ago, and we're seeing them all at once. But this one didn't even exist when that one started beaming its light at us. And this one may have died five billion years ago, but we won't know it for five billion more.' His voice, usually so soft, is rising now and there is a dangerous edge on it. I have never seen him this angry. 'So what does this map actually show us? Not the absolute reality of the universe but only a meaningless ragbag of subjective impressions. It shows the stars as they happen to appear to us just at this minute and we pretend that that is the actual cosmos, the true configuration.' His face has grown flushed. He pours more wine. His hand is trembling, suddenly, and I think he will miss the rim of the glass, but no: his control is perfect. We drink in silence. Another moment and he is calm again, benign as the Buddha, bathing me in the glow and lustre of his spirit.

'Well, we must do the best we can within our limitations,' he says gently. 'For the closer spans the map is not useless.' He touches something on his desk and the star-map undergoes a dizzying shift, the outer clusters dropping away and the centre of our own galaxy coming up until it fills the whole screen. Another flick of his finger and the inner realm of the galaxy stands out in bright highlighting: that familiar sphere, a hundred light-years in diameter, which is the domain of our Mission. A network of brilliant yellow lines cuts across the heart of it from star to star, marking the places where we have chosen to place our first receiver stations. It is a pattern I could trace from memory, and, seeing it now, I feel a sense of comfort and well-being, as though I am looking at a map of my native city.

Now, surely, he will begin to speak of Mission matters, he will start working his way round to the reason for my being here. But no, no, he wants to tell me of a garden of aloes he has lately seen by the shores of the Mediterranean, twisted spiky green rosettes topped by flaming red torches of blooms, and then of his visit to a lake in East Africa where pink flamingos massed in millions, so that all the world seemed pink, and then of a pilgrimage he has undertaken in the highest passes of the Sierra Nevada, where gnarled little pines ten thousand years old endure the worst that winter can hurl at them. As he speaks, his face grows more animated, his eyes take on an eager sparkle. His great age drops away from him: he seems younger by thirty, forty, fifty years. I had not realized he was so keen a student of nature. 'The next time you are in my country,' I tell him, 'perhaps you will allow me to show you the place along the southern shore where the fairy penguins come to nest in summer. In all the world I think that is the place I love the best.'

He smiles. 'You must tell me more about that some time.' But his tone is flat, his expression has gone slack. The effort of this little talk must have exhausted him. 'This Earth of ours is so beautiful,' he says. 'Such marvels, such splendours.'

What can he mean by that? Surely he knows that only a few scattered islands of beauty remain, rare fortunate places rising above the polluted seas or sheltered from the tainted air, and that everything else is soiled, stained, damaged, corroded beyond repair by one sort of human folly or another.

'Of course,' he says, 'I would leave it in a moment, if duty beckoned me into the Dark. I would not hesitate. That I could never return would mean nothing to me.' For a time he is silent. Then he draws a disc from a drawer of his desk and slides it towards me. 'This music has given me great pleasure. Perhaps it will please you also. We'll talk again in a day or two.'

The map behind him goes blank. His gaze, though it still rests on me, is blank now also.

So the audience is over, and I have learned nothing. Well,

322

indirection has always been his method. I understand now that whatever has gone wrong with the Mission – for surely something has, why else would I be here? – is not only serious enough to warrant calling me away from my House and my work, but is so serious that the Master feels the need of more than one meeting to convey its nature to me. Of course I am calm. Calmness is inherent in the character of those who serve the Order. Yet there is a strangeness about all this that troubles me as I have never been troubled before in the forty years of my service.

Outside, the night air is warm, and still humid from earlier rain. The Master's lodge sits by itself atop a lofty stepped platform of pink granite, with the lesser buildings of the Order arrayed in a semi-circle below it on the side of the great curving hill. As I walk towards the hostelry where I am staying, novitiates and even some initiates stare at me as though they would like to prostrate themselves before me. They revere me as I revere the Master. They would touch the hem of my robe, if they could. I nod and smile. Their eyes are hungry, God-haunted, star-haunted.

'Lord Magistrate,' they murmur. 'God be with you, your grace. God be with you.' One novitiate, a gaunt boy, all cheek-bones and eyebrows, dares to run to my side and ask me if the Master is well. 'Very well,' I tell him. A girl, quivering like a bowstring, says my name over and over as though it alone can bring her salvation. A plump monkish-looking man in a grey robe much too heavy for this hot climate looks towards me for a blessing, and I give him a quick gesture and walk swiftly onwards, sealing my attention now inwards and heavenwards to free myself of their supplications as I stride across the terraced platform to my lodging.

There is no moon tonight, and against the blackness of the highlands sky the stars shine forth resplendently by the tens of thousands. I feel those stars in all their multitudes pressing close about me, enclosing me, enfolding me, and I know that what I feel is the presence of God. I imagine even that I see the distant nebulae, the far-off island universes. I think of our little ships, patiently sailing across the great Dark towards the remote precincts of our chosen sphere of settlement, carrying with them the receivers that will, God willing, open all His heavens to us. My throat is dry. My eyes are moist. After forty years I have lost none of my ability to feel the wonder of it.

In my spacious and lavishly appointed room in the hostelry I kneel and make my devotions, and pray, as ever, to be brought ever closer to Him. In truth I am merely the vehicle by which others are allowed to approach Him, I know: the bridge through which they cross to Him. But in my way I serve God also, and to serve Him is to grow closer to Him. My task for these many years has been to send voyagers to the far worlds of His realm. It is not for me to go that way myself: that is my sacrifice, that is my glory. I have no regret over remaining Earthbound: far from it! Earth is our great mother. Earth is the mother of us all. Troubled as she is, blighted as she now may be, dying, even, I am content to stay here, and more than content. How could I leave? I have my task, and the place of my task is here, and here I must remain.

I meditate upon these things for a time.

Afterwards I oil my body for sleep and pour myself a glass of the fine brandy I have brought with me from home. I go to the wall dispenser and allow myself thirty seconds of ecstasy. Then I remember the disc the Master gave me, and decide to play it before bed. The music, if that is what it is, makes no impression on me whatever. I hear one note, and the next, and the one after that, but I am unable to put them together into any kind of rhythmic or melodic pattern. When it ends I play it again. Again I can hear only random sound, neither pleasant nor unpleasant, merely incomprehensible.

The next morning they conduct me on a grand tour of the Sanctuary complex to show me everything that has been constructed here since my last visit. The tropical sunlight is brilliant, dazzling, so strong that it bleaches the sky to a matte white, against which the colourful domes and pavilions and spires of the complex stand out in strange clarity and the lofty green bowl of surrounding hills, thick and lush with flowering trees bedecked in yellow and purple, takes on a heavy, looming quality.

Kastel, the Lord Invocator, is my chief guide, a burly, red-faced man with small, shrewd eyes and a deceptively hearty manner. With us also are a woman from the office of the Oracle and two sub-Adjudicators. They hurry me, though with the utmost tact, from one building to the next. All four of them treat me as though I were something extremely fragile, made of the most delicate spun glass – or, perhaps, as though I were a bomb primed to explode at the touch of a breath.

'Over here on the left,' says Kastel, 'is the new observatory, with the finest scanning equipment ever devised, providing continuous input from every region of the Mission. The scanner itself, I regret to say, Lord Magistrate, is out of service this morning. There, of course, is the shrine of the blessed Haakon. Here we see the computer core, and this, behind it under the opaque canopy, is the recently completed stellarium.'

I see leaping fountains, marble pavements, alabaster walls, gleaming metallic façades. They are very proud of what they have constructed here. The House of the Sanctuary has evolved over the decades, and by now has come to combine in itself aspects of a pontifical capital, a major research facility, and the ultimate sybaritic resort. Everything is bright, shining, start-lingly luxurious. It is at once a place of great symbolic power, a potent focus of spiritual authority as overwhelming in its grandeur as any great ceremonial centre of the past – ranking with the Vatican, the Potala, the shrine at Delphi, the grand temple of the Aztecs – and an efficient command post for the systematic exploration of the universe. No one doubts that the Sanctuary is the primary House of the Order – how could it be anything else? – but the splendours of this mighty eyrie under-score that primacy beyond all question. In truth I prefer the starker, more disciplined surroundings of my own desert domain, ten thousand kilometres away. But the Sanctuary is certainly impressive in its way.

'And that one down there?' I ask, more for politeness' sake

than anything else. 'The long flat-roofed building near that row of palms?'

'The detention centre, Lord Magistrate,' replies one of the sub-Adjudicators.

I give him a questioning look.

'People from the towns below constantly come wandering in here,' he explains. 'Trespassers, I mean.' His expression is cold. Plainly the intruders of whom he speaks are annoyances to him; or is it my question that bothers him? 'They hope they can talk us into shipping them out, you understand. Or think that the actual transmitters are somewhere on the premises and they can ship themselves out when nobody's looking. We keep them for a while, so that they'll learn that trying to break in here isn't acceptable. Not that it does much good. They keep on coming. We've caught at least twenty so far this week.'

Kastel laughs. 'We try to teach them a thing or two, all right! But they're too stupid to learn.'

'They have no chance of getting past the perimeter screen,' says the woman from the Oracle's office. 'We pick them up right away. But as Joseph says, they keep on coming all the same.' She shivers. 'They look so dirty! And mean, and frightening. I don't think they want to be shipped out at all. I think they're just bandits who come up here to try to steal from us, and when they're caught they give us a story about wanting to be colonists. We're much too gentle with them, let me tell you. If we started dealing with them like the thieves they are, they wouldn't be so eager to come creeping around in here.'

I find myself wondering just what does happen to the detainees in the detention centre. I suspect that they are treated a good deal less gently than the woman from the Oracle's office thinks, or would have me believe. But I am only a guest here. It's not my place to make inquiries into their security methods.

It is like another world up here above the clouds. Below is the teeming Earth, dark and troubled, cult-ridden, doom-ridden, sweltering and stewing in its own corruption and decay; while in this airy realm far above the crumbling and sweltering cities of the plain these votaries of the Order, safe behind their perimeter screen, go quietly about their task of designing and clarifying the plan that is carrying mankind's best outwards into God's starry realm. The contrast is vast and jarring: pink marble terraces and fountains here, disease and squalor and despair below.

And yet, is it any different at my own headquarters on the Australian plains? In our House we do not go in for these architectural splendours, no alabaster, no onyx, just plain green metal shacks to house our equipment and ourselves. But we keep ourselves apart from the hungry sweaty multitudes in hieratic seclusion, a privileged caste, living simply but well, undeniably well, as we perform our own task of selecting those who are to go to the stars and sending them forth on their unimaginable journeys. In our own way we are as remote from the pressures and torments of mankind as these coddled functionaries of the Sanctuary. We know nothing of the life beyond our own Order. Nothing. Nothing.

The Master says, 'I was too harsh yesterday, and even blasphemous.' The map behind him is aglow once again, displaying the inner sphere of the galaxy and the lines marking the network of the Mission, as it had the day before. The Master himself is glowing too, his soft skin ruddy as a baby's, his eyes agleam. How old is he? A hundred fifty? Two hundred? 'The map, after all, shows us the face of God,' he says. 'If the map is inadequate, it simply reveals the inadequacies of our own perceptions. But should we condemn it, then? Hardly, any more than we should condemn ourselves for not being gods. We should revere it, rather, flawed though it may be, because it is the best approximation that we can ever make of the reality of the Divine.'

'The face of God?'

'What is God, if not the Great Totality? And how can we expect to see and comprehend the Totality of the Totality in a single glance?' The Master smiles. These are not thoughts that he has just had for the first time, nor can his complete reversal of yesterday's outburst be a spontaneous one. He is playing with me. 'God is eternal motion through infinite space. He is the cosmos as it was twelve billion years ago and as it will be twelve billion years from now, all in the same instant. This map you see here is our pitiful attempt at a representation of something inherently incapable of being represented; but we are to be praised for making an attempt, however foredoomed, at doing that which cannot be done.'

I nod. I stare. What could I possibly say?

'When we experience the revelation of God,' the Master continues softly, 'what we receive is not the communication of a formula about a static world, which enables us to be at rest, but rather a sense of the power of the Creator, which sets us in motion even as He is in motion.'

I think of Dante, who said, 'In His will is our peace.' Is there a contradiction here? How can 'motion' be 'peace'? Why is the Master telling me all this? Theology has never been my speciality, nor the speciality of my House in general, and he knows that. The abstruse nature of this discussion is troublesome to me. My eyes rest upon the Master, but their focus changes, so that I am looking beyond him, to red Antares and blue Rigel and fiery blue-white Vega, blazing at me from the wall.

The Master says, 'Our Mission, you must surely agree, is an aspect of God's great plan. It is His way of enabling us to undertake the journey towards Him.'

'Of course.'

'Then whatever thwarts the design of the Mission must be counter to the will of God, is that not so?'

It is not a question. I am silent again, waiting.

He gestures towards the screen. 'I would think that you know this pattern of lights and lines better than you do that of the palm of your hand.'

'So I do.'

'What about this one?'

The Master touches a control. The pattern suddenly changes: the bright symmetrical network linking the inner stars is sundered, and streaks of light now skid wildly out of the centre towards the far reaches of the galaxy, like errant particles racing outwards in a photomicrograph of an atomic reaction. The sight is a jarring one: balance overthrown, the sky untuned, discordancy triumphant. I wince and lean back from it as though he has slapped my face.

'Ah. You don't like it, eh?'

'Your pardon. It seems like a desecration.'

'It is,' he says. 'Exactly so.'

I feel chilled. I want him to restore the screen to its proper state. But he leaves the shattered image where it is.

He says, 'This is only a probability projection, you understand. Based on early fragmentary reports from the farther outposts, by way of the Order's relay station on Lalande 21185. We aren't really sure what's going on out there. What we hope, naturally, is that our projections are inaccurate and that the plan is being followed after all. Harder data will be here soon.'

'Some of those lines must reach out a thousand light-years!'

'More than that.'

'Nothing could possibly have got so far from Earth in just the hundred years or so that we've been – '

'These are projections. Those are vectors. But they seem to be telling us that some carrier ships have been aimed beyond the predetermined targets, and are moving through the Dark on trajectories far more vast than anything we intend.'

'But the plan – the Mission – '

His voice begins to develop an edge again. 'Those whom we, acting through your House, have selected to implement the plan are very far from home, Lord Magistrate. They are no longer subject to our control. If they choose to do as they please once they're fifty light-years away, what means do we have of bringing them into check?'

'I find it very hard to believe that any of the colonists we've sent forth would be capable of setting aside the ordinances of Darklaw,' I say, with perhaps too much heat in my voice.

What I have done, I realize, is to contradict him. Contradicting the Master is never a good idea. I see the lightnings playing about his head, though his expression remains mild and he continues to regard me benignly. Only the faintest of flushes on his ancient face betrays his anger. He makes no reply. I am getting into deep waters very quickly.

'Meaning no disrespect,' I say, 'but if this is, as you say, only a probability projection – '

'All that we have devoted our lives to is in jeopardy now,' he says quietly. 'What are we to do? What are we to do, Lord Magistrate?'

We have been building our highway to the stars for a century now and a little more, laying down one small paving-block after another. That seems like a long time to those of us who measure our spans in tens of years, and we have nibbled only a small way into the great darkness; but though we often feel that progress has been slow, in fact we have achieved miracles already, and we have all of eternity to complete our task.

In summoning us towards Him, God did not provide us with magical chariots. The inflexible jacket of the relativistic equations constrains us as we work. The speed of light remains our limiting factor while we establish our network. Although the Velde Effect allows us to deceive it and in effect to sidestep it, we must first carry the Velde receivers to the stars, and for that we can use only conventional spacegoing vehicles. They can approach the velocity of light, they may virtually attain it, but they can never exceed it: a starship making the outward journey to a star forty light-years from Earth must needs spend some forty years, and some beyond, in the doing of it. Later, when all the sky is linked by our receivers, that will not be a problem. But that is later.

The key to all that we do is the matter/antimatter relationship. When He built the universe for us, He placed all things in balance. The basic constituents of matter come in matched pairs: for each kind of particle there is an antiparticle, identical in mass but otherwise wholly opposite in all properties, mirror images in such things as electrical charge and axis of spin. Matter and antimatter annihilate one another upon contact, releasing tremendous energy. Conversely, any sufficiently strong energy field can bring about the creation of pairs of particles and antiparticles in equal quantities, though mutual annihilation will inevitably follow, converting the mass of the paired particles back into energy.

Apparently there is, and always has been since the Creation, a symmetry of matter and antimatter in the universe, equal quantities of each – a concept that has often been questioned by physicists, but which we believe now to be God's true design. Because of the incompatibility of matter and antimatter in the same vicinity, there is very little if any antimatter in our galaxy, which leads us to suppose that if symmetry is conserved, it must be through the existence of entire galaxies of antimatter, or even clusters of galaxies, at great distances from our own. Be that as it may: we will probably have no way of confirming or denying that for many thousands of years.

But the concept of symmetry is the essential thing. We base our work on Velde's Theorem, which suggests that the spontaneous conversion of matter into antimatter may occur at any time – though in fact it is an event of infinitesimal probability – but it must inescapably be accompanied by a simultaneous equal decay of antimatter into matter somewhere else, anywhere else, in the universe. About the same time that Velde offered this idea – that is, roughly a century and a half ago – Wilf demonstrated the feasibility of containment facilities capable of averting the otherwise inevitable mutual annihilation of matter and antimatter, thus making possible the controlled transformation of particles into their antiparticles. Finally came the work of Simtow, linking Wilf's technical achievements with Velde's theoretical work and giving us a device that not only achieved controlled matter/antimatter conversion but also coped with the apparent randomness of Velde symmetry-conservation.

Simtow's device tunes the Velde Effect so that conversion of matter into antimatter is accompanied by the requisite balancing transformation of antimatter into matter, not at some random site anywhere in the universe, *but at a designated site*. Simtow was able to induce particle decay at one pole of a closed system in such a way that a corresponding but opposite decay occurs at the other. Wilf containment fields were employed at both ends of the system to prevent annihilation of the newly converted particles by ambient particles of the opposing kind.

The way was open now, though it was some time before we realized it, for the effective instantaneous transmission of matter across great distances. That was achieved by placing the receiving pole of a Simtow transformer at the intended destination. Then an intricate three-phase cycle carried out the transmission.

In the first phase, matter is converted into antimatter at the destination end in an untuned reaction, and stored in a Wilf containment vessel. This, following Velde's conservation equations, presumably would induce spontaneous transformation of an equivalent mass of antimatter into matter in one of the unknown remote antimatter galaxies, where it would be immediately annihilated.

In the second phase, matter is converted to antimatter at the transmitting end, this time employing Simtow tuning so that the corresponding Velde-law transformation of the previously stored antimatter takes place not at some remote and random location but within the Wilf field at the designated receiving pole, which may be situated anywhere in the universe. What this amounts to, essentially, is the instantaneous particle-by-particle duplication of the transmitted matter at the receiving end.

The final step is to dispose of the unwanted antimatter that has been created at the transmission end. Since it is unstable outside the Wilf containment vessel, its continued existence in an all-matter system is pointless as well as untenable. Therefore it is annihilated under controlled circumstances, providing a significant release of energy that can be tapped to power a new cycle of the transmission process.

What is accomplished by all this? A certain quantity of matter at the transmission end of the system is destroyed; an exact duplicate of it is created, essentially simultaneously at the receiving end. It made no difference, the early experimenters discovered, what was being put through the system: a stone, a book, a potted geranium, a frog. Whatever went in here came out there, an apparently perfect replica, indistinguishable in all respects from the original. Whether the two poles were situated at opposite ends of the same laboratory, or in different continents, or on Earth and Mars, the transmission was instant and total. What went forth alive came out alive. The geranium still bloomed and set seed; the frog still stared and leaped and gobbled insects. A mouse was sent, and thrived, and went on to live and die a full mouse-life. A pregnant cat made the journey and was delivered, three weeks later, of five healthy kittens. A dog – an ape – a man –

A man, yes. Has anyone ever made a bolder leap into the darkness than God's great servant Haakon Christiansen, the blessed Haakon whom we all celebrate and revere? He gambled everything on one toss of the dice, and won, and by his victory made himself immortal and gave us a gift beyond price.

His successful voyage opened the heavens. All we needed to do now was set up receiving stations. The Moon, Mars, the moons of Jupiter and Saturn, were only an eyeblink away. And then? Then? Why, of course, what remained but to carry our receivers to the stars?

For hours I wander the grounds of the Sanctuary, alone, undisturbed, deeply troubled. It is as if a spell of silence and solitude surrounds and protects me. No one dares approach me, neither as a supplicant of some sort nor to offer obeisance nor merely to see if I am in need of any service. I suppose many eyes are studying me warily from a distance, but in some way it must be obvious to all who observe me that I am not to be intruded upon. I must cast a forbidding aura today. In the brilliance of the tropic afternoon a darkness and a chill have settled over my soul. It seems to me that the splendid grounds are white with snow as far as I can see, snow on the hills, snow on the lawns, snow piled high along the banks of the sparkling streams, a sterile whiteness all the way to the rim of the world.

I am a dour man, but not a melancholy or tormented one.

333

Others mistake my disciplined nature for something darker, seeing in me an iciness of spirit, a sombreness, a harshness that masks some pervasive anguish of the heart. It is not so. If I have renounced the privilege of going to the stars, which could surely have been mine, it is not because I love the prospect of ending my days on this maimed and ravaged world of ours, but because I feel that God demands this service of me, that I remain here and help others to go forth. If I am hard and stern, it is because I can be nothing else, considering the choices I have made in shaping my course: I am a priest and a magistrate and a soldier of sorts, all in one. I have passed a dedicated and cloistered life. Yet I understand joy. There is a music in me. My senses are fully alive, all of them. From the outside I may appear unyielding and grim, but it is only because I have chosen to deny myself the pleasure of being ordinary, of being slothful, of being unproductive. There are those who misunderstand that in me, and see me as some kind of dismal monastic, narrow and fanatical, a gloomy man, a desolate man, one whom the commonplace would do well to fear and to shun. I think they are wrong. Yet this day, contemplating all that the Master has just told me and much that he has only implied, I am swept with such storms of foreboding and distress that I must radiate a frightful bleakness which warns others away. At any rate for much of this afternoon they all leave me alone to roam as I please.

The Sanctuary is a self-sufficient world. It needs nothing from outside. I stand near the summit of the great hill, looking down on children playing, gardeners setting out new plantings, novitiates sitting crosslegged at their studies on the lawn. I look towards the gardens and try to see colour, but all colour has leached away. The sun has passed beyond the horizon, here at this high altitude, but the sky is luminous. It is like a band of hot metal, glowing white. It devours everything: the edges of the world are slowly being engulfed by it. Whiteness is all, a universal snowy blanket.

For a long while I watch the children. They laugh, they shriek, they run in circles and fall down and rise again, still laughing. Don't they feel the sting of the snow? But the snow, I remind myself, is not there. It is illusionary snow, metaphorical snow, a trick of my troubled soul, a snowfall of the spirit. For the children there is no snow. I choose a little girl, taller and more serious than the others, standing somewhat to one side, and pretend that she is my own child. A strange idea, myself as a father, but pleasing. I could have had children. It might not have meant a very different life from the one I have had. But it was not what I chose. Now I toy with the fantasy for a time, enjoying it. I invent a name for the girl; I picture her running to me up the grassy slope; I see us sitting quietly together, poring over a chart of the sky. I tell her the names of the stars, I show her the constellations. The vision is so compelling that I begin to descend the slope towards her. She looks up at me while I am still some distance from her. I smile. She stares, solemn, uncertain of my intentions. Other children nudge her, point, and whisper. They draw back, edging away from me. It is as if my shadow has fallen upon them and chilled them as they played. I nod and move on, releasing them from its darkness.

A path strewn with glossy green leaves takes me to an overlook point at the cliff's edge, where I can see the broad bay far below, at the foot of Sanctuary Mountain. The water gleams like a burnished shield, or perhaps it is more like a huge shimmering pool of quicksilver. I imagine myself leaping from the stone balcony where I stand and soaring outwards in a sharp smooth arc, striking the water cleanly, knifing down through it, vanishing without a trace.

Returning to the main Sanctuary complex, I happen to glance downslope towards the long narrow new building that I have been told is the detention centre. A portcullis at its eastern end has been hoisted and a procession of prisoners is coming out. I know they are prisoners because they are roped together and walk in a sullen, slack way, heads down, shoulders slumped.

They are dressed in rags and tatters, or less than that. Even from fairly far away I can see cuts and bruises and scabs on them, and one has his arm in a sling, and one is bandaged so that nothing shows of his face but his glinting eyes. Three guards walk alongside them, carelessly dangling neural truncheons from green lanyards. The ropes that bind the prisoners are loosely tied, a perfunctory restraint. It would be no great task for them to break free and seize the truncheons from the captors. But they seem utterly beaten down; for them to make any sort of move towards freedom is probably as unlikely as the advent of an army of winged dragons swooping across the sky.

They are an incongruous and disturbing sight, these miserable prisoners plodding across this velvet landscape. Does the Master know that they are here, and that they are so poorly kept? I start to walk towards them. The Lord Invocator Kastel, emerging suddenly from nowhere as if he had been waiting behind a bush, steps across my path and says, 'God keep you, your grace. Enjoying your stroll through the grounds?'

'Those people down there – '

'They are nothing, Lord Magistrate. Only some of our thieving rabble, coming out for a little fresh air.'

'Are they well? Some of them look injured.'

Kastel tugs at one ruddy fleshy jowl. 'They are desperate people. Now and then they try to attack their guards. Despite all precautions we can't always avoid the use of force in restraining them.'

'Of course. I quite understand,' I say, making no effort to hide my sarcasm. 'Is the Master aware that helpless prisoners are being beaten within a thousand metres of his lodge?'

'Lord Magistrate!'

'If we are not humane in all our acts, what are we, Lord Invocator Kastel? What example do we set for the common folk?'

'It's these common folk of yours,' Kastel says sharply – I have not heard that tone from him before – 'who ring this place like an army of filthy vermin, eager to steal anything they can carry away and destroy everything else. Do you realize, Lord Magistrate, that this mountain rises like a towering island of

336

privilege above a sea of hungry people? That within a sixty-kilometre radius of these foothills there are probably thirty million empty bellies? That if our perimeter defences were to fail, they'd sweep through here like locusts and clean the place out? And probably slaughter every last one of us, up to and including the Master.'

'God forbid.'

'God created them. He must love them. But if this House is going to carry out the work God intended for us, we have to keep them at bay. I tell you, Lord Magistrate, leave these grubby matters of administration to us. In a few days you'll go flying off to your secluded nest in the Outback, where your work is undisturbed by problems like these. Whereas we'll still be here, in our pretty little mountain paradise, with enemies on every side. If now and then we take some action that you might not consider entirely humane, I ask you to remember that we guard the Master here, who is the heart of the Mission.' He allows me, for a moment, to see the contempt he feels for my qualms. Then he is all affability and concern again. In a completely different tone he says, 'The observatory's scanning equipment will be back in operation again tonight. I want to invite you to watch the data come pouring in from every corner of space. It's an inspiring sight, Lord Magistrate.'

'I would be pleased to see it.'

'The progress we've made, Lord Magistrate – the way we've moved out and out, always in accordance with the divine plan – I tell you, I'm not what you'd call an emotional man, but when I see the track we're making across the Dark my eyes begin to well up, let me tell you. My eyes begin to well up.'

His eyes, small and keen, study me for a reaction.

Then he says, 'Everything's all right for you here?'

'Of course, Lord Invocator.'

'Your conversations with the Master – have they met with your expectations?'

'Entirely so. He is truly a saint.'

'Truly, Lord Magistrate. Truly.'

'Where would the Mission be without him?'

'Where will it be,' says Kastel thoughtfully, 'when he is no longer here to guide us?'

'May that day be far from now.'

'Indeed,' Kastel says. 'Though I have to tell you, in all confidence, I've started lately to fear – '

His voice trails off.

'Yes?'

'The Master,' he whispers. 'Didn't he seem different to you, somehow?'

'Different?'

'I know it's years since you last saw him. Perhaps you don't remember him as he was.'

'He seemed lucid and powerful to me, the most commanding of men,' I reply.

Kastel nods. He takes me by the arm and gently steers me towards the upper buildings of the Sanctuary complex, away from those ghastly prisoners, who are still shuffling about like walking corpses in front of their jail. Quietly he says, 'Did he tell you that he thinks someone's interfering with the plan? That he has evidence that some of the receivers are being shipped far beyond the intended destinations?'

I look at him, wide-eyed.

'Do you really expect me to violate the confidential nature of the Master's audiences with me?'

'Of course not! Of course not, Lord Magistrate. But just between you and me – and we're both important men in the Order, it's essential that we level with each other at all times – I can admit to you that I'm pretty certain what the Master must have told you. Why else would he have sent for you? Why else pull you away from your House and interrupt what is now the key activity of the Mission? He's obsessed with this idea that there have been deviations from the plan. He's reading God knows what into the data. But I don't want to try to influence you. It's absurd to think that a man of your supreme rank in the second House of the Order can't analyse the situation unaided. You come tonight, you look at what the scanner says, you make up your own mind. That's all I ask. All right, Lord Magistrate? All right?'

He walks away, leaving me stunned and shocked. The Master insane? Or the Lord Invocator disloyal? Either one is unthinkable.

I will go to the observatory tonight, yes.

Kastel, by approaching me, seems to have broken the mysterious spell of privacy that has guarded me all afternoon. Now they come from all sides, crowding around me as though I am some archangel – staring, whispering, smiling hopefully at me. They gesture, they kneel. The bravest of them come right up to me and tell me their names, as though I will remember them when the time comes to send the next settlers off to the worlds of Epsilon Eridani, of Castor C, of Ross 154, of Wolf 359. I am kind with them, I am gracious, I am warm. It costs me nothing; it gives them happiness. I think of those bruised and slump-shouldered prisoners sullenly parading in front of the detention centre. For them I can do nothing; for these, the maids and gardeners and acolytes and novitiates of the Sanctuary, I can at least provide a flicker of hope. And, smiling at them, reaching my hands towards them, my own mood lightens. All will be well. God will prevail, as ever. The Kastels of this world cannot dismay me.

I see the little girl at the edge of the circle, the one whom I had taken, for a strange instant, to be my daughter. Once again I smile at her. Once again she gives me a solemn stare, and edges away. There is laughter. 'She means no disrespect,' a woman says. 'Shall I bring her to you, your grace?' I shake my head. 'I must frighten her,' I say. 'Let her be.' But the girl's stare remains to haunt me, and I see snow about me once more, thickening in the sky, covering the lush gardens of the Sanctuary, spreading to the rim of the world and beyond.

In the observatory they hand me a polarizing helmet to protect my eyes. The data flux is an overpowering sight: hot pulsing flares, like throbbing suns. I catch just a glimpse of it while still in the vestibule. The world, which has thawed for me, turns to snow yet again. It is a total white-out, a flash of photospheric intensity that washes away all surfaces and dechromatizes the universe.

'This way, your grace. Let me assist you.'

Soft voices. Solicitous proximity. To them, I suppose, I am an old man. Yet the Master was old before I was born. Does he ever come here?

I hear them whispering: 'The Lord Magistrate – the Lord Magistrate – '

The observatory, which I have never seen before, is one huge room, an eight-sided building as big as a cathedral, very dark and shadowy within, massive walls of some smooth moist-looking greenish stone, vaulted roof of burnished red metal, actually not a roof at all but an intricate antenna of colossal size and complexity, winding round and round and round upon itself. Spidery catwalks run everywhere to link the various areas of the great room. There is no telescope. This is not that sort of observatory. This is the central gathering point for three rings of data-collectors, one on the Moon, one somewhere beyond the orbit of Jupiter, one eight light-years away on a world of the star Lalande 21185. They scan the heavens and pump a stream of binary digits towards this building, where the data arrives in awesome convulsive actinic spurts, like thunderbolts hurled from Olympus.

There is another wall-sized map of the Mission here, the same sort of device that I saw in the Master's office, but at least five times as large. It too displays the network of the inner stars illuminated in bright yellow lines. But it is the old pattern, the familiar one, the one we have worked with since the inception of the program. This screen shows none of the wild divagations and bizarre trajectories that marked the image the Master showed me in my last audience with him.

'The system's been down for four days,' a voice at my elbow murmurs: one of the astronomers, a young one, who evidently has been assigned to me. She is dark-haired, snub-nosed, bright-eyed, a pleasant-faced girl. 'We're just priming it now, bringing it up to realtime level. That's why the flares are so intense. There's a terrific mass of data backed up in the system and it's all trying to get in here at once.'

'I see.'

She smiles. 'If you'll move this way, your grace – '

She guides me towards an inner balcony that hangs suspended over a well-like pit perhaps a hundred metres deep. In the dimness far below I see metal arms weaving in slow patterns, great gleaming discs turning rapidly, mirrors blinking and flashing. My astronomer explains that this is the main focal limb, or some such thing, but the details are lost on me. The whole building is quivering and trembling here, as though it is being pounded by a giant's hand. Colours are changing: the spectrum is being tugged far off to one side. Gripping the rail of the balcony, I feel a terrible vertigo coming over me. It seems to me that the expansion of the universe has suddenly been reversed, that all the galaxies are converging on this point, that I am standing in a vortex where floods of ultraviolet light, X-rays, and gamma rays come rushing in from all points of the cosmos at once. 'Do you notice it?' I hear myself asking. 'The violet-shift? Everything running backwards towards the centre?'

'What's that, your grace?'

I am muttering incoherently. She has not understood a word, thank God! I see her staring at me, worried, perhaps shocked. But I pull myself together, I smile, I manage to offer a few rational-sounding questions. She grows calm. Making allowances for my age, perhaps, and for my ignorance of all that goes on in this building. I have my own area of technical competence, she knows – oh, yes, she certainly knows that! – but she realizes that it is quite different from hers.

From my vantage point overlooking the main focal limb I watch with more awe than comprehension as the data pours in, is refined and clarified, is analysed, is synthesized, is registered on the various display units arrayed on the walls of the observatory. The young woman at my side keeps up a steady whispered flow of commentary, but I am distracted by the terrifying patterns of light and shadow all about me, by sudden and unpredictable bursts of high-pitched sound, by the vibrations of the building, and I miss some of the critical steps in her explanations and rapidly find myself lost. In truth I understand almost nothing of what is taking place around me. No doubt it is significant. The place is crowded with members of the Order, and high ones at that, everyone at least an initiate, several wearing the armbands of the inner levels of the primary House, the red, the green, even a few amber. Lord Invocator Kastel is here, smiling smugly, embracing people like a politician, coming by more than once to make sure I appreciate the high drama of this great room. I nod, I smile, I assure him of my gratitude.

Indeed it is dramatic. Now that I have recovered from my vertigo I find myself looking outwards rather than down, and my senses ride heavenwards as though I myself am travelling to the stars.

This is the nerve-centre of our Mission, this is the grand sensorium by which we keep track of our achievement.

The Alpha Centauri system was the starting point, of course, when we first began seeding the stars with Velde receivers, and then Barnard's Star, Wolf 359, Lalande 21185, and so on outwards and outwards, Sirius, Ross 154, Epsilon Indi – who does not know the names? – to all the stars within a dozen light-years of Earth. Small unmanned starships, laser-powered robot drones, unfurling great lightsails and gliding starwards on the urgent breath of photonic winds that we ourselves stirred up. Light was their propulsive force, and its steady pressure afforded constant acceleration, swiftly stepping up the velocity of our ships until it approached that of light.

Then, as they neared the stars that were their destinations, scanning for planets by one method or another, plotting orbital deviations or homing in on infra-red radiation or measuring Doppler shifts – finding worlds, and sorting them to eliminate the unlivable ones, the gas giants, the ice-balls, the formaldehyde atmospheres –

One by one our little vessels made landfall on new Earths. Silently opened their hatches. Sent forth the robots who would set up the Velde receivers that would be our gateways. One by one, opening the heavens.

And then – the second phase, the fabricating devices emerging, going to work, tiny machines seeking out carbon, silicon, nitrogen, oxygen, and the rest of the necessary building-blocks, stacking up the atoms in the predesignated patterns, assembling new starships, new laser banks, new Velde receivers. Little mechanical minds giving the orders, little mechanical arms doing the work. It would take some fifteen years for one of our ships to reach a star twelve light-years away. But it would require much less than that for our automatic replicators to construct a dozen twins of that ship at the landing point and send them in a dozen directions, each bearing its own Velde receiver to be established on some farther star, each equipped to replicate itself just as quickly and send more ships onwards. Thus we built our receiver network, spreading our highway from world to world across a sphere that by His will and our choice would encompass only a hundred light-years in the beginning. Then from our transmitters based on Earth we could begin to send – instantly, miraculously – the first colonists to the new worlds within our delimited sphere.

And so have we done. Standing here with my hands gripping the metal rail of the observatory balcony, I can in imagination send my mind forth to our colonies in the stars, to those tiny far-flung outposts peopled by the finest souls Earth can produce, men and women whom I myself have helped to choose and prepare and hurl across the gulf of night, pioneers sworn to Darklaw, bound by the highest of oaths not to repeat in the stars the errors we have made on Earth. And, thinking now of everything that our Order has achieved and all that we will yet achieve, the malaise that has afflicted my spirit since I arrived at the Sanctuary lifts, and a flood of joy engulfs me, and I throw my head back, I stare towards the maze of data-gathering circuitry far above me, I let the full splendour of the Project invade my soul.

It is a wondrous moment, but short-lived. Into my ecstasies come intrusive sounds: mutterings, gasps, the scurrying of feet.

I snap to attention. All about me, there is sudden excitement, almost a chaos. Someone is sobbing. Someone else is laughing. It is a wild, disagreeable laughter that is just this side of hysteria. A furious argument has broken out across the way: the individual words are blurred by echo but the anger of their inflection is unmistakable.

'What's happening?' I ask the astronomer beside me.

'The master chart,' she says. Her voice has become thick and hoarse. There is a troubled gleam in her eyes. 'It's showing the update now – the new information that's just come in – '

She points. I stare at the glowing star-map. The familiar pattern of the Mission network has been disrupted, now, and what I see, what they all see, is that same crazy display of errant tracks thrusting far out beyond our designated sphere of colonization that I beheld on the Master's own screen two days before.

The most tactful thing I can do, in the difficult few days that follow, is to withdraw to my quarters and wait until the Sanctuary people have begun to regain their equilibrium. My being here among them now must be a great embarrassment for them. They are taking this apparent deviation from the Mission's basic plan as a deep humiliation and a stinging rebuke upon their House. They find it not merely profoundly disquieting and improper, as I do, but a mark of shame, a sign that God Himself has found inadequate the plan of which they are the designers and custodians, and has discarded it. How much more intense their loss of face must be for all this to be coming down upon them at a time when the Lord Magistrate of the Order's other high House is among them to witness their disgrace.

It would be even more considerate of me, perhaps, to return at once to my own House's headquarters in Australia and let the Sanctuary people sort out their position without my presence to distract and reproach them. But that I cannot do. The Master wants me here. He has called me all the way from Australia to be with him at the Sanctuary in this difficult time. Here I must stay until I know why.

So I keep out of the way. I ask for my meals in my chambers instead of going to the communal hall. I spend my days and nights in prayer and meditation and reading. I sip brandy and divert myself with music. I take pleasure from the dispenser when the need comes over me. I stay out of sight and await the unfolding of events.

But my isolation is short-lived. On the third day after my retreat into solitude Kastel comes to me, pale and shaken, all his hearty condescension gone from him now.

'Tell me,' he says hoarsely, 'what do you make of all this? Do you think the data's genuine?'

'What reason do I have to think otherwise?'

'But suppose' – he hesitates, and his eyes do not quite meet mine – 'suppose the Master has rigged things somehow so that we're getting false information?'

'Would that be possible? And why would he do such a monstrous thing in the first place?'

'I don't know.'

'Do you really have so little regard for the Master's honesty? Or is it his sanity that you question?'

He turns crimson.

'God forbid, either one!' he cries. 'The Master is beyond all censure. I wonder only whether he has embarked upon some strange plan beyond our comprehension, absolutely beyond our understanding, which in the execution of his unfathomable purpose requires him to deceive us about the true state of things in the heavens.'

Kastel's cautious, elaborately formal syntax offends my ear. He did not speak to me in such baroque turns and curlicues when he was explaining why it was necessary to beat the prisoners in the detention centre. But I try not to let him see my distaste for him. Indeed he seems more to be pitied than detested, a frightened and bewildered man.

'Why don't you ask the Master?' I say.

'Who would dare? But in any case the Master has shut himself away from us all since the other night.'

'Ah. Then ask the Oracle.'

'The Oracle offers only mysteries and redundancies, as usual.'

'I can't offer anything better,' I tell him. 'Have faith in the Master. Accept the data of your own scanner until you have solid reason to doubt it. Trust God.'

Kastel, seeing I can tell him nothing useful, and obviously uneasy now over having expressed these all but sacrilegious suppositions about the Master to me, asks a blessing of me, and I give it, and he goes. But others come after him, one by one – hesitantly, even fearfully, as though expecting me to turn them away in scorn. High and low, haughty and humble, they seek audiences with me. I understand now what is happening. With the Master in seclusion, the community is leaderless in this difficult moment. On him they dare not intrude under any circumstances, if he has given the sign that he is not to be approached. I am the next highest ranking member of the hierarchy currently in residence at the Sanctuary. That I am of another House, and that between the Master and me lies an immense gulf of age and primacy, does not seem to matter to them just now. So it is to me that they come, asking for guidance, comfort, whatever. I give them what I can – platitudes, mainly – until I begin to feel hollow and cynical. Towards evening the young astronomer comes to me, she who had guided me through the observatory on the night of the great revelation. Her eyes are red and swollen, with dark rings below them. By now I have grown expert at offering these Sanctuary people the bland reassurances that are the best I can provide for them, but as I launch into what has become my standard routine I see that it is doing more harm to her than good – she begins to tremble, tears roll down her cheeks, she shakes her head and looks away, shivering – and suddenly my own façade of spiritual authority and philosophical detachment crumbles, and I am as troubled and confused as she is. I realize that she and I stand at the brink of the same black abyss. I begin to feel myself toppling forwards into it. We reach for each other and embrace in a kind of wild defiance of our fears. She is half my age. Her skin is smooth, her flesh is firm. We each grasp for

346

whatever comfort we can find. Afterwards, she seems stunned, numbed, dazed. She dresses in silence.

'Stay,' I urge her. 'Wait until morning.'

'Please, your grace – no – no – '

But she manages a faint smile. Perhaps she is trying to tell me that though she is amazed by what we have done she feels no horror and perhaps not even regret. I hold the tips of her fingers in my hands for a moment, and we kiss quickly, a dry, light, chaste kiss, and she goes.

Afterwards I experience a strange new clarity of mind. It is as if this unexpected coupling has burned away a thick fog of the soul and allowed me to think clearly once again.

In the night, which for me is a night of very little sleep, I contemplate the events of my stay at the House of Sanctuary and I come to terms, finally, with the obvious truth that I have tried to avoid for days. I remember the Master's casual phrase at my second audience with him, as he told me of his suspicion that certain colonists must be deviating from the tenets of Darklaw: 'Those whom we, *acting through your House*, have selected . . .' Am I being accused of some malfeasance? Yes. Of course. I am the one who chose the ones who have turned away from the plan. It has been decided that the guilt is to fall upon me. I should have seen it much earlier, but I have been distracted, I suppose, by troublesome emotions. Or else I have simply been unwilling to see.

I decide to fast today. When they bring me my morning meal-tray they will find a note from me, instructing them not to come to me again until I notify them.

I tell myself that this is not so much an act of penitence as one of purgation. Fasting is not something that the Order asks of us. For me it is a private act, one which I feel brings me closer to God. In any case my conscience is clear; it is simply that there are times when I think better on an empty stomach, and I am eager now to maintain and deepen that lucidity of perception that came upon me late the previous evening. I have fasted before, many times, when I felt a similar need. But then, when I take my morning shower, I dial it cold. The icy water burns and stings and flays; I have to compel myself to remain under it, but I do remain, and I hold myself beneath the shower head much longer than I might ordinarily have stayed there. That can only be penitence. Well, so be it. But penitence for what? I am guilty of no fault. Do they really intend to make me the scapegoat? Do I intend to offer myself to expiate the general failure? Why should I? Why do I punish myself now?

All that will be made known to me later. If I have chosen to impose a day of austerity and discomfort upon myself, there must be a good reason for it, and I will understand in good time.

Meanwhile I wear nothing but a simple linen robe of a rough texture, and savour the roughness against my skin. My stomach, by mid-morning, begins to grumble and protest, and I give it a glass of water, as though to mock its needs. A little later the vision of a fine meal assails me, succulent grilled fish on a shining porcelain plate, cool white wine in a sparkling crystal goblet. My throat goes dry, my head throbs. But instead of struggling against these tempting images I encourage them, I invite my traitor mind to do its worst: I add platters of gleaming red grapes to the imaginary feast, cheeses, loaves of bread fresh from the oven. The fish course is succeeded by roast lamb, the lamb by skewers of beef, the wine in the glass is now a fine red Coonawarra, there is rare old port to come afterwards. I fantasize such gluttonies that they become absurd, and I lose my appetite altogether.

The hours go by and I begin to drift into the tranquillity that for me is the first sign of the presence of God close at hand. Yet I find myself confronting a barrier. Instead of simply accepting His advent and letting Him engulf me, I trouble myself with finicky questions. Is He approaching me, I wonder? Or am I moving towards Him? I tell myself that the issue is an empty one. He is everywhere. It is the power of God which sets us in motion, yes, but He is motion incarnate. It is pointless to speak of my approaching Him, or His approaching me: those are two ways of describing the same thing. But while I contemplate such matters my mind itself holds me apart from Him.

I imagine myself in a tiny ship, drifting towards the stars. To make such a voyage is not what I desire; but it is useful focus for my reverie. For the journey to the stars and the journey towards God are one thing and the same. It is the journey into reality.

Once, I know, these things were seen in a different light. But it was inevitable that as we began to penetrate the depths of space we would come to see the metaphysical meaning of the venture on which we had embarked. And if we had not, we could not have proceeded. The curve of secular thought had extended as far as it could reach, from the seventeenth century to the twenty-first, and had begun to crack under its own weight; just when we were beginning to believe that *we* were God, we rediscovered the understanding that we were not. The universe was too huge for us to face alone. That new ocean was so wide, and our boats so very small.

I urge my little craft onwards. I set sail at last into the vastness of the Dark. My voyage has begun. God embraces my soul. He bids me be welcome in His kingdom. My heart is eased.

Under the Master's guidance we have all come to know that in our worldly lives we see only distortions – shadows on the cave wall. But as we penetrate the mysteries of the universe we are permitted to perceive things as they really are. The entry into the cosmos is the journey into the sublime, the literal attainment of heaven. It is a post-Christian idea: voyages must be undertaken, motion must never cease, we must seek Him always. In the seeking is the finding.

Gradually, as I reflect on these things yet again, the seeking ends for me and the finding begins, and my way becomes clear. I will resist nothing. I will accept everything. Whatever is required of me, that will I do, as always.

It is night, now. I am beyond any hunger and I feel no need for sleep. The walls of my chamber seem transparent to me and I can cast my vision outwards to all the world, the heavy surging seas and the close blanket of the sky, the mountains and valleys, the rivers, the fields. I feel the nearness of billions of souls. Each human soul is a star: it glows with unique fire, and each has its counterpart in the heavens. There is one star that is the Master, and one that is Kastel, and one that is the young astronomer who shared my bed. And somewhere there is a star that is me. My spirit goes outwards at last, it roves the distant blackness, it journeys on and on, to the ends of the universe. I soar above the Totality of the Totality. I look upon the face of God.

When the summons comes from the Master, shortly before dawn, I go to him at once. The rest of the House of Sanctuary sleeps. All is silent. Taking the garden path uphill, I experience a marvellous precision of sight: as though by great magnification I perceive the runnels and grooves on each blade of grass, the minute jagged teeth left by the mower as it bit it short, the glistening droplets of dew on the jade surface. Blossoms expand towards the pale new light now streaming out of the east as though they are coming awake. On the red earth of the path, strutting like dandies in a summer parade, are little shining scarlet-backed beetles with delicate black legs that terminate in intricate hairy feet. A fine mist rises from the ground. Within the silence I hear a thousand tiny noises.

The Master seems to be bursting with youthful strength, vitality, a mystic energy. He sits motionless, waiting for me to speak. The star-screen behind him is darkened, an ebony void, infinitely deep. I see the fine lines about his eyes and the corners of his mouth. His skin is pink, like a baby's. He could be six weeks old, or six thousand years.

His silence is immense.

'You hold me responsible?' I say at last.

He stares for a long while. 'Don't you?'

'I am the Lord Magistrate of Senders. If there has been a failure, the fault must be mine.'

'Yes. The fault must be yours.'

He is silent again.

350

It is very easy, accepting this, far easier than I would have thought only the day before.

He says after a time, 'What will you do?'

'You have my resignation.'

'From your magistracy?'

'From the Order,' I say. 'How could I remain a priest, having been a Magistrate?'

'Ah. But you must.'

The pale gentle eyes are inescapable.

'Then I will be a priest on some other world,' I tell him. 'I could never stay here. I respectfully request release from my vow of renunciation.'

He smiles. I am saying exactly the things he hoped I would say.

'Granted.'

It is done. I have stripped myself of rank and power. I will leave my House and my world; I will go forth into the Dark, although long ago I had gladly given that great privilege up. The irony is not lost on me. For all others it is heart's desire to leave Earth, for me it is merely the punishment for having failed the Mission. My penance will be my exile and my exile will be my penance. It is the defeat of all my work and the collapse of my vocation. But I must try not to see it that way. This is the beginning of the next phase of my life, nothing more. God will comfort me. Through my fall He has found a way of calling me to Him.

I wait for a gesture of dismissal, but it does not come.

'You understand,' he says after a time, 'that the Law of Return will hold, even for you?'

He means the prime tenet of Darklaw, the one that no one has ever violated. Those who depart from Earth may not come back to it. Ever. The journey is a one-way trip.

'Even for me,' I say. 'Yes. I understand.'

I stand before a Velde doorway like any other, one that differs in no way from the one that just a short time before had carried me instantaneously halfway around the world, home from Sanctuary to the House of Senders. It is a cubicle of black glass, four metres high, three metres wide, three metres deep. A pair of black-light lenses face each other like owlish eyes on its inner sides. From the rear wall jut the three metal cones that are the discharge points.

How many journeys have I made by way of transmitting stations such as this one? Five hundred? A thousand? How many times have I been scanned, measured, dissected, stripped down to my component baryons, replicated: annihilated *here*, created *there*, all within the same moment? And stepped out of a receiver, intact, unchanged, at some distant point, Paris, Karachi, Istanbul, Nairobi, Dar-es-Salaam?

This doorway is no different from the ones through which I stepped those other times. But this journey will be unlike all those others. I have never left Earth before, not even to go to Mars, not even to the Moon. There has been no reason for it. But now I am to leap to the stars. Is it the scope of the leap that I fear? But I know better. The risks are not appreciably greater in a journey of twenty light-years than in one of twenty kilometres. Is it the strangeness of the new worlds which I will confront that arouses this uneasiness in me? But I have devoted my life to building those worlds. What is it, then? The knowledge that once I leave this House I will cease to be Lord Magistrate of the Senders, and become merely a wandering pilgrim?

Yes. Yes, I think that that is it. My life has been a comfortable one of power and assurance, and now I am entering the deepest unknown, leaving all that behind, leaving everything behind, giving up my House, relinquishing my magistracy, shedding all that I have been except for my essence itself, from which I can never be parted. It is a great severance. Yet why do I hesitate? I have asked so many others, after all, to submit to that severance. I have bound so many others, after all, by the unbending oaths of Darklaw. Perhaps it takes more time to prepare oneself than I have allowed. I have given myself very short notice indeed.

But the moment of uneasiness passes. All about me are

friendly faces, men and women of my House, come to bid me a safe journey. Their eyes are moist, their smiles are tender. They know they will never see me again. I feel their love and their loyalty, and it eases my soul.

Ancient words drift through my mind.

Into thy hands, O Lord, I commend my spirit.

Yes. And my body also.

Lord, thou hast been our refuge: from one generation to another. Before the mountains were brought forth, or ever the earth and the world were made: thou art God from everlasting, and world without end.

Yes. And then:

The heavens declare the glory of God: and the firmament showeth His handiwork.

There is no sensation of transition. I was there; now I am here. I might have travelled no further than from Adelaide to Melbourne, or from Brisbane to Cairns. But I am very far from home now. The sky is amber, with swirls of blue. On the horizon is a great dull warm red mass, like a gigantic glowing coal, very close by. At the zenith is a smaller and brighter star, much more distant.

This world is called Cuchulain. It is the third moon of the subluminous star Gwydion, which is the dark companion of Lalande 21185. I am eight light-years from Earth. Cuchulain is the Order's prime outpost in the stars, the home of Second Sanctuary. Here is where I have chosen to spend my years of exile. The fallen magistrate, the broken vessel.

The air is heavy and mild. Crazy whorls of thick green ropy vegetation entangle everything, like a furry kelp that has infested the land. As I step from the Velde doorway I am confronted by a short, crisp little man in dark priestly robes. He is tonsured and wears a medallion of high office, though it is an office two or three levels down from the one that had been mine.

He introduces himself as Procurator-General Guardiano. Greeting me by name, he expresses his surprise at my most unexpected arrival in his diocese. Everyone knows that those who serve at my level of the Order must renounce all hope of emigration from Earth.

'I have resigned my magistracy,' I tell him. 'No,' I say. 'Actually I've been dismissed. For cause. I've been reassigned to the ordinary priesthood.'

He stares, plainly shocked and stunned.

'It is still an honour to have you here, your grace,' he says softly, after a moment.

I go with him to the chapter house, not far away. The gravitational pull here is heavier than Earth's, and I find myself leaning forwards as I walk and pulling my feet after me as though the ground is sticky. But such incidental strangenesses as this are subsumed, to my surprise, by a greater familiarity: this place is not as alien as I had expected. I might merely be in some foreign land, and not on another world. The full impact of my total and final separation from Earth, I know, will not hit me until later.

We sit together in the refectory, sipping glass after glass of a sweet strong liqueur. Procurator-General Guardiano seems flustered by having someone of my rank appear without warning in his domain, but he is handling it well. He tries to make me feel at home. Other priests of the higher hierarchy appear – the word of my arrival must be travelling fast – and peer into the room. He waves them away. I tell him, briefly, the reasons for my downfall. He listens gravely and says, 'Yes. We know that the outer worlds are in rebellion against Darklaw.'

'Only the outer worlds?'

'So far, yes. It's very difficult for us to get reliable data.'

'Are you saying that they've closed the frontier to the Order?'

'Oh, no, nothing like that. There's still free transit to every colony, and chapels everywhere. But the reports from the outer worlds are growing increasingly mysterious and bizarre. What we've decided is that we're going to have to send an Emissary Plenipotentiary to some of the rebel worlds to get the real story.'

'A spy, you mean?'

'A spy? No. Not a spy. A teacher. A guide. A prophet, if you will. One who can bring them back to the true path.' Guardiano shakes his head. 'I have to tell you that all this disturbs me profoundly, this repudiation of Darklaw, these apparent breaches of the plan. It begins to occur to me – though I know the Master would have me strung up for saying any such thing – that we may have been in error from the beginning.' He gives me a conspiratorial look. I smile encouragingly. He goes on, 'I mean, this whole élitist approach of ours, the Order maintaining its monopoly over the mechanism of matter transmission, the Order deciding who will go to the stars and who will not, the Order attempting to create new worlds in our own image – ' He seems to be talking half to himself. 'Well, apparently it hasn't worked, has it? Do I dare say it? They're living just as they please, out there. We can't control them at long range. Your own personal tragedy is testimony to that. And yet, and yet – to think that we would be in such a shambles, and that a Lord Magistrate would be compelled to resign, and go into exile – exile, yes, that's what it is!'

'Please,' I say. His ramblings are embarrassing; and painful, too, for there may be seeds of truth in them. 'What's over is over. All I want now is to live out my years quietly among the people of the Order on this world. Just tell me how I can be of use. Any work at all, even the simplest – '

'A waste, your grace. An absolute shameful waste.'

'Please.'

He fills my glass for the fourth or fifth time. A crafty look has come into his eyes. 'You would accept any assignment I give you?'

'Yes. Anything.'

'Anything?' he says.

I see myself sweeping the chapel house stairs, polishing sinks and tables, working in the garden on my knees.

'Even if there is risk?' he says. 'Discomfort?'

'Anything.'

He says, 'You will be our Plenipotentiary, then.'

* * *

There are two suns in the sky here, but they are not at all like Cuchulain's two, and the frosty air has a sharp sweet sting to it that is like nothing I have ever tasted before, and everything I see is haloed by a double shadow, a rim of pale red shading into deep, mysterious azure. It is very cold in this place. I am fourteen light-years from Earth.

A woman is watching me from just a few metres away. She says something I am unable to understand.

'Can you speak Anglic?' I reply.

'Anglic. All right.' She gives me a chilly, appraising look. 'What are you? Some kind of priest?'

'I was Lord Magistrate of the House of Senders, yes.'

'Where?'

'Earth.'

'On *Earth*? Really?'

I nod. 'What is the name of this world?'

'Let me ask the questions,' she says. Her speech is odd, not so much a foreign accent as a foreign intonation, a curious sing-song, vaguely menacing. Standing face to face just outside the Velde station, we look each other over. She is thick-shouldered, deep-chested, with a flat-featured face, close-cropped yellow hair, green eyes, a dusting of light red freckles across her heavy cheekbones. She wears a heavy blue jacket, fringed brown leggings, blue leather boots, and she is armed. Behind her I see a muddy road cut through a flat snowy field, some low rambling metal buildings with snow piled high on their roofs, and a landscape of distant jagged towering mountains whose sharp black spires are festooned with double-shadowed glaciers. An icy wind rips across the flat land. We are a long way from those two suns, the fierce blue-white one and its cooler crimson companion. Her eyes narrow and she says, 'Lord Magistrate, eh? The House of Senders. Really?'

'This was my cloak of office. This medallion signified my rank in the Order.'

'I don't see them.'

'I'm sorry. I don't understand.'

'You have no rank here. You hold no office here.'

'Of course,' I say. 'I realize that. Except such power as Darklaw confers on me.'

'Darklaw?'

I stare at her in some dismay. 'Am I beyond the reach of Darklaw so soon?'

'It's not a word I hear very often. Shivering, are you? You come from a warmer place?'

'Earth,' I say. 'South Australia. It's warm there, yes.'

'Earth. South Australia.' She repeats the words as though they are mere noises to her. 'We have some Earthborn here, still. Not many. They'll be glad to see you, I suppose. The name of this world is Zima.'

'Zima.' A good strong sound. 'What does that mean?'

'Mean?'

'The name must mean something. This planet wasn't named Zima just because someone liked the way it sounded.'

'Can't you see why?' she asks, gesturing towards the far-off ice-shrouded mountains.

'I don't understand.'

'Anglic is the only language you speak?'

'I know some Español and some Deutsch.'

She shrugs. 'Zima is Russkiye. It means Winter.'

'And this is wintertime on Winter?'

'It is like this all the year round. And so we call the world Zima.'

'Zima,' I say. 'Yes.'

'We speak Russkiye here, mostly, though we know Anglic too. Everybody knows Anglic, everywhere in the Dark. It is necessary. You really speak no Russkiye?'

'Sorry.'

'*Ty shto, s pizdy sarvalsa*?' she says, staring at me.

I shrug and am silent.

'*Bros' dumat' zhopay*!'

I shake my head sadly.

'*Idi v zhopu*!'

'No,' I say. 'Not a word.'

She smiles, for the first time. 'I believe you.'

'What were you saying to me in Russkiye?'

'Very abusive things. I will not tell you what they were. If you understood, you would have become very angry. They were filthy things, mockery. At least you would have laughed, hearing such vile words. I am named Marfa Ivanovna. You must talk with the boyars. If they think you are a spy, they will kill you.'

I try to hide my astonishment, but I doubt that I succeed. *Kill*? What sort of world have we built here? Have these Zimans reinvented the Middle Ages?

'You are frightened?' she asks.

'Surprised,' I say.

'You should lie to them, if you are a spy. Tell them you come to bring the Word of God, only. Or something else that is harmless. I like you. I would not want them to kill you.'

A spy? No. As Guardiano would say, I am a teacher, a guide, a prophet, if you will. Or as I myself would say, I am a pilgrim, one who seeks atonement, one who seeks forgiveness.

'I'm not a spy, Marfa Ivanovna,' I say.

'Good. Good. Tell them that.' She puts her fingers in her mouth and whistles piercingly, and three burly bearded men in fur jackets appear as though rising out of the snowbanks. She speaks with them a long while in Russkiye. Then she turns to me. 'These are the boyars Ivan Dimitrovich, Pyotr Pyotrovich, and Ivan Pyotrovich. They will conduct you to the voivode Ilya Alexandrovich, who will examine you. You should tell the voivode the truth.'

'Yes,' I say. 'What else is there to tell?'

Guardiano had told me before I left Cuchulain, of course, that the world I was going to had been settled by emigrants from Russia. It was one of the first to be colonized, in the early years of the Mission. One would expect our Earthly ways to begin dropping away, and something like an indigenous culture to have begun evolving, in that much time. But I am startled, all the same, by how far they have drifted. At least Marfa Ivanovna – who is, I imagine, a third-generation Ziman – knows what Darklaw is. But is it observed? They have named their world Winter, at any rate, and not New Russia or New Moscow or something like that, which Darklaw would have forbidden. The new worlds in the stars must not carry such Earthly baggage with them. But whether they follow any of the other laws, I cannot say. They have reverted to their ancient language here, but they know Anglic as well, as they should. The robe of the Order means something to her, but not, it would seem, a great deal. She speaks of spies, of killing. Here at the outset of my journey I can see already that there will be many surprises for me as I make my way through the Dark.

The voivode Ilya Alexandrovich is a small, agile-looking man, brown-faced, weatherbeaten, with penetrating blue eyes and a great shock of thick, coarse white hair. He could be any age at all, but from his vigour and seeming reserves of power I guess that he is about forty. In a harsh climate the face is quickly etched with the signs of age, but this man is probably younger than he looks.

Voivode, he tells me, means something like 'mayor', or 'district chief'. His office, brightly lit and stark, is a large ground-floor room in an unassuming two-storey aluminium shack that is, I assume, the town hall. There is no place for me to sit. I stand before him, and the three husky boyars, who do not remove their fur jackets, stand behind me, arms folded ominously across their breasts.

I see a desk, a faded wall map, a terminal. The only other thing in the room is the immense bleached skull of some alien beast on the floor beside his desk. It is an astounding sight, two metres long and a metre high, with two huge eye-sockets in the usual places and a third set high between them, and a pair of colossal yellow tusks that rise straight from the lower jaw almost to the ceiling. One tusk is chipped at the tip, perhaps six centimetres broken off. He sees me staring at it. 'You ever see anything like that?' he asks, almost belligerently.

'Never. What is it?'

'We call it a bolshoi. Animal of the northern steppe, very big. You see one five kilometres away and you shit your trousers, I tell you for true.' He grins. 'Maybe we send one back to Earth some day to show them what we have here. Maybe.'

His Anglic is much more heavily accented than Marfa Ivanovna's, and far less fluent. He seems unable to hold still very long. The district that he governs, he tells me, is the largest on Zima. It looks immense indeed on his map, a vast blue area, a territory that seems to be about the size of Brazil. But when I take a closer look I see three tiny dots clustered close together in the centre of the blue zone. They are, I assume, the only villages. He follows my gaze and strides immediately across the room to tap the map. 'This is Tyomni,' he says. 'That is this village. This one here, it is Doch. This one, Sin. In this territory we have six thousand people altogether. There are two other territories, here and here.' He points to regions north and south of the blue zone. A yellow area and a pink one indicate the other settlements, each with two towns. The whole human population of this planet must be no more than ten thousand.

Turning suddenly towards me, he says, 'You are big priest in the Order?'

'I was Lord Magistrate, yes. The House of Senders.'

'Senders. Ah. I know Senders. The ones who choose the colonists. And who run the machinery, the transmitters.'

'That's right.'

'And you are the bolshoi Sender? The big man, the boss, the captain?'

'I was, yes. This robe, this medallion, those are signs of my office.'

'A very big man. Only instead of sending, you are sent.'

'Yes,' I say.

'And you come here, why? Nobody from Earth comes here in ten, fifteen years.' He no longer makes even an attempt to conceal his suspicions, or his hostility. His cold eyes flare with anger. 'Being boss of Senders is not enough for you? You want to tell us how to run Zima? You want to run Zima yourself?'

'Nothing of that sort, believe me.'

'Then what?'

'Do you have a map of the entire Dark?'

'The Dark,' he says, as though the word is unfamiliar to him. Then he says something in Russkiye to one of the boyars. The man leaves the room and returns, a few moments later, with a wide, flat black screen that turns out to be a small version of the wall-screen in the Master's office. He lights it and they all look expectantly at me.

The display is a little different from the one I am accustomed to, since it centres on Zima, not on Earth, but the glowing inner sphere that marks the location of the Mission stars is easy enough to find. I point to that sphere and I remind them, apologizing for telling them what they already know, that the great plan of the Mission calls for an orderly expansion through space from Earth in a carefully delimited zone a hundred light-years in diameter. Only when that sphere has been settled are we to go farther, not because there are any technical difficulties in sending our carrier ships a thousand light-years out, or ten thousand, but because the Master has felt from the start that we must assimilate our first immense wave of outward movement, must pause and come to an understanding of what it is like to have created a galactic empire on so vast a scale, before we attempt to go onwards into the infinity that awaits us. Otherwise, I say, we risk falling victim to a megalomaniacal centrifugal dizziness from which we may never recover. And so Darklaw forbids journeys beyond the boundary.

They watch me stonily throughout my recital of these over-familiar concepts, saying nothing.

I go on to tell them that Earth now is receiving indications that voyages far beyond the hundred-light-year limit have taken place.

Their faces are expressionless.

'What is that to us?' the voivode asks.

'One of the deviant tracks begins here,' I say.

'Our Anglic is very poor. Perhaps you can say that another way.'

'When the first ship brought the Velde receiver to Zima, it built replicas of itself and of the receiver, and sent them onwards to other stars farther from Earth. We've traced the various trajectories that lead beyond the Mission boundaries, and one of them comes out of a world that received its Velde equipment from a world that got its equipment from here. A granddaughter world, so to speak.'

'This has nothing to do with us, nothing at all,' the voivode says coolly.

'Zima is only my starting point,' I say. 'It may be that you are in contact with these outer worlds, that I can get some clue from you about who is making these voyages, and why, and where he's setting out from.'

'We have no knowledge of any of this.'

I point out, trying not to do it in any overbearing way, that by the authority of Darklaw vested in me as a Plenipotentiary of the Order he is required to assist me in my inquiry. But there is no way to brandish the authority of Darklaw that is not overbearing, and I see the voivode stiffen at once, I see his face grow black, I see very clearly that he regards himself as autonomous and his world as independent of Earth.

That comes as no surprise to me. We were not so naïve, so innocent of historical precedent, as to think we could maintain control over the colonies. What we wanted was quite the opposite, new Earths free of our grasp – cut off, indeed, by an inflexible law forbidding all contact between mother world and colony once the colony had been established – and free, likewise, of the compulsion to replicate the tragic mistakes that the old Earth had made. But because we had felt the hand of God guiding us in every way as we led mankind forth into the Dark, we believed that God's law as we understood it would never be repudiated by those whom we had given the stars. Now, seeing evidence that His law is subordinate out here to the will of wilful men, I fear for the structure that we have devoted our lives to building.

'If this is why you really have come,' the voivode says, 'then you have wasted your time. But perhaps I misunderstand everything you say. My Anglic is not good. We must talk again.' He gestures to the boyars and says something in Russkiye that is unmistakably a dismissal. They take me away and give me a room in some sort of dreary lodging-house overlooking the plaza at the centre of town. When they leave, they lock the door behind them. I am a prisoner.

It is a harsh land. In the first few days of my internment there is a snowstorm every afternoon. First the sky turns metal-grey, and then black. Then hard little pellets of snow, driven by the rising wind, strike the window. Then it comes down in heavy fluffy flakes for several hours. Afterwards machines scuttle out and clear the pathways. I have never before been in a place where they have snow. It seems quite beautiful to me, a kind of benediction, a cleansing cover.

This is a very small town, and there is wilderness all around it. On the second day and again on the third, packs of wild beasts go racing through the central plaza. They look something like huge dogs, but they have very long legs, almost like those of horses, and their tails are tipped with three pairs of ugly-looking spikes. They move through the town like a whirlwind, prowling in the trash, butting their heads against the closed doors, and everyone gets quickly out of their way.

Later on the third day there is an execution in the plaza, practically below my window. A jowly, heavily bearded man clad in furs is led forth, strapped to a post, and shot by five men in uniforms. For all I can tell, he is one of the three boyars who took me to the voivode on my first day. I have never seen anyone killed before, and the whole event has such a strange, dreamlike quality for me that the shock and horror and revulsion do not strike me until perhaps half an hour later.

It is hard for me to say which I find the most alien, the snowstorms, the packs of fierce beasts running through the town, or the execution.

My food is shoved through a slot in the door. It is rough, simple stuff, stews and soups and a kind of gritty bread. That is all right. Not until the fourth day does anyone come to see me. My first visitor is Marfa Ivanovna, who says, 'They think you're a spy. I told you to tell them the truth.'

'I did.'

'Are you a spy?'

'You know that I'm not.'

'Yes,' she says. 'I know. But the voivode is troubled. He thinks you mean to overthrow him.'

'All I want is for him to give me some information. Then I'll be gone from here and won't ever return.'

'He is a very suspicious man.'

'Let him come here and pray with me, and see what my nature is like. All I am is a servant of God. Which I hope is true of the voivode as well.'

'He is thinking of having you shot,' Marfa Ivanovna says.

'Let him come to me and pray with me,' I tell her.

The voivode comes to me, not once but three times. We do no praying – in truth, any mention of God, or Darklaw, or even the Mission, seems to make him uncomfortable – but gradually we begin to understand each other. We are not that different. He is a hard, dedicated, cautious man governing a harsh troublesome land. I have been called hard and dedicated and cautious myself. My nature is not as suspicious as his, but I have not had to contend with snowstorms and wild beasts and the other hazards of this place. Nor am I Russian. They seem to be suspicious from birth, these Russians. And they have lived apart from Earth a long while. That too is Darklaw: we would not have the new worlds contaminated with our plagues of the spirit or of the flesh, nor do we want alien plagues of either kind carried back from them to us. We have enough of our own already.

I am not going to be shot. He makes that clear. 'We talked of it, yes. But it would be wrong.'

'The man who was? What did he do?'

'He took that which was not his,' says the voivode, and shrugs. 'He was worse than a beast. He could not be allowed to live among us.'

Nothing is said of when I will be released. I am left alone for two more days. The coarse dull food begins to oppress me, and the solitude. There is another snowstorm, worse than the last. From my window I see ungainly birds something like vultures, with long naked yellow necks and drooping reptilian tails, circling in the sky. Finally the voivode comes a second time, and simply stares at me as though expecting me to blurt out some confession. I look at him in puzzlement, and after long silence he laughs explosively and summons an aide, who brings in a bottle of a clear fiery liquor. Two or three quick gulps and he becomes expansive, and tells me of his childhood. His father was voivode before him, long ago, and was killed by a wild animal while out hunting. I try to imagine a world that still has dangerous animals roaming freely. To me it is like a world where the gods of primitive man are real and alive, and go disguised among mortals, striking out at them randomly and without warning.

Then he asks me about myself, wanting to know how old I was when I became a priest of the Order, and whether I was as religious as a boy as I am now. I tell him what I can, within the limits placed on me by my vows. Perhaps I go a little beyond the limits, even. I explain about my early interest in technical matters, my entering the Order at seventeen, my life of service.

The part about my religious vocation seems odd to him. He appears to think I must have undergone some sudden conversion midway through my adolescence. 'There has never been a time when God has not been present at my side,' I say.

'How very lucky you are,' he says.

'Lucky?'

He touches his glass to mine.

'Your health,' he says. We drink. Then he says, 'What does your Order really want with us, anyway?'

'With you? We want nothing with you. Three generations ago we gave you your world; everything after that is up to you.'

'No. You want to dictate how we shall live. You are people of the past, and we are people of the future, and you are unable to understand our souls.'

'Not so,' I tell him. 'Why do you think we want to dictate

to you? Have we interfered with you up till now?'

'You are here now, though.'

'Not to interfere. Only to gain information.'

'Ah. Is this so?' He laughs and drinks. 'Your health,' he says again.

He comes a third time a couple of days later. I am restless and irritable when he enters; I have had enough of this imprisonment, these groundless suspicions, this bleak and frosty world; I am ready to be on my way. It is all I can do to keep from bluntly demanding my freedom. As it is I am uncharacteristically sharp and surly with him, answering in quick snarling monosyllables when he asks me how I have slept, whether I am well, is my room warm enough. He gives me a look of surprise, and then one of thoughtful appraisal, and then he smiles. He is in complete control, and we both know it.

'Tell me once more,' he says, 'why you have come to us.'

I calm myself and run through the whole thing one more time. He nods. Now that he knows me better, he tells me, he begins to think that I may be sincere, that I have not come to spy, that I actually would be willing to chase across the galaxy this way in pursuit of an ideal. And so on in that vein for a time, both patronizing and genuinely friendly almost in the same breath.

Then he says, 'We have decided that it is best to send you onwards.'

'Where?'

'The name of the world is Entrada. It is one of our daughter worlds, eleven light-years away, a very hot place. We trade our precious metals for their spices. Someone came from there not long ago and told us of a strange man named Oesterreich, who passed through Entrada and spoke of undertaking journeys to new and distant places. Perhaps he can provide you with the answers that you seek. If you can find him.'

'Oesterreich?'

'That is the name, yes.'

'Can you tell me any more about him than that?'

'What I have told you is all that I know.'

He stares at me truculently, as if defying me to show that he is lying. But I believe him.

'Even for that much assistance, I am grateful,' I say.

'Yes. Never let it be said that we have failed to offer aid to the Order.' He smiles again. 'But if you ever come to this world again, you understand, we will know that you were a spy after all. And we will treat you accordingly.'

Marfa Ivanovna is in charge of the Velde equipment. She positions me within the transmitting doorway, moving me about this way and that to be certain that I will be squarely within the field. When she is satisfied, she says, 'You know, you ought not ever to come back this way.'

'I understand that.'

'You must be a very virtuous man. Ilya Alexandrovich came very close to putting you to death, and then he changed his mind. This I know for certain. But he remains suspicious of you. He is suspicious of everything the Order does.'

'The Order has never done anything to injure him or anyone else on this planet, and never will.'

'That may be so,' says Marfa Ivanovna. 'But still, you are lucky to be leaving here alive. You should not come back. And you should tell others of your sort to stay away from Zima too. We do not accept the Order here.'

I am still pondering the implications of that astonishing statement when she does something even more astonishing. Stepping into the cubicle with me, she suddenly opens her fur-trimmed jacket, revealing full round breasts, very pale, dusted with the same light red freckles that she has on her face. She seizes me by the hair and presses my head against her breasts, and holds it there a long moment. Her skin is very warm. It seems almost feverish.

'For luck,' she says, and steps back. Her eyes are sad and strange. It could almost be a loving look, or perhaps a pitying one, or both. Then she turns away from me and throws the switch.

* * *

Entrada is torrid and moist, a humid sweltering hothouse of a place so much the antithesis of Zima that my body rebels immediately against the shift from one world to the other. Coming forth into it, I feel the heat rolling towards me like an implacable wall of water. It sweeps up and over me and smashes me to my knees. I am sick and numb with displacement and dislocation. It seems impossible for me to draw a breath. The thick, shimmering, golden-green atmosphere here is almost liquid; it crams itself into my throat, it squeezes my lungs in an agonizing grip. Through blurring eyes I see a tight green web of jungle foliage rising before me, a jumbled vista of corrugated-tin shacks, a patch of sky the colour of shallow sea-water, and, high above, a merciless, throbbing, weirdly elongated sun shaped like no sun I have ever imagined. Then I sway and fall forwards and see nothing more.

I lie suspended in delirium a long while. It is a pleasing restful time, like being in the womb. I am becalmed in a great stillness, lulled by soft voices and sweet music. But gradually consciousness begins to break through. I swim upwards towards the light that glows somewhere above me, and my eyes open, and I see a serene friendly face, and a voice says, 'It's nothing to worry about. Everyone who comes here the way you did has a touch of it, the first time. At your age I suppose it's worse than usual.'

Dazedly I realize that I am in mid-conversation.

'A touch of what?' I ask.

The other, who is a slender grey-eyed woman of middle years wearing a sort of Indian sari, smiles and says, 'Of the Falling. It's a lambda effect. But I'm sorry. We've been talking for a while, and I thought you were awake. Evidently you weren't.'

'I am now,' I tell her. 'But I don't think I've been for very long.'

Nodding, she says, 'Let's start over. You're in Traveller's Hospice. The humidity got you, and the heat, and the lightness of the gravity. You're all right now.'

'Yes.'

'Do you think you can stand?'

'I can try,' I say.

She helps me up. I feel so giddy that I expect to float away. Carefully she guides me towards the window of my room. Outside I see a veranda and a close-cropped lawn. Just beyond, a dark curtain of dense bush closes everything off. The intense light makes everything seem very near; it is as if I could put my hand out the window and thrust it into the heart of that exuberant jungle.

'So bright – the sun – ' I whisper.

In fact there are two whitish suns in the sky, so close to each other that their photospheres overlap and each is distended by the other's gravitational pull, making them nearly oval in shape. Together they seem to form a single egg-shaped mass, though even the one quick dazzled glance I can allow myself tells me that this is really a binary system, discrete bundles of energy forever locked together.

Awed and amazed, I touch my fingertips to my cheek in wonder, and feel a thick coarse beard there that I had not had before.

The woman says, 'Two suns, actually. Their centres are only about a million and a half kilometres apart, and they revolve around each other every seven and a half hours. We're the fourth planet out, but we're as far from them as Neptune is from the Sun.'

But I have lost interest for the moment in astronomical matters. I rub my face, exploring its strange new shagginess. The beard covers my cheeks, my jaws, much of my throat.

'How long have I been unconscious?' I ask.

'About three weeks.'

'Your weeks or Earth weeks?'

'We use Earth weeks here.'

'And that was just a light case? Does everybody who gets the Falling spend three weeks being delirious?'

'Sometimes much more. Sometimes they never come out of it.'

I stare at her. 'And it's just the heat, the humidity, the lightness of the gravity? They can knock you down the moment you step out of the transmitter and put you under for weeks? I would think it should take something like a stroke to do that.'

'It *is* something like a stroke,' she says. 'Did you think that travelling between stars is like stepping across the street? You come from a low-lambda world to a high-lambda one without doing your adaptation drills and of course the change is going to knock you flat right away. What did you expect?'

High-lambda? Low-lambda?

'I don't know what you're talking about,' I say.

'Didn't they tell you on Zima about the adaptation drills before they shipped you here?'

'Not a thing.'

'Or about lambda differentials?'

'Nothing,' I say.

Her face grows very solemn. 'Pigs, that's all they are. They should have prepared you for the jump. But I guess they didn't care whether you lived or died.'

I think of Marfa Ivanovna, wishing me luck as she reached for the switch. I think of that strange sad look in her eyes. I think of the voivode Ilya Alexandrovich, who might have had me shot but decided instead to offer me a free trip off his world, a one-way trip. There is much that I am only now beginning to understand, I see, about this empire that Earth is building in what we call the Dark. We are building it in the dark, yes, in more ways than one.

'No,' I say. 'I guess they didn't care.'

They are friendlier on Entrada, no question of that. Interstellar trade is important here and visitors from other worlds are far more common than they are on wintry Zima. Apparently I am free to live at the hospice as long as I wish. The weeks of my stay have stretched now into months, and no one suggests that it is time for me to be moving along.

I had not expected to stay here so long. But gathering the information I need has been a slow business, with many a maddening detour and delay.

At least I experience no further lambda problems. Lambda,

they tell me, is a planetary force that became known only when Velde jumps between solar systems began. There are high-lambda worlds and low-lambda worlds, and anyone going from one kind to the other without proper preparation is apt to undergo severe stress. It is all news to me. I wonder if the Order on Earth is aware at all of these difficulties. But perhaps they feel that matters which may arise during journeys *between* worlds of the Dark are of no concern to us of the mother world.

They have taken me through the adaptation drills here at the hospice somehow while I was still unconscious, and I am more or less capable now of handling Entradan conditions. The perpetual steambath heat, which no amount of air conditioning seems really to mitigate, is hard to cope with, and the odd combination of heavy atmosphere and light gravity puts me at risk of nausea with every breath, though after a time I get the knack of pulling shallow nips of air. There are allergens borne on every breeze, too, pollen of a thousand kinds and some free-floating alkaloids, against which I need daily medication. My face turns red under the force of the double sun, and the skin of my cheeks gets strangely soft, which makes my new beard an annoyance. I rid myself of it. My hair acquires an unfamiliar silver sheen, not displeasing, but unexpected. All this considered, though, I can manage here.

Entrada has a dozen major settlements and several hundred thousand people. It is a big world, metal-poor and light, on which a dozen small continents and some intricate archipelagoes float in huge warm seas. The whole planet is tropical, even at the poles: distant though it is from its suns, it would probably be inhospitable to human life if it were very much closer. The soil of Entrada has the lunatic fertility that we associate with the tropics, and agriculture is the prime occupation here. The people, drawn from many regions of Earth, are attractive and outgoing, with an appealingly easy manner.

It appears that they have not drifted as far from Darklaw here as the Zimans have.

Certainly the Order is respected. There are chapels

everywhere and the people use them. Whenever I enter one there is a little stir of excitement, for it is generally known that I was Lord Magistrate of the Senders during my time on Earth, and that makes me a celebrity, or a curiosity, or both. Many of the Entradans are Earthborn themselves – emigration to this world was still going on as recently as eight or ten years ago – and the sight of my medallion inspires respect and even awe in them. I do not wear my robe of office, not in this heat. Probably I will never wear it again, no matter what climate I find myself in when I leave here. Someone else is Lord Magistrate of the House of Senders now, after all. But the medallion alone is enough to win me a distinction here that I surely never had on Zima.

I think, though, that they pick and choose among the tenets of Darklaw to their own satisfaction on Entrada, obeying those which suit them and casting aside anything that seems too constricting. I am not sure of this, but it seems likely. To discuss such matters with anyone I have come to know here is, of course, impossible. The people I have managed to get to know so far, at the hospice, at the chapel house in town, at the tavern where I have begun to take my meals, are pleasant and sociable. But they become uneasy, even evasive, whenever I speak of any aspect of Earth's migration into space. Let me mention the Order, or the Master, or anything at all concerning the Mission, and they begin to moisten their lips and look uncomfortable. Clearly things are happening out here, things never envisioned by the founders of the Order, and they are unwilling to talk about them with anyone who himself wears the high medallion.

It is a measure of the changes that have come over me since I began this journey that I am neither surprised nor dismayed by this.

Why should we have believed that we could prescribe a single code of law that would meet the needs of hundreds of widely varying worlds? Of course they would modify our teachings to fit their own evolving cultures, and some would probably depart entirely from that which we had created for them. It was only to be expected. Many things have become clear to me on this journey that I did not see before, that, indeed, I did not so much as pause to consider. But much else remains mysterious.

I am at the busy waterfront esplanade, leaning over the rail, staring out towards Volcano Isle, a dim grey peak far out to sea. It is mid-morning, before the full heat of noon has descended. I have been here long enough so that I think of this as the cool time of the day.

'Your grace?' a voice calls. 'Lord Magistrate?'

No one calls me those things here.

I glance down to my left. A dark-haired man in worn sea-man's clothes and a braided captain's hat is looking up at me out of a rowboat just below the sea-wall. He is smiling and waving. I have no idea who he is, but he plainly wants to talk with me, and anything that helps me break the barrier that stands between me and real knowledge of this place is to be encouraged.

He points to the far end of the harbour, where there is a ramp leading from the little beach to the esplanade, and tells me in pantomime that he means to tie up his boat and go ashore. I wait for him at the head of the ramp, and after a few moments he comes trudging up to greet me. He is perhaps fifty years old, trim and sun-bronzed, with a lean weatherbeaten face.

'You don't remember me,' he says.

'I'm afraid not.'

'You personally interviewed me and approved my application to emigrate, eighteen years ago. Sandys. Lloyd Sandys.' He smiles hopefully, as though his name alone will open the flood-gates of my memory.

When I was Lord Magistrate I reviewed five hundred emi-grant dossiers a week, and interviewed ten or fifteen applicants a day myself, and forgot each one the moment I approved or rejected them. But for this man the interview with the Lord Magistrate of the Senders was the most significant moment of his life.

'Sorry,' I say. 'So many names, so many faces – '

'I would have recognized you even if I hadn't already heard you were here. After all these years, you've hardly changed at all, your grace.' He grins. 'So now you've come to settle on Entrada yourself?'

'Only a short visit.'

'Ah.' He is visibly disappointed. 'You ought to think of staying. It's a wonderful place, if you don't mind a little heat. I haven't regretted coming here for a minute.'

He takes me to a seaside tavern where he is obviously well known, and orders lunch for both of us: skewers of small corkscrew-shaped creatures that look and taste a little like squid, and a flask of a strange but likeable emerald-coloured wine with a heavy, musky, spicy flavour. He tells me that he has four sturdy sons and four strapping daughters, and that he and his wife run a harbour ferry, short hops to the surrounding islands of this archipelago, which is Entrada's main population centre. There still are traces of Melbourne in his accent. He seems very happy. 'You'll let me take you on a tour, won't you?' he asks. 'We've got some very beautiful islands out there, and you can't get to see them by Velde jumps.'

I protest that I don't want to take him away from his work, but he shrugs that off. Work can always wait, he says. There's no hurry, on a world where anyone can dip his net in the sea and come up with a good meal. We have another flask of wine. He seems open, genial, trustworthy. Over cheese and fruit he asks me why I've come here.

I hesitate.

'A fact-finding mission,' I say.

'Ah. Is that really so? Can I be of any help, d'ye think?'

It is several more winy lunches, and a little boat-trip to some nearby islands fragrant with masses of intoxicating purple blooms, before I am willing to begin taking Sandys into my confidence. I tell him that the Order has sent me into the Dark to study and report on the ways of life that are evolving on the new worlds. He seems untroubled by that, though Ilya

374

Alexandrovich might have had me shot for such an admission.

Later, I tell him about the apparent deviations from the planned scope of the Mission that are the immediate reason for my journey.

'You mean, going out beyond the hundred-light-year zone?'

'Yes.'

'That's pretty amazing, that anyone would go there.'

'We have indications that it's happening.'

'Really,' he says.

'And on Zima,' I continue, 'I picked up a story that somebody here on Entrada has been preaching ventures into the far Dark. You don't know anything about that, do you?'

His only overt reaction is a light frown, quickly erased. Perhaps he has nothing to tell me. Or else we have reached the point, perhaps, beyond which he is unwilling to speak.

But some hours later he revives the topic himself. We are on our way back to harbour, sunburned and a little tipsy from an outing to one of the prettiest of the local islands, when he suddenly says, 'I remember hearing something about that preacher you mentioned before.'

I wait, not saying anything.

'My wife told me about him. There was somebody going around talking about far voyages, she said.' New colour comes to his face, a deep red beneath the bronze. 'I must have forgotten about it when we were talking before.' In fact he must know that I think him disingenuous for withholding this from me all afternoon. But I make no attempt to call him on that. We are still testing each other.

I ask him if he can get more information for me, and he promises to discuss it with his wife. Then he is absent for a week, making a circuit of the outer rim of the archipelago to deliver freight. When he returns, finally, he brings with him an unusual golden brandy from one of the remote islands as a gift for me, but my cautious attempt to revive our earlier conversation runs into a familiar sort of Entradan evasiveness. It is almost as though he doesn't know what I'm referring to.

At length I say bluntly, 'Have you had a chance to talk to your wife about that preacher?'

He looks troubled. 'In fact, it slipped my mind.'

'Ah.'

'Tonight, maybe – '

'I understand that the man's name is Oesterreich,' I say.

His eyes go wide.

'You know that, do you?'

'Help me, will you, Sandys? I'm the one who sent you to this place, remember? Your whole life here wouldn't exist but for me.'

'That's true. That's very true.'

'Who's Oesterreich?'

'I never knew him. I never had any dealings with him.'

'Tell me what you know about him.'

'A crazy man, he was.'

'Was?'

'He's not here any more.'

I uncork the bottle of rare brandy, pour a little for myself, a more generous shot for Sandys.

'Where'd he go?' I ask.

He sips, reflectively. After a time he says, 'I don't know, your grace. That's God's own truth. I haven't seen or heard of him in a couple of years. He chartered one of the other captains here, a man named Feraud, to take him to one of the islands, and that's the last I know.'

'Which island?'

'I don't know.'

'Do you think Feraud remembers?'

'I could ask him,' Sandys says.

'Yes. Ask him. Would you do that?'

'I could ask him, yes,' he says.

So it goes, slowly. Sandys confers with his friend Feraud, who hesitates and evades, or so Sandys tells me; but eventually Feraud finds it in him to recall that he had taken Oesterreich to Volcano Isle, three hours' journey to the west. Sandys admits to me, now that he is too deep in to hold back, that he himself actually heard Oesterreich speak several times, that Oesterreich claimed to be in possession of some secret way of reaching worlds immensely remote from the settled part of the Dark.

'And do you believe that?'

'I don't know. He seemed crazy to me.'

'Crazy how?'

'The look in his eye. The things he said. That it's our destiny to reach the rim of the universe. That the Order holds us back out of its own timidity. That we must follow the Goddess Avatar, who beckons us onwards to – '

'*Who*?'

His face flushes bright crimson. 'The Goddess Avatar. I don't know what she is, your grace. Honestly. It's some cult he's running, some new religion he's made up. I told you he's crazy. I've never believed any of this.'

There is a pounding in my temples, and a fierce ache behind my eyes. My throat has gone dry and not even Sandys's brandy can soothe it.

'Where do you think Oesterreich is now?'

'I don't know.' His eyes are tormented. 'Honestly. Honestly. I think he's gone from Entrada.'

'Is there a Velde transmitter station on Volcano Isle?'

He thinks for a moment. 'Yes. Yes, there is.'

'Will you do me one more favour?' I ask. 'One thing, and then I won't ask any more.'

'Yes?'

'Take a ride over to Volcano Isle tomorrow. Talk with the people who run the Velde station there. See if you can find out where they sent Oesterreich.'

'They'll never tell me anything like that.'

I put five shining coins in front of him, each one worth as much as he can make in a month's ferrying.

'Use these,' I say. 'If you come back with the answer, there are five more for you.'

'Come with me, your grace. You speak to them.'

'No.'

'You ought to see Volcano Isle. It's a fantastic place. The centre of it blew out thousands of years ago, and people live up on the rim, around a lagoon so deep nobody's been able to find the bottom. I was meaning to take you there anyway, and – '

'You go,' I say. 'Just you.'

After a moment he pockets the coins. In the morning I watch him go off in one of his boats, a small hydrofoil skiff. There is no word from him for two days, and then he comes to me at the hospice, looking tense and unshaven.

'It wasn't easy,' he says.

'You found out where he went?'

'Yes.'

'Go on,' I urge, but he is silent, lips working but nothing coming out. I produce five more of the coins and lay them before him. He ignores them. This is some interior struggle.

He says, after a time, 'We aren't supposed to reveal anything about anything of this. I told you what I've already told you because I owe you. You understand that?'

'Yes.'

'You mustn't ever let anyone know who gave you the information.'

'Don't worry,' I say.

He studies me for a time. Then he says, 'The name of the planet where Oesterreich went is Eden. It's a seventeen-light-year hop. You won't need lambda adjustment, coming from here. There's hardly any differential. All right, your grace? That's all I can tell you.' He stares at the coins and shakes his head. Then he runs out of the room, leaving them behind.

Eden turns out to be no Eden at all. I see a spongy, marshy landscape, a grey sodden sky, a raw, half-built town. There seem to be two suns, a faint yellow-white one and a larger reddish one. A closer look reveals that the system here is like the Lalande one: the reddish one is not really a star but a glowing substellar mass about the size of Jupiter. Eden is one of its moons. What we like to speak of in the Order as the new

Earths of the Dark are in fact scarcely Earthlike at all, I am coming to realize: all they have in common with the mother world is a tolerably breathable atmosphere and a manageable gravitational pull. How can we speak of a world as an Earth when its sun is not yellow but white or red or green, or there are two or three or even four suns in the sky all day and all night, or the primary source of warmth is not even a sun but a giant planet-like ball of hot gas?

'Settler?' they ask me, when I arrive on Eden.

'Traveller,' I reply. 'Short-term visit.'

They scarcely seem to care. This is a difficult world and they have no time for bureauc atic formalities. So long as I have money, and I do – at least these strange daughter worlds of ours still honour our currency – I am, if not exactly welcome, then at least permitted.

Do they observe Darklaw here? When I arrive I am wearing neither my robe of office nor my medallion, and it seems just as well. The Order appears not to be in favour, this far out. I can find no sign of our chapels or other indications of submission to our rule. What I do find, as I wander the rough streets of this jerry-rigged town on this cool, rainswept world, is a chapel of some other kind, a white geodesic dome with a mysterious symbol – three superimposed six-pointed stars – painted in black on its door.

'Goddess save you,' a woman coming out says brusquely to me, and shoulders past me in the rain.

They are not even bothering to hide things, this far out on the frontier.

I go inside. The walls are white and an odd, disturbing mural is painted on one of them. It shows what seems to be a windowless ruined temple drifting in blue starry space, with all manner of objects and creatures floating near it, owls, skulls, snakes, masks, golden cups, bodiless heads. It is like a scene viewed in a dream. The temple's alabaster walls are covered with hieroglyphics. A passageway leads inwards and inwards and inwards, and at its end I can see a tiny view of an eerie landscape like a plateau at the end of time.

There are half a dozen people in the room, each facing in a different direction, reading aloud in low murmurs. A slender dark-skinned man looks up at me and says, 'Goddess save you, father. How does your journey go?'

'I'm trying to find Oesterreich. They said he's here.'

A couple of the other readers look up. A woman with straw-coloured hair says, 'He's gone Goddessward.'

'I'm sorry. I don't under – '

Another woman, whose features are tiny and delicately modelled in the centre of a face vast as the map of Russia, breaks in to tell me, 'He was going to stop off on Phosphor first. You may be able to catch up with him there. Goddess save you, father.'

I stare at her, at the mural of the stone temple, at the other woman.

'Thank you,' I say. 'Goddess save you,' my voice adds.

I buy passage to Phosphor. It is sixty-seven light-years from Earth. The necessary lambda adjustment costs nearly as much as the transit fee itself, and I must spend three days going through the adaptation process before I can leave.

Then, Goddess save me, I am ready to set out from Eden for whatever greater strangeness awaits me beyond.

As I wait for the Simtow reaction to annihilate me and reconstruct me in some unknown place, I think of all those who passed through my House over the years as I selected the outbound colonists – and how I and the Lord Magistrates before me had clung to the fantasy that we were shaping perfect new Earths out there in the Dark, that we were composing exquisite symphonies of human nature, filtering out all of the discordances that had marred all our history up till now. Without ever going to the new worlds ourselves to view the results of our work, of course, because to go would mean to cut ourselves off forever, by Darklaw's own constricting terms, from our House, from our task, from Earth itself. And now, catapulted into the Dark in a moment's convulsive turn, by shame and guilt and the need to try to repair that which I had evidently made breakable instead of imperishable, I am learning that I have been wrong all along, that the symphonies of human nature that I had composed were built out of the same old tunes, that people will do what they will do unconstrained by abstract regulations laid down for them *a priori* by others far away. The tight filter of which the House of Senders is so proud is no filter at all. We send our finest ones to the stars and they turn their backs on us at once. And, pondering these things, it seems to me that my soul is pounding at the gates of my mind, that madness is pressing close against the walls of my spirit – a thing which I have always dreaded, the thing which brought me to the cloisters of the Order in the first place.

Black light flashes in my eyes and once more I go leaping through the Dark.

'He isn't here,' they tell me on Phosphor. There is a huge cool red sun here, and a hot blue one a couple of hundred solar units away, close enough to blaze like a brilliant beacon in the day sky. 'He's gone on to Entropy. Goddess save you.'

'Goddess save you,' I say.

There are triple-star signs on every doorfront in Phosphor's single city. The city's name is Jerusalem. To name cities or worlds for places on Earth is forbidden. But I know that I have left Darklaw far behind here.

Entropy, they say, is ninety-one light-years from Earth. I am approaching the limits of the sphere of settlement.

Oesterreich has a soft, insinuating voice. He says, 'You should come with me. I really would like to take a Lord Magistrate along when I go to her.'

'I'm no longer a Lord Magistrate.'

'You can't ever stop being a Lord Magistrate. Do you think you can take the Order off just by putting your medallion in your suitcase?'

'Who is she, this Goddess Avatar everybody talks about?'

Oesterreich laughs. 'Come with me and you'll find out.'

He is a small man, very lean, with broad, looming shoulders that make him appear much taller than he is when he is sitting down. Maybe he is forty years old, maybe much older. His face is paper-white, with perpetual bluish stubble, and his eyes have a black troublesome gleam that strikes me as a mark either of extraordinary intelligence or of pervasive insanity, or perhaps both at once. It was not difficult at all for me to find him, only hours after my arrival on Entropy. The planet has a single village, a thousand settlers. The air is mild here, the sun yellow-green. Three huge moons hang just overhead in the daytime sky, as though dangling on a clothesline.

I say, 'Is she real, this goddess of yours?'

'Oh, she's real, all right. As real as you or me.'

'Someone we can walk up to and speak with?'

'Her name used to be Margaret Benevente. She was born in Geneva. She emigrated to a world called Three Suns about thirty years ago.'

'And now she's a goddess.'

'No. I never said that.'

'What is she, then?'

'She's the Goddess Avatar.'

'Which means what?'

He smiles. 'Which means she's a holy woman in whom certain fundamental principles of the universe have been incarnated. You want to know any more than that, you come with me, eh? Your grace.'

'And where is she?'

'She's on an uninhabited planet about five thousand light-years from here right now.'

I am dealing with a lunatic, I tell myself. That gleam is the gleam of madness, yes.

'You don't believe that, do you?' he asks.

'How can it be possible?'

'Come with me and you'll find out.'

'Five thousand light-years – ' I shake my head. 'No. No.'

He shrugs. 'So don't go, then.'

There is a terrible silence in the little room. I feel impaled on it. Thunder crashes outside, finally, breaking the tension. Lightning has been playing across the sky constantly since my arrival, but there has been no rain.

'Faster-than-light travel is impossible,' I say inanely. 'Except by way of Velde transmission. You know that. If we've got Velde equipment five thousand light-years from here, we would have had to start shipping it out around the time the Pyramids were being built in Egypt.'

'What makes you think we get there with Velde equipment?' Oesterreich asks me.

He will not explain. Follow me and you'll see, he tells me. Follow me and you'll see.

The curious thing is that I like him. He is not exactly a likeable man – too intense, too tightly wound, the fanaticism carried much too close to the surface – but he has a sort of charm all the same. He travels from world to world, he tells me, bringing the new gospel of the Goddess Avatar. That is exactly how he says it, 'the new gospel of the Goddess Avatar', and I feel a chill when I hear the phrase. It seems absurd and frightening both at once. Yet I suppose those who brought the Order to the world a hundred fifty years ago must have seemed just as strange and just as preposterous to those who first heard our words.

Of course, we had the Velde equipment to support our philosophies.

But these people have – what? The strength of insanity? The clear cool purposefulness that comes from having put reality completely behind them?

'You were in the Order once, weren't you?' I asked him.

'You know it, your grace.'

'Which House?'

'The Mission,' he says.

'I should have guessed that. And now you have a new mission, is that it?'

'An extension of the old one. Mohammed, you know, didn't see Islam as a contradiction of Judaism and Christianity. Just as the next level of revelation, incorporating the previous ones.'

'So you would incorporate the Order into your new belief?'

'We would never repudiate the Order, your grace.'

'And Darklaw? How widely is that observed, would you say, in the colony worlds?'

'I think we've kept much of it,' Oesterreich says. 'Certainly we keep the part about not trying to return to Earth. And the part about spreading the Mission outwards.'

'Beyond the boundaries decreed, it would seem.'

'This is a new dispensation,' he says.

'But not a repudiation of the original teachings?'

'Oh, no,' he says, and smiles. 'Not a repudiation at all, your grace.'

He has that passionate confidence, that unshakeable assurance, that is the mark of the real prophet and also of the true madman. There is something diabolical about him, and irresistible. In these conversations with him I have so far managed to remain outwardly calm, even genial, but the fact is that I am quaking within. I really do believe he is insane. Either that or an utter fraud, a cynical salesman of the irrational and the unreal, and though he is flippant he does not seem at all cynical. A madman, then. Is his condition infectious? As I have said, the fear of madness has been with me all my life; and so my harsh discipline, my fierce commitment, my depth of belief. He threatens all my defences.

'When do you set out to visit your Goddess Avatar?' I ask.

'Whenever you like, your grace.'

'You really think I'm going with you?'

'Of course you are. How else can you find out what you came out here to learn?'

'I've learned that the colonies have fallen away from Darklaw. Isn't that enough?'

'But you think we've all gone crazy, right?'

'When did I say that?'

'You didn't need to say it.'

'If I sent word to Earth of what's happened, and the Order

chooses to cut off all further technical assistance and all shipments of manufactured goods – '

'They won't do that. But even if they do – well, we're pretty much self-sufficient out here now, and getting more so every year – '

'And further emigration from Earth?'

'That would be your loss, not ours, your grace. Earth needs the colonies as a safety valve for her population surplus. We can get along without more emigrants. We know how to reproduce, out here.' He grins at me. 'This is foolish talk. You've come this far. Now go the rest of the way with me.'

I am silent.

'Well?'

'Now, you mean?'

'Right now.'

There is only one Velde station on Entropy, about three hundred metres from the house where I have been talking with Oesterreich. We go to it under a sky berserk with green lightning. He seems not even to notice.

'Don't we have to do lambda drills?' I ask.

'Not for this hop,' Oesterreich says. 'There's no differential between here and there.' He is busy setting up coordinates. 'Get into the chamber, your grace.'

'And have you send me God knows where by myself?'

'Don't be foolish. Please.'

It may be the craziest thing I have ever done. But I am the servant of the Order; and the Order has asked this of me. I step into the chamber. No one else is with us. He continues to press keys, and I realize that he is setting up an automatic transfer, requiring no external operator. When he is done with that he joins me, and there is the moment of flash.

We emerge into a cool, dry world with an Earthlike sun, a sea-green sky, a barren, rocky landscape. Ahead of us stretches an empty plateau broken here and there by small granite hillocks that rise like humped islands out of the flatness.

'Where are we?' I ask.

'Fifty light-years from Entropy, and about eighty-five light-years from Earth.'

'What's the name of this place?'

'It doesn't have one. Nobody lives here. Come, now we walk a little.'

We start forward. The ground has the look that comes of not having felt rain for ten or twenty years, but tough little tussocks of a greyish jagged-looking grass are pushing up somehow through the hard, stony red soil. When we have gone a hundred metres or so the land begins to drop away sharply on my left, so that I can look down into a broad, flat valley about three hundred metres below us. A solitary huge beast, somewhat like an elephant in bulk and manner, is grazing quietly down there, patiently prodding at the ground with its rigid two-pronged snout.

'Here we are,' Oesterreich says.

We have reached the nearest of the little granite islands. When we walk around it, I see that its face on the farther side is fissured and broken, creating a sort of cave. Oesterreich beckons and we step a short way into it.

To our right, against the wall of the cave, is a curious narrow three-sided framework, a kind of tapering doorway, with deep darkness behind it. It is made of an odd glossy metal, or perhaps a plastic, with a texture that is both sleek and porous at the same time. There are hieroglyphs inscribed on it that seem much like those I saw on the wall of the stone temple in the mural in the Goddess-chapel on Phosphor, and to either side of it, mounted in the cave wall, are the triple six-pointed stars that are the emblem of Oesterreich's cult.

'What is this here?' I say, after a time.

'It's something like a Velde transmitter.'

'It isn't anything like a Velde transmitter.'

'It works very much like a Velde transmitter,' he says. 'You'll see when we step into its field. Are you ready?'

'Wait.'

He nods. 'I'm waiting.'

'We're going to let this thing send us somewhere?'

'That's right, your grace.'

'What is it? Who built it?'

'I've already told you what it is. As for who built it, I don't have any idea. Nobody does. We think it's five or ten million years old, maybe. It could be older than that by a factor of ten. Or a factor of a hundred. We have no way of judging.'

After a long silence I say, 'You're telling me that it's an alien device?'

'That's right.'

'We've never discovered any sign of intelligent alien life anywhere in the galaxy.'

'There's one right in front of you,' Oesterreich says. 'It isn't the only one.'

'You've found aliens?'

'We've found their matter-transmitters. A few of them, anyway. They still work. Are you ready to jump now, your grace?'

I stare blankly at the three-sided doorway.

'Where to?'

'To a planet about five hundred light-years from here, where we can catch the bus that'll take us to the Goddess Avatar.'

'You're actually serious?'

'Let's go, your grace.'

'What about lambda effects?'

'There aren't any. Lambda differentials are a flaw in the Velde technology, not in the universe itself. This system gets us around without any lambda problems at all. Of course, we don't know how it works. Are you ready?'

'All right,' I say helplessly.

He beckons to me and together we step towards the doorway and simply walk through it, and out the other side into such astonishing beauty that I want to fall down and give praise. Great feathery trees rise higher than sequoias, and a milky waterfall comes tumbling down the flank of an ebony mountain that fills half the sky, and the air quivers with a diamond-bright haze. Before me stretches a meadow like a scarlet carpet, vanishing into the middle distance. There is a Mesozoic richness of texture to everything: it gleams, it shimmers, it trembles in splendour.

A second doorway, identical to the first, is mounted against an enormous boulder right in front of us. It too is flanked by the triple-star emblem.

'Put your medallion on,' Oesterreich tells me.

'My medallion?' I say, stupidly.

'Put it on. The Goddess Avatar will wonder why you're with me, and that'll tell her.'

'Is she here?'

'She's on the next world. This is just a way station. We had to stop here first. I don't know why. Nobody does. Ready?'

'I'd like to stay here longer.'

'You can come back some other time,' he says. 'She's waiting for you. Let's go.'

'Yes,' I say, and fumble in my pocket and find my medallion, and put it around my throat. Oesterreich winks and puts his thumb and forefinger together approvingly. He takes my hand and we step through.

She is a lean, leathery-looking woman of sixty or seventy years with hard bright blue eyes. She wears a khaki jacket, an olive-drab field hat, khaki shorts, heavy boots. Her greying hair is tucked behind her in a tight bun. Standing in front of a small tent, tapping something into a hand terminal, she looks like an ageing geology professor out on a field trip in Wyoming. But next to her tent the triple emblem of the Goddess is displayed on a sandstone plaque.

This is a Mesozoic landscape too, but much less lush than the last one: great red-brown cliffs sparsely peppered with giant ferns and palms, four-winged insects the size of dragons zooming overhead, huge grotesque things that look very much like dinosaurs warily circling each other in a stony arroyo out near the horizon. I see some other tents out there too. There is a little colony here. The sun is reddish-yellow, and large.

'Well, what do we have here?' she says. 'A Lord Magistrate, is it?'

'He was nosing around on Zima and Entrada, trying to find out what was going on.'

'Well, now he knows.' Her voice is like flint. I feel her contempt, her hostility, like something palpable. I feel her strength, too, a cold, harsh, brutal power. She says, 'What was your house, Lord Magistrate?'

'Senders.'

She studies me as if I were a specimen in a display case. In all my life I have known only one other person of such force and intensity, and that is the Master. But she is nothing like him.

'And now the Sender is sent?'

'Yes,' I say. 'There were deviations from the plan. It became necessary for me to resign my magistracy.'

'We weren't supposed to come out this far, were we?' she asks. 'The light of that sun up there won't get to Earth until the seventy-third century, do you know that? But here we are. Here we are!' She laughs, a crazed sort of cackle. I begin to wonder if they intend to kill me. The aura that comes from her is terrifying. The geology professor I took her for at first is gone: what I see now is something strange and fierce, a prophet, a seer. Then suddenly the fierceness vanishes too and something quite different comes from her: tenderness, pity, even love. The strength of it catches me unawares and I gasp at its power. These shifts of hers are managed without apparent means; she has spoken only a few words, and all the rest has been done with movement, with posture, with expression. I know that I am in the presence of some great charismatic. She walks over to me and with her face close to mine says, 'We spoiled your plan, I know. But we too follow the divine rule. We discovered things that nobody had suspected, and everything changed for us. Everything.'

'Do you need me, Lady?' Oesterreich asks.

'No. Not now.' She touches the tips of her fingers to my medallion of office, rubbing it lightly as though it is a magic talisman. Softly she says, 'Let me take you on a tour of the galaxy, Lord Magistrate.'

One of the alien doorways is located right behind her tent. We step through it hand in hand, and emerge on a dazzling green hillside looking out over a sea of ice. Three tiny blue-white suns hang like diamonds in the sky. In the trembling air they look like the three six-pointed stars of the emblem. 'One of their capital cities was here once,' she says. 'But it's all at the bottom of that sea now. We ran a scan on it and saw the ruins, and some day we'll try to get down there.' She beckons and we step through again, and out onto a turbulent desert of iron-hard red sand, where heavily armoured crabs the size of footballs go scuttling sullenly away as we appear. 'We think there's another city under here,' she says. Stooping, she picks up a worn sherd of grey pottery and puts it in my hand. 'That's an artefact millions of years old. We find them all over the place.' I stare at it as if she has handed me a small fragment of the core of a star. She touches my medallion again, just a light grazing stroke, and leads me on into the next doorway, and out onto a world of billowing white clouds and soft dewy hills, and onwards from there to one where trees hang like ropes from the sky, and onwards from there –

'How did you find all this?' I ask, finally.

'I was living on Three Suns. You know where that is? We were exploring the nearby worlds, trying to see if there was anything worthwhile, and one day I stepped out of a Velde unit and found myself looking at a peculiar three-sided kind of doorway right next to it, and I got too close and found myself going through into another world entirely. That was all there was to it.'

'And you kept on going through one doorway after another?'

'Fifty of them. I didn't know then how to tune for destination, so I just kept jumping, hoping I'd get back to my starting point eventually. There wasn't any reason in the world why I should. But after six months I did. The Goddess protects me.'

'The Goddess,' I say.

She looks at me as though awaiting a challenge. But I am silent.

'These doorways link the whole galaxy together like the Paris Metro,' she says after a moment. 'We can go everywhere with them. *Everywhere.*'

'And the Goddess? Are the doorways Her work?'

'We hope to find that out some day.'

'What about this emblem?' I ask, pointing to the six-pointed stars beside the gateway. 'What does that signify?'

'Her presence,' she says. 'Come. I'll show you.'

We step through once more, and emerge into the night. The sky on this world is the blackest black I have ever seen, with comets and shooting stars blazing across it in almost comic profusion. There are two moons, bright as mirrors. A dozen metres to one side is the white stone temple of the chapel mural I saw on Eden, marked with the same hieroglyphs that are shown on the painting there and that are inscribed on all the alien doorways. It is made of cyclopean slabs of white stone that look as if they were carved billions of years ago. She takes my arm and guides me through its squared-off doorway into a high-vaulted inner chamber where a triple six-pointed triangle, fashioned out of the glossy doorway material, is mounted on a stone altar.

'This is the only building of theirs we've ever found,' she says. Her eyes are gleaming. 'It must have been a holy place. Can you doubt it? You can feel the power.'

'Yes.'

'Touch the emblem.'

'What will happen to me if I do?'

'Touch it,' she says. 'Are you afraid?'

'Why should I trust you?'

'Because the Goddess has used me to bring you to this place. Go on. Touch.'

I put my hand to the smooth cool alien substance, and instantly I feel the force of revelation flowing through me, the unmistakable power of the Godhead. I see the multiplicity of worlds, an infinity of them circling an infinity of suns. I see the Totality. I see the face of God clear and plain. It is what I have sought all my life and thought that I had already found; but I know at once that I am finding it for the first time. If I had fasted for a thousand years, or prayed for ten thousand, I could not have felt anything like that. It is the music out of which all things are built. It is the ocean in which all things float. I hear the voice of every god and goddess that ever had worshippers, and it is all one voice, and it goes coursing through me like a river of fire.

After a moment I take my hand away. And step back, trembling, shaking my head. This is too easy. One does not reach God by touching a strip of smooth plastic.

She says, 'We mean to find them. They're still alive somewhere. How could they not be? And who could doubt that we were meant to follow them and find them? And kneel before them, for they are Whom we seek. So we'll go on and on, as far as we need to go, in search of them. To the farthest reaches, if we have to. To the rim of the universe and then beyond. With these doorways there are no limits. We've been handed the key to everywhere. We are for the Dark, all of it, on and on and on, not the little hundred-light-year sphere that your Order preaches, but the whole galaxy and even beyond. Who knows how far these doorways reach? The Magellanic Clouds? Andromeda? M33? They're waiting for us out there. As they have waited for a billion years.'

So she thinks she can hunt Him down through doorway after doorway. Or Her. Whichever. But she is wrong. He who made the universe made the makers of the doorways also.

'And the Goddess?' I say.

'The Goddess is the Unknown. The Goddess is the Mystery towards which we journey. You don't feel Her presence?'

'I'm not sure.'

'You will. If not now, then later. She'll greet us when we arrive. And embrace us, and make us all gods.'

I stare a long while at the six-pointed stars. It would be simple enough to put forth my hand again and drink in the river of revelation a second time. But there is no need. That fire still courses through me. It always will, drawing me onwards towards itself. Whatever it may be, there is no denying its power.

She says, 'I'll show you one more thing, and then we'll leave here.'

We continue through the temple and out the far side, where the wall has toppled. From a platform amid the rubble we have an unimpeded view of the heavens. An immense array of stars glitters above us, set out in utterly unfamiliar patterns. She points straight overhead, where a Milky Way in two whirling strands spills across the sky.

'That's Earth right up there,' she says. 'Can you see it? Going around that little yellow sun, only a hundred thousand light-years away? I wonder if they ever paid us a visit. We won't know, will we, until we turn up one of their doorways some-where in the Himalayas, or under the Antarctic ice, or somewhere like that. I think that when we finally reach them, they'll recognize us. It's interesting to think about, isn't it?' Her hand rests lightly on my wrist. 'Shall we go back now, Lord Magistrate?'

So we return, in two or three hops, to the world of the dinosaurs and the giant dragonflies. There is nothing I can say. I feel storms within my skull. I feel myself spread out across half the universe.

Oesterreich waits for me now. He will take me back to Phosphor, or Entropy, or Entrada, or Zima, or Cuchulain, or anywhere else I care to go.

'You could even go back to Earth,' the Goddess Avatar says. 'Now that you know what's happening out here. You could go back home and tell the Master all about it.'

'The Master already knows, I suspect. And there's no way I can go home. Don't you understand that?'

She laughs lightly. 'Darklaw, yes. I forgot. The rule is that no one goes back. We've been catapulted out here to be cleansed of original sin, and to return to Mother Earth would be a crime against the laws of thermodynamics. Well, as you wish. You're a free man.'

'It isn't Darklaw,' I say. 'Darklaw doesn't bind anyone any more.'

I began to shiver. Within my mind sherds and fragments are falling from the sky: the House of Senders, the House of the Sanctuary, the whole Order and all its laws, the mountains and valleys of Earth, the body and fabric of Earth. All is shattered; all is made new; I am infinitely small against the infinite greatness of the cosmos. I am dazzled by the light of an infinity of suns.

And yet, though I must shield my eyes from that fiery glow, though I am numbed and humbled by the vastness of that vastness, I see that there are no limits to what may be attained, that the edge of the universe awaits me, that I need only reach and stretch, and stretch and reach, and ultimately I will touch it.

I see that even if she has made too great a leap of faith, even if she has surrendered herself to assumptions without basis, she is on the right path. The quest is unattainable because its goal is infinite. But the way leads ever outwards. There is no destination, only a journey. And she has travelled farther on that journey than anyone.

And me? I had thought I was going out into the stars to spin out the last of my days quietly and obscurely, but I realize now that my pilgrimage is nowhere near its end. Indeed it is only beginning. This is not any road that I ever thought I would take. But this is the road that I am taking, all the same, and I have no choice but to follow it, though I am not sure yet whether I am wandering deeper into exile or finding my way back at last to my true home.

What I cannot help but see now is that our Mission is ended and that a new one has begun; or, rather, that this new Mission is the continuation and culmination of ours. Our Order has taught from the first that the way to reach God is to go to the stars. So it is. And so we have done. We have been too timid, limiting ourselves to that little ball of space surrounding Earth. But we have not failed. We have made possible everything that is to follow after.

I hand her my medallion. She looks at it the way I looked at that bit of alien pottery on the desert world, and then she starts to hand it back to me, but I shake my head.

'For you,' I say. 'A gift. An offering. It's of no use to me now.'

She is standing with her back to the great reddish-yellow sun of this place, and it seems to me that light is streaming from her as it does from the Master, that she is aglow, that she is luminous, that she is herself a sun.

'Goddess save you, Lady,' I say quietly.

All the worlds of the galaxy are whirling about me. I will take this road and see where it leads, for now I know there is no other.

'Goddess save you,' I say. 'Goddess save you, Lady.'

The Face of the Waters
Robert Silverberg

'A marvellous book.' Arthur C. Clarke

It is the year 2450. Humanity is scattered among the stars, which teem with intelligent life – but Earth, the home world, is only a poignant memory. Thus all Earthmen are exiles.

An assortment of Earthmen has come to Hydros, a world with almost no landmass, only a great globe-encompassing ocean thinly sprinkled with tiny islands. The seas of Hydros swarm with apparently intelligent lifeforms of a hundred kinds, and one – a bipedal humanoid form – has created land of a kind for itself: floating islands woven from sea-borne materials, buffered by elaborate barricades against the ceaseless tidal surges of the sea.

For the Earthmen, Hydros is a world of no return, having no form of outbound space transportation that might lift them from the liquid surface of the planet. But they have come with a purpose. They travel across the endless ocean in search of the mysterious area from which no human has ever returned – the Face of the Waters. This brilliantly inventive novel tells their story.

Robert Silverberg is one of the greatest names in science fiction, winner of more awards than any other sf writer. *The Face of the Waters* is his most ambitious novel yet and an epic of imaginative adventure.

'Silverberg is our best.' *Fantasy and Science Fiction*

ISBN 0 586 21106 3

Kingdoms of the Wall
Robert Silverberg

'*This is the book of Poilar Crookleg, who has been to the roof of the World at the top of the Wall . . .*'

Kosa Saag casts its tremendous shadow over half the world. It is the Wall, an immense and solitary mountain, dominating the lowland landscape of teeming humanity. Strange and bewildering gods live at the summit, on the roof of the world: the First Climber brought back the gift of fire from them, and the secrets of growing and hunting food.

Poilar Crookleg has the blood of the First Climber in his veins. His father was a Pilgrim, and his father before him – but thousands of years have passed since the time of He Who Climbed, and many thousands of Pilgrims have disappeared, as Poilar's father did, or died, or gone mad, following His footsteps to the summit. Poilar's journey, through dreamlike new realms of danger and seduction, in a diminishing company of other young Pilgrims, is an epic journey of discovery.

'This is one of the few sf novels that I could not put down . . . deserves to become a classic.'   *Sunday Telegraph*

ISBN 0 586 21107 1

Raising the Stones
Sheri S. Tepper

Life on Hobbs Land was quiet and peaceful, which for some of the settlers was a sharp contrast to the worlds they had left behind. In particular, Maire Manone had abandoned Voorstod, a harsh and isolated land ruled by an unforgiving patriarchal religion whose adherents planned for the day when all humans would be forced to bow to their god. Maire had tried to forget Voorstod, but Voorstod had never forgotten her. Its men were even now on their way to Hobbs Land in the bloodthirsty anticipation of a holocaust . . . All in the name of god.

This is a major work by one of the new new stars of science fiction writing at her peak. Sheri Tepper brilliantly blends ecological puzzle, political intrigue and religious conflict in a story that has the power to reach the very heart and soul of the reader.

'In *Raising the Stones* Sheri S. Tepper has outdone herself. Secure in technique, incandescent in conception, and profound in insight, it is that rare thing – a book which makes the world we live in better than it was. As a writer myself, I'm left with one, rather frightening question: just how much growing can any writer possibly do?'   Stephen Donaldson

'Tepper knows how to write a well-made, on-moving story with strong characters . . . She takes the mental risks that are the life blood of science fiction and all imaginative narrative.'
Ursula Le Guin

ISBN 0 586 21212 4

The World at the End of Time
Frederik Pohl

The most accomplished work yet by one of the genuinely great names of science fiction.

Wan-To is the oldest, most powerful intelligence in the universe. But even Wan-To can experience loneliness, so he creates companions. Such offspring, however, can turn dangerous. When this happens he simply destroys the stars in which they may be hiding . . .

The colonists of the New Mayflower, recently landed on Newmanhome, know nothing of Wan-To. Until the planet's stars begin to shift and the climate starts to cool down, causing a desperate struggle to survive before the colony has even had a chance to develop.

ISBN 0 586 212755 2